RUNESCAPE®

THE FALL OF HALLOWVALE

ALSO AVAILABLE FROM TITAN BOOKS

RuneScape: The Gift of Guthix

ALSO AVAILABLE FROM TITAN COMICS

RuneScape: Untold Tales of the God Wars

RUNESCAPE®

THE FALL OF HALLOWVALE

ROBBIE MACNIVEN

JAGEX®

TITAN BOOKS

RUNESCAPE: THE FALL OF HALLOWVALE
Print edition ISBN: 9781803366050
E-book edition ISBN: 9781835411056

Published by Titan Books
A division of Titan Publishing Group Ltd
144 Southwark Street, London SE1 0UP
www.titanbooks.com

First edition: November 2024
10 9 8 7 6 5 4 3 2 1

Cover illustration: Mark Montague

A CIP catalogue record for this title is available from the British Library.

Printed and bound by CPI Group (UK) Ltd, Croydon CR0 4YY.

Dedicated to the fans of RuneScape –
I hope I've done the setting proud.

PART ONE

ONE

————◄◆►————

The eighth bell was tolling. Luken was late. He needed to reach the Hallowed Church and its great Sepulchre before Delen Akeron, archpriest of the unicorn, got himself killed.

The junior illuminator dodged around a series of street stalls and found himself fighting through a crowd of squabbling traders. A cart had thrown a wheel in the middle of the roadway, spilling several sacks full of turnips and radishes in the process. The driver was blaming one of the stall sellers for causing his donkey to shy, while the stall seller was cursing at the driver for blocking access to his wares.

He doubled back to bypass the gathering crowd and tried to work his way along the far end of the street. A duo of icyene psiloi, warriors clad in their bright silver armour, were watching the squabbling humans dispassionately, and most of the crowd didn't want to get too close to the tall, winged beings. Luken dared thread the gap, avoiding eye contact with the icyene and clutching his purchase – a sack full of joop powder – to his chest. The Hallowed Church's stocks of incense had been running low, and joop was a necessary ingredient for making more. Akeron had sent Luken to Hallowvale's marketplace to collect supplies before the evening service.

Luken had accepted the task grudgingly, not because he didn't fancy a trip into the heart of the great city that gave its name to the surrounding region – it felt like weeks since he had been out of the grounds of the Church and its Sepulchre – but because he worried about Akeron. Blessings of Saradomin or not, the archpriest had been growing ever frailer of late. Luken feared for the day when he was no longer able to fulfil his duties, and a new archpriest was elected from the other three Saradominist orders, one that would not have the patience Akeron had shown to him as his junior illuminator.

He successfully negotiated the edge of the crowd and pressed on, hitching the blue robes of his woollen himation so they did not trail in the muck and manure of the roadway. He darted in front of another cart on Agaristis Street and cut left across Candlemaker Row, into the church district that comprised much of the north-eastern quarter of Hallowvale.

The buildings here were among the oldest in the city, icyene-built, all stone arches, domes and columns. The streets were paved with proper cobbles, not rutted dirt, and every corner was overseen by graven statues and fluttering blue and gold standards bearing the star of Saradomin.

Luken forced himself to slow his pace, knowing Akeron would not approve of other clergymen seeing his junior illuminator sprinting through the sacred streets. He caught his breath and tried to tell himself he was being irrational. What terrible fate could possibly befall Akeron while he was absent? He'd barely been gone two bell-tolls. But he had promised to be back before eighth bell, and now he felt guilty. He was letting the archpriest down. Akeron needed him, even if he was too cantankerous to admit it.

He rounded the Temple of Enlightenment and began to cross the square beyond it. The Hallowed Church loomed before him, the heart of Saradominist worship in the city. It was a vast, domed structure, the tallest after the Everlight, the citadel and the acropolis, bigger even than the royal palace. Its façade supported by great pillars and its gilt doors flanked by towering statues of Saradomin, the bearded visage of the Father of Light and Wisdom carved with flawless perfection from blue azurenite by icyene craftsmen. Though Luken had lived in its shadow for as long as he could remember, the sight of it still made him slow his pace.

Something hit him from the right, almost knocking him over and making him scrabble at his joop bag. He had collided with a priest cutting across the square. The man growled something most unbecoming of a servant of Saradomin as Luken stammered an apology and hastened on.

Rather than enter through the main doors – they were locked at this time of day – he skirted along the pillars at the Church's front, feeling the eyes of the hypaspists on him every step of the way. Warriors from the four holy ordos – the wolf, owl, lion and unicorn – guarded the Hallowed Church night and day. Luken was afraid of them, of their great spears and swords and gleaming steel armour and equally hard silences. In all his years he had barely spoken to one, but thankfully being the archpriest's junior illuminator meant he went unchallenged. Still, he felt them watching him as he reached the alleyway that led down the Church's eastern flank.

He passed in through the building's arched side entrance, pausing briefly to scrape his shoes on the outer edge of the door so he didn't track mud into the holiest of spaces.

The exterior of the Hallowed Church was grand and imposing, but it was nothing compared to the interior. Its above-ground structure combined with the bulk of the Hallowed Sepulchre that lay beneath it, five lower levels forming sprawling catacombs of stone corridors and arches, pillars and statues and, of course, the tombs of the Hallowed Dead. Though lit by the radiant shards of Saradomin, Luken did not much like the under-levels, especially the ones reserved for the icyene.

He took the stairs that lay at the end of the entrance corridor, his every step watched by the statues of justiciars, priests and scholars that crowded along the walls. Familiar though he was with the place, he still felt as though they were all glaring at him.

As he climbed, he heard a rattle, echoing through the stone passages. He bit back a curse, and broke once more into an ungainly run.

He reached the upper hall in time to see Delen Akeron tottering at the top of an unfeasibly tall ladder, a hook-pole in one hand. He had just finished opening the last of the hall's dozen ceiling shutters, allowing the glorious brilliance of the Everlight to spill down into the chamber, illuminating the motes of dust drifting through the air.

"Archpriest!" Luken exclaimed, discarding the joop at the foot of the statue of Justiciar Phosani and charging to Akeron's rescue. The ladder swayed dangerously, Akeron snapping at him to calm down even as the archpriest clutched reflexively at the upper rungs.

Luken grabbed the ladder and steadied it, ignoring the diatribe from on high. Akeron began to descend unsteadily, the hook-pole in one hand combining with his long blue-and-white Saradominist robes to make his motions dangerously clumsy. Luken held his breath until he was able to help him down the last few rungs.

"You should not be opening the shutters alone, archpriest," Luken admonished. "What if you fell?"

"Then at least I'll finally be rid of your fussing, boy," Akeron growled, handing him the pole and adjusting his robes. No one seemed to know his age – nor dared to ask him – but the fact that the upper hall had borne a statue of him for as long as Luken could remember made him feel like the archpriest of the unicorn had been lambasting his junior illuminators and delivering uncompromising sermons since the Hallowed Church had been built, centuries before. Though increasingly gaunt, he was still tall and upright, with a full, white beard and bushy eyebrows framing eyes that were keen, quick and blue as azurenite.

When Luken thought of Saradomin in his prayers, he pictured Delen Akeron.

"Did you find the joop?" Akeron asked.

"Yes, archpriest."

"The good stuff? From Maken's stall?"

"Yes, archpriest."

Akeron held out one gnarled hand, and Luken obediently fished into the pocket of his himation and drew out the coinage left over from the purchase.

"You didn't buy yourself anything at the market?" Akeron demanded as he received back the money.

"No, archpriest."

Akeron grunted, looked down at the coins, then pressed them back into Luken's palm.

"Well, next time you can," he said, cutting off Luken's protests about it being money for the Church's upkeep. "Enough chit-chat. The floor needs swept and then that joop needs mixed, or it'll go up like a Day of Light bonfire instead of smouldering. Come on, boy, move yourself."

Luken nodded obediently and retrieved the broom he stored behind the statue of Justiciar Ekos Lysander. He began to sweep the bare flagstones of the upper hall, starting beneath the altar and working his way out in an arc. It was a process he had performed countless times, since he had been big enough to hold the broom.

As a baby, Luken had been abandoned on the steps of the Church and taken in by the Saradominist priesthood. There had been other orphans too, but almost all had decided to leave when they were old enough. Luken had stayed. He felt duty-bound to Akeron, who had always looked out for him when he had been younger, ensuring he was properly fed and ameliorating the punishments set by other priests.

In truth, the thought of leaving and abandoning the certainties and routines of life in the Church scared Luken.

So he swept, as he had swept so many times before, and lost himself in the peace of the cold, bright chamber.

The scrape of armour disturbed his labours. He looked up and froze. One of the hypaspists, a lion's pelt worn about his shoulders, was standing in the doorway to the upper hall.

"Word from the front doors, archpriest," he said. "A messenger, from the citadel. You are called to attend Her-Winged-Majesty on a matter of absolute urgency. He refuses to elaborate."

Luken cast an uncertain look at Akeron. Word from the citadel was a rare thing, even more so if it came directly from Queen Efaritay. Surely, she knew it was the Day of Light, and that the Church had to be prepared ahead of the service that would soon be filling its upper floors?

"Have the messenger take word that I will attend with all haste," Akeron said. Luken stared at him, wondering if he was missing something. As the hypaspist departed, he spoke up.

"What about the preparations for the service, archpriest?"

Akeron said nothing, looking instead towards the statue of Queen Efaritay, that stood to the right of the altar. Luken tried to change tack.

"I can finish the preparations while you are absent, archpriest. I'm sure I'll have it all set by the time you return."

To Luken's surprise, Akeron shook his head.

"No. You'll accompany me, boy."

"To the citadel?" Luken asked disbelievingly, feeling a sudden rush of equal parts anticipation and concern.

"We have been summoned to the citadel, so to the citadel we shall go," Akeron said, looking from the statue to Luken, his gaze fierce. "Now, get changed into something more befitting a faithful servant of Saradomin. Your robe hems are all mucky. It's not every day you get to meet the queen."

TWO

◆▸

The crash of steel meeting steel rang through the cold air, echoing back from stone vaults built by the hands of Saradomin's greatest servants.

Rhea pressed the attack. Phosani had turned aside her initial lunge – the justiciar of the wolf was fast, but Rhea could match her. She brought her spatha back in before Phosani could launch a riposte, jarring her opponent's sword aside and giving Rhea the angle she needed to stamp forward.

It was all in the footwork. It took her inside Phosani's guard and turned the block into a lunge. The tip of her sword hit Phosani's breastplate just to the lower-left of the bright gold of the star emblazoned across it, jarring off to the right.

Phosani swung a haymaker with her own spatha, crude but enough to keep Rhea at bay while the justiciar disengaged. She put a trio of paces between them, regaining a low guard, shoulders squared, feet spread.

Rhea quelled the urge to follow up immediately, instead taking a high guard and beginning to circle off to the left, slowly. She watched the justiciar intently as she moved, focusing on the tip of her blade, looking for the first hint that she was going to switch from defence to offence.

Phosani's face was inscrutable behind the bright steel of her spike-crowned helm, but Rhea could imagine it well enough, her noble features pursed, pale eyes glaring. She was being tested more than she was used to, but that was why she had chosen Rhea for this bout.

Phosani took a step forward and Rhea ceased her circling, trading a step back in response. Dry straw crackled underfoot. The vaulted, circular chamber around them had once been an icyene oratory, a Saradomin place of worship for the beings that had built Hallowvale. Echoes of that still persisted, in the slender, high stained-glass windows and the old icyene statues on their plinths, wings furled, hands folded and heads bowed.

But the oratory had been used as a drill chamber for centuries now, ever since the construction of the Hallowed Church had brought together all of Hallowvale's worshipers. The icyene had agreed to give this space over to the human ordos whose barracks shared its street, and now it was part sparring chamber, part armoury, its flagstones spread with straw and its edges crammed with training boards, dummies and racks bearing the arms and armour of the four ordos of human hypaspists that called the city home.

Phosani took another step, testing to see if Rhea would give more ground. She would not. The first, small retreat had been designed to build an assumption, and as soon as Phosani moved forward again Rhea shifted to meet her, high guard becoming a feint that disguised a two-handed stab, and aimed at the target of the star of Saradomin on her chest.

It was Phosani's turn to parry, matching Rhea for speed now – she had anticipated her subordinate's aggression. Rhea welcomed it, and they exchanged blows at close range, a swift cacophony of steel that made ugly echoes through the old chamber.

Phosani found the edge, scraping her blade along Rhea's and locking crossguards. The spatha they were using were crude swords, old and heavy and dull, good now only for training bouts. Phosani was a master of many weapons, and she used that weight to her advantage, driving aside Rhea's defence.

It was Rhea's turn to break off. Phosani tried to follow, but a slight misstep meant her lunge fell just short of connecting.

"Watch your footwork," Rhea advised as they circled again, catching their breath.

"Noted," Phosani responded, terse but measured. "Watch your recovery. These weapons make everything slower."

"Noted," Rhea said.

The two had been sparring in their full panoply for almost half an hour now, and neither had yet gained a true advantage. Rhea felt no pride matching the White Wolf. It was her duty to keep Phosani sharp. Rhea was the justiciar's longest serving hypaspist, the most battle-hardened of her Wolves, the whetstone to her blade. They pushed each other hard so that, when they entered combat again, it would be no greater challenge than when they fought across the old hall.

They met once more, Rhea leading as the dance of swords took them to the edge of the sparring area. Phosani succeeded in again locking their weapons, but rather than open Rhea's guard, she twisted the pommel up and cracked it against the cheek of Rhea's crested helm. She countered by snatching at Phosani's throat and kicked at her ankle, knocking her feet out from under her.

No rules here. When they met the Zamorakians again, there would be none then either.

The two went down together with a clatter of armour. Phosani was taller, but Rhea had been dragged down on top, and she knew she was stronger. She pinned Phosani's sword-wrist and dragged her own heavy blade, in a reverse grip, up beneath the edge of her opponent's helm, threatening to open her throat.

"Commander."

The words were not quite an exclamation, but they were not far off it. Rhea froze and grimaced, then rose up. She proffered Phosani her hand, and the justiciar of the wolf took it without hesitation, allowing herself to be dragged to her feet. They both turned to face the interloper.

Insela stood atop the steps leading down into the oratory. Like Rhea, she was one of Phosani's Wolves, though younger and less experienced. She was dressed in white chiton and a blue chlamys cloak, edged with silver. Strapped across her back was the crossbow she favoured in combat. Her dark hair was bound up, and her seemingly ever-watchful grey eyes darted between the two hypaspists.

Phosani paused to drag off her helmet and shake her hair free, a long cascade of silver that seemed to shine white in the cold, autumnal light spearing through the high windows.

"Speak," she instructed. The word sounded harsh, given an edge by the flush of combat that still gripped the pair, but the justiciar ameliorated it. "We were just finishing."

"A messenger has arrived at the barracks," Insela reported. "He came straight from the citadel, seeking you. Apparently, you are to report to Her-Winged-Majesty with all haste."

"Did he offer any elaboration?"

"No, commander, but he is waiting outside."

Rhea watched Phosani as she pondered the news. For a moment the tall warrior did not look so dissimilar to the statues of the winged beings watching over them. Rhea could see why there were the rumours of icyene ancestry in the justiciar's bloodline.

"Bring him in," Phosani instructed Insela eventually. As the crossbow-woman left, Phosani spoke to Rhea.

"If we are to go before the queen, you will accompany me."

"Of course, commander," Rhea said, noting the bitter look Insela gave her as she departed. "Should I help you out of your armour?"

"No," Phosani said. "Something tells me there won't be time for that."

✦ ✦ ✦

The citadel dominated the west of Hallowvale, a bristling crown of towers, battlements and buttresses that shone white in the Everlight's glory as Rhea and Phosani approached.

The main gate was flanked by icyene statues, towering mirrors of the armoured icyene warriors who stood guard outside the metal-sheathed doors. They were closed and barred, a fact that Rhea immediately noted as unusual. Though permanently defended, they usually stood open to allow the uninterrupted flow of dignitaries, officials and soldiery between the castle and the city. The fact that someone, presumably the queen, had ordered them shut suggested there was an immediate threat to Hallowvale.

Rhea resisted the urge to speculate with Phosani as they waited for the gate to open before passing into the citadel's main courtyard. The cobbled space was surrounded by towering fortifications, the walls hung with the standards of Hallowvale and the queen, the justiciar ordos, the icyene nobility and the Saradominist faith. An early twilight seemed to have gripped the space, the height of the surrounding defensive structures meaning even the Everlight had been driven out.

The place was bustling. The icyene garrison had been stood to, several ranks under inspection along the left side of the courtyard. Messengers were dashing back and forth, and as Rhea entered, she saw a flock of icyene psiloi take wing from the battlements above. They were heading north-west, skirting the lowering autumnal sun.

"We should have roused the Wolves before coming here," Phosani commented as they crossed the courtyard, barked icyene orders ringing out around them.

"I can return and muster them, commander," Rhea suggested.

"No. The messenger carried no instructions about that. Let us discover the cause of all this first."

They mounted the stone stairs leading to the citadel's keep, icyene royal guards resplendent in their silver-edged panoply admitting them. One led them inside.

The throne room of the citadel was a long chamber in the ancient style of New Domina, high, with tall, slender window arches and pillars carved with star constellations no human in the city would recognise. The throne itself sat atop a dais at the far end, its back fashioned like two icyene wings, spreading out and upwards and perfectly framed by a circular glass window bearing the star of Saradomin behind it. A lesser throne sat alongside – wingless, human craftwork, designed for Queen Efaritay's husband, Ascertes.

The chamber itself, while grand, was a lesser version of the throne room within the royal palace that lay to the southeast, but business was still often conducted in the citadel, close as it was to the city's main entrances and its centre. Rhea suspected the audience being held in the citadel also pointed to the threat the city was currently under – it was certainly a more secure location than the palace.

Both the queen and her human consort were present and seated. Before them was a circle of dignitaries, icyene and humans, standing separate from one another.

It seemed all the great and the good of the city had been summoned. The head of the Hallowvale icyene military, Strategos Archon Babel, was there with his senior subordinates, on the immediate right of the dais. The high priests of the lion, owl and wolf had also taken their places in the circle, as had a gaggle of minor nobles and the senior merchants, the emporoi.

Most notably, as far as Rhea was concerned, the leaders of the other hypaspist ordos had been called upon too. There was the ageing justiciar of the unicorn, Ekos Lysander, dressed for the time being in his Saradominist robes rather than armour. Beside him was the justiciar of the lion, Aliya, tall and imposing in her golden pelts, grasping the runic staff that marked her as the most potent arcane caster in the city. The only absence was Zachariah of the owl, who had been dispatched months ago by Saradomin himself on some secret task. His subordinate, a grizzled hypaspist by the name of Dorien, stood in his place. Phosani occupied the gap between them, nodding a greeting, while Rhea hung back, just outside the circle along with the other retainers.

The council was almost complete. Rhea half turned to see the last arrivals entering – the archpriest of the unicorn, old Delen Akeron, trailed by his fresh-faced, nervous-looking junior illuminator. They were both garbed in their formal robes, and the archpriest was clutching a staff topped with the star of Saradomin, a design echoed by the crown that gleamed on his brow.

They took their place, and an expectant hush settled. Efaritay rose gracefully from her throne, Ascertes following her. The entire assembly bowed.

"Sons and daughters of Hallowvale," the queen began, the light cascading through the star window making the perfect white feathers of her wings gleam. "My thanks for attending with such alacrity. Know that I would not have summoned with such abruptness, but a matter of gravest importance has arisen, and there is no time to delay."

None of the assembly made any comment, and Efaritay continued.

"I will be clear from the start, for the very survival of our city will likely depend on what we choose to do here today. Word has come from the north-western frontier. A Zamorakian legion, bearing the standards of the vyrelord Drakan, has broken through the defences. Just as their ancestors did, they are marching upon us."

✦ ✦ ✦

Shocked murmurs swept through the throne room. Luken simply stared. He had never seen Queen Efaritay this close, and was in awe of her pale, aquiline beauty, her grace, the calm precision of her voice, the way her feathers ruffled slightly when she spoke.

Her words were enough to break the spell. He blinked, looked at Akeron. Unlike almost everyone else in the circle, the archpriest's expression remained stoic.

Drakan. Luken had heard that name in stories, tales whispered during long winter nights in the Saradominist orphanage or written down in the musty old tomes he had studied as a child. He was the lord of all vampyres, nightmare creatures that feasted on the flesh and blood of mortals. Like the icyene, they were said to have come from beyond Gielinor, but they were different in every way – bat-winged, blood-drinking night-stalkers, hunters of the dark, servants of foul gods and killers of men. Luken hadn't believed in their existence, yet here he was, witnessing his queen speaking of them with utmost gravity. The reaction of the rest of the chamber left him in no doubt – the stories were true.

Justiciar Lysander, standing next to Akeron, was the first to speak.

"Are we certain of this? There have been rumours of disruption beyond the borders for weeks now, but a vampyre host?"

"It has been confirmed by Strategos Babel's prodromoi," the queen said, an elegant sweep of her arm indicating that Babel should speak. The icyene commander took a half-step into the circle – unnecessarily, Luken thought – and addressed the assembly.

"Three separate outfliers have come from the north, all eyewitnesses of the approaching host. The sky turns dark above them and the ground is black with their numbers. They bear icons of Zamorak and the heraldry of Lowerniel Drakan."

"And they have already broken through the border defences?" one of the emporoi merchants asked. "How can that be?"

"The border garrisons have been successively weakened to reinforce the armies besieging the Infernal Source," Babel said. "There was little intelligence of a Zamorakian legion mustering near Viggora's Folly. The tetrarchs were of the combined opinion that the city would not be threatened."

"Then the tetrarchs were mistaken," Zephiklos, priest of the owl, declared, referring to the senior military council that served Saradomin in his ongoing campaigns against Zamorak. "We have been left defenceless!"

"We are far from defenceless," Efaritay said before the council could descend into chaos. "Let us show the calmness and wisdom that are the tenets of our god. We have the garrison tagma, and we are blessed with the hypaspists of the ordos. The walls are strong and the Everlight is bright. Neither will be breached."

"But we must prepare to resist," Tarshen, the priest of the lion, said. "If it is true that the Zamorakians are led by vyre, there can be no negotiations. They will spare none of us if they are victorious! We must fight to the end!"

"And we shall," Efaritay said. "But we must choose our strategies carefully. Our first recourse should be to send for aid, from Forinthry and from Saradomin himself. Messengers stand atop the ramparts, waiting to take flight, but I would have the assent of this council before I order them on their way."

There were murmurs of agreement from both the human and icyene wings of the council. Luken found it amazing that the queen hadn't already sent her messengers, but he supposed he was being naïve – though Efaritay's lineage had ruled over Hallowvale since her mother and father had founded the city, she did so at Saradomin's command, and under the expectation that she would adhere to the guidance of Hallowvale's council.

"Do you think Saradomin can spare us aid?" another of the emporoi asked. "And even if he did, would it arrive in time?"

Phosani was the first to respond, her tone firm.

"Of course Saradomin will come to our aid. The only point of uncertainty is whether we can defend the land beyond the walls until he arrives. If it is true, and a whole Zamorakian legion marches against us, it is likely we will have to yield most of what lies outside the city to offset our numerical disadvantage."

There were more murmurs at that, but Lysander swiftly added his voice to Phosani's.

"I agree. As unpalatable as it may be, everything between the western gate and the Salve may have to be surrendered."

"What exactly does 'surrendered' entail?" another of the merchants asked. "Surely the people living there can be evacuated into the city?"

Lysander nodded, though Luken noted that Phosani gave no word or gesture.

He did his best to keep up with the conversation as it unfolded, but much of it was beyond him. He wasn't sure why Akeron had brought him.

For his own part, the archpriest listened silently, keeping his own counsel. Luken was waiting for some incisive comment, for Akeron to bring clarity not only to him, but to the whole assembly. But it never came.

A vote was held on a message to be sent to Saradomin, reporting the invasion and requesting relief be sent to Hallowvale. It passed unanimously.

"The hour grows late," Efaritay said afterwards. Luken realised she was correct. The throne room faced west, so didn't receive the Everlight's illumination directly. As the council had debated, lamp pillars had ignited of their own accord, keeping the chamber bathed in a warm glow as the last golden daylight glimmering through the Saradominist window behind the thrones had blinked out.

"I will adjourn this meeting for the night," the queen said. "We shall reconvene tomorrow morning, on the second bell, and finalise our strategy."

There was muttered assent. Luken looked at Akeron, who gave the slightest nod.

"Say nothing of what has transpired here today," Efaritay went on. "The news will be known in the streets soon enough, but we must control it for as long as possible. Panic will only undermine our efforts."

"May the light of Saradomin shine ahead of us, and light our way," Akeron said. They were the first words he had uttered.

"Will you lead us in prayer before we adjourn, hallowed archpriest?" the queen asked.

"As it pleases Your-Winged-Majesty," Akeron said, making the sign of the star and raising his staff. Like the rest of the assembly, Luken bowed his head quickly, and listened as the archpriest intoned the Third Prayer of Order and Wisdom, calling Saradomin's grace and good counsel down on them all. There, at last, was something Luken recognised, something he was familiar with. He took comfort from the words he had heard so often echoing around the Hallowed Church, and was briefly able to forget the tumultuous news and the great, imposing figures he was caught up amidst.

When it was ended, Efaritay dismissed the council. Akeron spoke briefly with the justiciar of the unicorn, Lysander, as they walked from the chamber, Luken keeping close behind the pair. They were old friends, and Lysander's duties in defending the Saradominist quarter meant he was a regular visitor to the Hallowed Church.

"Even if the message is delivered swiftly, how long will it take to muster a response?" Luken heard Lysander ask.

"All we can do is pray, my friend," Akeron responded. "That will be our best weapon, until we draw steel. That, and the light. Against the vyre, it is our only hope."

"Saradomin will come," Phosani said, interrupting the pair. The justiciar of the wolf had been about to leave the throne room ahead of them, but paused to speak to Lysander and Akeron. Her long silver hair matched the armour she wore. At her back was her retainer, a scarred, hard-faced hypaspist called Rhea. Her eyes were as cold and unyielding as the steel that sheathed her – he did his best not to quail behind Akeron as her gaze fell briefly on him.

"I would have expected greater faith from the archpriest of Hallowvale," Phosani went on.

"And I would have expected greater military practicality from a justiciar," Akeron replied. "I will include you in my prayers tonight, if it will ease your concerns."

Phosani said nothing more, but turned and left, her retainer in tow.

"Sometimes I think the White Wolf should have been the justiciar of the unicorn, and not I," Lysander said. "Truly, she loves the Lord of Light."

"One of her few redeeming qualities," Akeron said, dangerously loudly.

They passed out through the citadel, Luken finding himself craning his neck to stare up at the high walls and turrets surrounding them. More icyene were taking off, flying into the darkness that loomed to the west, beyond the radius cast by the Everlight. The night sky there was clouded, starless, a void that left Luken feeling cold and empty.

Akeron bade farewell to Lysander outside the gates, and they passed back into the constant glow of the Everlight, walking through the streets towards the Hallowed Church. There were few people abroad, and those they passed gave hasty bows to the archpriest before getting out of his way.

"Why did you stay silent throughout the council?" Luken dared ask as they went.

"I had nothing worthwhile to add," Akeron said. "At least, nothing that anyone would yet take heed of. You would do well to emulate me, boy."

"But surely they need Saradomin's guiding wisdom, the wisdom that only you can provide," Luken said, forging on despite Akeron's tone. "I mean, I didn't even know vampyres were real. I thought they were just monsters from the old stories, the kind the icyene tell about the things that haunt the night beyond the Everlight."

Akeron stopped, so abruptly that Luken bumped into him. As he started to apologise the archpriest gripped his wrist, the glow of the Everlight shining upon his fierce expression.

"Say nothing of vampyres, not out here," he said under his breath. "I fear many mistakes were made this evening, but

Her-Winged-Majesty was right about one thing. We cannot afford to scare the people."

Luken swallowed and nodded hastily, Akeron released him, and they carried on. He said nothing more until they reached the church district.

As they emerged into the square before the Hallowed Church, Luken realised that, despite the lateness of the hour, it was busy with people milling about. He was hit by a sudden rush of realisation. The evening service. Amidst everything that had happened, he had completely forgotten that Akeron had been set to lead the sunset prayers at the close of the Day of Light.

"Shall I send them away, archpriest?" he asked as they passed through the crowd, people bowing and genuflecting on either side.

"No," Akeron said, before raising his voice, addressing the people as he went. "The doors will be opened. A late service is better than none. Let us call on the Lord of Light, and look to the coming dawn."

THREE

◀◆▶

Ranis Drakan was forced to pause at the door of the watchtower. He had met the wicked tip of a spear, pressed to his throat.

"Let me past, you cretinous dolt," he snarled at the vyreguard standing just inside the entranceway, baring his fangs. His brother's elite warriors loved to impede him at every opportunity – he was becoming fairly certain it was a running joke among them.

"His-Dark-Self is feeding," the vyreguard replied, the spear not moving. "He is not to be disturbed."

"Is that so... Morgast," Ranis said in his most dangerous tone. The vyreguard's faceplate, crafted into a snarling, fanged grotesque, hid his identity, but Ranis took a stab at who this one was in an attempt at intimidation. "You'll regret delaying me when he finds out what I have to tell him."

"Well, I won't be held responsible for what happens to

you in there, my lord," the vyreguard said, his tone bordering on insolence. "And it's Vengen, not Morgast. He's guarding the other door."

Ranis hissed with impatience and smacked aside the spear before striding past the armoured imbecile.

The tower lay north-east of where the River Salve lost its way amidst the marshlands of Westmire, south of Viggora's Folly. It was one of dozens of similar defences that demarcated the frontier between Hallowvale and the Zamorakian-controlled lands further north. This part of the front line in the millennia-old war between Zamorak and Saradomin hadn't shifted for centuries. Until tonight.

There was a body lying in the doorway, a Saradominist soldier, ripped apart. Ranis paused to gaze longingly at the blood glistening across the stonework underfoot, then made himself carry on, stepping over the corpse and beginning to ascend the tower.

The blood could wait. He had to deliver this news before his sister did.

The vanguard of the Zamorakian legion had overrun the tower and pressed on south-east several hours before, at the onset of early night yet His-Dark-Self had chosen to linger, gripped by one of the unknowable fancies Ranis had long ago stopped trying to predict or interpret. Ranis had carried on with the main force, eager, like most other vampyres of note, to claim the honour of being the first to plant a foot on Hallowvale's soil.

It shouldn't have been this simple. The border defences had held the Zamorakians at bay for hundreds of years. Yet

Saradomin was now committing his all to what he thought would be a final battle against Zamorak at the Infernal Source. That had weakened his flank. It had fallen to the vyre to exploit that weakness, and so it had proven. This tower, and several others like it, had been left with only a skeleton garrison.

Now, it was a garrison of torn and bloodied corpses.

The lower chambers were deserted, already ransacked. Ranis stalked through them, until he heard a thump from above, something impacting against the wooden floorboards on the tower's highest level.

He climbed, his light step eliciting only the faintest creak from the timber underfoot.

It seemed a number of the garrison had made their last stand on the top floor. Ranis got a view of one man's legs as he entered the uppermost level, lying still, the rest of his body obscured by the figure crouched on top.

Most of the being's muscular upper torso was bare, and obscured by a great set of furled, bat-like wings. The pinions were etched with red markings and sigils, daubed in blood in the ancient language of Vampyrium. They recounted mighty and terrible deeds, litanies of horror and death the likes of which Ranis could only dream of. The markings met in the centre of the figure's upper back, arrows and circles forming the sigil borne on so many of fourteenth legion's banners.

The figure shifted slightly as Ranis crept in, still stooped over, making a faint, wet suckling noise. Despite his urgency, Ranis found himself pausing, mustering the courage to speak. He found his tongue eventually, and breathed a single word.

"Brother—"

What happened next was too fast for Ranis to follow. The figure moved, a blur of speed, the next thing he knew he was in the air, then pinned against the stone wall, his feet kicking uselessly, one armoured gauntlet clamping around his throat and nailing him in place like an insect on a specimen board.

He choked, hands instinctively going up to try to prise open the murder-grip, but it was utterly unyielding.

He found himself gazing into the red eyes of Lowerniel Drakan. There was nothing but bloodlust and hunger, and he was convinced his brother was about to rip his head off.

Just as suddenly as Ranis had been pinned, he was released. He dropped unceremoniously to the floorboards, though his reflexes allowed him to land lithely on his feet. He gasped, clutching his throat, trying to recover as Drakan spoke.

"Why do you disturb me?"

Ranis took a moment, finding his words as he forced himself to look up at his brother. Drakan had adopted the bestial aspect vampyres usually succumbed to when feeding, his high-boned, haughty features twisted into an animal countenance akin to that of a fanged bat. His lower jaw and broad chest were glistening with fresh blood. The scent of it made Ranis shiver with a sudden and potent hunger, but he suppressed it.

"I would not interrupt you if it wasn't urgent," he said, managing to meet his brother's gaze.

"Then speak."

"We have prisoners. Members of one of the garrisons

further south were fool enough to allow themselves to be taken alive."

"Is that so?" Drakan demanded. "And who took them?"

"Legionaries," Ranis said evasively, not wanting to mention that it had specifically been legionaries from the cohort that their sister, Vanescula, commanded. "But they are now in the care of my own brood. I have instructed none to touch them while they await your pleasure."

Drakan grunted. He turned aside, seemingly about to depart, but paused before leaving the room. Despite his best efforts, Ranis found himself staring at the bloody carcasses littering the floor. A terrible need churned inside him, a void that demanded to be filled.

"Go on, little brother," Drakan said, with something that might have been a smile. "Feed. You have earned it tonight."

✦ ✦ ✦

Lowerniel Drakan passed through his host. At its core was the fourteenth legion, a force of veteran Zamorakian soldiers who had long been bonded to his service. They came to attention as the phalanx of vyreguard that had closed in around him moved through their ranks, beating their swords against their shields in salute.

The common vyre surrounded Drakan's elite. Thralls, fang-masters and brood-warriors, a pallid swarm forged into a loyal and disciplined host by his iron will. There were lesser creatures too, undead wights and shambling corpses, and half-feral werewolves that prowled along the flanks of the host, hunting for scraps. Their snarls and growls silenced as Drakan passed by.

This was the army he had created, unleashed now with the blessings of Zamorak. The only being Drakan would even consider kneeling before had paid back his decision to betray the Stranger from Afar by promising him Hallowvale. And now, finally, the time had come to claim that reward. The gleaming city, with all its teeming, warm-blooded inhabitants, would be his. It would be the start of an empire on Gielinor, one that would cover the land in night and render Drakan lord of both the living and the dead.

At least, that was what Zamorak believed. That was why the dark god had agreed to Drakan's suggestion that a second front be opened in the east. He believed it would force Saradomin to abandon his siege of the Infernal Source and march back, to protect the city founded in his honour. Drakan did not care if he did or didn't. What mattered was not the city, but what lay beneath it, hidden in the dark, a secret that would allow him to found more than just another petty kingdom.

He discovered his sister, Vanescula, along with her brood, close to where the vanguard had halted. Their fangs were bared and talons out, facing off against Ranis's thralls, who had gathered around a small gaggle of prisoners, warding off the others of their kind.

The vyre quietened as Drakan moved among them, their aggressive hissing reduced to a low susurration. Vampyres respected power above all else, and none were more powerful than Drakan.

"Forgive us for disturbing you, brother," Vanescula said, doubtless noting the blood that had dried across his lower face and chest. "Ranis is being his usual, petulant self. My cohort were the ones who took these prisoners, but his thralls have seized them."

Drakan did not deign to respond, walking past her. He experienced brief disappointment in Vanescula. His sister was the only one who ever impressed him. She was measured where their younger brother, Ranis, was arrogant, watchful where he was aggressive, intelligent whilst he relied on a kind of low cunning. Drakan hoped the day would come when she would be like him – too powerful to be concerned about the opinions of others. Still, he had expected her to take the sting out of a situation like this, not worsen it with confrontation.

Ranis's brood had the good sense to part and admit him. Besides the vyre, the three prisoners were being guarded by their old comrades. A practitioner of the dark arts – possibly one of the necromancers that accompanied the legion, or Ranis himself, though he had little talent for it – had resurrected the slaughtered border guards, and now a dozen of them stood in close array around the three kneeling captives, their eyes smouldering with corpse-light, their bodies so fresh, blood still dripped from their wounds.

Drakan caused them to shuffle clumsily to one side with a single word. He stood, gazing down on the prize Ranis had stolen.

All three of the mortals were shivering and pale. None daring to look up. Drakan could smell their fear and hear the rapid beating of their hearts, driving warm, sweet blood through their soft bodies. It was intoxicating.

He reached down and snatched the hair of one, forcing the man to gaze upon him. Little more than a youth, fresh cheeks streaked with tears. His armour was simple leather, and he still had a pouch at his side bearing stones for a sling he had presumably abandoned. A prodromoi, a skirmisher in the Saradominist armies. This one, like the other two, had been considered unfit for the ferocious battles happening further west. They had been left behind, and had proven too cowardly or too foolish to end their own lives before they were taken.

Drakan stooped, and gazed deep into the youth's terrified eyes. They were wide, brown, devoid of anything but fear. Dumb, like cattle, Drakan thought.

He spoke words of power, hissed phrases taught to his kind long ago. There was a cadence to them, a lilting beat that matched the prisoner's heart, battering like a drum in Drakan's ears.

He watched the mortal slowly stop shivering, watched the fear leach out of his gaze, replaced by slack-jawed dullness. The hypnotic incantation finished, he spoke in the crude, grunting language the humans that followed Saradomin favoured.

"Where are the rest of the border forces?"

"Gone."

"Gone where?"

"West. Reinforcements."

Drakan already knew that, but he wished to test his level of control. The hypnotic arts had their uses, occasionally –

humans were susceptible, though the strong-willed could resist. This one was so broken he was barely coherent.

"Hallowvale's garrison – is it weak too?"

"No."

"How strong is the tagma?"

"Strong. The ordos are in the city."

That answer surprised Drakan. The human ordos were among the best of the Saradominist warriors. He had hoped most would be engaged at the Infernal Source.

"Which ones?"

"The Wolves. We saw them pass by a month ago."

"Is the city ready for a siege?"

"No."

"Were you expecting an attack from the north?"

"No."

"Are you ready to die?"

"No."

Drakan grunted, vaguely amused, and pressed a talon against the youth's brow, drawing the slightest bead of blood. The sudden pain broke the hypnosis. He began to shake again, and moaned with fear.

There was a thump from behind Drakan, and the hiss of a vyre's wings folding.

"Are they of any use, brother?" Ranis asked as he rejoined him, still wiping blood from his mouth.

"Matters are progressing," he told the lesser vampyre. "Continue the advance. And the next time you wish to steal your sister's glory, do not lie to me about it. I thought you would have learned that lesson by now."

A flash of anger crossed Ranis's face, but he wisely controlled it.

"As long as I have been of some assistance," he said, and offered a short bow. Drakan ignored him.

He had learned all he needed to. He unfurled his wings, and Ranis spoke again as he realised his brother was about to depart.

"You have no more use for them?"

Greedy, Drakan thought.

"Do with them what you wish," he said before taking flight, the screams of the prisoners following him as he returned to the watchtower.

Drakan alighted on the watchtower's parapets, perching on their edge. He looked to the south-east, towards the light glowing on the horizon, that sickening, aching, eternal false dawn that he knew belonged to the Everlight, the beacon tower that stood in the bay beyond the city of Hallowvale. It was the brilliance of Saradomin made manifest, anathema to all his kind.

To take the city would be one thing. To snuff out that beacon would be the greatest success Lowerniel Drakan had known since he had united the clans of Vampyrium. Yet all would be a means to an end. The prize he sought was far greater than breaking the Everlight, or even claiming the city. It was what lay beneath its streets, hidden and half-forgotten in the dark – true power, and the chance to remake all of Gielinor in his image.

FOUR

◀◆▶

Word of the approaching darkness broke among the people of Hallowvale the day after Queen Efaritay called her council. Perhaps one of the merchant emporoi let slip what had been discussed, or maybe the stories of the first refugees to arrive outside the gates began to reach the masses. Either way, the streets were soon in something close to turmoil.

Luken arose as he always did, washing and dressing in his dorm room before helping Akeron with his own ablutions. He did so in an exhausted fog, performing his duties by rote. The service had lasted well past middle-night, and he had lain awake for the remaining hours, the shutters of his chamber window slightly ajar to admit some of the Everlight's glow, keeping the deepest shadows at bay. The whole night, his mind had raced with thoughts of pale, red-eyed killers and armies of approaching nightmares.

He resisted the urge to ask Akeron more questions. The archpriest seemed as tired as he was, and liable to snap at him. As he finished tying his sandals, there was a knock at the door to the bedchamber. Luken answered and found himself confronted by one of the justiciar of the unicorn's hypaspists.

"Apologies for the disturbance, hallowed archpriest," the woman said, speaking to Akeron over Luken's head, "but there are large numbers of people gathering outside the main doors of the Church, and in the square beyond."

Akeron grunted, waving at Luken to bring him his star staff.

"Word must have gotten out," he said. "Even sooner than I feared."

"We are expected at the citadel for the reconvened council," Luken pointed out.

"Should I assemble an escort, hallowed archpriest?" the hypaspist asked.

"No," Akeron said. "Open the doors. Allow the people into the upper hall."

"But, archpriest, there is no sermon scheduled for today," Luken exclaimed, unable to avoid thinking about how he had finished sweeping the hall following Akeron's late service mere hours before.

"I am not archpriest of the unicorn only during the hours of my sermons," Akeron said sternly, a glare banishing his tired expression. "I am Saradomin's chief representative in this city. What would the Lord of Light think if the doors of his greatest temple remained barred while his children, scared and confused, are left outside?"

"But the council," Luken said in a half-hearted attempt at changing Akeron's mind.

"The council will convene again with or without us," Akeron continued. "And I heard quite enough of what they all had to say yesterday. Us being there will not make one blind bit of difference. But you know what will?"

Luken shook his head, nonplussed.

"Giving the people hope, reassurance and clarity. Light and wisdom, the blessings of our god."

"You're going to tell them what's coming?"

"They already know, some of them at least. But lying to them won't make it any easier when the Zamorakian hordes arrive outside the walls."

Luken felt a surge of mixed emotions, at once relieved and disappointed at being denied another visit to the citadel. He bowed his head in acquiescence.

"I will bring the star crown for you then, archpriest," he said.

"Open the doors," Akeron reiterated to the hypaspist. "And see the people through to the upper hall. I'm going to teach them not to be afraid of the dark."

✦ ✦ ✦

Fear gripped the streets of Hallowvale. Shops shut early and stall sellers packed away their wares in defiance of crowds of people attempting to stockpile food. Tempers flared. A massed brawl broke out in the market square, and only the arrival of a flock of armed icyene psiloi eventually broke it apart. Several shops along Pytheou Street were broken into.

There were reports of a fire in a tannery on Bastion Way, further adding to the alarm.

Amidst it all, the council reconvened in the throne room of the citadel. A large tapestry map had been spread out across the floor in the centre of the circle, showing the extent of the city and the lands surrounding it.

Rhea stood once more with Phosani, waiting for the queen to call the assembly to order. She had slept little, and had busied herself by putting a fresh edge on her kopis. She fully expected rest to be elusive for the foreseeable future. That did not concern her. The sharpness of her blade did.

Archpriest Akeron and Justiciar Lysander were both absent, and when the latter eventually arrived, he explained the continued absence of the former.

"The archpriest is holding an impromptu service at the Church," Lysander said. "One where he has informed the congregation of the approach of Drakan's host."

"Old fool," Babel snarled, the insult causing shocked expressions among a number of the humans present. Rhea caught Phosani glaring at the icyene as he continued. "He will create a panic."

"Judging by the situation on the streets as we came here, panic is already afoot," Lysander said, the look he gave Babel' as dark as Phosani's.

"Guidance and reassurance will likely be of great use in the coming hours," Phosani added. "The archpriest is doing his duty as a keeper and bringer of the light. Now, we must do ours, as warriors of that same light."

"The city must prepare for a siege," Efaritay said. Rhea felt the weight of her declaration, the seeming finality of it. There was silence before Babel spoke.

"Perhaps that will not be necessary. I believe our best course of action will be to march forth and meet the enemy in the field. The faster they reach the city, the quicker they may be able to take it. We should delay them for as long as possible."

"I agree. We cannot allow the vyre to march unopposed to our gates," Efaritay said. "But I would caution against committing the entire tagma against them in the open. It would accentuate our numerical disadvantage and risk disaster if we are defeated and unable to withdraw to the city's walls."

"What of the common people?" Lysander wondered aloud. "There are thousands living between the northern borders and the gates. Many will be unaware of what is happening. We should seek to evacuate them to the city."

"But how will we deal with the problem of supply?" one of the most senior of the emporoi merchants, Ranquel, asked. "And housing? The streets are already in turmoil! Where will these thousands go, and who will feed them?"

"The harvest is almost all in, and there are enough large, empty buildings in the city to provide accommodation, besides the market square," Efaritay said. "And if today's unrest does not abate, martial laws will be put into effect."

"Time is of the essence," Babel declared before Ranquel could respond to the queen's claims. "How long will it take us to spread the word and have people and wagons brought into the city? Days, certainly, if not weeks."

"What is the alternative?" Phosani demanded, still looking fiercely at Babel. "Abandon the people?"

"We need neither abandon, nor evacuate them if we meet the foe head-on."

"You would stake everything on a pitched battle, where we are at a disadvantage?"

"Our disadvantage is numerical only. This is our land. Most of us know every wood and hill and stream between here and the watchtowers. I could name three excellent defensive sites right now where the Zamorakians would have no option other than to attack us head-on."

"I believe our response needs to be measured," Efaritay said, her tone firm. "It is imperative we delay their incursion, but I will not commit all our forces to such a gambit. We will seek to harry their flanks while avoiding a pitched battle. The vyre will be weak during the daylight hours. On the other hand, we icyene can still match them in the air after dark. The light of Saradomin is within us."

"The humans are a liability," Babel said bluntly. "They are too prone to vampyric trickery. Are you suggesting we icyene fight unsupported?"

"We do not know that for certain," Phosani spoke up. "I have been in campaigns where the Zamorakian legions have included vampyres. It is true that the blessings of Saradomin repulse them. Even the presence of icyene is difficult for all but the most powerful of their kind to overcome."

"They detest the light in all its forms," Lysander added. "We should be thankful of the Everlight as well. No vyre will be able to penetrate it."

"So long as Saradomin's light shines, hope endures," Phosani said, speaking scripture from the Book of Light.

"Every warrior who goes into battle with the vyre should do so with Saradomin's blessings, now more than ever," Efaritay said. "Whether it will be enough, remains to be seen."

"It will be enough," Phosani declared.

"I pray so," Efaritay said. "It will be some time yet before the messengers dispatched to Saradomin last night return. Until then, I propose we delay the Zamorakians with hit-and-run strikes, while we continue to prepare Hallowvale for the inevitable."

Rhea half expected Babel to continue to push the idea of a pitched battle, but the strategos held his tongue. Efaritay put it to a vote, which passed almost unanimously.

"Justiciars, prepare your hypaspists," the queen ordered. "It is time to bring the people of Hallowvale to safety."

✦ ✦ ✦

The council was dismissed. Efaritay sent the royal guards from the chamber as well, leaving only her and Ascertes, seated on their thrones. As soon as the sound of the doors closing reverberated through the hall, the queen was up and pacing, sweeping down from the dais.

"How was I?" she asked after a few pensive moments.

Ascertes remained sitting, though his eyes never left his wife.

"You were strong," he said. "Decisive."

"If only that was enough," she replied.

Ascertes continued to watch her, seeking the right words.

He knew his wife was too sharp to be assuaged by platitudes and words of encouragement.

"They are divided," he said eventually. Efaritay ceased her pacing.

"What do you mean?"

Ascertes paused, uneager to undermine already fragile foundations.

"You know I value your insights in all things," Efaritay pressed. "Please, share your thoughts with me."

"Half of them are too confident," Ascertes finally admitted. "And half are too terrified. We want neither arrogance, nor fear. Now is a time for firm but considered action."

Efaritay stepped back up onto the dais, slowly, thinking aloud as she went.

"It is not surprising, I suppose. Half of them are warriors, and half are priests and merchants. The terror I can understand. But we cannot afford to be too bold. Not until we are sure the city has been secured and Saradomin has dispatched aid."

"Your decisiveness earlier has helped ensure that," Ascertes said. "You were right to go against Babel. He is rash."

"Strategos Babel is a skilled fighter and a fine commander, but he thinks only like an icyene," Efaritay said, halting before Ascertes' throne. "Head amongst the clouds. He envisages striking swift and true, like an arrow, not the butchery in the mud that a pitched battle would become. We do not have the numbers for that."

"You know my view of the hallowed strategos, my queen," Ascertes said, rising to stand before her, having to look up to meet the eyes of the tall icyene woman.

"Indeed," Efaritay said, answering Ascertes' smile with a slight one of her own. The glory of Hallowvale was built upon the coexistence of humans and icyene together, just as Saradomin intended. Still, there was always the potential for discord, and few would argue that the city belonged to the icyene first, and humans second. It was only an icyene who could rule, and icyene who occupied the senior military, administrative and bureaucratic roles. Human primacy existed only in the position of archpriest, the role rotating between the four Saradominist priesthoods of the wolf, lion, owl and unicorn, and even then, the icyene wielded vast influence. In the Hallowed Sepulchre, only icyene were permitted to be buried on the lowest levels, while the blessing of marriage at the city's acropolis was possible only if at least one of those being wedded was icyene.

Yet despite it all, Queen Efaritay had taken a human husband. Ascertes had first encountered her at a banquet celebrating the Day of Light. He had been young then, and she not quite yet in her prime, new to the throne. His family were minor nobility, originating from near the Lum River, but owned estates in Hallowvale just north of the city.

It had been passionate. A whirlwind which had snatched them both up and thrown them together in its midst. It was a match none had expected, and one which few icyene had approved of. Had she still been living, Efaritay's mother, by all accounts a particularly austere and harsh ruler, would have forbidden the union.

Ascertes had feared that Saradomin himself might forbid the marriage, wishing to secure Hallowvale with a strong icyene bloodline, but the god of light had passed no judgement – at least not to Ascertes' knowledge – and Efaritay had scorned the discontent of her own people, including the anger of Archon Babel, who had never veiled claims that Hallowvale would be better served by her marriage to him, and the political and military alliance that would create.

All that had been over twenty years ago. They had secured their succession with a daughter and a son, Larina and Safalaan. Ascertes had felt the years slowly beginning to grind on him, his strong jawline now less clear-cut and his hair thinning. Efaritay, however, had maintained a pristine icyene beauty, as pale and clear and perfect as a fresh spring morning. She was as enthralling to Ascertes then as she had been the day he had first laid eyes on her.

He kissed her. She returned it, then embraced him, her great white wings arching around to enclose him. There for a moment it truly was just the two of them, and the weight of all that had come before and all that must yet be done fell away.

"I love you," Ascertes said.

"And I love you," Efaritay affirmed. "From now until the end of time."

She paused, and the two enjoyed the silence for a little longer, but Ascertes sensed there was more she wished to say.

"Last night…" She trailed off.

"You did not come to bed," Ascertes recalled. "I am sorry. I should have stayed up with you."

Normally, the pair resided in the royal palace in the south-east of the city, but they had agreed to taking rooms in the citadel until the crisis had ended. Safalaan and Larina were due to be moved to join them as well – Captain Calix, commander of the icyene royal guard, had assured them that the citadel was the safest place to be.

"No," Efaritay said, releasing her husband and furling her wings. "I was not in the citadel. I had to leave for a while, to make a start on a project, one that I hope will make all the difference. But it must remain hidden, for now. It is too early, too fragile."

"Even for me to know?"

"A few more days, and I will seek your counsel on it."

"Then you have told me just to pique my anticipation? Tease."

"You know I cannot keep secrets from you." The queen smiled, placing a hand on his cheek.

"No hints?"

"It will be a weapon, I hope. One that no spawn of Vampyrium can stand against."

"That might just prove useful," Ascertes allowed, humour in his eyes.

Efaritay did not answer immediately. She turned away and resumed her anxious pacing, back down the dais and into the main body of the chamber, the stone eyes of a dozen great icyene ancestors gazing down on her.

"Alone, it will not be enough," she said. "We must marshall all our strength. If we are found wanting, all we hold dear will be destroyed."

FIVE

———◆———

Phosani's pack assembled in the barracks quadrangle on Lumenance Street.

Rhea inspected them prior to the arrival of the justiciar of the wolf. There were two hundred hypaspists in all, the elite of the human Saradominist ordos, heavily armed and armoured, and most of them battle-hardened.

They were clad in shining breastplates, greaves and vambraces, as well as helmets crested with a tuft of grey wolf's tail. Most were equipped with spears – dorata – and heavy round shields – aspides – as well as xiphos short swords.

The Wolves were the most aggressive of the four ordos. Leave it to the Owls to hold the line with their shield walls, or the Unicorns to strike light and swift – Phosani's pack attacked head-on, straight at the jugular, and once they had bitten deep they didn't let go until the foe had stopped twitching.

They'd done plenty of that over the past few years. Phosani, Rhea and most of the hypaspists arrayed before her had been at war with the Zamorakian legions for years. Over the past few months alone the campaign over Carralanger had seen more than their share of blood and suffering. They had returned to Hallowvale just over a month earlier, to rest and recruit, refilling ranks eroded and plucked at by a dozen battles. Despite the time spent mending arms and repairing armour, Rhea still noted combat damage as she walked the lines – notched spear hafts, scarred breastplates and scarred faces, gazing firmly ahead, not meeting her eyes.

She noted where repairs had not been enough, and went even harder on the new recruits, the young faces, uncut, unmarred, imposters standing in between old, familiar comrades. She barked at them to tighten buckles, straighten helmets, dress ranks, stand tall. She was hard on them all, because that was her duty. That was what the White Wolf required of her.

She also ensured every warrior carried a Saradominist star token. Almost all bore one already, either emblazoned on their armour or worn about their neck, for Phosani's hypaspists were a faithful band. Still, Rhea checked that they were burnished and displayed. The instructions from the council had been clear. The light of Saradomin would be as potent a weapon as those clenched in the Wolves' fists.

Phosani arrived not long after Rhea had finished her inspection. She was accompanied by Otrava who, alongside the crossbow-woman Insela, was the next in the ordo's chain of command after Rhea. Otrava and Phosani had been at prayer together, but Rhea sometimes wondered just how pious Otrava had been before she had encountered the White Wolf. Besides her martial efforts she was studying to be a potion-maker, Rhea liked her as little as she liked Insela – both had only joined the Wolves in time for their last campaign, amidst the ruins of Carralanger. Rhea had seen little of either of them in combat, and too much of them when it came to internal ordo politics. There were few things that Rhea despised more, and she found something unsettling in Otrava's hooded eyes. Like Insela, she always seemed to be watching.

The assembled hypaspists came to attention with a crash of steel as Rhea strode across the parade ground and saluted her commander, two fingers tapping the star of Saradomin on her own breastplate.

"The ordo of the wolf is assembled for war, justiciar," she reported, ignoring Otrava.

"How do they look?" Phosani asked, voice low enough to not carry to the front rank.

"Blunt," Rhea said without hesitation. "But what can you expect from a blade that hasn't seen a whetstone in months?"

"We did our best to avoid that," Phosani said. "Drills, inspections."

"You asked me for my opinion. You know as well as I that campaigning is the only sure way of keeping a soldier fit and ready."

"We shall have to pray to noble Saradomin that the whetstone does not shave off too much," Otrava said. Rhea held her gaze coldly before Phosani spoke.

"Thank you, Rhea. You may take your place. You as well, Otrava."

Rhea saluted again and marched to her post, near the right of the front rank. She nodded to Klaxar, the first warrior on her left, a short, dark-skinned Uzerian she had fought almost every battle alongside. Rhea had never known her own family – they had all perished in a Zamorakian raid while she was still a child – but the likes of Klaxar and the hypaspist who stood in the file behind her, Mardin, were like sister and brother to her. The ordo had long been the only family that mattered.

"Wolves of Saradomin," Phosani called, standing before the assembled host. "By now, you will all have heard the rumours, but allow me to speak plainly. We all know the legions of Zamorak do not rest, and that has been proven true once again. An invasion of Hallowvale is underway, led by vampyric filth, spawned from the darkness. This is a foe feared by any true child of Saradomin, but not by the Wolves!"

There were growls of affirmation as Phosani continued.

"We ride out now to bring the people of Hallowvale to safety. The vampyre is a heinous foe, able to corrupt and confound, but they cannot withstand the light! They fear it, and that means they will fear us, for we are Saradomin's shining sword, and we will burn away their foulness!"

"The light," the assembled hypaspists barked as one, their declaration of faith ringing around the quadrangle and out across Lumenance Street. "The light!"

"To horse," Phosani ordered. "Let us carry that light from these walls, and scourge away this darkness."

✦ ✦ ✦

The city's tagma marched from the western gate, in the shadow of the citadel. Luken had a prime view of the martial display from the gatehouse, standing shivering next to Akeron as the archpriest gave his blessings to the departing soldiers. The priests of the wolf, owl and lion were present as well, their voices overlapping in the wind, stentorian tones calling out the litanies of the Book of Light and making the sign of the star again and again with hand and staff. Their prayers competed with the snapping of the blue and gold banners that had been hoisted above the gatehouse, a final reminder to the departing warriors of Hallowvale that their god was watching over them.

Luken held one of the Hallowed Church's copies of the Book of Light aloft for the soldiers below to see if they glanced up. While the sight of rank after rank stretching out below him along the road from the city had been thrilling at first, he had quickly grown miserable. The autumn wind had a wintery bite to it, and it felt as though he had done nothing over the past day and a half besides attend to Akeron while he said his prayers for the masses. The old archpriest's voice was beginning to crack, a sure sign that he had preached one sermon too many.

Out in the distance, beyond the Everlight's reassuring brilliance, it seemed as though an early twilight had settled over the land, reducing everything to muted shades of brown, green and grey. Low, wrathful clouds were broiling up to the north. Luken had already asked if the vampyres were summoning them to hide their pale faces from the sun – all the stories agreed that such creatures were weaker during the daylight, and could not endure the holy Saradominist glow of the Everlight in particular. Akeron had refused to answer. All Luken knew was what he had heard the old man preach, that the vyre were the spawn of the darkness, and that faith in the holy light of Saradomin would banish them.

Faith and, it seemed, a strong sword-arm. Luken couldn't imagine how any foe could stand against the host he was seeing march from the city.

"Go forth, defenders of Hallowvale," Akeron was calling, intertwining dogma with encouragement. "Go forth, and carry the light with you! His is the light that makes all things known! Trust in it, trust in victory!"

Luken felt the weight of the old tome in his cold hands, and found himself looking for any hint of daylight breaking through the distant clouds, and sign that their god was coming to their aid.

There was none.

◆ ◆ ◆

The tagma marched west then north as the day grew old, dividing as it went. The ordo of the wolf were dispatched along the road to Korkyria by Babel, with instructions to evacuate the hamlets and farmsteads scattered across the area. Phosani in turn divided her command between herself, Rhea, Otrava and Insela, hoping to fulfil her duties as quickly as possible and rejoin the main host.

Rhea led Klaxar, Mardin and two dozen hypaspists to a trio of farms occupying a small valley west of the Deepwood. Middle-day had passed, and the sun was sinking fast, driven by the lateness of the year. A cold wind, herald of the coming winter, was cutting across the rutted, tree-lined track they were taking, snatching the last golden-brown leaves from skeletal branches and sending them whipping and flurrying about the riders.

Death was in the air. Rhea could sense it all around, a bitter promise. She continued to scan the grey sky through the branches as they went, one hand resting on the hilt of her kopis. They didn't know just how far south-east the Zamorakians had penetrated. During the day their masters would be slow and weak, and the general consensus seemed to be they would make little ground before nightfall. But Rhea had been in too many campaigns to fall into the trap of assuming an enemy's strength or movements. The common legionaries of the Zamorakian host were humans, and presumably unafraid of the sun. Advancing towards a foe without at least knowing their approximal location – and dividing while doing so – sat ill with her.

The occupants of the first two farms they came to were shocked to find their yards filled with armoured ordo warriors. They had heard nothing of the invasion, nor the queen's instructions to head for Hallowvale. Rhea had them fill their wagons with what produce they could and set out before moving on, sending a trio of hypaspists with each family with instructions to abandon the wagons if they were slowing them down too much. Recent rains had turned the tracks and pathways through the countryside into mud, which wasn't helping the Saradominist mobilisation.

As they rode into the yard of the third farmstead, Rhea felt something was wrong. It was too quiet. There was no one in the fields, no animals in their pens, no lowing of livestock from the barn. The only movement was one of the stead's window shutters, banging repetitively in the wind.

"Mardin, Klaxar, with me," she ordered as she dismounted and tied her reins to the farmyard's hitching post. "Almar, Juko, search the barn. The rest of you, establish a perimeter. Watch the skies as well as the trees."

As the hypaspists obeyed, Rhea approached the front door. She knocked, her fist ringing against the stout wood. The only answer was the ongoing, nerve-fraying clatter of the shutters.

Rhea tried the handle. It was unlocked. She looked back at Klaxar and Mardin. Neither said anything, but Klaxar hefted her twin-headed labrys axe.

Rhea eased the door open with one hand, the timber creaking painfully, while slipping her kopis free from its scabbard with her other.

She knew immediately that they were too late. The entrance led into a kitchen space in total disarray, the table overturned, pots and pans scattered, plates shattered, a stool smashed.

Silently, she directed Klaxar and Mardin in as well, treading as lightly as possible on the floorboards. Her heart was racing, and she took a second to calm her breathing before carrying on.

A pantry lay undisturbed beyond the kitchen, and with it a set of stairs. She began to climb them, her kopis poised before her. She timed each step to the banging of the shutter, not wanting the creaking to give her away to anything that might still be above them.

At the landing she heard a shout. From outside, plucked at by the wind.

"On me," she barked, dashing back down. Klaxar and Mardin burst from the other rooms and charged out into the mud of the farmyard.

The shout had come from the barn. Rhea reached it just as Juko came stumbling from its doors, retching. She swept past him, calling out Almar's name as she went.

It was dark within, the pallid, watery daylight filtering in through slats in the woodwork. The air was earthy, filled with the reek of livestock. Rhea's first step landed on something wet and yielding. She came to a halt, arm straight and kopis raised, letting her eyes adjust.

Almar was standing in the middle of the space. He was one of Rhea's veterans, which was why she had assigned one of the fresher faces, Juko, to accompany him. He turned as Rhea entered, his expression unreadable in the half-dark.

"We found the farmers," he said. Rhea looked down, realising she'd stepped in an unidentifiable mess of offal. She moved to Almar's side, and he gestured into one of the stalls that lined the barn's walls.

The place was heaped with bloody remains. Most of them seemed to be the barn's cattle, but not all. Rhea felt a surge of anger and revulsion, emotions she forced herself to quash.

Right now, they weren't useful. She needed to be cold, and focused.

She stooped over the carcasses, the stink of blood hitting her.

"They look like they were savaged by feral animals," she said after a few moments, trying to piece together what had happened. "Either the vyre are ever more bestial than the stories claim, or..."

She trailed off, turning over different possibilities in her mind. If the vampyres had gotten this far south, perhaps accounts of their hatred of the daytime had been exaggerated? If they could fly during the day, they could reach the city walls in just a few hours more.

Klaxar called for her from the barn's front door. She rejoined her companion outside. Juko was still composing himself, face white as an icyene's wings. Rhea ignored him as Klaxar pointed out something in the mud leading to the barn doors.

"Prints," the hypaspist said.

He was right. The mud was a mess, and clearly there had been a struggle in the yard before the farmstead's inhabitants had been forced into the barn.

"They had dogs with them," Mardin commented, crouching over a different set of prints – paw markings. Rhea followed them a short way in reverse, back towards the farmhouse, before stopping and staring.

Halfway across the yard, the pawprints became the marks of human feet.

Realisation struck, colder than any autumn wind.

She ran back towards the barn just as a cry rose from within it, shouldering her way past Juko and shouting as she went.

"Werewolves!"

SIX

———◆———

There was one in the barn with Almar. It had borne the veteran hypaspist down, all claws and bristling fur and savagery. Almar cried out again, trying to snatch at where his doru spear had fallen amidst the bloodied hay, but the beast had its jaw clamped around his throat, a twist of its head sending blood jetting.

Rhea charged the werewolf with a roar. It twisted away from her strike at the last moment, snarling, its muzzle bloody. She barrelled into it, using her momentum to bear it down and drive her kopis into its midriff.

Anger and hate lent her strength. She ripped the curved blade free and slashed at the beast's neck. It went still under her.

She heard a thud. There was no time to check on Almar, there was a second werewolf in the barn. They had concealed themselves among the rafters, lurking in the darkness there, the stink of their butchery masking their scent.

The creature made for the door at the far end of the barn, claws scrabbling on the floor. Rhea made it to her feet, but Klaxar was already storming past her with a shout of her own, swinging her labrys. It connected with the werewolf's upper back as the beast made it out into the daylight. It let out a pained yelp, before Klaxar ended it with another swing.

Rhea searched the rafters, but they were empty now. She cursed herself for not looking up sooner. The mistake had cost Almar his life. The hypaspist lay, neck glistening, face strangely pale and calm, almost reproachful-looking as it stared with unseeing eyes past Rhea. She mastered the worst of her anger and sorrow, then made the sign of the star over him.

Juko and Mardin had entered, weapons drawn. Rhea snapped at the former to retrieve Almar's doru and xiphos as well as the Saradomin icon he wore around his wrist, before standing and stepping over the body.

She joined Klaxar at the far end of the barn, ducking out into the cold wind. Like the corpse of the werewolf that Rhea had killed, the one Klaxar had brought down was reverting to its human form, bones cracking and popping and fur shedding. The corpse it left behind was skinny and pale.

"They were youths," Rhea said darkly. "Probably stayed behind to scavenge the remains, but the main pack won't be far."

As though in answer, a terrible sound rose from the woodland beyond the fields, a noise that called for a primal response in every human that heard it – the howl of a wolf. It was joined by more, until the mournful wailing was ringing out over the fallow acres, an answer to the dying shriek of Klaxar's victim.

"Lord of Light," she murmured, staring at the dark tree line.

"Get to the horses," Rhea said. "Everybody. Make for the road. Now!"

✦ ✦ ✦

The ordo of the wolf fled before their namesake.

Rhea's first instinct had been to stand and fight. She trusted her hypaspists, and trusted that they could have defended the farmstead against any beastly pack, even outnumbered. But if they had done so, they would likely have abandoned their horses to be slaughtered, and that would have left them cut off. Night was coming, and Rhea had no doubt the vyre would soon be abroad.

So they rode, back along the track, aiming for the end of the valley and the road beyond it, where the rest of the tagma would be close.

Rhea took up the rear with Mardin. It had pained her to even leave Almar's body behind – she wouldn't allow any others under her command to be picked off.

The howling grew louder, harrying them over the rush of the wind and the thunder of hooves. Rhea felt her fear, the instinctive response to the realisation that they were being hunted. She tried to use it, tried to drive her mount on, daring to snatch a glance to her left and right.

There were shapes beyond the trees lining the track, feral, loping things, half-formed, part beast, part man. They were gaining.

More than that, Rhea knew. They were trying to hem them in and cut them off.

"We can't outride them," Mardin shouted as he galloped alongside her.

She knew he was right. They were faster than their horses. Another few minutes and they would be overtaken from either side, and then it would be a case of the creatures bursting in among the riding column, ripping at the hamstrings and bellies of their horses and leaping astride the falling hypaspists. It would be a massacre.

Rhea sawed on her reins, thighs clamped to her mount's flanks as it reared in the roadway. Mardin came up short as well, turning back to her, shouting.

"What are you doing?"

"Buying time for the others," Rhea snapped. "Keep going, for light's sake!"

"Not without you," Mardin responded.

There was no time to argue, or to curse him for a fool. She'd sent Klaxar with the head of the column, to lead them to the main road. There was no one she'd trust more to get them through.

She shot a glance either side, then back to the track. The werewolves were closing in with horrifying, unnatural speed, their howls ringing through the air. At the very least, she and Mardin seemed to have drawn their attention.

"Better on foot," she said, dropping down to the ground.

As Mardin did likewise she clapped a hand to her horse's rear, sending it racing off after the others.

"Not the place I thought we'd meet our end," Mardin said morosely as he hefted his doru. Brown and gold leaves flurried down around them, the howling and snarling of the pack filled the air as they closed in on the two dismounted hypaspists, beginning to circle them.

"Better than growing old, losing your wits and dying in some piss-soaked bed," Rhea told her friend, shifting her stance in the mud, guarding his left side while he protected her right. The hammering of her heart drove out the last of her doubts and fears. All that was left was to do what she did best – fight.

She gestured at one of the werewolves that had led the pack down the pathway, its pelt thick and streaked with grey, drool running from its wicked, bared canines.

"Come on then, beast," she shouted to it, giving it a snarl of her own.

She was ready for the werewolf's lunge, holding her kopis low, point upwards, but instead of attacking, it twisted to one side with a yelp. A shaft of wood had materialised as though by sorcery in its shoulder, the end fletched with white feathers.

As Rhea watched, more arrows came whipping down from above, fully like a sudden hailstorm. They struck the circling werewolves with unerring accuracy, driving them into a frenzy of yelping and barking. The largest one, the one Rhea had seen hit first, snapped the haft of the arrow buried in its shoulder with one hand and, in an unerringly human-like gesture, rose onto its hind legs. It howled up at the low clouds, clouds that now acted as a backdrop to a dozen flying figures.

Icyene. They were prodromoi skirmishers, lightly armoured and wielding short bows which they now used to rain arrows down on the pack. Each one had a glimmering sheen about them, a luminescence that fought back against the day's steadily deepening gloom.

Rhea hadn't known such a sense of relief for a long time.

The werewolves, flightless and unarmed, were helpless against the circling skirmishers. A second arrow struck the pack's leader, and he turned and delivered a series of barks. With the fluidity of bonded hunters, the beasts broke off and loped away into the surrounding fields, scattering. They left several of their number lying in their wake, studded with arrows, twitching as, in death, their veneer of humanity returned.

The icyene didn't pursue. One swooped down, landing with grace and poise on the path just in front of Rhea and Mardin. Bow still in one hand, he tapped his leather breastplate in salute. Rhea returned the gesture, limbs feeling suddenly weak as the passions of combat deserted her.

"My name is Xavix," the icyene said. "Well met, hypaspist of the wolf."

"Rhea," she replied. "Light be with you, Xavix."

"We've been scouring the skies, but they remain clear for now," he continued. "That will doubtless change come the night, but this isn't the first were-pack we've tracked today."

"That pack will regroup—"

"Which is why you should rejoin the main host as soon as possible. Orders are to concentrate north-east of Korkyria. The town has mostly been evacuated now. One of my fliers has gone to tell your column to bring your horses back."

"I owe you a battle-debt," Rhea admitted, inclining her head and making the sign of the star.

"Something tells me you will have ample opportunity to return it soon enough, Wolf," the icyene replied.

SEVEN

◆▶

At some point, the candle in Luken's sleeping cell guttered and went out.

That was when the monsters came for him. Horrid, pale things, all wicked claws and bloodshot eyes and long, distended canines.

He didn't know whether he screamed in the dream, or in reality. He found himself sitting bolt upright in bed, slicked with cold night sweat.

The candle on his bedstand was still burning, despite the efforts of his nightmares. The shutters were ajar too, the Everlight warding off the night. He didn't dare close his eyes.

Eventually, he felt his pulse levelling off, his breathing returning to normal. He rolled over, staring at the door – still shut, the lock still in place. He tried to banish the last vestiges of the nightmare but could not.

When he had been younger, his nights had regularly been plagued by terrors. He would wake up all the occupants of his shared dorm with his screams. He sometimes found himself out of bed, halfway down the corridor outside, convinced he was being chased by the insubstantial shades his youthful mind imagined haunted the old dormitories appended to the Hallowed Sepulchre.

The terrors had lasted for years, and drawn the ire of both his fellow orphans, and the clergy charged with the children's upbringing. Only Akeron had shown him any patience. Once he had called Luken to the library that formed part of the church district. The rank upon rank and tier upon tier of shelves piled high with a seemingly endless collection of books, scrolls and parchments had filled Luken with awe.

Stern but attentive, Akeron had walked among the shelves with him and confided in Luken: as a young man he too had suffered from nightmares that had torn his sleep apart. He told him that reading just before bed had helped settle his mind, and that with time the affliction had passed.

Akeron had spoken with the dorm overseer, and Luken was permitted to burn a small candle and read a text of his choice after the rest of the children had been put to bed. Akeron's prescription had not only worked, but he had discovered a fascination with books, particularly fables, histories and Saradominist stories. His mind distracted, the nightmares had faded.

Until tonight.

He reached under his bed for one of the jumble of books there, pulling out De Matina's *Fables of Light and Dark*. He thought better of it, putting it back. He'd read it too many times, and besides, the first few tales in the compilation featured the vyre.

He threw back the sheets in frustration and rose.

The dormitories were cold, a relief at the height of summer, bitterly unpleasant any other time of year. He drew his night gown around himself and picked up his candle and holder from the stand.

He could think of no way to clear his head other than to visit the Church. Even in the dead of night the outer doors were guarded, but he had direct access via the inner passages between the living quarters and the main building across the street. While the lower levels and corridors were part of the Sepulchre, and still unnerved him, especially in the dark, he liked to visit the upper hall sometimes, and take in the majesty of the pillars and mosaics by candlelight. There was a power and majesty to it even more serene and pronounced when its shutters were drawn, and it lay deserted in the dead of night.

He hesitated before unlocking his dorm's door. He steeled himself, mouthed a prayer to the Lord of Light, and slowly unlatched the door.

Nothing in the corridor stirred. After peering left and right, he stepped slowly out and closed his door behind him. His candle flickered, a little bulwark in the darkness that pressed in from either end of the passageway.

He headed right, padding with silent, bare feet across the cold flagstones. To reach the passage that would take him into the Sepulchre and then the Church proper, he first needed to pass the archpriest's own sleeping chamber. He could normally do so with little difficulty – he was quiet, and Akeron's hearing wasn't what it once was. On this occasion though, he froze as soon as he turned the corner and caught sight of the door.

It lay ajar, the Everlight spilling out into the corridor. That wasn't what Luken had expected at all. He didn't know the exact time but doubted he had been asleep for long. The old man needed his rest, especially at a time like this.

Pursing his lips, Luken continued to the doorway, steeling himself before easing round for a glance inside.

Akeron's chambers were almost as spartan as his own. The archpriest had access to a grand master bedroom in the upper floors, but he had never taken up residence there, preferring to retain the room he had used since his days as a common priest of the unicorn. Luken admired such stoicism, even if he felt that Akeron deserved better. He knew there was no point in trying to change his mind.

He caught sight of the archpriest sitting at his writing desk, facing the room's window, silhouetted by the Everlight's glory. He was slightly bent over, reading from one of the piles of books heaped and scattered across the table. Like Luken, and in spite of the cold, he was dressed in his night shift, and the unkempt state of his bed implied he had risen in a similar state of mind to his junior illuminator.

Luken's sense of guilt redoubled – he had no wish to spy on the archpriest in the middle of the night. He was about to withdraw when Akeron moved, so suddenly it made Luken jump. He turned, twisting in his chair and fixing him with a glare through straggling, white hair.

"Archpriest," Luken stammered, unable to find the words that would adequately explain his presence. Akeron seemed to slump slightly, as though he had feared it would be someone else. Without looking back at his desk, he thumped whatever book he had been reading shut and pushed it away.

"What are you doing awake?" he demanded, voice a dry croak.

"I couldn't sleep," Luken said miserably, feeling suddenly foolish. "I thought I might walk the Sepulchre."

He trailed off as Akeron rose with a crack of stiff joints and hobbled across the room to the door.

"You should not be up during the night, even with the Everlight aglow," he growled as he came. "And certainly not out of your chamber and wandering the halls and corridors. Have you been asleep these last few days?"

"No, archpriest," Luken began to say, but Akeron continued to admonish him, voice a low, dangerous rasp.

"The shadows are no longer safe, Luken. Take your candle, go back to your room, lock your door, and pray to great Saradomin that he sends his hosts to save us. For I fear that is our only hope."

Before Luken could find the right words to respond, Akeron had reached the door and closed it in his face. There was a cold scrape, the sound of the lock being drawn into place, then silence.

Luken felt suddenly alone, and terrified. He scrambled back to his room, using one hand to shield the flickering flame of his candle, trying not to think about what would happen if it went out. When he reached his chamber he locked the door, threw open the shutters, and pulled the covers over him.

He did not find a modicum of sleep until the first bells of the lesser shrines outside were tolling.

✦ ✦ ✦

Queen Efaritay took off from the balcony of her bedchamber in the citadel. She flew low and fast, leaving behind Ascertes, sleeping soundly with Larina and Safalaan on either side of him. She had sung a song of Hallow, a soft lullaby that had woven its comforts through their dreams, easing them and helping them into a deep slumber.

The pang of guilt at having to enchant her own family was subsumed by Efaritay's determination, by the urgency she battled so hard not to show every day, even to him.

The air outside was cold, the illumination of the Everlight clear and pale. In the east, dawn was beginning to show itself. To the west, darkness reigned beyond the radius cast by the tower. She turned her back on it, sweeping over the city streets with short, firm beats of her wings.

The worst of the panic that had gripped Hallowvale seemed to have passed. The city lay quiet, bathed in the Everlight's brilliance. The humans had looked to the calmness and leadership of the icyene, had found their faith in Saradomin, or had simply decided that the best recourse was to lock their doors and shutter their windows. Efaritay feared the last was the most common explanation.

Hallowvale was divided, and in truth she knew it always would be. She had done all she could since taking the throne to lessen the differences between humans and icyene. Her marriage to Ascertes had been born out of love, but she had taken a private satisfaction in the shockwaves it sent through the icyene nobility, how it had partially upended the social order of the whole city. In the years since, she had continued conciliation between Hallowvale's two strata, trying to lift the humans and prove to them this was a place that belonged to all who worshipped Saradomin, not just the icyene.

But her kin would only stand for so much. Laws surrounding the use of the acropolis or burials in the Hallowed Sepulchre remained beyond her influence. Besides the justiciar ordos, icyene still controlled the city's military, still ruled its supreme court, and still passed many of its laws. The only truly senior role held by a human was the old archpriest of the unicorn, and even that was only because many icyene held their own, private worship, away from the humans that frequented the upper levels of the Hallowed Church. The views of Archon Babel were tainted with bitterness by his feelings towards her, but she knew their underlying root was shared by many icyene – the humans were inferior, a wingless breed who did not bear Saradomin's light within them, and could only pay lip service to the god that favoured the icyene above all others.

Now the connections she had struggled to build were going to be tested in the most difficult environment imaginable – a siege.

She knew she could not assume help was coming, even if it seemed inconceivable that it was not. It was her duty, her responsibility, to prepare Hallowvale for the worst. To endure weeks, perhaps months, of protracted conflict. There would be further difficult choices. Already, supplies were a concern, as were the refugees beginning to fill the city's western quarters, in the shadow of the citadel. She had to navigate all those issues while never once appearing uncertain or lost. If it seemed she was, the humans would lose heart, and icyene, like Babel, would begin to disregard her authority.

Such were the burdens of the crown. For a few moments, Efaritay made herself forget it all, focusing instead on the sense of freedom that came with flight, and the comforting brightness of the Everlight. It was more than just a beacon to the icyene – it was a symbol of home, its illumination a sacred reminder of Hallow. The nights there had been deadly, but the long days had enabled her people to thrive. They had brought the sacred light of their home with them to Gielinor, and as long as it shone, there was cause to believe the darkness would not overcome them.

Even now, though it had been steadily losing its lustre over the decades, its radius creeping back to the edges of the city walls, the Everlight still gave Efaritay more hope than any of Hallowvale's towering defences. The queen swept down into the square that lay outside the city's arboretum. She knew she should not leave the citadel without her guards, let alone without telling anyone, but she had never taken well to having a gaggle of guards and attendants following her. She was certain she was safe, for now.

The arboretum lay at the heart of Hallowvale. The domed building had been constructed by Efaritay's father – she had memories of visiting as a child, while it was still being raised. Horticulture had been his passion, one that the duties of kingship had rarely allowed him to indulge, and which Efaritay's mother had not approved of. The building had barely been completed, and the plants within still young, when his light had left him and he had passed away.

In Efaritay's mind, the arboretum was now a monument to his memory, each plant within a living shrine. On the day of her wedding to Ascertes she had issued a decree that for much of the year the building would be open to all within Hallowvale who wished to visit, regardless of station or whether they were human or icyene – it would not be the preserve of just the royal household and the icyene nobility. It had been another small step on what she hoped was the path to unity, but privately it was one that pleased her more than any number of grander, more sweeping decrees.

Two icyene from her personal guard, Miletus and Iklea, were on duty outside the arboretum's tall doors. Efaritay hoped their presence would not draw attention to the building, but she also had no wish to leave what was now within unprotected. They saluted her as she passed, and she made an icyene gesture of greeting, before unlocking the doors.

Helius, the master of the arboretum, had given her the keys to the dome. She walked inside, stepping through the entrance hall before arriving in the central chamber.

Radiance was beaming in through the window arches in the dome, the Everlight reinforced by the rising sun. It left the greenery surrounding her dappled in strips of light and dark, the heavy fronds, leaves and brilliantly coloured flowers perfectly silent and still.

She walked amidst them, humming softly to herself. There were plants here not only from the furthest corners of Gielinor, but from Hallow as well, carefully transported to this new home. They reminded her of a place she barely remembered, and of a time before she had come to understand just how heavy the burden of leadership was.

The arboretum had been enchanted so that, regardless of the season or the weather beyond the dome, its contents remained forever in bloom. Efaritay allowed herself time to drink in the beauty of the life blossoming around her, before directing her path to the far end of the chamber.

There, she found what she had come for.

It was a sapling, small and slender. Its bark was white and its branches, though fragile-looking, were jagged. A few delicate leaves clung to it. It sat in dark, loamy earth between two Hallow skyroots, in a space Efaritay had carefully cleared and tended.

She inspected the small tree carefully, from leaf tips to roots. It looked as though its seed had been planted one, maybe two summers ago. In reality, Efaritay had buried it just a few days previously.

She sang to the plant, her eyes closed, her pale, slender fingers gliding gently over its branches and trunk. As she did so, she reached within herself, grasping the light at her core, sharing it with her creation. With the old, arcane words of Hallow, she nourished the sapling and heard it respond with the creak of its timber and the rustling of its leaves.

It was new to this world. It did not yet understand its duty, its purpose, but with time it would answer her call without hesitation.

The icyene queen's song ended and she opened her eyes and stepped back, feeling light-headed. Growth magics were draining, and she felt an ache in her core, the sort of exhaustion she might have experienced if she had been flying for days. She wished she had the strength to push on, but it would do, for now.

The tree now stood perhaps a foot taller, its trunk stouter, more firmly rooted. She knew its jagged branches would not grow up to be beautiful, like the skyroots that flanked it like majestic guards. But, unlike everything else beneath the dome, beauty was not what it had been planted for. Its purpose was not to bring another little piece of the glory of bright Hallow to Gielinor. It was to defend what already existed here, to act as a weapon to be wielded against the most terrible foes imaginable.

With it, they might yet stave off the coming dark.

PART TWO

EIGHT

◆

Rhea grunted as the spear's haft thumped into her breastplate, driving her back.

The bastard she was up against was big and well-armoured in dark Zamorakian chainmail and leather. His half-helm left his jaw exposed, mouth a rictus snarl as he drove at her.

Human teeth, not fangs. That, at least, was a blessing.

She dropped back as the Zamorakian legionary lunged with his spear, thankful she had the space to do so. The battle had degenerated into a feral scrap with no hint of order or linear formations. If she had been packed into the ranks she wouldn't have had room to evade, but then again, the Zamorakian likely wouldn't have made the lunge in the first place – Klaxar would probably have cut him from collar to sternum with her labrys by now.

The spear's tip fell short. She went back on the offensive, as fast as she had been with Phosani in the sparring ring, kopis cutting up at the man's throat. He dropped a shoulder, but it still slashed a red mark across his jaw.

She stepped in again, expecting him to falter and for her to drive her blade through his neck or crotch or under his arm, any one of the weak points in his black steel. But instinct and battle-fever drove the man to strike back at her, fuelled by pain. Rhea was only half inside his guard, and the spear's wicked tip ripped along her flank, gouging her breastplate.

Before she could respond, she saw movement behind her opponent. A flash of steel and the man let out a bellow of pain. His left leg abruptly gave way amidst a gout of crimson, and there was a clatter as he fell, his size working against him. The back of his knee had been neatly sliced open.

Phosani had gotten in behind the Zamorakian, and as he fell she raised her xiphos, two-handed, and drove it down through the back of the man's neck, severing his spine with a brutal thud.

"I had him," Rhea grunted, panting, the flush of battle overcoming her natural deference towards the White Wolf.

"I know," Phosani responded, tugging her sword free and stooping to wipe it on the dead Zamorakian's leggings.

Rhea took the opportunity to look left and right, seeking fresh foes. Icyene prodromoi had detected the movement of a Zamorakian column along a lesser track running parallel to the main Hallowvale road. As predicted, the invading host was too large to take any one route to the city. Between that and the vampyres' aversion to fighting during daylight hours, the invasion was not progressing at pace.

The icyene outfliers had detected this cohort of human Zamorakian legionaries, trying to make ground during the twilight without support. Phosani and her Wolves had laid an ambush, and fallen upon the foe amidst the lengthening shadows. The clash had been short and brutal. The Zamorakians had thought themselves safe as night drew near, the Saradominists withdrawn from the area. Now their bodies littered the forest track, Phosani's Wolves moving among them, finishing the last of them. There were to be no prisoners, ostensibly because of the need to retreat quickly before the vyre were able to arise. Rhea did not lament that. Her view of Zamorakians, sharpened by decades of warfare, contained little in the way of empathy anyway, but when it came to the scum that willingly served vampyres, there could be no mercy.

Phosani called for her salpinx blower and had him send out the signal for the Wolves to gather. Rhea looked along the track until she spotted Mardin and Klaxar, both bloodied but unharmed. She felt a brief sense of relief, there and gone again. Years ago the safety of her fellow hypaspists at the close of a battle had been almost an afterthought. She had been young, brash, revelling in the test of arms and the superiority of being a justiciar's warrior. Now though, with so many campaigns behind them, everything felt so much more precarious. Mardin and Klaxar were her oldest companions, and though she did her best not to ponder it in those horrid, quiet times between drilling, marching and fighting, it seemed impossible to her that all three of them would see out this war together.

But at the least they should see out the rest of the evening. This was only the latest of three successful ambushes the Wolves had launched in the past four days. Like the other justiciar forces and their supporting icyene, they were harrying the invaders' flanks without ever giving them the satisfaction of a pitched battle. She knew that such a style of warfare likely sat ill with some of the other ordos, but Phosani's Wolves relished the hunt, and Rhea had long ago dispensed with ideas of honour when it came to combat. Perhaps she had just spent too long battling the Zamorakians and their brutal ideology, but as far as she was concerned, war had little room for noble concepts. It was their duty to win it as quickly as possible, so that further bloodshed might be averted.

As the Wolves collected their wounded and began to move back south along the track in the deepening twilight, Phosani clapped a hand to Rhea's shoulder, pausing under a redbough tree that one dead Zamorakian soldier was slumped against.

"I want you to ride back to the citadel, tonight," she said. "Take a few of your hypaspists, and an icyene to watch the skies. Report to Her-Winged-Majesty directly and tell her what has been happening here. I don't have time to write a full account, but I trust you to clearly convey the situation."

"Couldn't Otrava or Insela do that, commander?" Rhea asked, hoping she didn't sound churlish, but unable to simply accept the unexpected order. As she spoke, she looked over at where Insela was plucking the last of her crossbow bolts from a splayed Zamorakian's throat, checking it for damage before slipping it back into her quiver.

"I have asked you, Rhea," Phosani said with a woodenness that surprised her. "You are the one I trust to bear word to the queen. Tell her we are bleeding the Zamorakians as they would have sought to bleed us, and that their progress has been slowed to a crawl."

"Do I tell her also that her icyene are struggling, forced to support us during the day then defend us from above at night?" Rhea asked tersely. "Do I tell her that despite our victories, the enemy's numbers are barely decreased, and that they continue to make progress towards the city? That we don't have time to cut off heads, and that they simply raise their own dead and add them to their ranks once more?"

"Give a truthful and clear account," Phosani said, showing no reaction to her tone. "We shall continue to harry them here. Do not worry – there will be plenty left to kill on your return."

Rhea spent a second longer trying to articulate her desire to stay with her fellow Wolves, to continue to share in their dangers and slaughter the invaders. But all those considerations were subordinate to her duty. She forced herself to salute, fingers tapping the Saradominist star on her chest.

"As you command, my justiciar."

+ ✦ +

An icyene prodromoi named Xephios acted as Rhea, Klaxar and Mardin's warder as they rode through the night for Hallowvale. He remained above them like a guiding star, his light a reassurance that, if there were flocks of vampyre abroad in the dark, none were close. Still, even with his presence, it was a relief to see the perpetual illumination of the Everlight ahead.

Rhea took in the sight of Hallowvale as they crested the last rise before its gates, an island of light in a sea of night, its tall walls and bristling towers gleaming, the blue and gold Saradominist standards atop its jagged crown bolts of brilliant colour. She felt an unexpected wave of awe, and paused her mount so she could look out over the city.

Xephios went ahead, then swept back down, alighting before the trio of hypaspists. For a moment the Everlight was behind him, making his wings shine almost blindingly and giving him a halo.

"I have informed the guards at the gate of your approach," he said.

"My thanks," Rhea said. "Will you be entering the city as well?"

"No. I wish to return to my prodromoi. They will have need of me."

Impressed by his sense of duty, and more than a little jealous, Rhea wished for Saradomin's blessings upon the icyene before he took off, a star arcing back out into the dark.

They rode for the gates. Rhea was tired, but she pushed through it. Now was not the time to think about how little she'd eaten, how little she had slept, or the fact that she hadn't been out of her armour's panoply for days.

She had been given a duty to perform. The sooner it was done, the sooner she could rejoin the pack.

They entered the city without issue, riding the short distance from the western gate up to the citadel's eastern entrance. Dawn was coming on, vaguely discernible as the light in the east strengthened, but the streets remained quiet. Rhea thought about the panic that had gripped them when news of the invasion had first broken. Now, it was as though Hallowvale had resigned itself to the prospect of a siege, and all the harrowing misery such a thing entailed.

Rhea had known sieges before. In her early years with the Wolves she had fought in the defence of Hadrenport, a nine-month investment of the coastal city by a powerful Zamorakian host. Her abiding memories were of hunger, so achingly terrible they'd been reduced to eating rats and gnawing on leather bindings torn from the books of the city's library. That was when she had truly bonded with Klaxar. The relief, when the siege had finally been broken, was something Rhea had never been able to articulate – only those who had shared in the defence could understand.

She had fought in siege lines too, outside Pergamon and Salmis. Such duties were hardly less brutal. She had almost died of the dysentery that had decimated the besiegers at the former, and had been part of the storming party that had assaulted the breach at the latter. She still had nightmares about the broken, blood-slick stonework and the broken bodies underfoot. That was where her old friend, Hephas, had been killed, struck through the eye by a Zamorakian crossbow bolt.

A siege is a time of misery and suffering, though Rhea feared that in Hallowvale, it would be on a scale beyond anything she had known before. The city was vast compared to any of the others she had fought in. It was difficult to imagine the size of the opposing force necessary to even threaten it. How could these great walls and towers and their winged, light-blessed guards possibly be overcome?

She knew that was foolishness. In her decades of war, she had seen mighty forces laid low. The Zamorakians themselves had reckoned Pergamon impregnable, but Rhea had stood upon its highest tower, seen the horned banner of Zamorak cast down in a ripple of torn crimson silk, and watched as the sun climbed up above a breach that had almost been walled up again with the dead.

She feared it would be worse in Hallowvale.

They were admitted to the citadel, where they dismounted and were shown by icyene guards to the throne room. Despite the earliness of the hour it seemed the queen was already holding an audience – the three of them were required to wait outside.

Rhea and Mardin remained dutifully standing, the latter twisting his torso left and right slightly as he sought to work riding aches from his body, but Klaxar chose to sit with a clatter on one of the marble benches along the side of the antechamber. She was in a surly mood, a mirror of Rhea's – the more senior hypaspist was just better at hiding it.

"Quite the contrast," Klaxar muttered, nodding from the trio of Wolves to the two guards standing at the throne room's doors. Rhea quickly worked out what she meant. The difference between the mud-spattered, bedraggled hypaspists and the towering icyene in their gleaming and silver armour could not have been more marked.

Rhea didn't reply, refusing to be drawn into jibes. She had learned to respect icyene battle-prowess over the years, and besides, she suspected the royal guards would see combat soon enough.

While she waited, she focused her thoughts on what she would tell the queen, using it to overcome her tiredness. Despite the successes of the past few days, the Zamorakians hardly seemed to care about the Saradominists nipping at their heels. Their numbers were simply too great. Rhea considered how to phrase the truth without sounding like a harbinger of despair.

Eventually, the doors to the throne room were opened and one of the queen's household servants came out.

"Your name?" he asked Rhea brusquely, simply ignoring Mardin and Klaxar. She told him and he gestured curtly.

"Follow."

Rhea entered the throne room once more and stepped forward as the servant called out before withdrawing.

"Samyra Rhea, hypaspist of the ordo of the wolf!"

The queen already had an audience, though it was smaller than the full council meetings Rhea had attended with Phosani. Almost all of those present were icyene, military leaders and nobles. Archon Babel was among them, and looked as though he had been interrupted by her arrival. There was a rustling of furled wings as Rhea halted before the dais and bowed to Efaritay and her husband.

"Welcome, brave Rhea," the queen said, as serene and calm-sounding as ever. "I am told you bring word from your justiciar? How fares her efforts at checking the invader?"

"The tidings are mixed, my queen," Rhea admitted, deciding that simple, direct answers would be her greatest ally in this battle. In truth she did not know why Phosani had chosen her. She had no art with words, no talent at gilding the truth. She was a soldier, and this was unfamiliar, dangerous territory.

"Go on," Efaritay said, and Rhea realised she had been hesitating for too long.

"Our efforts meet with frequent success. The enemy's outlying forces have been repeatedly ambushed and struck down. We make them pay in blood for every step they take towards this city. Our own casualties are minimal. The icyene are giving everything to ensure the skies remain safe and our light does not go out when night falls."

During the latter comment she glanced at Archon Babel, but his expression remained disdainful. She carried on.

"But the enemy's progress remains largely unchecked. Their numbers are such that they are not even attempting to remedy their mistakes. They don't need to. Our own efforts require us to be constantly on the move, constantly wary of reprisals. There is little time to rest or eat. This mode of warfare is unsustainable, and soon one of our sections will make a mistake. That will likely lead to casualties we cannot afford."

"This is what I feared, Your-Winged-Majesty," Babel said before anyone could respond to Rhea's comments. "The enemy will not be stopped by this form of resistance, not before they reach the walls. We should gather our strength and make a stand."

"What is your opinion of the Zamorakian forces you have fought so far?" Efaritay asked Rhea, seemingly ignoring Babel.

"Not high," Rhea admitted. "I have not yet encountered vampyres in the night, mostly thanks to the efforts of the icyene. During the day they are vulnerable, and they do not seem to be too numerous. The vast majority of the Drakan host are humans, bearing the heraldry of the fourteenth legion. They are well-equipped but do not seem battle-hardened. They are no match for either icyene or we hypaspists, at least not one-to-one. I believe the vyre are using them as fodder to bear the weight of the fighting and preserve their own numbers."

"Another reason to face them directly," Babel said. "Their only advantage is numerical. I know of several locations we might stymie them before they progress any further. The Hill of the Hetakeron, or the rise just east of Hephaston's old mill. We can use the terrain to negate their numbers."

Rhea was watching the queen as Babel spoke, and she noticed something she had rarely seen in Hallowvale's ruler – anger. It seemed as though she was about to snap at her fellow icyene and, sensing it, Babel became suddenly quiet. But Efaritay composed herself, and the moment passed.

"All options, tactical and strategic, will be considered," she said with perfect poise. Rhea noted that Ascertes was less restrained, the human glaring at Babel. The strategos returned the expression.

This was not Rhea's place, and it made her uncomfortable. Politicking, clashing personalities, even the antagonism between human and icyene – she did not care for it. Despite her tiredness, she found herself wishing she were back facing the Zamorakians again, blade to blade, instead of enduring this duel of terse words and pointed looks.

There was a noise from beyond the doors to the chamber. Rhea recognised the raised voice of the icyene who had first announced her. The doors swung open and all heads turned as the servant swept back in, followed by a second icyene. She wore the light leather armour of a prodromoi, but the heraldry on her breast didn't belong to Hallowvale's garrison tagma. It was the crest of Saradomin's personal host, the Optimatoi.

Rather than announce her, the servant hurried ahead of her, bowed hastily to the queen and king, and mounted the dais to whisper in Efaritay's ear. Rhea watched her carefully, but her face betrayed nothing, nor did her voice when she spoke.

"The council will briefly adjourn."

There was nothing more to it. The throne room's guards led the assembly out into the antechamber. Neither Mardin nor Klaxar showed any surprise at Rhea's abrupt reappearance.

"She arrived with an outer tower guard," Klaxar told her, softly, as the council split off into muttering groups. "Told that hatchet-faced servant she had come directly from Saradomin, and that she had orders to deliver a message to the queen as soon as she arrived."

"The news we've been waiting for," Mardin mused.

"We have an answer to our prayers," Klaxar added, her tone laconic. "Whether it's a nice answer or not…"

It didn't take long for the messenger to reemerge from the throne room. A hush fell across the antechamber, but she said nothing, made no eye contact, her face giving nothing away as she left. The doors closed behind her. There was no sign of the council being readmitted.

"Perhaps we should depart?" Mardin wondered. "They might spend hours considering whatever they just heard."

Rhea was tempted. She had done what she had been sent to do. With fresh horses from the stables, they could be back with the ordo before middle-night. The strains of strategic decisions could be left to others.

"Don't you want to know what the word is?" Klaxar asked.

"We might not be informed of it," Mardin pointed out. "Unless the queen wants us to take a message back to the justiciar, but an icyene would be quicker."

"We will remain a little while longer," Rhea decided. "But if there is nothing more to do here, I will leave word that we have returned to the ordo."

The trio were just about to depart when the doors to the throne room were opened once more, and the guards ushered the council back in. Rhea left her companions, a sudden sense of foreboding creeping over her as she took her place before the thrones. There was a coldness now to Efaritay's expression, no longer merely guarded.

"I have received news direct from blessed Saradomin, at the Infernal Source. The Lord of Light has made his will known."

Several of the icyene murmured devotional utterings before the queen continued.

"There will be no immediate relief. The siege of the Infernal Source is at a crucial stage, and the entire war hinges on it. The other fronts are stretched thin, and a shift of troops is likely exactly what Zamorak is looking for. It is the strategic council's opinion that Drakan's invasion is intended as a diversion."

Shocked silence followed the claim. Rhea felt numbness, almost resignation – the same feeling she had experienced when facing what seemed like certain death on the battlefield, as she had when the were-pack had almost caught her and Mardin. Even Babel's bullish attitude seemed to have evaporated. Efaritay went on.

"I have been instructed to prepare Hallowvale for a siege. We are to trust in the presence of the ordos and the glory of the Everlight, for the time being. Once the Infernal Source has fallen, support will be sent immediately."

"It isn't a diversion," another of the icyene nobles muttered. "They don't understand the extent of the invasion."

"I have sent the messenger back stating as much," Efaritay said. "I remain certain that aid will be forthcoming. Hallowvale cannot be abandoned."

"But will it arrive in time?" said another member of the military council.

"My queen," Babel said, and Rhea briefly thought Efaritay was going to snap at the strategos to remain silent, but she gestured curtly for him to continue instead.

"Let me assemble the tagma and meet the enemy. These raids along their flanks are not slowing them. If they reach the walls, and the illumination of the Everlight, we will be at the mercy of whatever they have planned next. The city is not ready for a siege, and it cannot be made ready in such little time, but if we go on the offensive and check them, the initiative will no longer be theirs. We will buy ourselves time, time to bring more of the country people within the halls, time to stockpile more supplies, and time for a proper response from great Saradomin. We may even break the invaders before they go any further. I trust in my icyene warriors. Each is worth half a dozen humans, werewolves or vampyres."

"It is a matter I am willing to suggest to the wider council," Efaritay began to say, but Babel dared to interrupt, during a particularly vicious glare from Ascertes.

"With all respect, Your-Winged-Majesty, we do not have time for further debate. It is well within your power to issue the necessary orders. Myself and the rest of the garrison not yet deployed to the north stand ready. We can be on the road before middle-day."

Efaritay held Babel's gaze while responding, though her words were not directed at him.

"Rhea," she said. "You are the only human present, and if I am not mistaken you are a veteran of these wars. You are Justiciar Phosani's chief lieutenant, are you not?"

Rhea briefly considered Otrava and Insela, and wondered how true that was anymore, before choosing the simplicity that served her so well when speaking to superiors.

"Yes, Your-Winged-Majesty."

"Then I would hear your opinion on the proposal that we face the enemy in the open."

Rhea had not expected to be addressed directly. She had been hoping to withdraw, not wishing to be dragged into arguments between the icyene. If Saradomin truly wasn't sending aid, the ordo would have need of her now more than ever. She hesitated, the eyes of the tall, winged beings fixed on her.

"I am a fighter, not a strategist, my queen," she found herself declaring. "I would not presume to interrogate the proposals of an icyene strategos."

For once, Babel's expression was not one of scorn or disdain, but Efaritay looked displeased.

"In these circumstances, such humility does you little credit," she warned.

"Nevertheless, I have nothing to add beyond the report I have already delivered."

She offered a short bow and, in an attempt at softening her defiance, continued. "I exist to slay your foes, and the foes of blessed Saradomin, to defend his light and those who cleave to it. Those are my oaths as a hypaspist of the wolf. Beyond them, I make no presumptions. Send me against the enemy, Your-Winged-Majesty, and I will fulfil my purpose. I cannot do that here."

Efaritay was silent for a while, gazing into the distance, as though communing mentally with some unknown, invisible being. Finally, she nodded.

"Then let it be so. We will meet the enemy on ground of our own choosing, beyond the walls. You will not command the host however, Strategos Babel, at least not solely."

Babel once more looked shocked, and then outraged, likely

assuming he would have to share command with Lysander or Phosani, but it was Efaritay's turn to continue over her fellow icyene's protestations.

"I will be with the Hallowvale tagma. Rhea has spoken well. There is a time to shape strategy, and a time to implement it, and the latter is done best on the field of battle. If we are to stake our survival on one engagement, it is only right that I place myself in the line with my city's brave warriors."

There were murmurs among the gathering, and Rhea noted the look of dismay Ascertes gave his wife. He leaned against the edge of his throne to whisper to her, but she brushed him off.

"We shall march within the hour. Strategos Babel, you shall remain here until then, and we will discuss further matters of strategy. The rest of this council is dismissed."

"My queen, with your permission, my hypaspists and I would return immediately to the fray," Rhea said. "We will be needed now more than ever."

"I have no doubt that is true," Efaritay said. "But you must have ridden through the night to deliver this report. I may be an icyene, but I am not oblivious to the efforts and sacrifices made by humanity, or the need for them to eat and sleep more than my kind. You will take on sustenance and rest, before you collapse."

"Is that an order, Your-Winged-Majesty?"

"Yes. A servant will prepare a place for you and your companions in the citadel's main guardhouse. Eat, sleep, and then you may return to your Wolf kin."

Rhea swallowed her frustration and bowed. Accepting the order finally allowed her rigid thoughts to turn to rest. It felt unworthy, like a betrayal, yet she was relieved. She hadn't slept properly in days.

"You are dismissed," Efaritay told her. "Go with Saradomin's blessings."

"May the light bless you likewise, Your-Winged Majesty," Rhea said. As she withdrew, she tried not to think about the cold irony of those words.

The light had abandoned them.

NINE

———◆———

Efaritay knew what Ascertes was going to say as soon as the council had been dismissed.

"You can't go," he declared, rising from his throne.

"I must," Efaritay replied, not looking at him.

"What happens if you fall?" her husband demanded. "Or worse, are captured!"

"Then rulership of Hallowvale will fall to you. It will be your duty to defend our home until Saradomin arrives."

"I am not icyene, I cannot be king," Ascertes exclaimed. "And besides, Saradomin isn't coming!"

It felt like sacrilege to say it, and it stung Efaritay deeply. Until today, it was something she had simply refused to consider, but the foundations of her certainties had been shattered, and everything was collapsing around her. She couldn't acknowledge that, even to the man she loved. She had to remain strong, not only for Ascertes, Safalaan and Larina, but for the entire city.

"You can be king," she told Ascertes, dismissing his first claim while trying not to think about his second. "The laws of Hallowvale are clear on the matter. If the queen perishes and there is no heir yet of age, the king will assume full royal authority. Nowhere does it specify that said king must be icyene."

"Those laws were written assuming both the king and queen would be icyene," Ascertes pointed out. "They never thought a day would come when a queen of Hallow would wed a human of Gielinor."

"Then they were short-sighted fools," Efaritay said. "I am going with the tagma. It is my duty. It is your duty to remain here and lead in my absence. That is the end of it."

"Tell our children that," Ascertes said fiercely.

Efaritay stood as well, towering over him.

"I will," she said. "They too must learn to do their duty."

She knew she was being cold. It was a shield she used to protect herself. She turned away from Ascertes and paced round behind their thrones, until she was standing before the circular window that framed them. Light shone through the stained glass, making the star of Saradomin in its centre gleam like gold, bathing her in its brightness.

"He will come," she said softly as she gazed into the heart of the star. "He must. This is his city. We are his chosen people. He would not leave us alone in the dark."

Ascertes rounded the thrones from the opposite end and stood alongside her, looking at her rather than the glass crest.

"Did your mother leave you in the dark?" he asked. The question momentarily shocked Efaritay into silence. Ascertes knew of her difficult relationship with the woman who had born her. She had believed that only strictness could prepare her for the burden of rulership. As monarch, she had claimed, there could be no room for doubt, uncertainty or fear. And among her many firm lessons, she had locked Efaritay in a lightless room for hours, telling her that she would only be let out when it was clear she no longer feared the dark.

In a way, it had worked. Lightlessness no longer held a terror of its own for her, at least not as much as it did for many of her kind. But none of the other 'lessons' had ever rung true. If anything, she felt more unsure of herself than she had when she had been a child, imagining a future where she was a wise and benevolent monarch. She couldn't admit it though, even to Ascertes.

"Those we love cannot always be there for us," Ascertes said, his tone becoming gentler as he saw just how far he had pushed her. "Sometimes they even choose not to be. That is the way of the world."

Efaritay sighed. She felt suddenly exhausted. She embraced Ascertes, then held him by the shoulders as she gazed down into his eyes.

"And that is why I must go," she told him. "My city is at war. I am tired of this room and these debates. It is time for me to lead."

Ascertes did not argue but sighed and leaned against the back of his throne. She found herself thinking how old he had become, almost without her noticing. Humans lived such painfully short lives. She had known that when she had married him, had accepted that she would outlive him by many centuries.

But perhaps now, that would not be the case.

She resolved not to ponder such things, and instead took his hand and squeezed it.

"We should go," she said. "Out into the city. I have something I want to show you."

◆ ◆ ◆

Efaritay permitted the guards to accompany the royal couple as they passed from the citadel to the city centre. They rode on horseback, an unusual act for icyene, but one that Efaritay insisted on whenever she was beyond the walls of the citadel or the palace with her husband. Wingless as he was, she would not leave him behind while she took flight.

They passed through the wide streets between the crag and the arboretum. Like the palace district in the south-east of the city, this part of Hallowvale was populated almost wholly by icyene. It was one of the first areas to be built, and its tall, colonnaded stone buildings, the broad, tree-lined boulevards and the statues, fountains and small squares stood in contrast to the timber and slate structures and narrow, winding streets that marked the more human-dominated areas.

The royal party rode swiftly, so as not to attract a crowd, the echo of hooves striking cobbles reverberating back from the grand buildings flanking them. They reached the square before the arboretum, where they dismounted and entered in through the main doors.

"Is this the secret you've been keeping from me?" Ascertes asked as they went. "The… weapon you mentioned?"

"You'll see," Efaritay responded simply, pausing for a short while in the entrance hall. She had summoned Vulkat, Forgemaster of Hallowvale, to meet them. He arrived with commendable speed, his expression one of slight concern as he bowed and presented Efaritay with an object, bundled up in purple velvet.

Efaritay took and unwrapped it. She had seen it when first completed, though only by the ruddy glow of Vulkat's furnaces. Here, in the open, the brilliance of the Everlight caught it and made it shine like shards of purest sunlight.

It was a spearhead, broad and flat-bladed, with wickedly barbed edges. Alongside it was a base spike made from pure silver. All that was missing was a haft to connect them.

"Your work is without compare, noble Vulkat," she told the icyene smith.

"Nothing pleases me more than to meet with your approval, my queen," he said. "May it shine with the light of Saradomin himself, and bring death to his enemies."

"Come join us, and you shall see it made whole," Efaritay said, gesturing for the forgemaster to walk alongside them as she turned and led Ascertes into the main chamber of the arboretum.

The blisterwood tree was barely a sapling anymore. Ascertes stood looking at it, the light through one of the dome's windows lancing down to make its bark shine white.

"You have been growing this," he said to Efaritay. "It is from Hallow?"

"Yes," she replied. "Its name is the blisterwood. The seed comes from a grove in my family's old palace in New Domina. Like many of the plants from my home, it loves the light, and bears it within. And that in turn makes it inimical to the spawn of Vampyrium."

"So the weapon you spoke of is a tree," Ascertes said, his doubtful expression giving way to a wry smile. "I should have expected as much."

"Nature goes to war for survival every day," Efaritay pointed out. "It is not so unthinkable that it should be able to lend us a tool for our own use."

She returned the spearhead and spike to Vulkat and stepped up to the tree, greeting it. She heard its subtle, creaking response, and ran her fingers once more along its bark, communing with its essence, a young but stalwart thing with strength that ran from the darkness of its deep roots to the heady light its branch tips bathed in. It craved that light, just like the icyene, just like all who called Saradomin god. It hungered for victory over the coming night as much as any of them.

The blisterwood was ready. She sang to it softly, letting it show her the branch it wished to gift to her – a strong appendage, the stoutest of all those her magics had so rapidly grown. She accepted it, took the spearhead back from Vulkat and, holding the weapon by its neck, just below the jagged edges at the base of the blade, she used it to cut away the branch. It passed through with a single firm stroke, the tree offering no resistance while the new blade cut true.

Efaritay grasped the branch before it could fall. The wood

was still living, still imbued with the power it had borne up from a mere seedling. She worked her hands over it, encouraging it to straighten, ensuring it ran true. As she had hoped, the spear tip and its base spike were perfect fits.

Her words rose, calling on the light, binding it with the living blisterwood. The haft began to glow with an inner luminescence, until it was blinding to all but icyene eyes. Ascertes was forced to avert his gaze as the spear tip too began to glow, turning white-hot.

Efaritay's words reached a crescendo, the weapon vibrating. It looked as though it would ignite or splinter into pieces, but then the brilliance began to recede, the spell complete.

She had seared all three components together, from the silver spike to the white, living blisterwood haft to the wicked tip. The spear was finished, imbued with the magics of the light.

She tested its weight, spinning it around her body before lunging with it, one-handed. It was light, perfectly balanced, the blade humming as it seemed to cut the very air itself.

"It is magnificent, Your-Winged-Majesty," Vulkat said. "What name shall you give it?"

Efaritay tossed the spear from one hand to the other and back again, then turned back to the blisterwood tree, gazing up at it, listening.

"The Sunspear," she said.

"It is beautifully crafted," Ascertes acknowledged, able to look at the shining weapon once more. "But one spear won't win a war."

"If I plunge it through the withered heart of Lowerniel Drakan, it might," Efaritay pointed out. "Or do you not believe the stories our peoples share, of great heroes doing great deeds in the past millennia of this war? Did Promeclese not turn back the Chthonian beasts? Did a single clay golem not deal a mortal wound to Zamorak's mighty demon lieutenant, Thrammon, when Uzer fell?"

"You wish to be a hero then," Ascertes said with a bitter edge. "Why not give the spear to Babel? Light knows, he fancies himself a wise general."

"Perhaps I will, but that won't stop me from setting out with the tagma," Efaritay declared. "Nor will this be the only weapon crafted from blisterwood timber. The tree is ready now. Its sap is poisonous to the vyre, and its splinters mean certain death. At the very least there will be enough to equip the royal guard. That may be enough to give us the edge. And if we are besieged, I will grow this tree until it dwarfs all around it, and it will become the bane of every monster that braves the brilliance of the Everlight."

TEN

◆

An icyene was close.

Drakan had been stalking it for almost an hour. It was injured, lost, separated from its flock. It could still fly, but not well, or for long. A Zamorakian arrow had pierced one of its wings.

Most importantly, it was afraid.

Drakan followed it from treetop to treetop. He would know instinctively when the moment came to strike, but for now he kept his distance. This was the part he savoured, the mounting tension prior to the satisfaction of the kill. It was what he had first come to Gielinor to indulge – who would not want to hunt strange creatures in worlds far from his own?

These icyene were some of the most dangerous of the prey he had stalked, but they had a great weakness, one that aligned perfectly with the strengths of the vampyre.

Icyene were afraid of the dark. It was only natural, or so Drakan had heard. Much as with Vampyrium, the nights of the place they called home were filled with terrors, but unlike Vampyrium, these creatures had created an eternal daytime through magical artifice, just like the Everlight in the bay overlooking Hallowvale. It was detestable, but the ingenuity of it almost impressed Drakan.

Accustomed as they were to eternal illumination, they feared the dark, though they would never admit it to their lesser servants, like the humans.

Drakan could taste that fear now, taste it as surely as the scent of the icyene's blood, staining the perfect white of its feathers. It was intoxicating to him, yet he controlled his urges, keeping a steady pace and a regular distance, close enough so that he did not lose track of the creature, close enough for his chosen prey to know that death was near, but far enough that his prey would believe it had noticed him purely through its own guile, as if it had outsmarted Lord Drakan. He loved to falsely give the hope of escape, before snatching it away in a fatal instant. He had killed many thousands in this way, but icyene were particularly special. Stalking and slaying them was an enjoyment beyond compare.

And yet, it was one that could also be ruined. In the night air he heard a keening, detectable only to his kind – his brood were calling to him, pleading for his presence. He recognised Vanescula's tone.

There were few he would have cut a hunt short for, but she was one of them. Snarling with frustration, he lunged into a proper pursuit, letting caution give way to the rush of the chase.

The icyene put in a last desperate effort, perhaps still convinced it might escape. It did its best to fly, a guttering flame to Drakan's blood-shot senses, struggling upwards in the engulfing dark.

He caught it midair. He could have impaled it using the Spear of the Blood Hunt, but he had left it in the care of the captain of the vyreguard, Korgax. He preferred to hunt in the traditional style of Vampyrium, with claw and fang.

The icyene's shriek was brief, cut short by a brutal twist of Drakan's arms and upper body as the pair plummeted towards the earth. They were dead before hitting the forest floor, while Drakan was still airborne and rising again, darting like a barbed arrowhead back towards where his host had gathered.

The fourteenth legion was on the move still. The vampyre broods were mostly aloft, while the werewolves roamed the countryside and the human cohorts took the roads and tracks leading south-east, marching towards the light. Drakan knew the latter forces were being pushed hard, forced to scout ahead or protect makeshift vampyre nests during the day then carry on at night. He did not care. What mattered was reaching Hallowvale, and claiming what lay beneath the city.

He followed the after-echoes of the shriek he had heard earlier, still shivering through the night. At their epicentre, he found a building beside the road the legion was in the process of passing. A cohort section had broken off and appeared to be working to dismantle it, wrapping ropes around its pillars or hacking at its foundations with the tools brought to facilitate the siege of Hallowvale.

It was a wayside shrine, Drakan realised as he circled it from above, one of the small stone structures that dotted the main road to Hallowvale. At places like these travellers could stop, give thanks to Saradomin for guiding them this far, and pray for him to continue to lead them to the light of his shining city.

The mangled, drained carcass of the chapel's priest was lying outside, at Vanescula's feet. Though she had surely fed, there was no sign of blood on her lips, or staining her armour. She was always so careful when she ate.

She knelt as he alighted before her and furled his wings.

"Why have you called upon me, sister?" he demanded, motioning for her to rise.

"I would speak with you on a matter of importance, great vyrelord," she answered, staying down on one knee, head bowed.

Drakan bared his fangs. He was unused to such obeisance from her. It did not suit her.

"I was hunting. What do you want?"

"To speak openly," she responded, only now rising to face him – though much leaner, she was one of the few vyre who were almost tall enough to look him in the eye.

"You know I would never call into question your orders before anyone else, even Ranis," she said. "But you know also that I have doubted this venture from the beginning. I have held my tongue since you first told me of it, but we are approaching a point of no return. Every step we take deeper into this accursed queendom leaves us more isolated."

"Are you afraid, sister?" Drakan said scornfully. He was not in the mood to assuage doubts.

"Do not seek to shame me into silence, as you would do one of your legionary commanders," Vanescula responded with commendable viciousness. "You will hear my counsel now, whether you wish to or not. I have held my tongue long enough."

Drakan spread his broad arms.

"Then speak. I am listening, for now."

"Why are we here?"

The question was not one any of Drakan's subordinates had asked him, he assumed because the answer seemed obvious. He gave Vanescula the courtesy of not responding with those obvious answers – blood, the supposed glory of Zamorak, the snuffing out of the detestable Everlight and the slaughter of the citizens of Hallow. Instead, he waited for her to continue.

"This seems like a doomed venture," she said. "Not that anyone else appears to have noticed. They are all in awe at the number of vyre you have gathered despite our losses over the centuries, and the hosts of mortals and beasts you put at their disposal. They are drunk on the prospect of tearing wings from icyene and collecting more mortal cattle. Do you know that Ranis got half of his own brood wiped out by an icyene ambush on one of the first nights after we broke through the frontier? Off hunting, like you, albeit with none of your patience or talent."

"Are you petitioning me to reprimand him? I'm sure you could do that yourself."

"You know he would only heed either of us for so long before going back to his ways. I am merely noting the scraps and treats you feed to the others to keep them in line, to stop them from thinking too much about where this road leads."

"And where does it lead, sister?" Drakan asked. In truth he had known this moment would come. Vanescula was the only one who both saw beyond the immediate, and questioned what she was told.

"To Hallowvale, a siege, and victory," she said, almost surprising him. "The other vyrelords are right enough to trust the size of the forces at our disposal, and everything we have seen so far points to the Saradominists being unprepared. Defeating the power of the Everlight will be no simple task, but it can be done, with time. But that is where my doubts begin, dear brother. We do not have time."

"You expect a response from Saradomin," Drakan said.

"How could there not be? Hallowvale is his city, a shining jewel, where night is unknown. We must assume that even now, he marches to its relief."

"If he does then Zamorak will strike him from behind. He cannot easily take the Infernal Source while relieving Hallowvale."

"Then what happens when he has triumphed at the Infernal Source? He will come here with all his forces. We will be annihilated."

"Everything you have said is true," Drakan admitted. He walked to the side of the chapel, gazing at a section of human legionaries heaving vainly on a rope wrapped around one of its pillars, trying to bring it down.

"And that is why I am certain there is something more," Vanescula said, following him. "You know that even if you take Hallowvale, you cannot hold it, not unless unforeseeable events of vast magnitude intervene in our favour. There must be another reason we are here. You are not merely sacrificing yourself as a diversion to aid Zamorak. That has never been your way, or the way of our family. Drakans serve Drakans, first and last."

"You are clever, Vanescula, and that is why you so often bear my favour," Lowerniel said. "It is why I forgive little indiscretions, like this conversation. Why I indulge them, in fact. I will tell you why we are here, because you are clever enough to not tell anyone else, yet. Is that clear?"

"It is," Vanescula said.

"Hallowvale is not the city of light the Saradominists portray it as. The icyene came long ago and built their temples and arenas and palaces, but there was another before them. A being older and more powerful than any that now walk Gielinor, including Zamorak or that fool Saradomin. He knew the power of blood, among other things. He sought to siphon off the ancient, arcane energies that formed a nexus beneath the place that would become Hallowvale. He bound elemental magics in an arcane artefact, partly separated from this reality as we know it, but linked to it. A place that can still be accessed, I believe, from below the city."

He had piqued Vanescula's interest. He enjoyed watching her as she worked it out, probing and discounting possibilities. When she spoke she still sounded uncertain, almost disbelieving.

"Do you refer to the Blood Altar?"

"I do," Drakan said. "I have followed stories of it, interrogated prophesies and read the runes in the viscera of arcanists and sorcerers from Forinthry to Uzer. All point to the altar's existence under Hallowvale."

"A nexus of blood magics," Vanescula mused. "The most valuable thing our kind could possess. And you believe all those old stories, those prophesies?"

"We shall see," Drakan said. "But to find out, we must reach the city. Nothing else matters."

He gestured at the humans struggling pathetically with the rope, trying to drag down a pillar. A flick of a talon and the black-armoured legionaries scrambled back, leaving Drakan to pick up the rope. He wrapped it around his broad forearms and began to pull. It strained taut, creaking, and there was a cracking sound. The pillar came away in a burst of crumbling old stone, and part of the chapel's roof came down with it, splitting the Saradominist star over the lintel.

Drakan tossed the rope aside and addressed his sister once more.

"Say nothing of this to anyone, not Ranis, nor even the handmaidens of your own brood." He paused, looking at the panting, fearful mortals he'd dismissed, wondering how many of the brute, Infernal-speaking beasts understood the hissed language of Vampyrium.

"Kill these ones too," he told his sister. "And one more thing."

"Yes, brother?"

Drakan fixed her with his bloody red glare, his wings beginning to unfurl.

"Never disturb me while I'm hunting again."

✦ ✦ ✦

Akeron had just finished reading from the Third Homily of the Book of Light when he collapsed.

Luken saw him begin to falter, and was dropping his censer and rushing to his side before he hit the floor.

He had been watching him throughout the service. He had been unsteady for days, and had broken off a reading that morning. Luken had urged him to rest, but he had refused.

"I'll rest when I'm interred in the grand hallowed coffin, boy," he had growled, before ordering Luken to collect his golden-threaded chasuble.

There was an audible gasp from the congregation as the archpriest fell, and one woman cried out in alarm. Luken's censer clanged off the mosaic floor and rolled, spewing its sweet-stinking smoke. He grabbed onto Akeron and checked his breathing. The old man's eyes fluttered.

"Help me!" Luken barked at the nearest church attendants, who were just staring. They came forward, but were brushed aside by two armoured hypaspists of the unicorn, who made to lift Akeron between them.

Before they could do so, the archpriest's eyes snapped open and he grabbed Luken's forearm in a shaking, white-knuckled grip.

"The altar," he snarled. "We must protect the altar!"

In confusion, Luken looked towards the upper hall's altar, then back at the archpriest, not knowing what to say.

"Make way," one of the hypaspists said, dragging Luken away from Akeron so they could raise him properly.

Luken stood, finding himself suddenly unable to move. He was unaware of the commotion throughout the rest of the chamber, the other guards clearing out the congregants, or the other attendants and illuminators gathered round. His eyes were fixed on Akeron as he slipped back into unconsciousness, and was lifted, suddenly looking so weak and frail.

Luken remained, staring in Akeron's wake even after he was gone, until one of the altar boys tentatively shook his arm.

"I'm sure he'll be alright," the youth said.

Luken couldn't find the words to respond. He brushed the boy aside and hurried to his dorm.

◆ ◆ ◆

One of the hypaspists came to find Luken.

"The archpriest is asking for you," he reported.

"He's awake?" Luken asked hopefully.

"Yes, though largely incoherent. Come."

Luken followed the hypaspist to the infirmary building across the square from the Hallowed Church. Unlike the other ordos, the hypaspists of the unicorn had remained within the city, continuing to garrison the sacred Saradominist sites.

The archpriest had been given a private ward within the infirmary. Luken rushed to his bed, and gripped the old man's hand.

"Took you long enough, boy," Akeron growled. The admonishment – so like the archpriest – caused a surge of relief in Luken.

"I told you not to hold the service tonight," he said.

"Last I checked, you were the under illuminator and I was the archpriest," Akeron said. "No. For once in your life, be silent and listen."

Luken leaned in so Akeron could wheeze almost directly into his ear.

"Are we alone?"

Luken felt suddenly uneasy. He glanced over his shoulder, but the hypaspist who had brought him into the ward had withdrawn outside the door.

"Yes, we are."

"What I have to tell you is vital," Akeron said. "I may not be around much longer to repeat it."

Luken began to protest about that claim, but Akeron snarled at him.

"I said listen, boy! The Zamorakians aren't only coming here to take this city and snuff out its light. They want something, something that's been buried here since before the first stones were laid. A force of darkness, born out of blood.

"It takes the form of a stone called the Blood Altar. It lies in a cursed chamber in a place outside this plane of existence. It can only be accessed by tunnels beneath the royal palace, in the south-east of the city. The Everlight was built there not only to act as a beacon for the icyene, but to help protect and contain the altar, to ward off the darkness that may seep from it, and keep unholy things that may wish to claim it far away. Its location is known only to me, Justiciar Lysander, and now you. It must remain that way."

"How can it be that the icyene don't know?" Luken asked. "Surely the queen or her council are aware of it?"

"The queen's parents were the last to know," Akeron said. "But that was almost half a millennium ago. They decided then that the knowledge would be held only by the archpriest as well as the justiciar of the unicorn, as the foremost servants of Saradomin in Hallowvale. In telling you, I have not broken that oath. Under illuminator you may be, but you are still a member of the clergy. Swear to me now upon the light that you will tell no other what I have told you."

"I swear it," Luken said, almost without thinking. He was still recovering from shock at the idea that a dark artefact was lying almost beneath their feet, in the very heart of Saradomin's most sacred city. How could it have existed so close to the likes of Queen Efaritay and remained undetected?

"Surely it has to be destroyed, this altar," he said.

Akeron had drifted, eyes straying back up to the ceiling, but at Luken's words he refocused.

"It is too dangerous. Some of the greatest minds and most devout churchmen have dedicated their entire lives to attempting to find how the Blood Altar might be unmade, but most agree that the risk outweighs the chances of success. It is believed whatever powerful being first constructed it intended it as a siphon, to drain the darkest magical energies from this corner of Gielinor. Attempting to break it may unleash the very evil we seek to destroy."

The archpriest lay still and silent, and Luken briefly thought he was lapsing into a state of semi-consciousness again, but when he spoke again his voice was still clear. Luken realised he had been lost in remorse.

"I have not done enough to continue their work. That is to my shame. When I inherited the diocese from Archpriest Apolos, the quest for the destruction of the altar had become little more than myth and legend. I visited it, once, to be formally entrusted with maintaining its secrets, but I made little effort to succeed where so many others had failed. May Saradomin forgive me for my idleness. I had barely thought about it for years before news of the invasion came."

Luken thought back to when word had broken, in the council chamber, and how distracted Akeron had seemed then and in the days that followed.

"You've been looking for answers," he said. "All those books in your chambers."

"Too little, too late," Akeron said bitterly. "Next to the wisdom of those who have performed these duties before me, I am a mere fool. I have found nothing to point towards how the Blood Altar might be safely destroyed. My only hope is breaking the physical link that allows others to access it."

"Would not great Saradomin know?" Luken asked, feeling foolish for suggesting something that seemed so obvious.

"If he does, he has chosen not to destroy it," Akeron grumbled. "It is not our place to question his decisions."

Luken bit his tongue, afraid he was about to utter something heretical.

"We should tell him the altar is in danger then," he suggested.

"He will know if Hallowvale is threatened, then the altar is likewise threatened. It is too late to send further word anyway. The vyre could be at the gates before a messenger even reaches him. We have only two options. Make an attempt at destroying it, or destroy the monsters coming to claim it."

"What will happen if the vyre take it?"

"I do not know for sure," Akeron admitted, his voice growing weaker. He was flagging. "But nothing good. The altar's essence is blood magics, the same energies that drive the vyre. If they claim it and corrupt it, even the Everlight might not be enough to contain them. The lighthouse is failing anyway. Another disaster I have allowed to unfold on my watch."

"There is yet time, archpriest," Luken said, squeezing Akeron's hand, desperate for him to maintain his focus. "Tell me what I must do? You know I will not rest until it is done!"

Akeron grunted and closed his eyes before answering. "The exuberance of youth. We were all like you once, boy. But that spirit of yours may yet make the difference."

He paused, and Luken feared he had drifted off to sleep, or worse, but after a while he opened his eyes once more and looked at Luken closely, as though making one final decision on whether or not to go on.

"You must search the library, and beyond," he said. "From the Hallowed Texts to the Lesser Scrolls. Look for any mention of the Blood Altar, or of unholy artefacts, of blood magics and worship of the darkness. Any hint as to how the sorceries binding and preserving the altar can be safely unmade. If you find anything, bring it to me. And pray. Pray that Saradomin gives me the strength to rise up from this damnable bed and resume my duties. We are running out of time."

ELEVEN

———◆———

Rhea, Mardin and Klaxar were given one of the citadel's now-empty guardrooms to sleep in, a place of bare stone and rows of wooden cot beds with straw sacking. She lay down on one, pausing only to unbuckle her kopis, and was asleep in moments.

Her rest was deep and dreamless, but she awoke abruptly to find Mardin already up, looking through a crack in one of the room's shutters. Klaxar was snoring heavily on a bed in the far corner.

Rhea sat up, brushing hair from her eyes. She took a second to find herself, then rose stiffly and joined Mardin at the window.

"Have you slept?" she asked.

"No," he admitted. "I was thinking about the farm. The one the beasts got to before us."

Rhea grunted. A family hauled into their own barn to be butchered and devoured like so much livestock, yet she had barely given it a second's thought since. It had been subsumed, first by the encounter with the were-pack itself, then by the days of hard riding and hard fighting.

She had seen terrible things in the years of campaigning. There seemed to be little rhyme or reason as to which ones lingered with her, and which were dragged down into the darkness of her psyche. Slaughter and pain and grief, yet it was often the smaller incidents that returned in her nightmares.

A dog that had belonged to one of the ordo's squires, refusing to leave his master's side even after the youth had been slain by wights resurrected by a Zamorakian necromancer.

The expression on the elderly mother of one of Rhea's slain companions, shifting in a few, pained seconds from confusion to grief to a cold, hard mask of acceptance when she realised her daughter's fate.

Snowfall, descending softly and peacefully over a field littered with broken weapons and shields and torn standards and equally torn bodies, covering the carnage with pristine whiteness, as though trying to hide what horrors mortals and monsters had unleashed upon one another.

Those little things stayed, and the greater horrors were submerged, and eventually they all became one. Rhea was thankful for the marching and the fighting and the killing only because it stopped her dwelling on any of it, gave her a purpose that allowed her to avoid the terrible, quiet moments such as these.

The only way to escape the horrors was to make more of them.

"Do you really believe he won't come?" Mardin asked. He had no need to say who.

Rhea looked at him. He was a veteran of as many campaigns as her, his face scarred by a Zamorakian axe and a werewolf's talons. He was a fighter, a killer, a good soldier. But just then, the Everlight's brightness spilling through the shutter crack as he gazed out across the city, he looked forlorn, almost childlike. Lost, Rhea realised.

She could understand why. To many of his followers, Saradomin was more than some distant, unreachable deity, some abstract theological concept. He walked among them, the light made flesh, their saviour against the darkness threatening to swallow up all of Gielinor. They had both seen him twice, once when he had addressed the combined tagmata ahead of the Paddewwa campaign, and once during the battle of White Mountain, where his awesome might had broken the back of the Zamorakian host, turning the tide just when all seemed lost. "Trust in the light" was the common phrase among Saradominist soldiers. Trust it will always rise and banish the dark.

Yet now it seemed it would rise no more. Rhea had never been a deeply religious person. She was devoted to Saradomin, but it was the devotion a good soldier showed towards their commander, not the devotion of a priest to their god. She could understand why the likes of Phosani were dedicated heart, body and soul to Saradomin – when he had addressed them all before Paddewwa, she had felt as though his words had a brilliance all of their own, one which burned away the doubts and fears and left only clarity. When she had seen him fight at White Mountain, it had been feats of strength and power that had awed her, shrugging off the frenzied blows of the Zamorakians, smiting whole ranks with a light that could sear away flesh and melt bones.

Rhea had experienced power of godhood but could never bring herself to trust in it above the strength of her own sword-arm. Looking at Mardin though, contemplating the knowledge that his deity might not hear his prayers after all, Rhea could understand his fear.

"If Saradomin does not come, we will have to find our own light," she told him firmly. "The city must not fall. The Everlight must not go out. If it does, every battle we've fought, every friend lost, every sacrifice made, may be for nothing. The war could turn against us, irrevocably."

"That's why he must come," Mardin said. "That's why we have to believe."

Rhea was tempted to say she put more stock in actions than beliefs, but she held her tongue. Mardin didn't need that right now. She had rarely seen the grizzled warrior so shaken.

"You should rest," she said. "Don't make me order you, the way Her-Winged-Majesty ordered me."

There was a terse knock at the door. Klaxar surged upwards, snatching her labrys axe from where she'd propped it beside her bed, her eyes wild. Rhea glanced at her, feeling the sudden, unexpected urge to laugh.

"Enter," she called instead. An icyene stepped into the guardroom, clearly struggling to mask his distaste for the three shabby humans he found within.

"Orders for Justiciar Phosani, direct from Her-Winged-Majesty," he declared, and held out a piece of parchment, folded and sealed. "They are instructions to muster at the mill formerly belonging to Hephaston, west of the city gates. That is where the rest of the tagma will be concentrating."

Rhea took the parchment, securing it in the pouch at her side.

"A battle, huh?" Klaxar said, sounding as though she had just awoken from the longest and most peaceful sleep of her life. "A proper one, no more of this skulking about in the woods. About time."

"So it would seem," Rhea said, stooping to retrieve her kopis and belt. As she buckled it on, she tried not to think about what would be left behind in that battle's aftermath, or how she was going to tell Phosani that the god she loved so much had abandoned them.

✦ ✦ ✦

Rhea and her companions rejoined the ordo of the wolf in the dark, just east of Hephaston's mill.

It had taken time to locate the main encampment, in the night encroaching beyond the furthest reaches of the Everlight's radius. They had ridden towards the last rally point, but Rhea had deemed it too close now to the enemy's ongoing advance, and Klaxar had found hoof prints that implied the ordo had shifted further east.

They had turned in that direction and ridden through the dark, haunted by the eerie shrieks and cries and the lights dancing in the sky. Icyene and vyre doing battle, Rhea knew, as they had done every night since the frontier had fallen.

Eventually they found an outpost of half a dozen members of the ordo. They were taking shelter from a sudden autumnal rainfall beneath a broad hyca tree at the side of the road. Swords sprang from scabbards before they saw just who had stumbled upon them.

"Further up the track," the commander of the little band, a hypaspist named Attikus, told Rhea. "The justiciar has been waiting for you."

The three of them rode on, finding the Wolves sheltering in a copse close to Hephaston's watermill. The mill itself was a derelict stone structure, abandoned a generation ago when old Hephaston had perished without an heir to take on its working. It stood at the base of a hill around which a stream, known now as Hephaston's Run, passed. The area directly to the south had become waterlogged and marshy thanks to the inactivity of the mill. The woodland was to the hill's north.

Rhea dismissed Klaxar and Mardin and greeted Phosani when she found her. As expected, the justiciar was not resting but had joined the reinforced night watch that protected every Saradominist camp throughout the hours of darkness. Rhea joined her at a sputtering fire, its glow flickering over the justiciar's damp features. She looked tired.

"You came straight from the citadel?" she asked, and Rhea wondered if there was reproachment in her tone.

"The queen bade us rest a few hours after delivering the report," she admitted. "Despite my objections."

Phosani offered no comment, and Rhea went on.

"I bear orders from the queen. I was present during her last council meeting, where I delivered the report."

"Are we to continue our delaying tactics?"

"No. Her-Winged-Majesty has resolved to meet the enemy in a pitched battle."

Phosani looked at Rhea sharply.

"Did you counsel against this?"

"I offered a description of the campaign thus far," Rhea said. "It was not my place to debate with the likes of Strategos Babel."

Phosani let out a small hiss of annoyance. "Babel has been wrong about this from the beginning. We should seek to delay them, yes, but committing our entire tagma to a pitched battle? The arrogance of the icyene blinds them to reality. This is not some legion of spavined Zamorakian fodder. They have vyre."

Rhea held her tongue, instead pulling out the parchment she had received from the icyene messenger before departing.

"This comes from the queen herself, commander. I believe it is instructions to rejoin the tagma."

"What's the muster point?" Phosani asked as she broke the seal and opened the paper, having to stoop and hold it at an angle so the firelight illuminated it.

"We're already at it," Rhea said as Phosani read. "The old mill is where the tagma will concentrate. I believe this is where Babel intends to make his stand. The terrain is favourable at least."

Phosani grunted, still reading. When she finished, she

crumpled the paper up before it could get any wetter and tossed it into the fire. It hissed softly before catching.

"Why this sudden change in strategy?" she demanded. "Was Babel really able to convince the queen?"

Rhea didn't know what to say, so she did what she liked to do best, and attacked head-on.

"Word was received by the council while it was in session," she said. "From the Lord of Light. We are not to expect immediate relief in the event of a siege. The conquest of the Infernal Source remains the main goal."

Phosani was silent, and Rhea found it difficult to read her face – the rain was worsening, and the fire was starting to sputter and die.

"There must have been some mistake," the justiciar said.

"I saw a messenger arrive, and the queen was clear afterwards about what had been delivered."

"Did you hear what this messenger actually said? Did you read any letter they carried?"

"No, commander."

"Tell me exactly what happened."

Rhea could sense the anger in the justiciar, the desire to lash out. She had expected as much, though she still had to curb the instinct to respond in kind.

"I had just delivered my report when a messenger arrived, an icyene prodromoi with the Optimatoi's crest. She wished to speak with the queen immediately. The entire council was dismissed, and we waited in the antechamber outside the throne room until we were permitted to return. Her-Winged-Majesty informed us that word had come from the Lord of Light that no troops could be spared from the Infernal Source. After that Strategos Babel's suggestion about delaying the enemy with a pitched battle was agreed upon."

"What has happened at the Infernal Source?" Phosani wondered. "There must have been some setback. Perhaps Zamorak himself has entered the fray?"

Rhea said nothing. She felt uncomfortable, she realised. Consoling a fellow hypaspist in a moment of doubt was one thing, but attempting to soften this sort of blow struck against her commander was another entirely.

"Saradomin will come," Phosani said, and scuffed at the edge of the fire with her boot. The flames rekindled, lighting her drawn features briefly. "He must come."

"Do you have any further orders?" Rhea asked, ashamed at the fact she was trying to get away, but unwilling to linger anymore. She had done her duty. Now she needed time to prepare for what they all knew was coming.

"Nothing for now," Phosani said. "Go and sleep, if you've not had enough already. We will move when it's dawn, occupy that hill ahead of the rest of the tagma's arrival."

"Understood, commander," Rhea said, saluting without thinking before withdrawing – two fingers, against the star of Saradomin on her breastplate.

The gesture was lost in the dark.

✦ ✦ ✦

The hypaspists of the owl were the first to join the Wolves above Hephaston's mill. They arrived in the misty, wet dawn, the feathered mantles they wore clasped around their shoulders drenched. Aliya's Lions reached the muster point a little after middle-day. Combined their numbers were still fewer than Phosani's ordo – most of them were serving at the Infernal Source.

Flocks of icyene continued to come in throughout the day as word slowly spread to them that the queen wished to concentrate her forces. Rhea recognised a number of them, and recognised too that their numbers were much reduced. The hypaspists of Hallowvale, the icyene, had paid in blood for facing the vyre head-on and during the darkest hours of the night.

Justiciar Lysander and a section of the hypaspists of the unicorn were the last members of the ordos to arrive. They were few in number as well – most had been left behind to continue their sacred duty, guarding the Saradominist temples in Hallowvale.

The banners atop the crest of the hill overlooking the mill and stream were complete, the wolf and lion pelts, the shimmering unicorn horn and the feathers of the owl arrayed side-by-side. Lysander met with Phosani and they shared what seemed like an earnest conversation. Rhea could not overhear what passed between them. Otrava and Insela were the ones attending the White Wolf.

The rain ceased, though the skies remained low and bleak, the day so grey that the illumination of the distant Everlight remained visible against the clouds to the east. It seemed to grow as Rhea gazed towards it, and it took her a while to understand exactly what it was she was looking at.

The Queen of Hallowvale had arrived. She materialised from out of the light, and carried it with her. Gone was the austere and guarded stateswoman Rhea had seen in the throne room of the citadel, replaced by a warrior-queen. Her blue robes and mantle had been replaced by a shorter white chiton, worn beneath a breastplate of burnished steel and a helmet of the same metal, topped by a blue and white crest. To her left arm was strapped a large, round wooden shield, an aspis, also sheathed in steel, as were her vambraces and greaves. The armour panoply shone brilliantly not just in the distant glow of the Everlight, but from the spear that Her-Winged-Majesty was carrying in one hand. Rhea had never seen its like before – it was as though a shard of the Everlight had been broken free and fashioned into a weapon.

With the queen came her guards, similarly attired, so that it seemed as though a constellation of glittering stars had broken free from the firmament and had come sweeping down through the dull clouds, intent on carrying the light of the heavens to the surface of Gielinor. One of them bore the royal standard, a blue and gold bolt of silk that streamed lustrously as they flew.

Rhea felt the moroseness that had been growing over her lift, and for a few precious moments everything, from the cold and the damp to the bleak news from Saradomin, was forgotten. She looked up at her queen, her light fell upon her face and dazzled her eyes, and briefly she shared in the faith that Phosani, Mardin and the other true Saradominists of the ordos held so dear.

The hypaspists hurried to make space for the icyene on the crest of the hill. Efaritay alighted with effortless grace, her guards doing likewise around her a heartbeat later with barely a scrape, furling their glorious wings.

Without instruction the hypaspists knelt, bending their knees in the dirt. Rhea went down with the rest, averting her gaze from the light. All was still and silent, and she found herself closing her eyes and allowing herself to exist in just that period of time, that fragment of peacefulness amidst the whole fractured mess. That, she supposed, was as much a prayer to Saradomin as anything spoken by her fellows.

"Rise," Efaritay said, her voice carrying easily. "I will not labour you with speeches or declarations, not yet. You all know your duty. The rest of the tagma approaches. We will make our stand here, upon the hill of Hephaston."

She gestured, and the icyene guardswoman bearing the royal standard stepped forward and planted it atop the hill's crest, between the banners of the ordos. Efaritay raised her spear and it shone, its brilliance reflected back from the weapons of her followers as the hypaspists drew swords or shook spears, their voices ringing out over the bleak, damp countryside.

"Hallowvale! Hallowvale! Hallowvale!"

TWELVE

———◆◆———

Ranis hunted among the fourteenth legion until he found the cohort bearing his sister's banner. Vanescula was present among the human Zamorakian soldiery almost as much as her own brood. She was dutiful like that, unlike Ranis, who had barely seen his own legionary cohort since crossing the frontier.

She was overseeing them as they finished breaking camp in the twilight and began to march, forming up behind the cohort ahead of them in the slow-moving Zamorakian column occupying the main road south. While some of the legion's subdivisions were still advancing during the day, most marched at night now, so that they could better fall under the protection of their vyre overlords.

As Ranis moved along the roadside towards her, he saw a figure leave her side. While he didn't catch the man's face, as he approached he saw him shift and change, his sensitive hearing catching the ugly, wet snapping of bones and a feral snarl. What had once been a man loped off on all fours into the gathering dark. Ranis stopped a short distance away.

Vanescula sensed his presence.

"Approach," she said while watching the front ranks of her cohort as they stepped off from their muster point, cattle in tight ranks and black armour.

"I hope I wasn't interrupting anything," Ranis said as he advanced to her side.

"Why are you here?" she demanded.

"Does a younger brother need a reason to check the welfare of his older sister?" Ranis asked.

"Speak," Vanescula snapped, showing her fangs. "Even if we had the time, you know I would not indulge your games."

"I came to seek your counsel," Ranis admitted, holding up a hand defensively. "I have need of your wisdom."

Vanescula's cold expression refused to brighten. Ranis knew she was too clever to be drawn by flattery, but assuaging vyre nobility came naturally to him.

"You are scheming, and you wish for my approval," Vanescula said. "Or perhaps you hope to indict me in whatever plans you are concocting by informing me of them, so you can use me as a shield, or blackmail me into assisting you. And no, don't—"

She held up a finger sharply as Ranis began to protest.

"Do not reply with false dismay or outrage! Leave behind the platitudes and gratitude as well. I warned you, I have neither time nor patience for you this night."

Ranis pursed his thin lips and mustered himself for a reply.

"You are colder than ever, sister. Very well. I will speak plainly, and tell you that the situation we find ourselves in is intolerable."

Vanescula looked back at the passing ranks, their helms turned towards her in salute.

"Elaborate," she demanded.

"You are as much a hunter as any other Drakan," Ranis said, ignoring the host going by. "You know how to stalk powerful prey. Slowly and patiently. Harass it, bleed it, never give it any rest. Drain its strength while conserving yours. That is what the light-loving cattle are doing to us, sister. They raid, ambush, they harry, snapping about our heels. We bleed as we go forward, slowly, drop by drop, yard by yard."

"If you wish for a change of strategy you should speak to His-Dark-Self," Vanescula said. "I command this cohort, not the legion."

"Do not feign weakness. You have greater influence over him than any other."

Vanescula laughed at that. "I'm not sure if I should take that as a compliment or not."

Ranis refused to let the conversation descend into just another round of jibes and bared fangs.

"Have you been aloft since we crossed the frontier?" he asked instead.

"What?"

"Have you flown? During the night? Have you sought prey, as it is natural for our kind to do?"

Vanescula said nothing. Ranis fought not to appear

triumphant. Chiding her would not help bring her onto his side. He had to press his point instead.

"You do not fly because you do not wish to face the icyene. They are everywhere. They slaughtered half my brood on one of the first nights."

"That is because you were arrogant and impatient, as ever," Vanescula said heartlessly. "If you wish to take wing against those monsters then you are welcome to."

"And when did you last feed?"

"A few nights ago. Some Saradominist priest who refused to abandon his wayside shrine."

Ranis paused again. He hadn't anticipated her having fed so recently, and it undermined his argument. Sensing his weakness, Vanescula pushed back.

"And how about you, dear brother? When did you last feed? You do not seem to be gnawed by hunger, riven with the blood-need. Have a few legionaries from your cohort gone missing over the past few days? Just a few extra casualties from the raids, unaccounted for. You know we're forbidden from feeding on our own soldiers?"

Ranis scoffed and waved the accusation away.

"This is all taking too long, and costing us too much. You know it as well as I, though you feign ignorance."

"And just what are you proposing? Or rather, what would you have me propose to our brother?"

"We should march the legion night and day until we are at the walls. The Saradominists seem ill-enough prepared as it is. If we hurry, we may take the city by storm. There would be no need for a siege. No need to fear Saradomin cutting us off from the west and coming to Hallowvale's relief. We should bring together all vyre as well, and engage the icyene at night, when they must face us at our strongest or risk us picking off their human servants."

"This is the grand strategy you have concocted?" Vanescula asked. "I am at least relieved to note I'm not the only Drakan who worked out the dangers of Saradomin coming to the aid of his city."

"The sooner we take Hallowvale, the sooner we can prepare it for the inevitable counterattack," Ranis went on, daring to hope his sister was accepting his point. "When Saradomin comes east, Zamorak will strike from the north, and this war will turn. More importantly, we will have secured a new home on Gielinor, a better one than Vampyrium. But to do all that, we need to move with speed. Lowerniel is treating this like a glorified hunting trip."

Vanescula just laughed. Ranis frowned, feeling his pride prickle.

"What's so funny?"

"You have an excellent sense of timing, Ranis, I'll give you that. Or your friends among the pack have managed to get word to you quicker than mine. That would be disappointing."

Ranis thought about the werewolf he had seen leaving Vanescula just before his arrival.

"What have you heard?" he demanded, feeling suddenly cautious. Something had clearly happened that he was unaware of, and there were few things Ranis hated more than other people knowing things he did not.

Vanescula was quiet, watching him closely and with the faintest hint of amusement.

"Cease your teasing," Ranis snapped. "Tell me!"

She laughed before speaking.

"Oh, very well. It seems your wishes have been granted by no less than Queen Efaritay herself. The packs ranged far to the south today, farther than any of them had managed before. They found that the parties that have been hounding us have retreated. Not just that, but they are concentrating their strength just to the north-west of the city walls. The queen is there and seemingly all their host."

Ranis felt an unexpected thrill, twinned with simple relief.

"Then they mean to do battle," he said, trying not to get ahead of himself. "A pitched battle, in the open."

"So it would seem."

"We could not hope for better. Slaughter them, and the city will be left almost defenceless. It will fall within days once we reach it, if we can only destroy the Everlight."

"And just how do you plan on doing that? I'm sure our brother would appreciate your genius."

"That is a matter for when we reach Hallowvale."

"Afraid I will steal your cunning and claim it as my own?"

"I'm sure you have ideas of your own. What's important now is that we meet these fools before they realise their mistake and withdraw back to their walls."

"Bold Ranis, rushing off to seek martial glory in the field of combat," Vanescula said. "This is an unexpected turn."

"Do not taunt me," Ranis said, though his mood had lifted too much for him to snap. "You must see as clearly as I that this is a stroke of good fortune."

"I will consider it as such once the battle is won and the foe slaughtered."

"They cannot possibly stand against our might," Ranis exclaimed. "Against the might of Drakan!"

Vanescula looked back at the Zamorakian soldiers marching by, then raised a clenched fist. The legionaries, their heads already turned in salute, began to cheer as their commander acknowledged them.

"Perhaps it is time you attended to your own cohort, brother," she said without looking away from the passing ranks. "It seems as though you'll be leading them into battle soon enough."

✦ ✦ ✦

Efaritay summoned the leaders of the Hallowvale host for a council of war. A camp had sprung up along the eastern slopes and in the fallow fields beyond. The tagma had spent the day stockpiling underbrush from the forest to the north, setting it out across the western slopes and along the banks of the stream beneath. As twilight began to replace the day's gloom, they did their best to kindle the damp wood. Eventually, the flames caught, and a ring of flickering illumination banded the hill, warding away the dark as it came prowling in.

The commanders of the ordos and their subordinates gathered again along with the officers of the tagma's human phalanxes and the icyene in charge of the psiloi flocks. Efaritay received them beneath the royal standard, with Babel at her side, a brazier combining its light with the lambent glow emanating from the Sunspear.

She had spoken with the strategos at length before bringing their subordinates together. He was in his element, laying out his plans to turn the hilltop into an impregnable fortress. Efaritay had humoured him because she broadly agreed with the tactics he was suggesting, and because she knew she had given herself little other choice now that she had backed his strategy.

Back at the citadel, Ascertes had continued to try to talk her out of leading the tagma to face the Zamorakians in the field. She had eventually commanded him to be silent. She was not proud of her loss of control, but she dared not admit the truth, even to her husband. The word from Saradomin had stunned her. Privately, in the aftermath of the council meeting that had been interrupted by the arrival of his messenger, she had written a fresh letter to him and had it dispatched by the swiftest remaining icyene wing. It was a desperate plea for him to reconsider, coupled with a description of the full extent of the invasion Hallowvale was facing.

She should have been clearer from the beginning. She should have waited until she knew the enemy's strength and made it known, instead of sending the vague initial reports of an incursion across the northern frontier.

She had blundered, perhaps fatally. The only hope was to delay the Zamorakians. She had become terrified of her own paralysis, of simply sitting behind Hallowvale's walls and hoping that they could outlast the night.

In times of war, any action is better than no action, or so Efaritay's mother had claimed. So she had acted, and now she had to trust in Babel, and the warriors under their command.

She allowed him to describe the coming battle to the rest of the tagma leadership. Now was no time to undermine him, and his plan seemed sound enough. The terrain was as good as Babel had claimed during the council sessions. The hill above the old mill was steep, and the Zamorakians would be forced west by the forest. The approach there was complicated by the presence of the stream which, though fordable, would slow any attack before it even hit the slope. The flooded, swampy land to the south meant there would be no easy outflanking, certainly none that any force on the hill would remain unaware of. The main road to Hallowvale passed by the mill itself over a small stone bridge, south of the hill, but the Zamorakians would not be able to manoeuvre along it with the Saradominist in such a position of strength nearby – they could descend and strike at any time.

The phalanxes of pike-armed human phalangites – six formations in total – would array themselves midway up the hill, covering the slope in an arc from the south, west and north. The icyene flocks would protect the skies and rain arrows down on the Zamorakians as they were forced to wade the stream that had once fed Hephaston's mill and then climb the slope to get at the Saradominist lines. The ordos would be held in reserve, the hypaspists of the lion, owl and unicorn – all few in number – remaining mounted while those of the wolf were dispersed on foot at the centre of the line. Lastly, Efaritay and her royal guard would hold the crest of the hill, a final reserve that, according to Babel, would not be risked. It was only then that Efaritay interrupted.

"I will deploy the guard as I see fit, strategos. If the battle is to turn upon a single clash of arms, I intend to be in the midst of it. That is both my duty, and my right, as queen."

"With all respect, Your-Winged-Majesty, we cannot endanger you," Babel began to say, but Efaritay shook her head.

"This battle will not be easy. We are gravely outnumbered. If we are to be victorious, we all have to take on the greatest of dangers, including myself. That is why I am here."

Babel was wise enough not to argue any further. He finished giving his instructions, and accepted the questions of his subordinates. Matters of disposition and supplies were dealt with, and the chain of command was clarified – Babel accepted that each human phalanx should report to him and Efaritay directly, rather than having to go first to other icyene officers. Justiciar Aliya spoke of the sorcerous threat of the vyre, particularly the danger that they and their Zamorakian minions might seek to resurrect the dead in the midst of battle. She promised to work to unmake such efforts, and swore that the rune-casters accompanying her would closely support the main battle line.

It seemed all was set, until the White Wolf called out with one last, abrupt, question.

"Is it true that Saradomin is not coming?"

Surprise passed across Babel's face, and he glanced uncertainly at Efaritay. She answered herself, addressing Phosani.

"Not immediately, but have no doubt that relief will be dispatched. If we delay the Zamorakians here, we will buy time for their arrival."

Phosani nodded, her expression hard, and Efaritay hoped her assurances had sounded truthful. She wished she could convince herself.

THIRTEEN

◄◆►

The prodromoi spotted the Zamorakian host approaching as darkness overtook twilight's last glimmer. They skirted round from the west, at first just a few pinpricks in the dark, uncertain out beyond the firelight of the pyres burning along the hill's lower slopes. They grew steadily however – torches borne by the Zamorakian legionaries – until they became a constellation below the hill.

The sky above was riven with vyre, their unnatural shrieking drifting on the cold air as they called to one another. The icyene took flight, wary of an immediate attack, but there was none. Dawn rose, as grey and wet as the day before, leaching a hint of colour into the torpid autumnal landscape.

The Zamorakians lay like a blot before Hephaston's hill. They stood in battle array, block after block of dark-armoured warriors beneath the banners of their vyrelords. More were still marching from the roadway and spreading out into the surrounding fields and meadows as the daylight strengthened, stretching off in the distance. There was no hint of their vampyric masters – they were shunning the brightest hours of daylight.

It was as bad as Efaritay had feared. None of the reports of the size of the enemy host had been exaggerated. She looked to the hill, and to the phalanxes arrayed along the slopes, a bristling forest of pikes silhouetted against smouldering flames as the last of the night's pyres burned themselves out. She had to trust in their strength, and her own. The position was sound. Doubts now would only serve to betray her.

The Zamorakians continued to amass as the day drew on but showed no sign of attacking. Dorien, in command of the detachment of Owl hypaspists, came to the royal standard not long after middle-day to suggest a sortie against the Zamorakian flank, while they were still gathering.

Babel, to his credit, refused the suggestion, saving Efaritay the trouble of overruling him. They were outnumbered enough as it was without risking troops in more raids, and the hilltop had been chosen specifically as a defensive bulwark. They would not play into the enemy's hands.

But that meant waiting for the onset of darkness. More firewood had been gathered throughout the day and the clouds, while bleak, withheld their rain. Those were the only blessings. As twilight returned and the pyres were again kindled into light, Babel returned to the hill's crest after inspecting the line.

"With your permission, my queen, we will stand the entire tagma to throughout the night," the strategos said.

During the day sections had been rotating between guarding the slopes, gathering wood or resting, but there could be no doubt that every warrior would be needed during the hours of darkness.

"Agreed," Efaritay said, wishing, as the peals of the salpinx rang out across the hill, that she had found the time for a few hours of sleep while there had still been daylight guarding them.

It would be a long night.

◆ ◆ ◆

The horn called the ordo of the wolf to the hunt.

Rhea walked among the pack as they made final preparations, doling out threats and encouragement. She exchanged cold jests with the other veterans, and gave terse advice to the pups that had only joined them since their return to Hallowvale.

Ensure swords were loose in the scabbards. Tighten buckles. Re-tie laces. Always get the man or woman who would be to the left or right of you in the line to check over your panoply, once you had it all on. Look to them, trust in them. Don't be the link that broke. The phalanx was only as strong as its weakest member.

Phosani returned as Rhea was still moving through the pack. She had been absent with Otrava and Insela, attending a final meeting with the other ordo leaders. Rhea hadn't been asked to accompany her to any of the councils since the queen's arrival. It stung, but a part of her was also relieved. She felt as though, in being the one who had first told Phosani that there would be no relief from Saradomin, she had somehow belittled or challenged the White Wolf's faith. She had no wish to endure her justiciar's current coldness any more than she had to.

"Is the pack ready?" Phosani asked, her silver hair shimmering in the glow of the campfires.

"It's about to be," Rhea reported. "Are the Zamorakians on the move?"

"Unclear," Phosani said. "Take your post."

The hypaspists assembled into a column of march, Rhea taking her position beside Mardin and in front of Klaxar, in the front rank. Phosani went ahead along with the salpinx blower, Insela and Otrava, the latter carrying the wolf standard. They set off, marching to take their place in the line.

As they went, Rhea found herself glancing up into the sky, at the last, faint glimmer of daylight struggling against the horizon.

Abruptly, she found herself wondering whether she would see another dawn.

✦ ✦ ✦

The officers of the fourteenth legion attended their commander, along with the nobility of Vampyrium. Drakan was standing in a field on the edge of the Zamorakian encampment, gazing silently into the distance. Before him, the pyres kindled by the Saradominists across the slopes rose, defiant against the prowling night, crowning the hill with a circlet of flame. It was already graced by a halo, the pallid illumination of the far-off Everlight, hidden by the crest but strong enough this close to the city to silhouette the promontory.

The Saradominists had made the hill their sacred queen. Drakan resolved to trample her and drench her in blood.

"Vanescula," he said.

Though he had his back to them, he could sense the mass of officers and vyrelords and ladies behind, standing at a cautious distance as they waited for instructions. He could hear the delicious heartbeats of the humans, and the high-frequency keening of the vampyres, a union of butchers and cattle he had forged for the sole purpose of claiming the prize that awaited him beneath Saradomin's prized city.

"My vyrelord?" Vanescula asked as she joined him. He spoke to her without averting his gaze from the fires on the slopes.

"Take the hill. Kill them all."

Vanescula bowed and withdrew. Drakan heard her as though in a dream, addressing his lesser subordinates.

"We attack tonight. The second through seventh cohorts will array and drive directly for the hill crest. The first, eighth, ninth and tenth cohorts will remain in reserve. Be sure to halt once you've crossed the stream and dress ranks before advancing up the slope. You may have to do so again once you breach their watch fires. My vyrelords, take your broods to wing. We will tear apart the icyene, and once it is done, descend on the rear ranks beneath us. Rip them to pieces from above. Ulf, your packs should range north and south, circle the hill. If the Saradominists attempt to withdraw, it will be up to you to close in and harry them. Turn any retreat into a rout. You have discretion to hunt as you see fit. Questions?"

Drakan had no interest in giving such instructions himself. The minutia of battle was better handled by someone like his sister. At heart he was a hunter, not a general.

Vanescula dismissed her kindred and the legion's officers, and they hurried away to their broods and cohorts. Drakan sensed her linger a while, as though she wished to speak with him, but he was in no mood for discussion, and after a while she silently departed.

He stood alone, enjoying the quiet, the anticipation. Again, that sweet moment, before the hunt began. Soon that hill would run red with glorious slaughter, and they would all feast. He would have to show restraint though. That would be the true test of his generalship, not petty tactical wrangling or stirring the cattle to feats of arms. To control his vyre in the aftermath, to ensure they hunted down any survivors and made the victory complete while avoiding the temptation to gorge themselves on blood and carcasses – none but Drakan could have hoped to exhibit such mastery of the vyre, such self-discipline. It was a triumph he would have to repeat when Hallowvale itself fell, if his true plans were to reach fruition.

The silence was broken, stirred by the peal of cornu horns and the barking of orders. He heard the tramp of feet in the mud as the front ranks of his cohorts stepped off. He unfurled his wings, tensed, and took flight, shooting up into the night sky. As he did so, he called out, summoning the vyreguard to him. The other broods rose as well, filling the night air with the hiss of leathery wings and their predatory snarls and rattles.

Drakan roared, an exaltation of bloodlust and anticipation. It was answered by a shriek from the vyre, and then a great shout from the humans marching below.

The fourteenth legion would take the hill before the dawn.

+ ✦ +

"They're advancing, my queen," the prodromoi said, panting.

Efaritay thanked the scout and dismissed her, refusing to let the rush of nervous anticipation show as she looked at Babel.

"As I predicted," the strategos said. "We must stand firm throughout the night. Survive until the dawn, and it will be the herald of our victory. Look to the coming of the light."

"Look to the coming of the light," Efaritay repeated, refusing to ponder the irony of the sacred phrase, the discordance of knowing Saradomin was not coming.

There was time now for neither doubt nor despair.

"Have the flocks take wing," Babel ordered the salpinx blower. The notes carried cold and clear, and there was a rustling of wings as the psiloi arrayed around the hill's crest took flight, launching themselves into the dark to join the prodromoi retreating from beyond the stream.

Efaritay pulled on her helm, hefted the Sunspear and called for her shield.

"You should remain here, my queen," Babel said. "At least stay with the reserve. We may have use of your royal guard at the most critical point."

"You will have use of them now," Efaritay declared. "You will stay and oversee the battle, Strategos Babel. That is your duty. But my duty is up there, with them."

She pointed with the Sunspear, up at the flocks answering the salpinx's commands, taking flight, like hundreds of fireflies dancing against the backdrop of the black sky.

"As my queen wishes," Babel said, offering a bow. "Go with the light, Your-Winged-Majesty."

"And you, strategos," she said, before calling out to her guards.

"To me, defenders of Hallowvale!"

She took flight, joining the circle of light in the sky that now mirrored the ring of flames around the hill.

FOURTEEN

The Zamorakian cohorts marched against Hephaston's hill.

They reached the stream that bordered the base of its western slope. It wasn't wide, but it was running cold and quick thanks to the recent rains. The legionaries dammed it up with their own bodies as they waded across, struggling to keep their ranks.

That was when the first arrows began to fall among them. Prodromoi shots, striking with unerring accuracy from out of the night sky, punching through throats and faces, dropping bodies and darkening the waters with blood.

That would not stop the fourteenth legion – the prodromoi were few, their deadly rain a light hail against the bulk of the attacking cohorts. And besides, it lasted only a few minutes before the airborne icyene archers were driven back ahead of the oncoming vyre broods.

"Push on," Zamorakian centenarii and ordinarii barked,

shoving and cajoling their legionaries onwards as they clambered up out of the bitter waters. "Up the slope! Move!"

There was no point in halting to dress the ranks yet. Another obstacle stood between the Zamorakians and the enemy phalanxes, a wall of flames stacked up along the lower slopes, designed to give early warning of any surprise attack and help keep the night at bay.

The Zamorakians drove up the slope and into the flames, kicking and trampling, the ruddy glow gleaming from drawn spatha, black parma shields and chainmail. A few tumbled back in agony as they were burned, and some were even ignited, screaming horribly as they fell amidst consuming flame. Their comrades beat them aside with their shields and pushed on, crushing the pyres as they would crush the Saradominists, breaking apart the crown of flames.

As they went, the death-rain returned. This time it wasn't the work of the icyene, but of the sphendonitai, human slingers and archers scattered loosely behind the phalangites on the upper slopes. The pyres had not served only to light the hillside, but to show the sphendonitai the fullest extent of their range. The Zamorakians had entered it.

Arrows and stones slashed down against helmets and shields. The humans had none of the accuracy of the icyene, but they had greater volume.

"Shields up," the centenarius bellowed. "Re-form! Re-form your damned ranks!"

Lit by the flickering of trampled embers, the cohorts sought to order themselves after their drive through water and flame. Some, raw recruits who had served in the legion for mere months or weeks, panicked. Most did not. The fourteenth legion had fought at Agabus, at Uzer and at Tanner's Hill, and during the retreat to Saranthium. They had endured worse hails than this.

The cohorts reordered their ranks, shields up and overlapping, creating an outer shell against which slingshots rattled and arrows buried themselves, quivering.

"Advance!" came the shouted order, and they did so, beginning to climb once more. Now the only obstacle between them and the hill's crest was the steel and wood, flesh and bone and blood of the Saradominist phalanxes. The Zamorakians and their banners and icons of horns, bats and wolves went up the slope, disdaining the missiles falling amongst them.

Rhea watched them come. The ordo of the wolf was the heart of the Saradominist line, a block of hypaspists bedecked in the pelts of the predator they venerated. The Zamorakians were a dark, glittering mass beneath them, partly silhouetted by what remained of the pyres behind them.

Orders rang out from the phalangites to the left and right, and a thundering shout went up as they lowered their pikes ahead of the advancing legionaries, forming a bristling wall of steel-spiked shafts.

"Shields," Rhea heard Phosani demand from among the ordo's ranks. She repeated the shout, spreading the order to the right of the formation.

Shields were brought up and clashed together, presenting those Zamorakians directly below not with an array of sarissa pikes, but the snarling heraldry of the wolf-and-star.

The hypaspists beat the hafts of their doru spears against the edges of their shields, setting up a clattering racket.

"When they come, kill the bastards," Rhea snarled at her fellow Wolves. "Kill them all."

There was no need for more eloquent encouragement, and there were no cheers or shouts of defiance. When all the faith and fury and high Saradominist ideals were stripped away, the men and women packed shoulder-to-shoulder around her were hardened killers, just like the Zamorakians coming for them.

Light or dark, now they would see who killed better.

Barely a dozen yards separated the two sides. The Zamorakians seemed to falter though, and Rhea swiftly saw why. Light arced over the Saradominist line, meeting the blackness that was surging and broiling above the Zamorakians. Before the humans of both armies met, the icyene and the vyre crashed against one another in the skies above, their meeting accompanied by a terrible, howling shriek from the vampyres that chilled Rhea's blood and seemed to make even the Zamorakians quail.

She had only a few moments to watch the clash. The legionaries now let out a roar of their own and began to press the last few yards.

No more orders, no more doubts. Heart hammering, Rhea planted her feet on the slope and switched her grip on her doru from overhand to underhand, raising it and, as the gap closed, driving it over the top of her shield.

It clattered against the edge of one of the Zamorakian shields and jarred up and off a steel helmet. She recovered and made to lunge again, feeling her own aspis shield take a hit, presumably from a spatha.

The thunder of the Zamorakian line meeting the Saradominists around her eclipsed even the crash of the icyene and the vyre.

A spatha slammed into Rhea's aspis, numbing her forearm. She ploughed down with the spear again, scraping and shattering mail but failing to find flesh. The press made wielding it underhand difficult to get a downward angle, so she switched back, shortening her grip, stabbing past where a black-painted parma was overlapping with her own shield and shoving against it.

This time it felt as though she had punched through something more yielding than mail, leather or padded cloth. The pressure against her aspis vanished and she had to lean back into Klaxar to avoid stumbling forward into the gap.

It was gone soon, whoever she had wounded dragged back, their place in the struggling front rank refilled. The Zamorakians faced an uphill battle in the most literal sense, the phalangites able to push down on them with their shields and drive down with their spears. Those thrusts that didn't scar helmets or scrape off armoured shoulders gouged faces and necks. The Zamorakian legionaries struggled to drive through the interlocking shields or swing high enough to slash over them.

"Push together," Rhea bellowed, stabbing again past the rim of her aspis, trying to lunge so that even if the legionary pressing directly against her avoided the doru tip, one in the second or third rank caught it.

The hypaspists took a step forward, then another, and suddenly the pressure was gone again, the Zamorakians tumbling back down the slope. Their line had lost its coherency somewhere, and it had crumbled.

Rhea's veins sang with the joy of battle, and she had to check herself before instinct and momentum led her to rushing after the retreating foe.

"Hold the line," she roared, hearing Phosani, Otrava and Insela giving the same commands to the left. "Don't break formation!"

The hypaspists of the wolf knew better than to make that mistake. They kept their position on the slope, shields scarred but unbroken, still interlocking.

It was the right decision. The Zamorakians didn't retreat far. The cohort that had engaged the hypaspists went perhaps fifty yards back down the slope before their officers rallied them, barking and snapping. Ranks re-formed, shields raised once more against the resumed barrage of slings and arrows.

Rhea spun her doru so it was tip-down and shook it, getting rid of the worst of the blood and ensuring it didn't run down the haft and make her fingers wet and sticky.

There was no more time to recover. The phalanx directly to Rhea's right was still engaged with a cohort to their front. The phalangites were thrusting their pikes down the slope and into the Zamorakian formation, who were in turn trying to hack and chop their way through the multiple layers of steel-tipped poles to reach the Saradominists beyond. They were having some success – legionary cohorts had experience meeting phalangite pike blocks, and included among their ranks warriors armed with axes and polearms that they used to hack the heads from the pike hafts, leaving nothing but wooden sticks in the grasp of their opponents. They were pushing through, some getting as far as the phalangite front ranks, where their spatha swords and heavier armour were allowing them to wreak havoc.

Rhea turned to look for Phosani, and found her seemingly thinking the same thing.

"Turn the flank to your right," the justiciar shouted through the formation at her.

"Three files, on me," Rhea immediately barked, taking the six warriors behind her and the two files immediately to her left. "Swords only. Get close, slaughter them."

No further instructions were necessary. The hypaspists drove their spears into the slope, drew their swords, and broke formation with Rhea at their head, rushing suddenly towards their right, and the exposed right flank of the Zamorakian cohort struggling with the phalangites.

To their credit, the legionaries saw the threat coming. The rightmost files tried to turn outwards and lock their parmas, but to do so they were forced to work their left arms bearing the shields out of the formation. There were still gaps and Rhea crossed the last few yards of the slope at a sprint, kopis rasping from its scabbard, a snarl on her lips.

Then she was in among them. A Zamorakian, his shield trapped against his file partner, tried to bring up his spatha, but could only scream as a vicious downward swing of the kopis cleaved through his shoulder and uppermost ribs. Rhea's sword was supposed to be a cavalry weapon, its wicked, curved lower edge and the blunt weight of its back making it a brutally efficient chopping blade. Wielding it on foot required height, strength and stamina, all of which Rhea had, even so she knew it would not be long before she tired with it and was forced onto the defensive. She did not intend to be wielding it long enough for that to happen.

She kicked the Zamorakian in the gut and dragged the kopis free, the horrific wound jetting blood, making the man's chainmail glisten darkly in the firelight. She then rammed herself onwards into the gap, hacking, slamming aside a swing with her shield as she went, going on instinct.

Like wolves in amongst the flock, the hypaspists savaged the right flank of the cohort. Speed and violence were the key to victory, and Rhea knew it.

She screamed in the face of another Zamorakian, who spat at her and attempted to drive his spatha into her gut. She couldn't bring her shield round in the press, but had to trust in her breastplate to turn the stab. It left the Zamorakian exposed as Rhea was driven forward by the force of the hypaspists behind her, sawing her kopis across his throat, ripping through his chainmail.

More strikes fell against her, the Zamorakians scrambling to get at her past their comrade as he clamped a hand to his injured neck and choked on blood. A spatha clanged from her helm, another chopped into her shoulder, biting but not deep enough. She shoved with her shield, trying to clear the space to defend herself, knowing that in a few heartbeats more she would be overwhelmed.

Then came a familiar bellow. A labrys swung past her,

cleaving the skull of the next Zamorakian open, his helmet's black crest turned sticky with brain matter. Klaxar was there, hewing like a deranged woodsman. Mardin struck as well, the hammerhead of the sagaris he was wielding turning a parma to splinters.

The legionaries broke. Their flank torn up, and with the phalangites continuing to hold firm, their ranks disintegrated and they scattered back down the slope.

Rhea stumbled and felt Mardin's hand on her shoulder, steadying her. She heard a pealing note, the ordo's salpinx calling them back.

"Rally on the Wolf standard," she panted to the hypaspists who had followed her. "Move!"

She cast a glance back along the slope as she went, seeing that all along the hillside, the Zamorakians had been repulsed.

It would only be a brief reprieve. The cohort first broken by the Wolves was advancing again, slow and steady, backlit by the pyre's remnants.

Rhea and the others rejoined the ranks, snatching up spears and locking shields. As they did so, there was sudden movement in front of the hypaspist line.

A shape came tumbling down from above, impacting into the slope and rolling a short distance. Rhea realised with a jolt of horror that it was a body, an icyene, armour and flesh gouged and wings broken. The Zamorakians hesitated. Both sides stared at the corpse in shock, before all eyes looked skywards.

Overhead, the battle raged.

FIFTEEN

———◆———

Ranis shrieked and slashed aside the spear darting towards him, a beat of his wings propelling him in under the icyene's guard.

They collided in midair, the vampyre trying to rip off the warrior's helm and tear her throat out with his fangs. He was so focused on the kill, and half-blinded by the thing's light, that he didn't notice her dagger – the first he knew of it was agony in his side, just below his ribs.

The pain drove him on. He savaged her neck, spitting out her foul blood.

Even just being this close to an icyene burned him, as though the creature was daylight made flesh. It hurt his skin and made his eyes ache, his predator vision reduced to a blur of brilliance.

They were repulsive things, and Ranis was driven to slaughter them. He kicked away from the one he had killed, allowing her to plummet into a death spiral, before snatching the knife from his side and sending it after her. The wound ached, unlike anything a mortal's weapon would do to him. Even their steel was cursed.

Clutching his flank, Ranis beat his wings, trying to gain height and break away from the melee. A swirling aerial battle had broken out between the vampyres and the icyene above the hilltop. Below, their mortal followers hacked and stabbed and struggled against one another in the mud, but Ranis knew it was up here that the battle would be decided. Up here the masters fought.

He cast about for what remained of his brood, but he could neither find nor sense them. All around was chaos, vyre and icyene colliding and grappling, a deadly dance of death that formed a maelstrom above the embattled hill. Some plunged to the ground, struggling in their death throes, until an impact against the hill's flank killed both. Some survived, broken and injured, their fate decided by the warriors nearest to wherever they had dropped.

Ranis thrilled at the carnage, at the blood that suffused the air with its coppery stink, at how warriors tore at one another both above and below, weapons and claws and fangs mangling flesh and breaking bone and splitting skulls. It was a storm of violence, addictive to a creature like him.

He forced himself to maintain control. He was Lowerniel's brother, second in line to House Drakan. He ruled this slaughter – the slaughter did not rule him.

He looked down upon the chaos, trying to pick which part to dive back into. There was a light at the heart of it, one fouler than all the rest. To a vampyre's vision, all icyene emitted light, but this one was achingly brilliant, as though a fragment of the Everlight itself had been brought to battle by the Saradominists.

It could only be Queen Efaritay.

Just the thought of her made Ranis's wound ache more. Briefly he indulged the idea of rallying the broods about him and leading them against that light. He imagined ripping and tearing his way into that soul-singeing brilliance, overcoming the Saradominist queen, breaking her neck and ripping away her wings, drenching himself in her cursed blood.

Those thoughts made him forget his wound. But they were foolishness, he knew. There was no sense in risking himself, not here and now, when the greater prize – Hallowvale itself – remained to be won.

His brother would want to butcher Queen Efaritay himself, and Ranis knew better than to deny him.

He twisted left and right, testing his injury, but its pain had faded. Baring his fangs, he stooped down into a dive.

◆ ◆ ◆

High above, Drakan circled. The vyreguard were with him – at a respectful distance – but no icyene rose to challenge them.

The Saradominists were holding. Though outnumbered, the natural abilities of the icyene made them repellent to the vampyres. Against an ordinary mortal the speed and the strength of a vyre was easily superior, but against icyene they were fighting half-blinded. Even to Drakan, watching the fight below was like trying to focus on the individual snowflakes in a blizzard, each icyene a dancing point of light.

Still, he could sense the presence of his kin by their shrieks and hisses, rather than through sight alone. He heard an exclamation of pained fury from Ranis – he had been injured, though seemingly only enough to stoke his wrath.

Vanescula let out a more urgent cry, and Drakan sought her out, dropping lower while hissing at the vyreguard to stay high. He found her twisting one way and then another as she exchanged blows with an icyene psiloi.

He saw why she was struggling – at some point one of her wings had been clipped, its membrane damaged. She was struggling to stay aloft while fending off her attacker, and the psiloi was pressing his advantage.

Drakan would not permit that. He swept closer, then pulled up, judging the distance and Vanescula's erratic flying. He hefted the Spear of the Blood Hunt, drew back, and cast the wicked weapon like a javelin.

It had hardly left his fist before he was beating his wings again, swooping down on Vanescula and her opponent. The Blood Hunt struck true, slamming through the icyene's shoulder and down through his torso, transfixing him vertically. He began to fall as Vanescula, shocked, was hit by the wake of her brother's passing.

Drakan plunged down after the icyene and snatched the base of the spear still protruding from his shoulder, sweeping downwards with his wings at the same time. Briefly, the corpse's plunge was arrested as the weapon was yanked brutally free, accompanied by an arc of crimson that drizzled away into the night. He ran his tongue along part of the gore-slick haft, tasting the icyene's foul blood, before gripping it properly and rising once more to join Vanescula.

"I was fine," she said, already recovered from the shock of Drakan's deft intervention.

"Take your brood back," he ordered her.

"I do not need your protection," Vanescula spat. Drakan bared his fangs in response, just as riven with the blood-hunger as she was, only controlling it better.

"There are few of our kind I would mourn the loss of this night, but you are one of them. Go to the legion and see that they press the attack. The icyene will endure to the death if it means guarding their cattle, but if the hill's defences break, the icyene break too. The mortals will not resist you as these creatures do. Take the hill for me. Then we take the city."

"Their queen is here," Vanescula said, indicating where the light shone at the heart of the battle. "Slay her and we will deal a mortal blow to their morale."

"None will face her but I," Drakan declared. "Now go, and command the legion."

She hissed wrathfully, but offered no further protest as she broke off and wheeled away with an unsteady beat of her injured wings.

Drakan went in the opposite direction, climbing again. He resumed his circling, watching the Saradominist host like a huntsman observing his flagging prey. Most of all, watching the light at their heart, the brilliance that could only be Queen Efaritay.

+ ◆ +

Efaritay twisted in the air, looking for another foe. The royal guard were all about her, a flying phalanx slaying any vyre that dared approach their queen. She refused to hide at the heart of the flock though. With a flurry from her wings, she shot forward, deeper into the fight.

She had seen the face of battle before. Her parents had considered military experience a vital part of her upbringing, and she had been assigned to serve in the tagmata not long after she had come of age.

Privileged as she was, she had been sent to join the Optimatoi but had pleaded with Saradomin himself that he send her into battle, rather than use her as a glorified messenger. She had killed her first foe at Six Forks, and her last almost twelve years later, at the battle of Highpass.

That had been several centuries ago now, and Efaritay had never led a host of her own, nor fought with a weapon of arcane might in her fist.

The Sunspear was incredible. It shone brilliantly from tip to base, like a new sun, reborn in her grasp. Many vyre seemed unable to even approach it, let alone fight against it. She had plunged it through one pallid, shrieking creature's breast, and witnessed its flesh ignite and its bones turn to ash, the monstrosity crumbling as assuredly as if it had been exposed to the Everlight's direct illumination.

The blisterwood haft sang to her in her grip, exalting in the defeat of the enemies of the light. She knew power the likes of which she had never experienced, coupled with a certainty she had feared would never return. Saradomin was with them right now after all, in Efaritay's grasp, striking down all who would challenge her.

She plunged into a fresh swarm of vampyres and they twisted away from her, howling, blinded and burning. One was strong enough to meet her airborne charge, and crashed against her aspis, but she knocked it aside and beheaded it with a sideways swipe of the Sunspear, its body burning up even as it plunged like a small, fiery comet down towards the melee playing out across the slopes.

"They cannot stand before the light of Saradomin," she exclaimed to the icyene around her, wheeling in the air and brandishing the Sunspear. "Even in the depths of night, they have no power over us!"

The closest of her royal guard, a veteran named Heria, began to respond, but never got a chance to finish. Something struck her, something so big and so fast that Efaritay felt the wind of its passing, the raw power, but caught only an impression of it with her eyes. Marble-white musculature, vast wings, and blood, Heria's blood. The guard was suddenly just gone.

Whatever it was, it had come down from above, and was now rising back up at her just as fast and as hard. Efaritay wrenched her body around so she was at an angle to meet it. This time, she saw red eyes and red fangs. She thrust downwards with the Sunspear in the desperate hope the creature would impale itself.

It didn't. It slammed into her aspis, the shield almost splitting in two. Efaritay was thrown to the side in midair, winded, her left arm numb. She spun and lashed out with the Sunspear to keep it at bay while she recovered, wings working hard.

And there, she finally got a proper view of it. Vampyre, the largest and most monstrous one Efaritay had ever seen. Its lower body and much of its left arm was sheathed in black and gold armour, the rest all bare musculature, draped in precious stones. Its wings were vast and daubed in blood markings. More blood, fresh, glistened from its maw. Its face was bat-like, bestial. Its crimson eyes were the most terrible thing Efaritay had ever seen.

In one fist it grasped a wicked spear, while in the other it was still clutching one of Heria's torn-off wings. It casually tossed the gore-matted feathers away as it glared at her.

"So, this is the queen of the icyene," it rasped in a cold, strange accent.

"Lowerniel Drakan," Efaritay responded. Her heart was racing, her body flushed with fear, and a ferocious determination.

"I am not accustomed to negotiations, not when it comes to creatures as… detestable as you," Drakan said, seemingly unconcerned by the fact that Efaritay's royal guard had closed in around them. He also seemed wholly unafraid of the brilliance of the Sunspear, its light making his pallid skin glow white and glittering back from those awful, predatory eyes.

"But you have come here to face me rather than cower behind your walls and your little lighthouse," he continued. "And I respect that, Queen Efaritay."

At no point had Efaritay imagined speaking with the master of the Drakan. Perhaps she should bargain, negotiate, even stall for time, but all she could think of was her hatred for these creatures.

"I will destroy you," she spat. "I will drive the Sunspear through your withered heart and stake your body out to burn in the rising sun. You and all your foul kin."

Drakan responded with a bloody, fanged grin and spread his arms.

"Well, here I am," he said. "Let us see who is dead come the dawn."

SIXTEEN

——◆——

Ascertes stood at the balcony outside his bedchamber in the citadel, and gazed west.

The light of day was gone, and on this far side of the city, the brightness of the Everlight was only a faint glimmer. There was illumination out there though, a flickering that danced and strove against the deepening night.

He had instructed any messengers from Efaritay or Babel to wake him, no matter the hour. There had been no word, but he knew what he was looking at.

Sleep was impossible. Standing and doing nothing was barely more tolerable. That was his lot. He had been left behind, stranded and adrift, while his wife went to war. He knew he should be thankful that he was married to such a woman, and proud that she was leading the defence of their home. Yet those emotions were subsumed by frustration and concern. By fear, and by shame at the fact that he wasn't doing more.

He heard the sound of his bedchamber door being quietly opened. He turned, expecting to find an icyene prodromoi bearing word. But instead, he was confronted by the sight of his children.

Larina stood in the doorway, Safalaan partially hidden behind her. Ascertes felt anger and concern at the fact that they were out of bed without their chaperone, but it quickly evaporated.

"We couldn't sleep," Larina admitted in a small voice.

Ascertes strode to the door and embraced them together before bringing them inside.

"Neither could I," he said. "But that's alright. Maybe we can all try and sleep in here tonight."

He closed the door to the chamber, then tutted, striding to the bed and pulling off one of the leopard pelt covers.

"You shouldn't walk about at night in just your gowns," he pointed out, noticing how cold the little duo were. He wrapped the blanket around them both. "And especially not without Esme."

"She fell asleep in her chair," Larina said, referring to their chaperone. "We didn't want to wake her."

"Well in future, you must. I've told you, and so has your mother, that a time is coming when it won't be safe to wander alone, even here in the citadel."

"We don't like staying here," Safalaan piped up. "It's cold and draughty. When are we going back to the palace?"

"I don't know," Ascertes said. "But I hope it won't be too long."

"Where is mam?" Safalaan went on. When others were

present, the children were expected to refer to Efaritay formally, as the queen or Her-Winged-Majesty. Ascertes permitted them to dispense with that whenever they were alone.

"I told you, she is leading the army," Larina said tersely to her little brother.

"She isn't a fighter though?" Safalaan said incredulously.

"Oh, she is." Ascertes smiled. "Your mother is many things. A ruler, a councillor, a warrior. That is what it means to be a true leader. She must be many things, to many different people. And tonight, she must be a fighter."

"Is she fighting right now?" Larina asked.

Ascertes ushered them out together with him onto the balcony, making sure the blanket remained wrapped tightly around them.

"Do you see those lights?" he asked his children, pointing towards the glimmering in the distance. "That's mam. Out there, with all the bravest soldiers in Hallowvale. Leading them."

"She is shining," Safalaan said, awe in his voice.

"She is. She is light made manifest. The light of Saradomin. The light that burns away the darkness, and shines from everything good. And that light is within you too."

"In me?" Safalaan asked. "In Larina too?"

"In both of you. You are her son and daughter, made from my flesh and blood, but from hers as well. She is within you, and that includes her light."

"But is she fighting?" Larina reiterated.

"Yes," Ascertes admitted.

Safalaan and Larina looked out over the balcony's edge, silent for a while as they pondered what they were looking at, and what their father had told them.

"Will she be alright?" Larina asked.

"Have you ever met someone stronger or braver than mam?" Ascertes said.

They both shook their heads without averting their gaze from the distance.

"That's why I think she'll be alright," Ascertes said. He patted Larina on the shoulder.

"Come. We'll see nothing more standing here. Your mother won't forgive me if she gets back and finds out we've stood in the cold on the balcony all night! Get into bed, and I'll read you a story. A pair of stories, your choice, if you can agree for once!"

Safalaan broke from the blanket and scurried inside eagerly, but Larina lingered, still looking out towards the west. Ascertes patted her shoulder.

"She'll be alright," he reiterated, and tried to believe it. "Come inside."

Larina nodded, and allowed Ascertes to take her back in. Before crossing the threshold, he stole one last look beyond the balcony, and prayed silently to the light that it would bring his wife home.

◆ ◆ ◆

The Zamorakian necromancers sought to raise the dead.

A great number of animated corpses already followed Drakan's host, but the commanders of the Zamorakian legion disdained them as a crude and unsubtle weapon that offered little help to their disciplined formations.

Still, they could not deny the power of dark magics, and the night itself seemed to stir around the legion's sorcerers as they gathered at the foot of the hill and began their incantations.

Across the slope, the dead began to stir. The efforts of the dark sorcerers were met and challenged, as Justiciar Aliya led her rune-casters in an unbinding from the hill's crest, channelling their efforts and breaking the weaker of the Zamorakian spells as swiftly as they spun them. The corpses of the newly slain continued to twitch, but did not rise.

* ✦ *

Vanescula found the mortal commanders of the fourteenth legion close to an old, partly ruined mill to the south of the hilltop. They had chosen it for their command post, the legion's bat standard planted above the old stonework. A continual stream of messengers were hurrying back and forth from the structure.

She strode in through the remnants of the doorway, the guards saluting her.

"What is happening?" she demanded, interrupting the gaggle of senior officers in the ruined room's centre. They turned, most beginning to hastily salute.

"Answer me," Vanescula barked. Her left wing ached where the icyene's spear had torn it, and she burned with embarrassment at the fact that she had required her brother to save her. Worse, the blood-fever was still gripping her, and she was desperate to kill. Only her willpower was stopping her from enacting that desire on the soldiery before her.

"The attack on the hill continues, Lady Drakan," one of the magisters – Marrelus, she thought his name was – declared. "The cohorts have gained the lower slopes but have not yet broken the Saradominist line."

"Why not?"

"Their phalanxes are well-sited and holding their coherency. Attacking uphill isn't helping. Nor is the darkness. We are struggling to coordinate."

Vanescula hissed, not bothering to mask her frustrations from the mortals.

"Why have you not flanked them? Use our numerical superiority. If we encircle the hill and attack across it, they will have to spread their line thin. The breakthrough will come."

"The terrain is not conducive," Marrelus answered, showing commendable bravery by doing so. "The south, just past us here, is a bog, and the north is dense woodland. The packs are traversing it, but if we try to move the reserve cohorts as well the sun will be up before they are in position."

Vanescula sought to calm herself. She considered Marrelus's claims, and what Drakan had ordered her to do.

"The icyene are committed in the air," she said. "They won't be able to assist the phalanxes. I will call my brood, and we will break through their line."

The humans exchanged glances, but none seemed to want to argue.

"Send a message to the first cohort, tell them to look for my arrival," she ordered and, without another word, strode back out into the night.

SEVENTEEN

---◆---

Efaritay roared and lunged. The royal guard launched themselves forward as well, swords and spears vicing in at Drakan from all angles.

With one powerful sweep of his wings, the vampyre rocketed upwards, leaving the icyene to stab and slash the air.

Efaritay followed him. She shouted the name of her god as she went, lunging the Sunspear at the pale horror, knowing nothing besides a desire to kill this monstrous threat to her home and family.

With a speed and grace that belied the vyrelord's size, Drakan turned in his ascent and drove down with his own spear at the icyene queen. He turned his body to one side as he did so, the Sunspear slicing harmlessly past him, while Efaritay's shout became a grunt as her aspis took the force of Drakan's weapon, the momentum of both warriors conducted via steel and timber.

The aspis splintered into pieces, the spearhead narrowly missing Efaritay's arm, sliding past her. The pair twisted by one another and Efaritay beat her wings to give herself room to recover her guard, but Drakan drove immediately back in. He snatched her, his armoured hand clamping around her upper right arm, the clawed gauntlet drawing blood. Suddenly there was nothing between her and those wicked red fangs. She found herself unable to move, slender prey caught and paralysed in the predator's iron grip.

Then Drakan half turned, hissing in pain. The swiftest among Efaritay's guards had managed to follow her up and one, Dionysen, slashed his xiphos across the vyrelord's shoulder. He let go and turned, lashing out with terrifying speed.

Dionysen tried to dodge, but Drakan's spear caught one of his wings, slicing clean through it. The icyene cried out in pain and began to drop, trailing blood and feathers.

More of the royal guards threw themselves at Drakan, as they did so Efaritay pulled away and drove back in with a shout. She held the Sunspear two-handed, feeling the blisterwood's power, its desire to burn this abomination out of the sky.

Drakan swept his weapon back around, the hafts cracking off one another with a sound like a thunderclap. Efaritay's lunge was knocked aside, and as she recovered the vampyre had already pivoted to rake his armoured claws along the face of another guard, ripping flesh from bone.

He was so fast, so strong. Efaritay tried to stab again, and again she was parried, then thrown back with a powerful beat of Drakan's pinions. The terrible creature swung his spear so hard that its long blade beheaded one of the guards as the icyene stabbed in with a xiphos, blood arcing away through the night air.

As it did so, Efaritay heard a low, ticking, chittering sound coming from the vampyre.

She realised he was laughing.

He was enjoying this. Revulsion filled her. The Sunspear blazing in her fist, she launched herself back at the monster with a shout.

She stabbed, and beat her wings furiously when Drakan blocked, driving herself with all her strength against the vyre. It was enough to finally break his poise, and though he grabbed another guard by the throat with his gauntleted fist, a second and then a third were able to land blows, striking his shoulders and arms. Finally, Efaritay saw that pale, marble-like skin cut, saw it bleed black, rotten blood.

Drakan bellowed and kicked her away, swinging his spear in a wide arc that drove off his attackers. The light of the Sunspear shone back from his red eyes and made his blood glisten as he turned in the air, the icyene circling him warily.

Efaritay faced him, panting, filled with determination. They had wounded the beast. That meant they could kill it.

"I have enjoyed tonight, Your-Winged-Majesty," Drakan spat. "But I fear we will not see a personal resolution between us before the dawn."

"There will be a resolution," Efaritay declared, spinning the Sunspear in one hand before dropping into a low guard. "Your invasion ends tonight."

"No," Drakan said, eyes not leaving Efaritay's. "I will see you again, and when I do, you will kneel in supplication."

"Never," Efaritay shouted, and attacked once more. But the vampyre was gone. He swept his wings downwards, shooting into the black belly of the clouds above like a bolt loosed from a crossbow. By the time Efaritay had arrested her forward motion and swept her wings back to try and follow him, he was gone.

✦ ✦ ✦

Vanescula called her brood to her and joined the first cohort. They were the best the fourteenth legion had to offer, bonded and sworn to the service of the Drakans. Each legionary, upon his acceptance into the cohort, shed his blood for Drakan to consume, creating a bond between them and the lord of the vyre. To most other vampyres it was a meaningless little ritual, but the human soldiers took great pride in it.

The first cohort especially saw themselves as direct inheritors of the demons that had once made up the Zamorakian hosts, even going so far as to ape their forebearers with their horned helms.

Once with them, Vanescula received arms and armour befitting what she was about to do. Like the icyene, vyre usually wore light armour of leather and padded cloth when fighting airborne, and many preferred to use claws and fangs as weapons. Now though, Vanescula took up a black-crested steel helm and breastplate and a heavy wooden parma shield, as well as a clawed mace, its head fashioned like a grinning, fanged skull. Her brood were similarly attired, so that they were almost as heavily equipped as Drakan's infamous vyreguard.

Unlike Ranis, she was not too proud to address the mortal soldiers before they stepped off. Still, they were veterans, and she kept it simple for them.

"We're going up that hill, and we're killing everything that gets in our way! Promotion and a bounty for the first to reach the crest! For Zamorak, and House Drakan!"

As they cheered, Vanescula hissed at her brood and they closed in around her, a wedge of black-lacquered steel that set off towards the slope. The first cohort followed, war hounds unleashed.

Vanescula waded through the stream, her fangs gritted. Like all vyre, she naturally detested water. She felt its bitter cold biting and gnawing at her legs and waist, but forged on, climbing the far bank. Her brood were strong and loyal enough to follow her without hesitation.

The ground beyond was a mess, thousands of drenched feet having churned the first dozen yards of slope to slick mud. The vampyres forged through it and then over the trampled and guttering remnants of the fires the Saradominists had set. Beyond they found scattered bodies and lone individuals from the other cohorts – those unlucky legionaries who had been struck down by the first flurry of slingshots and arrows, or those who had been injured further up the slope and had managed to drag themselves away before their strength deserted them. Vanescula kicked one aside as she went, her whole focus on climbing the slope and reaching the flesh and blood and glory awaiting her.

The cohort ahead had been driven back by the phalanx beyond them, and were still re-forming. Vanescula wondered how many times they had attacked while the vyre were fighting above – three times, four? They were tenacious, as she would expect from the fourteenth, but so were the Saradominists.

The first cohort's horn blower sounded the cornu, alerting those ahead of them to the approach of their comrades. Vanescula pushed her way into the broken formation, fangs bared, struggling with the urge to kill. She needed to close with the enemy, to shed their blood, rich and sweet compared to the foul icyene essence.

She paused long enough for the foremost ranks of the first cohort to clear the broken formation, then led them on. Ahead the phalanxes waited, backlit by more fires built near the hill's crest. They were resting their pikes, but once more presented them as the fresh cohort rose to the attack, an overlapping hedge of wicked steel.

"Plumbata," Vanescula shouted. "On my signal, prepare to cast!"

"Vyrelady, what of your kindred above us?" the first legion's ordinarius, a battle-scarred veteran named Sagitus, called out.

She glanced upwards, at the ferocious clash overhead. The slope allowed the Saradominists to cast their arrows and slingshots at a shallower arc while shooting downhill, avoiding the risk of hitting the icyene grappling with the vampyres. The plumbata were weighted darts – ideally they would be thrown high to plummet down through helmets and shoulders, but at distances as short as the gap between the first cohort and the Saradominists, they could still be launched straight.

"Cast them," Vanescula repeated. "There is no better way to break a phalanx. Cast, and follow me!"

She broke into a run, driving herself up the final few yards. It seemed as though she was about to impale herself on those long poles of timber and steel, but then the air around her was whistling with metal of a different sort. Plumbata, dozens of them, hurled at a range of no more than two dozen paces. At such distance and with a target as large as the phalanx, almost every one found a mark. The ordered row of pikes was suddenly broken and ragged as Saradominists fell screaming, struck through by the wicked darts. Their comrades scrambled to fill the sudden gaps, forced to trample over their own dead and dying in their haste to stop the formation breaking apart.

Vanescula saw the fear and terror in the eyes of the mortals, not just at the fact that their formation had been broken open, but at the realisation that they were being assaulted by armoured vyre warriors.

She didn't take the time to savour the emotion. She attacked, tapping into the predatory speed her kind were able to unleash when they weren't being blinded by icyene light-curses.

The world seemed to slow around her as her body went into overdrive, her mind processing everything at a pace no mortal could match. In little more than a few rapid heartbeats she had woven her way through the broken wall of pikes, smashing one aside with her shield and splintering the shaft of another with a blow from her mace.

To her prey, Vanescula and her brood became a blur of speed. Even encumbered by heavy armour, they ripped into the phalanx before any of the humans could respond. Vanescula broke two heads to fragments with her mace, then a third that staved the steel of a pikeman's helmet into his skull.

The phalanx was decimated. The other vyre, though slower and weaker than their mistress, were still far more than any of the pikemen could resist. They were torn to pieces or ripped open. At such close range the pikes were worse than useless.

Then the first cohort struck. The defensive hedge of steel had completely fallen apart, and the veteran legionaries stormed into the bloody wound torn by their overlords.

Vanescula was the first to punch out the back of the formation, a strike of her mace shattering the ribs of the warrior in the final rank opposing her. She came to a halt, panting heavily, turning to look back at her brood. Perhaps ten seconds had passed since her first kill. She could taste sweet blood but couldn't even remember using her fangs.

The phalanx broke. They ran, back up the hill, throwing their pikes aside, tripping and scrambling in the slope's mud.

Vanescula felt the thrill of victory, quickly eclipsed by the need to keep going. The vampyres had torn a hole, but the phalanxes to the left and right were still intact, still resisting. And ahead, she could see the hill's crest, surmounted by the banners of Hallowvale, illuminated in the fires ranged around them.

"On," she roared at her brood and the cohort, together as one. "On!"

✦ ✦ ✦

Rhea's doru splintered. She had driven it so hard against a parma that it had smashed through, gouging the face of the legionary carrying it but also splitting the spear's haft.

She left it where it was and reached for her kopis. It wasn't well-suited to the crushing press of a phalanx meeting a cohort, where there was little room to swing its wicked, weighted edge, but then the enemy's spatha weren't ideal weapons in this kind of melee either. The kopis was at least shorter, and it allowed her to drive it through the gaps between her shield and the enemy's.

She did just that, thrusting with her right arm while heaving with the rest of her weight against her left, Klaxar's hand on her shoulder, adding to her efforts. It was a shoving and hacking match, as brutal and unsubtle as any combat a member of the Wolves had fought in. Three times they'd driven back the cohort opposing them, and three times the Zamorakians had re-formed and come again. Rhea hated them, but she would never deny that they were good soldiers.

A spatha bit into her shield and stayed wedged there. The upper rim of the aspis had been hacked and chopped almost to pieces. She jammed her kopis under and to the right, twisting it from side to side as she sought to push it home into anything she could reach.

"Head," she heard Klaxar bark in her ear, and stooped as much as she was able. She half felt, half saw the passage of her companion's labrys, the heavy double-headed axe cleaving over the top of the locked shields and hewing into the heads and shoulders beyond. There was a shriek of pain and Rhea was pushing, pushing before she even felt the resistance against her momentarily go, knowing Klaxar had dealt another fearsome wound and she had to take advantage of it.

The spatha lodged in her shield was dragged free and came again, not hacking this time but trying to drive over and angle down into her face using the aspis rim as a guide along the flat of the blade. She managed to turn aside in time, the point jarring off her cheek guard. She snarled and sensed Klaxar swinging again. More screaming. She saw movement in the gap between her shield and Mardin's next to her and tried to get her kopis across and up, before realising the man who had so carelessly exposed himself was already dead – his skull was a gory mess, but the press of the two embattled lines was so tight that his corpse was being held in place, pinned against the shields of the hypaspists.

It was hard to tell just how long it had been since the Zamorakians had first crossed the stream and climbed the slope, but Rhea's limbs were aching, and that was a sure sign they had been fighting for a long time. When fatigue began to weigh through the mindless rush of battle, she knew she was approaching her limit.

Klaxar bellowed and swung again, and suddenly the pressure was gone, not just from Rhea's aspis, but all across the line. The cohort had broken off for the fourth time, scrambling or limping back down the slope. The body she had been holding off slumped on top of the ones already heaped in front of the ordo of the wolf, like flotsam washed up and piled against a seaside wall.

"Spear," Rhea panted, half turning while she had the opportunity. Phondax, in the rear rank, passed his doru forward, replacing her broken one.

"All still in one piece then?" Mardin growled. He had taken a gash to the shoulder, but it seemed light.

"Moreso than anyone I've hit so far," Klaxar quipped, tapping the dripping edge of her labrys lightly against the back of Mardin's helm and grinning at him.

"They're tenacious tonight," the older hypaspist observed, as though talking about a particularly dogged display while watching a sporting event during the Dominion Games.

There was no time for further levity. Rhea caught a shrill series of salpinx blasts, off to her right. She immediately recognised it as the call to rally. That was never a good sign.

She broke formation enough to get a look past the ordo's right flank, and saw that her worst fears had been correct. Seemingly from nowhere, the phalanx to their immediate right had broken. She had been half aware of Zamorakian reinforcements flooding up the slope in that direction, but the desperate melee had kept her occupied and blind to events unfolding elsewhere across the slope.

Somehow, the Zamorakians had completely broken the phalangites. They were streaming past, into the gap in the hill's defences. The flank of the ordo of the wolf, just feet from Rhea, was completely exposed.

There was no time to look to Phosani or wait for orders. She grabbed Mardin by the shoulder while shouting to all those around her.

"We need to re-fuse the line! Now! Use me as your mark!"

She raised her spear and ran to her right, the edge of the formation breaking apart as the hypaspists tried to adjust. What had once been a line was now being bent at a right angle, its side running up the slope rather than across it.

The closest section of the cohort realised what was happening, and saw their chance. They rushed the hypaspists with a roar.

✦ ✦ ✦

Strategos Babel saw the collapse of Zenaphon's phalanx. He also saw the reason for it, the vyre who hacked their way into the midst of the phalangites with shocking speed and force.

"Message to the ordo of the owl," he said calmly to one of the runners gathered with him on the crest of the hill. "Dismount and advance down the slope. Plug that gap. And tell the humans I will be with them."

The youth nodded and took off into the fire-shot darkness, flying low. Babel turned to address the psiloi arrayed around him. There were fifty of the armoured icyene, a final reserve. He had anticipated that not all the vyre might be committed to the aerial battle, and that any who fought on foot alongside their human minions would massively outclass even the likes of the hypaspists. Only the icyene could truly stop them.

"The line is broken," he told his warriors. "We must mend it. Follow me, and we will turn this night into day."

He took his doru and aspis from his retainer and raised the spear before setting off down the slope, on foot, breaking into a sprint. The phalanx attacked by the vampyres was in total disarray, phalangites scattering across the hilltop. There was no time to rally them, and nor did Babel wish to – they were only humans, and once their courage was gone he knew they were useless. The icyene would win this.

"For Hallowvale," he shouted and, as the distance closed, he lunged and beat his wings. The icyene took flight just before impact, using it to give them a further advantage in speed and height.

With a crash that echoed out across the hilltop, the icyene and the vampyres collided.

✦ ✦ ✦

The Zamorakians had no time to reorganise after their breakthrough, and the hypaspists around Rhea hadn't yet had a chance to lock up. The two sides met across the slope, not in close formation, but in a true melee.

Rhea knew they had to stand firm, or the whole line would collapse. She met the first legionary with a lunge of Phondax's doru, stepping into the strike. The Zamorakian, a tall woman who had lost her helmet at some point, anticipated the hit and swept Rhea's spear aside with her scarred parma, but that was what Rhea had wanted. She used their twinned momentum to half turn to the right, bringing up her aspis as she did, twisting it so it was side on. The edge connected with the Zamorakian's flushed face, cutting off her war cry with a brutal crunch. She went down as assuredly as if Klaxar had struck her with her labrys.

Rhea stepped over her and ended her quickly with a downward stab of her doru to the throat, recovering the spear just in time to meet the next Zamorakian.

This was a different kind of killing. This was not a formed phalanx meeting a cohort, that battle of raw strength, weight and mass, not a shoving and hacking match. This was what Mardin liked to call 'proper fighting'. Rhea embraced it, driven by cold determination born of the knowledge that the battle was close to being lost.

Turn the spatha of the next Zamorakian with her doru, step in close, drive him back with the haft, held crossways. A kick to the ankle, slam the aspis into the side of his helmet, get him down on his back. Stab, recover, turning already to take the next legionary's strike against her shield. Push her left arm up so it likewise drove the Zamorakian's sword up, opening his guard, letting her jab the doru in under his arm. Twist and drag the spearhead free of flesh and ribs, recover. Meet the next one.

It was mechanical, mindless, muscle memory and instinct. She was a killer, so she killed, hard and fast, knowing only that she couldn't give herself time to stop and think. She was vaguely aware of Klaxar and Mardin and others around her, fighting their own battles, giving their all to close the gap.

Unfamiliar horn notes pierced the blur, a legionary cornu blowing orders Rhea did not recognise. Their meaning became apparent soon enough. She kicked a shuddering, bleeding Zamorakian off her doru – her fifth or sixth, she wasn't sure – and brought her battered aspis up, teeth bared, already reacting to the next attack, only to find that there wasn't one. There were no more Zamorakians rushing at the Wolves. Instead they were going past, down the slope. Breaking. Running. Running from the light that had blazed from the hill's crest and into their midst.

✦ ✦ ✦

Vanescula had expected the possibility of more icyene in reserve, but still the brightness of the winged creatures against her vision caused her to stumble, hissing in shock and pain. They fell upon her brood like burning stars, and only instinct allowed her to bring her parma up in time to take a crashing impact from a psiloi spear. Its tip punched through the wood, splintering the shield's upper half and driving her back a pace down the slope.

She twisted the parma so it jammed the spear and swung her mace, splitting the haft. The icyene who had collided with her was already dropping the weapon and drawing a xiphos short sword, but Vanescula refused to give it the time to regain the initiative. She swung with her mace, half-blind but working on raw instinct and aggression. The strength of her blows dented then splintered the icyene's shield, forcing it to retreat.

"Feathered wretch," Vanescula howled, slamming aside the psiloi's shield with her own and aiming her next swing between the icyene's wings. She was rewarded by a wet crunch, and the light that burned within the accursed creature suddenly glimmered and dimmed.

There was no time to enjoy the kill. Her brood were struggling to weather the storm of brilliance that had fallen upon them. She could hear Valclaw shrieking with pain, and Ineska stumbled into her – the light had burned out her eyes, leaving her blind. Vanescula shoved her back towards the rear ranks.

There were humans joining the icyene now too, armoured Saradominist infantry, these ones carrying spears and shields rather than the unwieldy pikes. They wore feathered mantles draped around their shoulders or over their shields – Vanescula recognised them as hypaspists, more of the enemy's elite. Even they could not have stood against her alone, but with the light of the icyene in her eyes she was sluggish, unable to tap into the predatory speed and strength that made her kind so deadly to most other races.

Another icyene came at her, a blur of brilliance. She warded away its blows with her parma, giving ground, snarling and spitting. Varkax threw himself at the icyene from the right, giving his mistress the time she needed to withdraw deeper into the assailed cohort.

Victory had been so close, as sweet as blood on her lips. Now though, it had slipped away. The Saradominists had thrown in their reserves. She looked into the sky, searching for a sign that her kin had broken the icyene above, but the storm of death was unabated, and the Saradominist phalanxes further to the left and right remained unbroken.

She shoved her way through the press to where the first cohort's standard was being held aloft, and snatched the arm of the horn blower beside it.

"Sound the retreat," she hissed.

EIGHTEEN

—◆—

The salpinx called Rhea back to Phosani.

The justiciar was beaten and bloody. A blow had dented her helmet, torn away part of the visor and left her face gouged. Her shield must have been split in two at some point, for the one she now carried wasn't her own. The lower corner of the wolf pelt she wore over her shoulders was sopping wet and matted with gore from where she had repeatedly wiped her xiphos clean against it.

In the weak, guttering firelight she looked the way Rhea felt – exhausted, yet defiant.

"Well done," Phosani said to her. "If you hadn't refused the flank when you did, the whole line might have collapsed."

"I did what any Wolf would have done," Rhea said stoically. "I killed."

"And you will do so again," Phosani replied, looking

down the slope. Rhea followed her gaze and took in the sight of the Zamorakian cohorts. They had retreated to the same point they had fallen back to after every previous, failed assault, just above the ash and charred wood of the lower pyres. They were still re-forming.

So were Saradominists above them. The gap had been closed, Zenaphon's broken phalanx rallied and returned to their previous position. They had been reinforced by the ordo of the owl.

There were icyene in the front ranks now too, and not just with the phalangites. After leading the counterattack, Strategos Babel had taken a risk and dispersed his small reserve of psiloi among the frontline phalanxes. If the legionary cohorts were led by vyre fighting on foot, the icyene would counter them.

"They must be tiring," Phosani said as she surveyed the Zamorakians. "Every time they re-form, it takes them longer."

That was true enough. Rhea watched as legionary officers shouted and cajoled their warriors slowly back into order, facing them up the slope once more. There were no more missiles falling on them from the sphendonitai higher up – Rhea assumed they had been ordered to conserve the last of their ammunition.

"Even their masters are spent," she mused. While the vampyres and the icyene still fought overhead, it was no longer a frantic cloud of aerial combat. The two sides had largely broken apart, and only the edges of the two hosts were skirmishing with one another.

"But they will keep coming," Phosani declared, referring to the human Zamorakians below. "The vyre spend the lives of their followers like a gambling addict at the card table."

"If they do not stop, then neither shall we," Rhea said, not caring how stubborn she sounded. She had passed beyond tiredness now, entering that cold and numb place where she knew the only option was to keep going.

Phosani's response was interrupted by a commotion from the crest of the hill. They both looked back up the slope, wary of some fresh danger.

Instead, Rhea saw that the light that had framed the crest throughout the night – the Everlight – seemed to be growing stronger. At first she thought perhaps it was reinforcements come from Hallowvale, the last of the icyene, shining in the dark. But as it continued to strengthen, spreading its glow over the hilltop and down the western face, she recognised it as something even better.

The dawn was breaking over Hephaston's hill.

Someone, somewhere, cheered. The sound began to multiply, voices hailing the light. Bloodied spears were beaten against battered shields, and soon the whole hilltop, which moments before had been a place of tired silences and bitter resignation, resounded with sounds of hope and defiance.

Rhea couldn't help but join in, giving wordless allegiance to the new day, to the light that surely meant the killing and the dying was done, for now. The vyre were the first to flee, wheeling away in a great flock, shrieking mournfully.

The horns carried by the legions started to blow. The cohorts reversed, turning their faces away from the light.

They retreated with the night, marching west, re-fording the stream at the base of the hill. By then the vyre had vanished, going to ground ahead of the new day. The legion, however, went only so far as the encampment they had pitched west of the stream.

Rhea leaned against her spear, fighting the abrupt urge to lie down in the bloody dirt. The battle-fever had left her, and in its wake was only a hollow kind of exhaustion. Still, she stayed on her feet. Everyone else was as tired as she was. She refused to be the first to give way.

"Orders, commander?" she asked Phosani.

"They remain unchanged," the justiciar said. "Hold the line. I will seek out the strategos. You have command of the Wolves until then."

Rhea managed a salute before Phosani left, then turned again to watch the day break over the hill and illuminate the carnage left behind by the longest night of her life.

Efaritay was forced to plant the base of the Sunspear into the dirt to support herself – if she didn't, she would have collapsed as soon as she alighted back on the hillside.

Her whole body ached, especially her wings and back. None of the icyene who had met the vyre at the start of the attack had found a chance to touch down until now, and the hours of aerial combat had almost broken their endurance. Even members of the royal guard fell to their hands and knees as they landed, some shaking, one vomiting. The flocks were ragged, exhausted, but they were also victorious.

That was what Efaritay told herself. Dawn was upon them, like a blessing from great Saradomin himself. Efaritay dragged off her helm and felt the warmth on her face, banishing the night's chill.

It was small comfort. She couldn't drive out the idea that the savage combat had been nothing but a game to Drakan, that he could have torn her apart if he wanted to. If so, then why was she still alive? None of the possibilities were reassuring.

She tried to put the doubts behind her, calling out to the remnants of her guard.

"Blessings of Saradomin be upon you all," she said, finding her voice still strong despite the fatigue weighing her down. "Without you, I would surely not have survived the night."

"Long live Hallowvale," the royal standard bearer, Gaia, managed. "Long live the queen!"

The rest of the guard joined in the acclimation, and suddenly their fatigue was gone, if only for a while.

As welcome as the dawn was, its light had illuminated the grim state of the hilltop. The east slope and the camp beyond had become a sprawling hospital for the wounded, a place where sobbing and screaming filled the morning air. The ground of the opposite slope was almost wholly hidden by the bodies still covering it, Zamorakian legionaries from the stream up to the high-water mark where cohort and phalanx had contended. There the dead from both sides were heaped indiscriminately, and few had the strength to pull them apart yet.

Efaritay suppressed the urge to try to snatch some sleep. There was too much to be done.

"Call for the officers to assemble," she told the guard's salpinx blower, before trudging across the crest to where Babel was waiting.

A junior psiloi had already reported to her how, while she had been locked in the desperate struggle with Drakan, Babel had led a counterattack that had quite likely stopped the hill from being overrun.

"Well met, strategos," she said. Babel, his helmet off, bowed to her.

"The light has delivered us," he said. "I am told you faced the master of our foe?"

"I did," Efaritay said, not wishing to elaborate. "What of the fighting on the slopes? Where do we stand?"

"Do you wish me to summarise, or wait?" Babel asked, nodding towards the first of the tagma's officers as they climbed wearily to the crest to join them.

"I will wait," Efaritay said, watching more of the commanders gather. She was relieved to see the leaders of the ordos and their immediate subordinates were still all living. She pushed herself to address them, again discovering the strength that had made her speak to the royal guard. It was leadership in its most basic form. It was her duty, a requirement, no matter how tired she was.

"Warriors of Hallowvale," she said. "The foe has been checked. For the first time since they crossed the frontier, they have not gained a single inch more of Hallowvale's sacred soil. That is thanks to you, your warriors, and their sacrifices. You have my eternal thanks, and I'm sure the thanks of all those we are defending."

There were murmurs of gratitude. Efaritay looked to Babel.

"Strategos, what news?"

Babel took a step forward.

"There have been reports of movement in the marshes to the south, and the woods to the north. Werewolves, but there may be legionary infantry heading in that direction too. They are undoubtedly seeking to encircle us and cut us off from Hallowvale. If we remain here, we will be besieged as assuredly on this hilltop as we would be in the city."

"So, the position is becoming untenable," Efaritay said, failing to keep the coldness from her voice as she looked at Babel. "Yet you claimed we could hold them here?"

"We have done," Babel said. "And I believe we could last another night."

"And what about the night after that?"

"Make no mistake, we have checked them," Babel responded, looking not at Efaritay but at his subordinates, as though challenging them to disagree. "We have inflicted two or three times more casualties upon them than they have upon us. Do that again and we will have evened the odds."

"I fear you are speaking out of pride now rather than strategic sense," Efaritay said, any reservations she had once had about challenging Babel over military matters in front of his officers now gone. "The plan was never to sell our lives here. It was to try and halt the invasion, permanently."

"If we remain for another night, I doubt the defence will hold," Phosani added. Like the others, she had removed her helmet, and her long silver hair gleamed in the morning light. "Justiciar Aliya did well to keep their dark magics at bay, but it is only a matter of time before they commit their undead slaves to the fray. Superior our warriors might be, but we would be overwhelmed."

"I am ordering a withdrawal, back to the city," Efaritay decided. "We must begin as swiftly as possible, while we have the daylight."

"And surrender the hill we have bled for?" Babel demanded, pride and exhaustion causing him to forget himself before his queen. "How could you conscience such a thing?"

"We are about to be outflanked and enveloped," Efaritay said just as harshly. "It does not require the rank of strategos to see that. Those who have died here would not be served by our needless sacrifice."

"Withdrawing will be difficult with so many wounded," Calix, captain of the icyene royal guard, said. "We will have to force march if we are to reach the radius of the Everlight before sunset. If the vyre fall upon us after dark, while we are strung out along the road…"

"That is why I will brook no delay," Efaritay said. "The hypaspists will guard the flanks and rear and the icyene will keep watch from above. The wounded will be kept in the midst of the phalanxes. Leave the camp behind, and any goods that might slow us down."

"We will need a rearguard," Phosani pointed out. "More than just a force to protect the back of the column. Warriors to remain on the hilltop, and buy as much time as possible."

"I volunteer for that honour," Justiciar Lysander said immediately. The aged justiciar looked around, as though challenging anyone to contest it with him.

"Are you certain?" Efaritay began to say, but Lysander carried on firmly.

"My Unicorns were the only ones who didn't wet their blades last night. We will keep this hilltop throughout the day. Monokeros is still at Hallowvale with the temple guards. He is a fine warrior and a true servant of Saradomin. He will command the remnants of the Unicorns and oversee the defence of the holy district when the siege begins. I have also instructed him to ensure the temple is sealed if the worst should happen."

"Very well then," Efaritay said, trying to find the right words to honour the justiciar. "I will see that Saradomin himself hears of your courage, and that of your hypaspists. There is no greater glory than to lay down your life for the light."

"Well spoken, Your-Winged-Majesty," Lysander said with a smile, recognising the pious quote from the Book of Light.

"We will make good the justiciar's sacrifice by marching," Efaritay said, her resolve hardened by Lysander's bravery. "Every minute matters, every step counts. Forget how tired you are. It is our duty now to ensure every warrior who looks to us for leadership makes it back to Hallowvale. Let the Everlight be our guide. While it shines, there is hope."

✦ ✦ ✦

The tagma began to leave the hill they had bled so much for. The ordo of the owl provided a mounted vanguard, followed by the wagons and transports for the encampment. The phalanxes began to move off next, shifting with well-drilled proficiency from battle line to column of march, following the slope round the crest and down to the track leading past Hephaston's mill.

There were skirmishes. The Owls charged and drove off a pack of werewolves that tried to impede them, then fought to keep the ravenous half-beasts away from the flanks of the wagon train. Running battles developed, and at one point the icyene shadowing the column from above had to swoop down to prevent a breakthrough that could have led to a massacre.

The ordo of the wolf were the second last formation to leave the hill. By then the Zamorakian cohorts were beginning to stir from their encampment, and as Rhea barked at the Wolves around her to pick up their feet, she could see the black-clad legionaries beginning to shake themselves into order beyond the stream.

The Wolves left behind their dead, thirty-one in all, according to the muster that morning. It reminded Rhea of Almar, abandoned for the were-packs to be ripped apart in the farm somewhere out there, in land now controlled by the vyre. Every one of the bodies had been beheaded, a cruel necessity that was thought to make it harder for the Zamorakian necromancers to defile the corpses by raising them to fight against their old comrades. There was nothing more that could be done – Rhea had left behind the mortal remains of many good soldiers and close friends before. She could only hope she would not be seeing them again, at least in this life.

The Wolves saluted the hypaspists of the unicorn as they passed them. That was a harder thing to do than leaving behind the dead. Rhea felt anger and resentment at the fact that Lysander and his warriors had claimed the honour of being the last off the hilltop, yet there was also that small, disgusting seed of relief that reminded her that, though harrowed and honed down by years of fighting, she was still only human. She had seen too much of the war to truly believe she would survive it, but still, she wanted to live, wanted to beat the odds just one more time, always one more.

Lysander returned the salute of the Wolves with a raised spear. His hypaspists had formed a small knot atop the crest of the hill. The other banners were gone now, and even the last of the icyene were departing from overhead. Yet as long as the ordo of the unicorn, no matter how few in number, held the hill, the Zamorakians could not easily fall upon the rest of the tagma as it hastened back to Hallowvale.

Rhea took one last look at the slope where they had held throughout the night, then snapped at the head of the column to pick up the pace.

"It's a long way to the city," she barked out. "A long way to the Everlight. We need to reach it before nightfall, or none of us will see home again. So, pick up your feet, and march!"

✦ ✦ ✦

Ranis had lain down to rest in the woodland behind the legion's main encampment. He had found a hollow, partially covered by an ancient, fallen tree, enough to shield him from the cursed, sickening effects of strong daylight. He hugged the gory remains of the phalangite he'd plucked from the ground as they had retreated, smeared with the man's blood, in a sluggish fugue. His side still hurt. He needed darkness, he needed rest.

Something woke him from his torpor. He sensed one of the few remaining members of his brood, Yulslav, crouching on the fallen tree above him, hissing.

He managed to sit up. Everything ached.

Yulslav looked as awful as he felt. He was covered in dry blood, dirt and leaves, and appeared to have crawled to Ranis's resting place along the forest floor.

"What do you want?" Ranis demanded, voice a dry croak.

"The Saradominists," Yulslav rasped back. "Retreating."

Just hours earlier such news would have filled Ranis with fierce exhilaration, but now he could barely even focus on what Yulslav meant.

"Go to the cohort," he managed. "Order them. Attack, attack, attack. I want my banner on the hill first."

"Yes, master," Yulslav said.

+ ✦ +

Drakan watched the hill's abandonment from the edge of the forest.

The sunlight made his skin ache, but he ignored the discomfort. The light held no power over him.

209

Vanescula was with him, looking even more pale and drawn than usual. She had found him and approached without saying anything, hanging a little back, in the forest's shadows.

"Forgive me," she said eventually.

"For what?"

"I did not break them, as you instructed."

Drakan hushed his sister, not taking his eyes off the hill. The last Saradominist infantry were leaving its slopes. Only a small number remained, gathered on the crest. A little morsel left behind for his pleasure.

"You met their queen?" Vanescula asked.

"I did."

"And she still lives?"

"She does."

Drakan did not begrudge his sister's company, but he also had no desire to explain to her why he had spared Queen Efaritay. Not yet, anyway.

He had not sent any instructions to the legion, but some of the more competent officers, seeing the Saradominist withdrawal, had started re-forming their cohorts. One in particular began to advance seemingly without orders.

"That's Ranis's cohort," Vanescula observed. "He wants the glory of taking it. A hilltop now mostly abandoned."

"Someone needs to win the lesser victories," Drakan said. "And Ranis craves them. He is welcome to them."

He looked properly at Vanescula. She was clearly struggling in the daylight, even beneath the forest's shade.

"Go and rest," he ordered her. "We will catch them soon enough. When darkness falls, they will be ours."

Vanescula did not argue, but withdrew to whatever bolt-hole she had found for herself. Drakan remained watching the hill, scenting the fresh blood being spilled there as Ranis's cohort charged the last of the defenders.

It had been a good night's work, but it was still only a beginning.

NINETEEN

———◆◆►———

Luken managed to stifle a yawn until he was out beyond the doors of the library, blinking in the illumination of the Everlight. He had completely lost track of time, though the closed doors and shutters of the street implied it was the city's sleep cycle.

Early or late, he still felt frustration as he began to head back towards the Church. Akeron had entrusted him with a great and terrible secret. Since their talk in the infirmary, he had spent almost every waking hour – and now, more than a few sleeping ones – in the library that lay just west of the Church, searching the towering stacks for any hint at how to destroy the Blood Altar. Musty old tomes, crackling rolls of vellum, mould-blotched scrolls and slender pamphlets, he had trawled through dozens if not hundreds, until his eyes ached and his body had started cramping up from being perpetually hunched over a reading slab.

He had found very little that made sense to him, let alone evidence of an arcane way to undo the altar's magic. He was no mage or rune-sorcerer, and the magics arts were entirely unfamiliar to him.

He had told Akeron as much the day before, when he had visited him in the infirmary again. The archpriest seemed to be regaining his strength, though the stern matron charged with overseeing him had point-blank refused to permit him to leave. Akeron had told Luken to keep looking. There had to be something in the library, he claimed. Something that, apparently, generations of Hallowvale's greatest minds had missed.

As soon as Luken turned into his dorm corridor, he saw that the door to Akeron's bedchamber, locked since he had been taken to the infirmary, was lying open.

Luken padded silently across the cold flagstones towards it. He was just about to peer around the corner when someone approached from within the room, making him yelp.

It was Akeron. He looked every bit the infirmary escapee – his white hair and beard were tousled, his eyes baggy, his shoulders hunched. Most of his body was hidden by several infirmary gowns he appeared to have thrown over himself. He was clutching the star staff, that sacred symbol of his office, using it like a crutch.

"Archpriest," Luken exclaimed, his initial fright replaced by the abrupt and inappropriate desire to hug the old man. Instead he managed a bow, relief at Akeron's return tempered by his frail state. "Should... should you be up?"

"The good brothers and sisters of the infirmary and I are in an ongoing debate about that one," Akeron said. "But that is of no concern to you. Where have you been?"

"The library, as you instructed," Luken said. "I'm going to return as soon as I've had a few hours' sleep!"

"Sleep can wait," Akeron said, ushering Luken back out into the corridor. "I must take you to the Blood Altar. Before I die."

"You're not going to die," Luken exclaimed.

"Of course I'm going to die, boy," Akeron snapped. "Even the icyene die! And before I travel into Saradomin's light, it is my duty to show you the cursed place you have been made guardian of. In a moment of weakness, it seems I have made you the inheritor of that particular duty. There's no sense telling you of the Blood Altar and not showing you how to reach it."

"We're going now?" Luken asked, wondering about Akeron's state of mind as much as his physical frailty. "Just the two of us?"

"Yes, just the two of us, haven't you been listening?" Akeron said. "You must tell no one else of this! No one! Not a priest of Saradomin, not the wisest icyene philosopher, not a justiciar, besides Lysander. If the queen herself demands to know the secret you carry, you are not to tell her. If you are threatened with death, torture, slow dismemberment, you must still not speak a word. The altar is powerful and dangerous beyond your understanding, and if dark forces lay claim to it, it could spell the doom of the whole of Gielinor."

Luken gulped but managed to nod. Akeron patted his shoulder.

"Now come, before the city awakes," he said. "Go downstairs and wake up one of the carriage drivers."

They took the transport south through the sleeping city, Luken saying nothing as he tried to come to terms with the weight of his responsibility. He wished Akeron hadn't told him, but it was too late for that.

They alighted outside the royal palace. It had been shut up since the royal family had left it for the greater safety of the citadel. Still, it looked magnificent in the glory of the Everlight, with its soaring walls and columns of marble pillars, each carved like a huge icyene, the figures standing with arms folded in the traditional repose of Saradominist contemplation, unfurled wings acting as the supports for the roof above. All of it shone, pristine white in the Everlight's glow. The tower itself stood in the distance, almost directly behind it, a column of dazzling power that soared into the sky overhead, banishing the night with glittering radiance.

The palace doors stood shut and barred, the parade of stairs leading to them deserted. Akeron took Luken left, towards the wall that encircled the flanks and rear of the royal residence, securing it where it bordered onto the bay that lay to the south and east of Hallowvale.

They arrived at the narrow path that led down between the walls and the shore. Progress was slow, and almost without thinking about it, Luken took Akeron's arm, allowing him to lean on both the junior illuminator and the star staff. The archpriest didn't protest.

The pathway took them under the east wall of the palace, walking the narrow strip of shingle between the bay and the fortifications. The Everlight lay directly across the water from them, surrounded by a series of small, verdant islands littered with icyene structures. They were some of the oldest buildings in Hallowvale, with the acropolis, the stadium that held the Dominion Games and the city's amphitheatre all vying for space along with the *oikoi* households where the noblest icyene families had once lived. The white pillars, triangular roofs and stairways echoed the architecture of both the palace and the Everlight itself, standing proud at the centre of the little archipelago. Luken found he could not look up at its pinnacle, so bright was the radiance shining from it.

"Perhaps the light is the key," he said as they went, tugging his robe tighter around him with his free hand to ward off the cold sea breeze. "The Everlight is the work of great Saradomin himself, is it not? Its light is his light, a shard of his essence giving out eternal luminance. That's what the sacred texts say."

"They are correct," Akeron agreed.

"So what if we brought that light down into where the altar lies? Used the raw power of Saradomin himself to destroy it?"

"And just how would we get the Everlight down there?" Akeron asked. "I told you already, the Blood Altar does not lie in a chamber beneath the palace, at least not in literal terms. We cannot reach it by tunnelling to it, or tearing down its walls to expose it to the glory of Saradomin's creation."

"But what if we could remove the core of the Everlight and bring it to the altar?" Luken wondered out loud.

"Remove the Everlight?" Akeron repeated, looking sharply up at Luken as they went. "With a horde of vyre bearing down upon the city? Think about what you're suggesting, boy!"

Luken pursed his lips, feeling foolish. Akeron tapped him on the arm, and he realised the old man wished to pause.

"Here we are," he said.

There was an opening in the wall beside them, a circular space slightly larger than a fully grown man. The bottom of it was discoloured and glistening with scum. Luken got a whiff off it and grimaced.

"The sewer outflow from the palace," Akeron said before noticing Luken's expression. "What, did you think icyene smell like rose petals when they use the chamber pot? Or that it isn't as bad when the king and queen go?"

"I'm not sure I'll be able to look at any of them the same again," Luken admitted. Akeron grumbled something then urged him towards the opening.

To Luken's relief, the section of tunnel that joined with the palace's waste system didn't last long. The downside was that the connecting passage Akeron then directed him into was much lower and narrower, forcing him to stoop slightly. Where the drainage system had clearly been crafted by humans or icyene, made from the same stonework as the wall it was tunnelled through, this tunnel had been roughly hewn through the bedrock below the palace. The only sign of intelligent design were torches, set in sconces at regular intervals.

As they approached the first, groping along using the last of the light filtering in through the sewage tunnel, a flame kindled and ignited seemingly from nowhere, lighting the torch and illuminating the path.

"Dormant icyene magics," Akeron said. "Like the ones that often light the interior of the citadel or the palace. Do not be afraid."

He fished into the gowns he was wearing and drew out a map, which he unrolled and studied beneath the torch's light. Then, muttering to himself, he urged Luken on along the tunnel, each torch ahead of them sparking into light while the ones they left behind quickly dimmed and went back out.

"Are these passages known of by the royal family?" Luken asked. "Or the royal guards?"

"Of course," Akeron said. "They can be used as a means of escape if the palace is overrun, but what they don't know is that not all the passages are what they seem."

They reached a crossroads, with Akeron consulting the map again and choosing the left-hand route, then the right at another fork. Luken was doing his best to breathe normally and not think about the tons of rock pressing in all around him. He hadn't been troubled much by claustrophobia since he'd been instructed to help clean and tend to some of the lowermost crypts in the Hallowed Sepulchre, but the tightness of the tunnels were resurrecting old fears.

Akeron again indicated for Luken to pause. They stood still in a nondescript stretch of passageway, the rugged stone picked out by the flames of the nearest torch.

The archpriest folded away his map and pulled the gowns away from his throat. He had something on underneath, a necklace which he now held up before the junior illuminator.

Luken peered at it in the flickering light. It seemed to be a metal token, strangely shaped, with a piece of ruby at its centre, crafted into what looked like a drop of blood. It glinted in the light.

"This is a blood talisman," Akeron said. "An arcane artefact, forged on the altar and bound to it. Scholars believe it is not unique, but it is the only one currently in our possession, and the only means we reliably have of accessing the altar."

"How does it work?" Luken asked warily.

"You must clasp it, and centre your thoughts on your own heartbeat," Akeron said. "Allow no distractions. It is better if only one uses it, but it can transport two if their focus is great enough. You can use it at any point along this stretch of tunnel, and it will take you to the skulls."

Luken felt reluctant to touch the talisman, let alone question what Akeron meant by skulls, but the archpriest's scowl was enough of an incentive. He held the lower part of the amulet in forefinger and thumb as Akeron grasped the upper, then closed his eyes and tried to pinpoint the rapid tattoo of his heart.

It took some time, but he made himself breathe slow and regular, and eventually caught the rush of blood in his ears, then the beating deep within his chest.

"Open your eyes," Akeron instructed. Luken did so, and discovered that they were no longer in the tunnel.

Somehow, between the beating of their hearts, they had been transported into another stone chamber. It was as rugged and subterranean as the passages they had left behind, illuminated not by torchlight, but by Akeron's staff.

Light shone from the star tipping it, and Luken instinctively made the sign of the Lord of Light.

Its glow picked out what Luken at first took to be two gigantic skulls, their backs fused together, set in the middle of the chamber.

"They are made of stone," Akeron said, removing the blood talisman from Luken's grip. "This is not the Blood Altar, but it is the final gateway between us and that liminal space. Reach out and touch them with me, and we will be transported."

Doing his best to swallow his fear, Luken approached the skulls with Akeron, placing his hand tentatively on one while Akeron reached for the other. He closed his eyes as he did so, as he had done when gripping the talisman.

This time, he felt the air around him change.

His eyes snapped open. The first thing he noticed was the infernal heat that had suddenly replaced the cold of the tunnels, followed by a heavy, coppery stench.

They stood in a low, wide chamber, its floor formed from flagstones while its walls and ceiling were comprised of rough-hewn bedrock. Four stone columns supported the ceiling, and between them was a dais, illuminated by four pillars of fire. The middle of the dais was dominated by a large block of stone, smooth and almost circular.

The place had a dark, fire-shot grandeur to it, but one architectural feature in particular left Luken in no doubt that the talisman had transported them into the right place.

Blood was running from the stone in the chamber's centre. It seemed to pour continuously from within the altar itself, running down its sides and into four channels cut in the flagstones. They radiated out around the supporting pillars and into what could only be described as a lake that lay around the chamber's edge, between where the floor ended and the rock walls began.

Luken retched. The whole place stank of blood, the air filled with its coppery reek, with its heat and cloying potency.

Akeron stepped away from him and hobbled up the short flight of stairs to the altar. Luken noted he had extinguished the light of his staff. He hurried after him, not wishing to be separated from the archpriest. He didn't want to be left behind, stranded and sealed within the terrible chamber.

"The Blood Altar," Akeron declared. Luken joined him in gazing down on the top of the stone slab. He saw that the blood was welling and bubbling up from a teardrop-shaped space carved in the stone's centre.

"Where does it come from?" he asked.

"Who can say?" Akeron responded. "It is magic of a most ancient and potent kind. I am no sorcerer or rune-crafter, but whoever created this place must have possessed power beyond anything seen in Gielinor today. Perhaps it was one of the old gods, before even the coming of Saradomin."

Despite the chamber's burning heat, Luken felt a chill run through him.

"And nothing can be done to break it?" he asked, almost afraid to suggest such a thing in the altar's presence.

"No blow, sorcerous or otherwise, has ever harmed the stone, and no effort to shift it has ever succeeded," Akeron said. "Likewise with the pillars that support the chamber. One of the archpriests of yore, Venerable Herodiphon, sought to build a platform over the blood and tunnel out through the walls, but when he returned to check the progress of the workers he left behind, he found no trace of them. They had vanished, along with all their tools, and the walls were untouched."

"Perhaps we should not linger here then," Luken suggested.

"No, we should not," Akeron agreed. "You have seen it now. You know how to reach this place, should the need ever arise. Pray to the light it does not."

"I shall, archpriest," Luken said fervently, just wanting to be gone.

"Take the talisman," Akeron instructed, holding up the token once more. "And think of where we stood before coming here. The tunnel."

Luken snatched at the talisman and closed his eyes again. He felt as though he was choking on the close, blood-stinking air, and was horrified by the idea that the arcane amulet wouldn't work, that they would be stuck in the sealed, nightmarish chamber for eternity. He tried to focus on the passageway, desperate to find himself back amongst even those low tunnels.

He found himself gasping cold, clear air. He opened his eyes, and went weak with a surge of relief as he discovered it had worked. They were back in the passageway, seemingly bypassing even the grim skull chamber.

Akeron lowered the talisman, and swayed. Luken snatched his arm again, seeing as he did so just how pale the archpriest had become.

"We need to get you back to the Church," he said firmly. For once, Akeron didn't protest.

Holding the archpriest tightly, Luken steered him back along the tunnel.

TWENTY

———◄◆►———

The tagma was close to breaking.

Rhea had seen it before. During the retreat from Al Zakqa, she had witnessed what an army in its death throes looked like. Discipline began to collapse. Soldiers no longer marched with purpose, or even resignation, but limped and dragged themselves along like condemned men. Weapons and armour were cast aside. Those who had been carrying them followed soon after, those without the mental and physical strength abandoned at the roadside. Orders became fewer and harsher, and less readily obeyed.

Eventually, there would be no organisation, no formation, just a tired, frightened mass. It would be an army no more, just a broken mob.

That was what Rhea began to witness on the road back to Hallowvale. The main body of the tagma was ahead of her; she saw its detritus and its stragglers abandoned along the way. They had marched out of the city, fought all night against horrors few of them had ever even imagined before, and now were marching back again, without rest, hunted every step of the way by ravenous half-beasts.

She knew there was little she could do to stop the rest of the tagma from breaking, but she would sooner have her blood drunk by a brood of vyre than let it happen to the Wolves. The need to lead them, to provide a figurehead they could focus on, was enough to make Rhea forget her own exhaustion.

"Hold your ranks, damn you," she barked, calling out the cadence of the march. "None of you have permission to go this damn slow! Pick your feet up!"

To their credit, the Wolves stayed together, right up until Alcindies. He was one of the younger ones, new to the ranks, a Hallowvale recruit who had earned approval from his superiors while serving as a hoplitai and had been offered a place in the ordos. He had chosen the Wolves. Rhea had made a point of watching him, as she had done with all their recruits, alert to the possibility that he may not possess the ferocious spirit demanded by the ordo. From what Rhea had seen, he was dutiful and understood the honour of his position, and she had noted the blood on his doru when the Wolves had re-formed that morning as the sun rose.

But now she had found Alcindies' limit. There was a clatter as he collapsed, breaking the marching column. Rhea immediately doubled back and hauled him to the side of the rutted roadway.

"Get up," she snapped. Alcindies groaned.

"Leave him," said a voice. It was Insela. She was bringing up the rear of the formation, and now paused by the road as the last of the hypaspists struggled past.

"Is he part of your section?" Rhea demanded, only glancing at her.

"No."

"Then let me dispense discipline as I see fit."

"He isn't part of your section either."

Rhea shot the arbalist a venomous look. Insela simply shrugged and turned away, hurrying to catch up with the column.

She pulled off Alcindies' helmet and struck him with her palm, then unstopped the water gourd at her hip and poured the last of its contents down his throat. He choked and spluttered, pulling away from her grip and sitting up.

"Don't think for a second I'm carrying you, pup," Rhea growled.

She saw the fire rekindle in the young warrior. He accepted her proffered hand and she pulled him back to his feet.

"March," she said simply.

Alcindies obeyed, beginning to limp after his fellow Wolves. Rhea waited until he had gone a few paces before starting to follow, keeping behind him, ready to snatch him if he stumbled.

She couldn't help but glance back as they went. The roadway had just passed out of a section of woodland, and as Rhea looked she caught movement beneath the boughs. She didn't need to stop and focus to know what it was.

The were-packs were closing in, and worst of all, she and Alcindies were now the last Saradominists still following the column. They had almost been left behind.

"You're doing well, pup," she lied to Alcindies, desperate to keep him moving. She caught horrible noises drifting from the woodland, the screams of those who had fallen behind and, unlike Alcindies, hadn't managed to find their feet again.

Darkness was beginning to fall, save for ahead, where the Everlight still shone, still beckoning above the ragged column. They had to reach it before the shadows – and worse – caught up with them.

They walked. It couldn't be called marching any longer. Rhea found herself lapsing into silence, the metronome of scuffing feet a dull constant. Her aches and pains began to resurface once more, and with it the thoughts that she knew would lead to her destruction – couldn't she stop, just briefly? How much easier would it be if she cast away her helmet, her shield, even her kopis?

She gritted her teeth and kept going. As though frustrated at her defiance, she heard a howl rising up from behind her, the terrible half-human, half-bestial wailing of the werewolves.

They were getting closer. She snatched another glance back, and saw them clearly now, loping out onto the roadway. The shadows seemed to stretch alongside them, creeping out from under the boughs, eager to eat up the last of the daylight.

The rearmost ranks of the ordo were a few dozen paces ahead. The gap between them and Alcindies was growing, step by step, while the one between Rhea and the werewolves was shortening.

"Keep going," she told Alcindies, looking back again. The closest of the werewolves, fully transformed into their bestial visage, were breaking into loping strides, canines bared.

Rhea knew they weren't going to make it. As soon as she stopped and turned, she would be dead. She might kill one or two, but in doing so she would be left behind, and surrounded.

She remembered that cold resignation on the road from that nameless farmhouse where Almar had died. The memory caused her to look up, and again she saw her salvation.

Icyene were circling overhead, little glimmers against the darkness that was spreading like spilled ink through the low clouds. An arrow came whizzing down out of the gloom, the first drop of an impending storm, impaling itself with a thud in the roadway just ahead of the oncoming werewolves.

The beasts had learned. They came up short, snarling and circling, but getting no closer.

Rhea was too tired to acknowledge the icyene's protection. She just kept walking.

"The eyes of Saradomin's servants watch over us," she told Alcindies, not even knowing if he had heard her, or if he was truly aware of how close to death they were. All that mattered was that he kept walking.

"This is the last rise," she went on, recognising the road's incline. They trudged up it in the wake of the rest of the ordo, and found themselves looking down on Hallowvale, shining like a white mountain in the sunset, bathed in the

Everlight's glory. Rhea didn't think she had ever seen a more beautiful sight.

✦ ✦ ✦

The tagma's rearguard struggled into the glow of the Everlight just as the last of the day vanished. There was a haunting shriek from the vyre rising after them, flocking in the darkness just beyond the ring of brilliance protecting the city. The packs added their howling to the discord, a chilling cacophony that the horn blowers atop the city's towers answered defiantly.

Rhea limped into the long shadow cast by the western gatehouse, using her doru like a crutch. Alcindies was still in front. Somewhere through the fatigue that had stripped away her thoughts, Rhea realised she was the last one to pass through the gates.

Perhaps she should have paused, looked back, made some defiant gesture to reinforce the challenge of Hallowvale's horns. But she did not have the strength. Instead, she just carried on, in under the towering stonework.

The gates slammed shut behind her, the locking bars heaved into place.

The siege of Hallowvale had begun.

✦ ✦ ✦

Ascertes' heart was racing as he dashed out into the main courtyard of the citadel. He knew that as king he should show restraint, control, affect a statelier presence, but right then he didn't care about any of that.

The courtyard was almost full. Icyene were still alighting from above. They looked tired. Many were blood-spattered or bore fresh wounds.

Ascertes strode in among them, casting about for the royal standard and the more familiar faces of his personal guard.

After a few frantic seconds he found them and, even more importantly, he found his wife. Efaritay, her helmet missing but the Sunspear still in her grip, looked at him, and for a second there was a terrible hollowness to her expression, the look of a warrior who had been pushed beyond breaking point.

Then recognition reached her, and she smiled. Ascertes threw his arms around her.

"I thought I would never see you again," he found himself admitting.

Efaritay embraced him back, and eventually he managed to release her, realising he was probably embarrassing her. Icyene had a strong sense when it came to impropriety, and the nearest warriors were giving them space and firmly looking in every other direction.

"Saradomin has delivered me back safely," Efaritay said. "Would that I could say that about so many brave others."

"It is your own skill and the courage of Hallowvale's warriors that has delivered you," Ascertes responded. "How went the battle?"

He had heard nothing yet of what had occurred beyond the walls, had merely seen the lights of the icyene returning as darkness fell. He had ordered Larina and Safalaan to stay in their chamber until he knew more, worried that they had been defeated and Efaritay possibly slain.

"We made a stand as Babel advised, on the rise above Hephaston's mill," Efaritay said. "The Zamorakians attacked at night, in full force. We held them until the dawn, but could not have withstood a second assault."

"The host is intact?" Ascertes asked. He had seen the tagma's vanguard reaching the western gate from the citadel's ramparts. They had looked ragged and bloody. "Did Babel survive?"

"The retreat was done in good order," Efaritay said. "Babel was alive when last I saw. He is bringing in the last flocks."

The queen had just finished speaking when all her strength seemed to leave her. Ascertes had to snatch at her and support her, grabbing onto the Sunspear with his other hand as well. The queen's standard bearer, Gaia, swept forward.

"With respect, my liege, Her-Winged-Majesty is exhausted," the loyal retainer said, supporting Efaritay under her other arm. "She needs rest."

"Yes, of course," Ascertes responded, chiding himself for not considering just how tired Efaritay really was. He signalled to two of the royal guards who had remained behind in the citadel, and they hurried down the steps from the doors to take over from Ascertes and Gaia.

"Take her to her chambers," he said. "And tell my children they may see her. When she is fully awake, inform her I am marshalling the defence."

✦ ✦ ✦

The vyrelords gathered on the ridge overlooking Hallowvale's citadel and western walls. Ranis was among them. Like the others, he found he could hardly even look towards the city. To his sight it was like a newborn sun set down upon Gielinor, a wall of white brilliance so intense he could barely discern the individual features of towers, parapets, spires and rooftops. Even Vanescula, he noted, was not gazing directly at the city, but was instead pretending all her attention was focused on Drakan.

Alone among the vampyres, His-Dark-Self seemed untroubled by the nightmarish luminance. Drakan stood before his hissing, cringing broods and faced the city. He seemed lost in contemplation.

"We should press the attack," Ranis said loudly, deciding to take the initiative. "They are exhausted, broken. Assault the walls now and we will take this city before the sun's return. This is our best opportunity."

Some of the lesser vyrelords, including Alexei Jovkai and Nadezhda Shadum, chittered with agreement.

"Would you be the first to fly into the light?" Vanescula demanded.

"We have a mortal legion for a reason," Ranis sneered. "They will storm the walls and snuff out the Everlight, and once it is gone, the city will be defenceless against us!"

"And how will the legion be able to achieve any of that?" Vanescula said. "They don't yet have any ladders, siege towers, rams! The city is defended by walls, how will they climb them? The Everlight is on an island, will they swim to it? Think, brother!"

"Be silent," Drakan said sharply, and the vyrelords obeyed, not so much as a hiss disturbing the sudden stillness.

Ranis watched his brother as he inhaled slowly and deeply, seeming to scent the air, as though hunting for the smell of blood. Drakan nodded once, apparently satisfied, then turned to face his kin, his powerful frame backlit by the cursed Everlight.

"There will be no assault tonight. Instruct the officers of the legion that they are to commence siege operations. Ensure the city's walls are invested. Is that clear?"

The vampyre nobility gave their affirmation.

Ranis departed, saying nothing more. He had known an immediate attack on the city was impractical, but he had wanted to keep the others distracted, make them think he was desperate for a swift resolution. He didn't want them to sense that he now had something more at play, something he had brought with him from the hill where they had fought the last battle.

His cohort was moving into position to the north-west of the citadel. With typical Zamorakian military efficiency, the fourteenth legion had already arranged plans for the siege of Hallowvale prior to the invasion. Every part of Drakan's host knew where it should stake out its encampments. From the north-eastern coast all the way round to the south-western shoreline, over the coming night and day the icyene-made city would be invested, surrounded on its landward side. Then, true offensive operations could begin.

Ranis detested sieges. For him they meant inactivity, boredom, sitting on one side or the other of the walls, watching mortals grub in the dirt and construct their little toys of timber and steel. There was little killing to be done, and that meant little in the way of blood. The vyre preferred to descend on their foes from above and slaughter at will. Walls were no defence against the children of Vampyrium. But at Hallowvale, the light changed everything. Ranis was just thankful its radiance did not reach far beyond the city. Out here, the night still ruled.

His cohort had pitched their first tents, the black silken pavilions used by the officers. One was reserved for Ranis, though he was rarely with the mortals nominally under his command and, like most vyre, preferred to find his own resting place when the sun returned. Now though, the black pavilion had discovered a new and vital purpose.

The legionary guards posted outside it bowed. Ranis ignored them and ducked within. He felt the delight he had experienced when he had first met the captive. Surely now, he would be able to prove himself beyond all doubt and establish his place in the vyre hierarchy as second only to his brother.

Though he barely remembered giving the order, he had certainly been right to demand his cohort attack the Saradominist rearguard atop the hill. He had hoped simply to win prestige, but his legionaries had brought back something potentially even more valuable. A prisoner, now tightly bound to the pole supporting the centre of the tent. Ranis bared his fangs in a smile.

PART THREE

TWENTY-ONE

———◆————

Rhea paused as she walked the ramparts of the citadel, and looked out at the gathering twilight.

After the desperate retreat to Hallowvale, almost a week had passed without incident. The Zamorakians had moved like some vast, black-scaled snake slowly constricting around the city, cutting it off from everything north and west of the walls. Only the seaward side remained open – Rhea supposed they should be thankful the enemy hadn't brought a fleet.

The city had been quiet and still. On Babel's advice, orders had been issued that kept people confined to their homes except for short periods. Guards had been set on food stores and patrolled the streets to guard against looting, unrest, or the possibility of infiltrators. Hallowvale felt eerily deserted, though Rhea knew it was an illusion. It was strange to think of the many thousands huddled in their oikos, blind to what was happening on the walls or beyond them, praying fervently for deliverance from the darkness that had risen up to choke their city.

Praying to a god who wasn't coming.

The legion had started to dig. Night and day, work shifts laboured to create trenches that encircled the walls. They had started felling the nearest woodlands too, the dull thud of axes striking timber providing a constant, dull backdrop. Already the tree lines that Rhea had once recognised from the walls were gone, reduced to bristling carpets of stumps.

The wood was being used to raise up palisades along with the trenchworks, reinforcing them and turning the Zamorakian encampments into miniature fortresses, protecting against any attempt by the defenders to sally out, or against any external efforts to relieve the siege. They were links in the chain designed to strangle Hallowvale to death.

Rhea knew that was not all they needed the wood for. From where she stood, she could see engines taking shape amongst the encampments or in the trenches – onagers and covered battering rams, and the frames that would become siege towers, rising up from among the enemy's tents.

It was all progressing with slow, predictable inevitability. Rhea had spent her life fighting the Zamorakians, and she knew how their legions operated – methodically and precisely. Siege work came naturally to them, and would progress through a series of stages as they worked to overcome Hallowvale's defences.

"They'll be coming soon," said a voice to her right. She looked over, and saw that Damacleso had approached her and was now following her gaze, out over the Zamorakian lines.

He was an Imcando dwarf, one of the pyrophoroi responsible for manning the arcane war engines sited atop some sections of the city walls. There were few of them among the garrison tagma – most of the Imcando were in the west with Saradomin, deploying their great and terrible machines at the heart of the fight. A few had remained assigned to Hallowvale, though Rhea hadn't spoken with any until the Wolves had been assigned to the westernmost sections of the citadel's ramparts, which also included the area where Damacleso's war machine and its small crew were stationed. The weapon, a pyrokutor, looked to Rhea like a strange collection of bronze and copper pipes and canisters. She had little idea about what it could do, but she had built up something of a guarded rapport with its operators – Rhea appreciated dwarf bluffness.

"Shoddy makers of tools, you humans," he went on. "But those Zamorakians will build enough catapults to turn even these icyene walls to rubble, given enough time. Thankfully, time is something they won't have."

"Only if Saradomin does come," Rhea pointed out.

"You think he won't?" Damacleso asked sharply. The Imcando were well known for their devotion to the Lord of Light. Most of them would put the faith of an archpriest to shame.

"I was there when his message arrived, saying he could not send relief," Rhea said, unwilling to choose being politic over the cold truth.

"Have faith, Wolf," Damacleso said, his tone almost reproachful. "As surely as the sun will rise with each dawn, so our Lord of Light will come to this, his hallowed city."

"Perhaps," Rhea allowed. "But there is no sign of him yet. At best, we will face many days and nights of bloodshed before his arrival."

"You don't sound like you're looking forward to it," the dwarf said.

"Should I be?" Rhea asked, taken aback. Damacleso grinned.

"It's going to involve burning a lot of bastard Zamorakians. I haven't had a chance to do that in long enough."

Rhea couldn't help but laugh.

"Something for us all to look forward to then," she said, offering the Imcando a slight bow, then doing the same to his war engine before moving further along the parapets.

Phosani was waiting for her at the base of the north-westernmost tower. Rhea saluted her by touching the star on her breastplate.

"Anything to report?" the justiciar asked.

"Nothing, commander. Our section remains secure. No movement along the front, besides the usual. The Zamorakians facing us have widened one of their saps. Acletas claims it's on the edge of his effective range. He thinks they're going to move the onagers forward into it soon, maybe even tonight."

Acletas was the ballista captain, in charge of the two artillery pieces sited on the towers assigned to the protection of the Wolves. None of the weaponry mounted atop Hallowvale's walls had begun to launch projectiles yet, conserving ammunition until the trenchworks being dug by the enemy were no longer at extreme range.

"If not tonight, it will begin soon," Phosani said, adding nothing more. Like so many of the others, she had been uncommonly morose since the retreat to the city. Rhea had rarely seen morale so low. At this stage she could only hope a return to action triggered the Wolves' defiance.

"We'll be ready when it does," she tried to reassure her commander. "No Zamorakian filth will take this wall, not while the Wolves hold it."

"Perhaps," Phosani said and then, unexpectedly, added – "have you seen the dead?"

"The dead?" Rhea asked, not knowing what the White Wolf meant.

"Working among them? The risen dead. They had walking corpses at the start of the invasion, and they must have resurrected plenty at Hephaston's mill."

"It's difficult to tell from this distance," Rhea said, acknowledging Phosani's line of thinking. "But no. The legions don't like to use the undead in their assaults, they think them too weak, and the wards inscribed in the stonework of the walls should keep them back, even if the Everlight doesn't. But that doesn't explain why they aren't using them to dig trenches."

"They must be massing them somewhere," Phosani pondered. "But where, and why?"

Rhea didn't know, so held her tongue. The obvious answer, she feared, was that they would find out soon.

✦ ✦ ✦

Acletas's prediction proved correct. That night, the bombardment began.

The first warning was a cracking sound, the noise clapping back off the walls and rooftops like thunder. It had come from the south, beyond the citadel, somewhere around the western gate into the city. Rhea, who had been about to be replaced by Otrava as wall section commander for the night, looked to the left, but could see nothing past the nearest tower.

The cause of the sound soon became obvious. There was a second cracking noise, this one much closer. Rhea felt the stonework beneath her shiver, and realised the wall had just been struck by a projectile.

The Zamorakians had finished their siege engines.

"Stand to," Rhea barked at the salpinx player accompanying her. Horns rang, calling the defenders to the ramparts. It was a precaution, but Rhea doubted it would be necessary – there would be no nighttime assault, only a hail of stone and steel.

The artillery sited across the walls began to return the punishment. They were shooting blind, out into the twilight on the edge of the Everlight's radius, but the likes of Acletas had positioned his weaponry carefully during the daytime, presetting the aim to cover the areas that would be occupied by the finished Zamorakian war machinery. Ballistae and catapults began to launch their projectiles out into the dark, blind as to their success.

Rhea paced the walls as they rapidly filled with soldiery, ordering them to watch their spacing and remain behind the protection of the parapets. It was possible to see the projectiles launched at the walls as they arced into the illumination of the Everlight. She watched one stone slam into the north-western tower, just below its ramparts, gouging at the masonry and kicking up a puff of dust. Another hurtled low overhead, the rumble of its passing followed by a dull crunch as it struck a rooftop somewhere within the city.

"Their aim isn't up to much," Mardin quipped as Rhea passed his and Klaxar's part of the wall. "So much for Zamorakian military engineering."

Rhea didn't indulge in the battle humour. Mardin knew as well as she did that the opening salvos were simply designed for the weapon operators to find their range and adjust their tension and elevation.

"I wouldn't linger here too long, Wolf," Damacleso called as she carried on down the line, the dwarf and his crew standing behind the bellows and copper piping of their curious war machine.

"They'll be targeting engines like this," the Imcando went on, smacking one knot of pipework. "And the ones atop the towers. Knock them out, then the assault goes in."

"I know," Rhea said. As though to underscore Damacleso's claim there was a ringing clang. Rhea assumed a ballista bolt had just struck the stone embrasure shielding its front and ricocheted away.

"You think it'll still be in one piece when they come?" she asked, indicating the pyrokutor.

"Saradomin willing," Damacleso said piously. "Never underestimate Imcando engineering, Wolf!"

✦ ✦ ✦

243

The barrage carried on throughout the night and into the dawn.

The return of the daylight showed that there was no Zamorakian assault force packing the saps and trenchworks beneath the walls. Most of the defenders were stood down, including Rhea. She went to sleep in the barrack block assigned to her and the rest of her section in the citadel, the once-empty chambers and guardrooms now crammed with the garrison force. At first, the sound of projectiles occasionally striking the other side of the wall was enough to wake her, but not for any length of time. She had long ago learned not to worry about the possibility of death from a random stone or bolt.

For days the bombardment continued. The walls were scarred, some sections of parapet wholly demolished, the towers pounded. One by one the Saradominist artillery fell silent, the engines wrecked and the crews killed or wounded.

Those projectiles that missed the walls struck the city instead. Roofs were staved in, towers and spires scarred, streets gouged. People died, indiscriminately. Refugees, both those who had come into the city ahead of the invasion, and people already within the walls, began crowding the oikoi and buildings in the east of the city, out of range of the Zamorakian bombardment. The wharf warehouses and the docks were overcrowded. There were reports of looting and lawlessness, but few soldiers could be spared from the walls to keep the peace. Plumes of smoke rose from across the city, caused by arson or damage from the barrage, the ashy clouds diffracting the constant light of the Everlight.

Rhea endured it as they all did, silent but for the orders she gave. She ate, she slept, she watched the siege lines slowly spreading below her, and she waited.

And on the fifth day, the first tower fell.

TWENTY-TWO

———◆▶———

Efaritay felt the arboretum shudder around her, causing leaves to rustle and timber to groan, as though the plants at the heart of Hallowvale were in fear.

Another catapult stone had struck the square outside. The arboretum itself had been hit several times since the bombardment began, its dome proving resilient enough to deflect all but one of the impacts. A single rock had smashed through, bringing down a cascade of masonry on the west side and splintering half a grove of hycar trees.

Efaritay had lamented their destruction at first, before feeling a surge of shame. Hallowvale was beset by the legions of darkness, and death was raining down upon her subjects all over the city, yet she was sorrowing over a stand of trees?

She sang to the blisterwood. It felt as though she had done little else since making it back to the city. The tree itself had grown mighty, equal now to the skyroots flanking it, its white branches thick and jagged.

It had become her sole focus since the start of the siege. During the day she had spent recovering, Ascertes had thrown himself into organising the defences. After the chaos of the retreat and the initial fears that the Zamorakians would conduct an immediate assault, everything had suddenly become slow and turgid. Efaritay had found herself with little to do, and after the weeks of tension since the start of the invasion, the new responsibilities Ascertes had taken on seemed to have given him new drive and focus.

Efaritay felt as though he had robbed her of it. She had taken to visiting the arboretum each day rather than the walls, deciding she could do more good there, growing and repairing the blisterwood. There were more cuttings, jagged offshoots that grew from the outer branches like white-bladed knives. She had started giving them to the royal guard, and one to Ascertes, to use against the vyre should they ever somehow pierce the Everlight's protection.

A part of her knew she was merely avoiding reality. Since the battle above Hephaston's mill, she had been living in a daze. Her dreams were riven by the slaughter she had witnessed, and she couldn't shake her memories of the clash with Drakan, of his raw strength and speed; even the light of the Sunspear and its blisterwood haft had done nothing to stop him. She was haunted by the beast's mocking disregard for the efforts of her and her guards to slay him. He had treated it like a game.

How could they hope to fight such a monstrosity? Every time she sought reassurance, her thoughts went to Saradomin, then despair. There had been no word from the west. She toyed with the idea that the vyre had intercepted the messenger, that the Lord of Light was just then leading a host to break the siege.

Was she lying to herself? Was the truth not that she was hiding here, shutting herself away with just the trees her father had planted for company?

The arboretum shook again. Another impact, closer this time. Dust cascaded down from the jagged gap already ploughed through the dome's roof.

She focused her energy on the blisterwood, soothing it, encouraging another shard from one of the boughs to break off in her hand. Doing so left her feeling even more drained, but it was preferable to standing atop the walls and simply waiting.

The queen inspected the wood she had taken, spinning it and testing it, finding it as hard and sharp-tipped as a knife. It was warm as well, a living weapon. Drive it into a vyre and the creature would burn as assuredly as though it had been struck by the full power of the Everlight.

She wondered if that would be the case with Drakan.

She could almost feel the vyrelord's terrible presence, his predatory gaze. Despite herself she turned, hunting through the shadows beneath the surrounding boughs, snatching up the Sunspear from where it rested against the blisterwood's flank. She hadn't gone anywhere without it since it had been forged. It felt like a part of her now, the only thing keeping the dark at bay.

But no, no winged threat beneath the eves, no gleaming red eyes amidst the shadows. She took a slow breath. What would her mother think of her, seeing how weak she had become, just when strength was needed most of all.

"Thank you," she said out loud to the blisterwood tree, holding up the shard it had gifted her with this time. "We must continue to resist. We must not give up hope. Saradomin will come. The light will not go out."

The tree made no response.

Efaritay departed.

✦ ✦ ✦

The first tower to fall was the one to the immediate right of Rhea's section, the most north-westerly in the citadel.

Its upper half gave way with a cracking sound. Its top had already been abandoned, broken to stone splinters by the focused bombardment of most of the Zamorakian artillery pieces on the northern and western sections of the siegeworks. The lower half of the structure remained intact, but by the time the dust settled there was a ramp of settling rubble up to the jagged remains of its upper levels.

The Zamorakians cheered. Rhea heard it start among their catapults and spread through their works, the sound of their jubilation drifting up to the walls.

"Bastards," Klaxar muttered.

The next tower fell a few hours later, this one on the south-west of the citadel, where its walls ran down to the western gatehouse leading into the city proper. By this point there was definite activity in the saps, more so than usual.

The salpinx rang out, and the tagma stood to.

✦ ✦ ✦

"Are they coming?" Ascertes asked as he arrived on the citadel walls. The walkway was bustling with hypaspists hurrying to their positions and archers stringing bows and loosening sheaves of arrows.

The king had been holding a strategic session with Babel in the citadel's throne room, discussing matters of supply and rationing, but as soon as he had heard the collapse of the north-west tower he had hurried up to the walls.

He felt as though he had barely left them since the siege began. He hadn't been fully out of his armour panoply since that first day. He had devoted himself to the defences, but there had been little to do but endure the bombardment. Until now.

"Yes, my king, they're coming," Phosani, justiciar of the wolf said. She and her pelt-clad hypaspists commanded much of the citadel's walls, and while Ascertes didn't want to appear weak by voicing his relief at their presence, he was privately glad such a veteran force had been assigned by Babel to hold the most vital part of the Hallowvale's defences. Phosani was nothing if not grim and taciturn, seemingly now more than ever. It was hard to imagine any force, even the vyre, taking the walls when her and her warriors defended them.

He stood beside the White Wolf and gazed out over the Zamorakian siege lines. There was movement throughout the trenchworks, and the three siege towers that had been constructed directly opposite the citadel's western curtain wall were now beginning to sway and lumber ponderously into motion. They had been completed over the past few days, their fronts covered with taut animal hides and what, from a distance, looked like slender red and white banners that rippled in the breeze. They started to roll over planks laid across the saps, entering the bare ground between the trenchworks and the walls.

"It's a full assault," Phosani said. "They think they have broken us, now they will try and storm the walls."

Ascertes cast about, looking for an order to give, feeling out of place simply standing as the tagma readied itself. But everything was falling into position. They had all been waiting long enough for this.

There was a rustling of feathers, and with a shout the icyene who had been assembling behind the walls launched themselves skywards, rising up above the ramparts. Ascertes tracked them, looking for any hint that the queen was among them, but he could see no sign of her helmet's crest or the brilliance of the Sunspear.

He was afraid. His mouth was dry, his hands sweating and shaking. He tried to wipe them on the hem of his undershirt, visions of his spear slipping from his grip invading his mind. That would be such a stupid way to die. Not befitting of Queen Efaritay's husband. He wondered where she was, looking again along the walls and up to the skies for her.

He had hardly seen Efaritay since she had made it back to Hallowvale. Whenever they had spoken, she had seemed almost in a daze. The battle before the retreat had shaken her and he didn't know how to dispel the shadow that had fallen over her.

She had taken to spending all her time in the arboretum. Ascertes knew he had to tell her to find her strength, her courage, but he had never been the one who had to do that. It had always been the other way round.

The trio of siege towers had entered the dead ground before the walls. The Zamorakians advanced along with them, blocks of infantry behind and on either flank. They had their shields up and interlocked, a slow-moving testudo that looked almost impervious to arrows and slingshots. Their cornua blared, a deep, ugly note that countered the clear peals of the salpinx.

The sphendonitai manning the walls began to loose their projectiles. Arrows and slingshots rained down on the approaching towers and infantry, clattering off timber and parma shields. The icyene who had taken wing above the walls added their own arrows to the hail.

The response was immediate. From slats along the front and sides of the siege towers, Zamorakian crossbowmen started to shoot back. Ascertes saw the first volley rattle and clack off the parapet to his left and right. A sphendonitai reeled away just after loosing his own shot, clutching at the bolt buried in his shoulder.

"Behind the parapet, Your Majesty," Phosani advised. He shook his head, refusing to leave the gap in the ramparts and render himself blind to what was coming.

He felt helpless, able only to watch the slow, methodical Zamorakian advance. It was immediately clear that with the artillery they had mounted on the citadel's towers destroyed, they would not be able to check the legionaries before they hit the base of the walls.

But it wasn't only machinery that defended Hallowvale. Ascertes heard a series of arcane phrases being called from amongst the troops packed behind the ramparts to his left. He made out one of the tagma's rune-casters, dressed in the orange himation robes of a fire summoner, holding aloft her staff. The runestone embedded in its blackened head flared, sorcerous flames coruscating above it into a fireball. With a shriek that sounded as though she herself were burning, the summoner swung her staff and launched the ball of flame at the nearest of the three towers.

It raced through the air. For a second Ascertes feared it was going to miss. But it struck the tower near its pinnacle and exploded in a roaring surge of flame and smoke. When it had cleared, part of the tower was still burning, and the fire leapt and spread.

A cheer went up from the defenders, one that Ascertes joined. The tower's progress faltered as those pushing it stopped. Soon the whole top was burning like a huge torch, black smoke roiling off it.

As the cheering around him faded, Ascertes heard the screaming of the Zamorakians trapped inside. Several managed to get out through the top, plummeting with terrible screams to the ground below.

The instinctive horror that Ascertes felt at such a fate was swiftly seared away by the rising battle-lust. He no longer felt afraid, but exultant, gripped with defiance and determination.

"We'll burn them all!" he found himself shouting. More cheers went up, and he looked towards the fire summoner once more, finding her replacing the burned-out runestone in her safe with another, the sizzling shard that remained of the first gripped in her thickly gloved hands. Her face was flushed with the heat she was channelling.

She began to chant again, the warriors nearest her raising their shields to cover the openings in the parapet, protecting her from the hail of crossbow bolts now battering at that section of wall. Ascertes held his breath as she swept her staff in an arc above her head once more, conjuring a second fireball and launching it at the next tower.

Every face on the walls seemed to follow the blazing comet as it arced towards its target. A cheer was on the lips of several of the sphendonitai around Ascertes just before it struck.

The acclimations died amidst a cracking sound. A disc of pitch black materialised from nowhere in front of the siege tower, just ahead of the fireball. The blazing fury was swallowed up in the blackness, continuing to hurtle away into the void that then disappeared as swiftly as it had been conjured, leaving no evidence of its own existence, or that of the fireball.

The necromancers that accompanied the Zamorakian legions were working to protect the assault. The fire summoner stared at the tower then, with a grim expression, began to chant again.

More crossbow bolts cracked against the parapets. Ascertes saw several of the icyene above them hit. Efaritay wasn't among the flocks.

The Zamorakians were nearing the walls. He heard Phosani and her lieutenants bellowing commands, ordering their hypaspists to close up and keep their shields high. One of the siege towers was angled to reach the wall just to Ascertes' right, another to his left. He gripped his doru tighter, then heard what sounded like a monstrous intake of breath from off to his right. He turned in time to see the pyrokutor being unleashed.

The Imcando war machine had survived the Zamorakian bombardment, protected by its own section of parapet, and the fact it was sited on the walls rather than one of the towers. Its dwarf rolled its muzzle forward past the scarred embrasure, angled it as best he could and, with the depression of bellows and the turning of a great wheel in its brass flank, it fired.

There was a roar like the wrath of the gods unleashed, and a wave of heat washed over Ascertes, making him flinch. A stream of liquid purple flame launched from the blackened muzzle of the pyrokutor, slamming with wood-splintering force into the right side of the siege tower just to the war machine's right.

The effect of the weapon was instant, and horrific. The purple flames transmitted in an eyeblink across half of the tower, running like wildfire through a tinder-dry forest. In mere seconds the entire structure was blazing, the Zamorakians around its base scattering desperately, some of them struck by gobbets of the burning substance.

No one cheered. He stared in fascinated horror as the tower collapsed in on itself in a roaring plume of smoke and purple fire, an acrid stink accompanying its demise. The tower struck by the fire summoner's magics was still crackling fitfully, yet the pyrokutor had demolished the second construct in mere moments. The dwarfs were already resetting the nightmarish weapon, pumping the bellows and pouring a viscous-looking liquid from a clay amphora into one of its tanks.

"With me," Ascertes heard Phosani shouting. The White Wolf was leading a section of her hypaspists left across the walls, towards where the final siege tower was now looming above the parapets. It was clear the pyrokutor wouldn't be ready in time, and even if it was, it wouldn't be able to get an angle on the third tower.

Ascertes found himself following the Wolves. The ramparts in front of the siege tower were packed with Saradominist soldiery now, shouting and beating their spears on their shields. Arrows were thudding against the tower's flanks, adding to the bristling forest already studding it.

He realised what he had noted earlier covering the front of the tower weren't red and white banners. Up close, he saw they were wings – icyene wings, torn from those killed or captured earlier in the invasion and now nailed as trophies to the war engine.

The ramp fell. There was the crack of wood meeting stone, followed by a roar and the thunder of feet as the Zamorakians stormed out onto the walls. They were met by spears, thrusting up into the attackers, scoring off parma or driving through thighs and stomachs.

Momentum carried the assault over the battlements and onto the walkway. Several hypaspists were trapped under those they had impaled, as the legionaries behind stepped on their comrades to leap down amongst the Saradominist ranks.

The carnage was absolute. Warriors were forced against one another, no room to hack and barely space to stab, the injured and the dying held up by the tightness of the press. Ascertes had seen battles before, but he had never been involved in a storm assault. He was carried forward as the hypaspists charged in on either side of the Zamorakians forcing their way onto the walls. His spear, held upright, was useless, so he simply let go of it and managed to shove back against the flow until he could at least draw his xiphos.

There was a scream as someone – Ascertes couldn't see who – was shoved off the wall. A crossbow bolt slashed just overhead, another ricocheted from the top of the parapet just to his right. He saw a flash of steel, followed by a jet of blood. The hypaspist in front of him slumped back against his shield, his shoulder carved open by a spatha. Ascertes screamed, trying to twist away, but couldn't find the space to move back, so the dead man remained trapped as the legionary, with no room of his own to pull his weapon free and hack again, sawed the blade down savagely until the Saradominist half collapsed.

Ascertes now faced the hypaspist's killer. The Zamorakian snarled, face flushed red with battle frenzy, struggling to free his blade from the corpse trapped between him and Ascertes.

The king of Hallowvale drove his xiphos through the man's throat. Blood jetted across the short sword's blade, and the Zamorakian made an ugly choking noise, eyes wide and bulging, mouth opening and closing again before turning crimson.

Ascertes yelled and yanked his sword free. The legionary fell against the hypaspist he had killed, black-crested helmet knocking against Ascertes' aspis. Another Zamorakian was about to leap from the ramparts, almost on top of him, but an icyene arrow from above punched down through the back of his neck, causing him to fall off into the gap in the crenelations.

The sphendonitai and prodromoi were sending a blizzard of missiles into the ramp connecting the siege tower to the walls, turning the small space into a deathtrap. Experienced in storm drills, the Zamorakian legionaries were forming a testudo as they left the tower's protection, shields raised overhead and on either side, but the sheer volume of shots was finding gaps, sending men sprawling across the wooden boards or tumbling, screaming, from the sides before they could reach the wall.

"Kill them," Ascertes heard a voice bellowing. The crushing press around him seemed to redouble as the ordo of the wolf hacked and stabbed at those legionaries who had gained the wall, any finesse and discipline lost. The ramparts were being turned into a butcher's block, the stones underfoot slippery with blood, the dying trampled with the dead.

Ascertes wanted to shout, but the breath was being crushed out of him. He was driven forward, into the maelstrom, right beneath where the tower ramp had lowered. He knew he was as likely to be crushed to death as he was to be slain by a Zamorakian sword.

A legionary fell on top of him, a sphendonitai arrow in her eye. He heaved her off with her shield, just in time to meet the next Zamorakian. This one was very much alive, roaring as he slammed his spatha down from where he stood on the edge of the parapet. It bit into the rim of Ascertes' aspis as he tried to free his right arm from where it was pinned to his side by the press, caught between the need to kill his attacker and defend himself from another frenzied swing.

There was a bark of effort from his left, and the legionary suddenly toppled back off the parapet with a scream, his left foot chopped off at the shin – the bloody appendage remained sitting on the stonework. Ascertes stared at it, before he was shoved back, dangerously close to the edge of the wall.

A tall hypaspist had taken his place, the wolf pelt she wore over her shoulders matted with blood. When the next Zamorakian tried to jump down, she simply smashed him aside with her shield, knocking the next on the immediate left off the siege tower's ramp.

"Spears," the hypaspist shouted, her voice carrying clear over the chaos. "Use your damn spears! Drive them back!"

The other hypaspists around Ascertes stabbed their dorus up at the Zamorakians still pouring across the ramp. With their shields up over their heads protecting themselves from the prodromoi shooting from above, the legionaries had little to protect their legs and lower torsos. After a few frantic seconds a hedge of spear tips were meeting the onrushing Zamorakians, those behind shoving their comrades in front onto the wicked steel. Impaled or thrown over the ramp's edges – they had nowhere else to go.

There was a roar, and Ascertes felt a blast of heat hit him, making him flinch. Fire roiled and snarled against the flank of the tower before quickly igniting along its right side, running along it almost to the ramp. The Wolves raised their shields, warding away the wave of heat, and Ascertes understood that the fire summoner had been able to unleash the power of her runestone again. Whatever dark sorceries had protected the tower the first time had been unmade or overwhelmed.

"Hold firm," he heard Phosani shouting from somewhere to the right. The last legionaries were flinging themselves desperately against the spears and shields of the hypaspists, left with a choice between steel and fire. They died all the same.

Finally, the flood of bodies stopped coming. The Zamorakians within were either all dead, or had managed to scramble back down the ladders and out of the doomed construct. The top of the siege tower was starting to burn, the heat of it forcing the Saradominists to yield that part of the wall. Ascertes dragged in a breath as the pressure around him finally began to ease, only to choke on ash and smoke.

It was impossible to walk past the parapets without treading on the dead. He stumbled on a splintered parma, close to the edge of the wall. A hand grasped his arm and tugged him back.

"Careful, Your Majesty," said the woman. Ascertes recognised the tall, scarred Wolf who had saved him from the Zamorakian on the ramparts. His mind had been unable to process how he knew her at the time, but now her name came to him, recalled from meetings in the throne room. She was one of Phosani's lieutenants.

"Rhea."

"I'm honoured that you remember me, my king," the Wolf said, inclining her head slightly. Ascertes fought for the right words, then reached to his waist.

"Then let me honour you further," he said. He had remembered the shard of the blisterwood tree, tucked into his belt. Efaritay had assured him that one cut with it would be enough to immolate any vampyre, but to him it seemed like a desperate measure, and currently of little use fighting human Zamorakian legionaries in ferocious clashes of steel. Even with the blisterwood, he had none of the light abilities of the icyene – he suspected if he ever did encounter a vyre, he'd be as good as dead anyway.

Still, he could think of no other way of thanking Rhea for saving his life. He suddenly felt as though the gift was foolish, but pressed it into her hand anyway.

"I think that Zamorakian would have staved my head in if you hadn't brought him down," he said truthfully. "Consider this a gift from both the queen and I. If you ever encounter the vyre, may it prove useful."

Rhea looked at the shard of white wood in her shield hand, her expression inscrutable, then offered another short bow.

"My thanks, Your Majesty. With your permission, I will see to my hypaspists. The next assault will likely be soon."

"Of course," Ascertes said, thankful the grizzled warrior was excusing herself. She began to stride along the wall, shouting for volunteers to get the wounded down off the walkway.

Ascertes spent a short while staring at the burning siege tower. It began to collapse, charred timbers giving way, a geyser of flames and ash heralding it as it fell down from the wall. The nearest sphendonitai and hypaspists moved in to begin the grisly work of clearing the bloody walkway, tossing the Zamorakian corpses over the wall and beginning to ferry the Saradominist dead down to the city, so they did not impede the efforts of their still-living comrades.

Ascertes watched them, and smelled the blood and burned skin and hair, and heard the moaning of those wounded still being helped away, and the sobbing of a young sphendonitai who had just found a friend or relative among the dead. He thought about Rhea's parting words, and looked out beyond the parapet. The Zamorakian saps were once more full, a second assault wave ready, this one bearing ladders.

It was only the beginning.

TWENTY-THREE

Ranis invited Lady Verzik Vitur to visit the prisoner.
He had been working on the old man for some time.
It had been clear from the reports of his cohort as well
as the excellence of his panoply that he was an honoured
warrior. Ranis hadn't wanted to reveal that he had a captive
before he had extracted what he wanted from him, but his
cohort's commander had believed the prisoner was a senior
officer among the Saradominists.

The admission of the man's name and rank was the first
indication that he was beginning to break. He was Lysander,
justiciar of the unicorn. Ranis had never bothered to learn
the intricacies of the Saradominist command structure, but
he knew the ones who identified with different beasts were
considered elite and devout.

Lysander had not shared his name willingly. Ranis had
hypnotised him, using vampyre abilities that were part
arcane, part raw predation. Drakan was, of course, the

master of such arts, but Ranis could bend prey to his will too, provided their strength was eroded.

He had done that by tearing Lysander's flesh and breaking his bones. Had he been an icyene, Ranis could not have doused the light within him even with previous injuries, but this one? For all his faith, he was only human. And though he had resisted every demand Ranis had made of him, he had not been strong enough to stop himself from falling under the vyre's spell.

That was when Ranis had understood just what he had won.

"You are a tease, my vyrelord," Verzik Vitur declared before entering the tent. "Luring me out here without telling me the reason. Our broods will start to gossip!"

"As though they don't already, my dear," Ranis said, feigning the same affection as Vitur. Their partnership was symbiotic, though each might have called the other parasitic. As Lowerniel Drakan's younger brother, Ranis needed allies among the vyre nobility who could be relied upon, a political power base that would stop him from becoming an irrelevance when compared with his sister. On the other hand, any vyrelord who could call him an ally ostensibly had a direct route to Drakan, even if it was clear that Ranis overplayed how much respect and influence he could demand from his brother. Vitur appreciated such a balance more than most, and had consequently become one of Ranis's most reliable allies among the ever-shifting politics of Vampyrium.

Vitur reminded Ranis of a leech in more ways than one, a parasite perpetually gorged with blood. Unlike Ranis or

Vanescula, she was more heavy-set, and grew bloated when she fed. Even on campaign she dressed more like a court noblewoman than a warrior, wrapped in fine purple silks, velvets and furs, her face powdered and rouged. Ranis had never quite established if it was all merely an affectation, designed to lure others into thinking her vain and vacuous, or if she truly did think she could emulate the beauty of other species' nobility.

"I smell blood," Vitur said as she pushed her way into the tent. "You haven't brought me a treat, have you?"

"Not precisely," Ranis said as he gestured at the prisoner. "This is Lysander, justiciar of the unicorn, captain of the armies of Saradomin. He was... wise enough not to fight to the death on that hilltop a few weeks ago. I have had him here ever since."

Vitur chirred with intrigue and delight, shifting her bulk closer. Lysander was still bound, head bowed, his flesh caked with dried blood and his face swollen and discoloured. He groaned and stirred as the two vyre inspected him.

"My my, you've kept this quiet, haven't you?" Vitur said as she got dangerously close to the prisoner. Ranis remained by her side, ready in an instant to restrain her if she suddenly gave in to the desire to feed.

"I merely wished to make sure I had acquired something valuable before advertising it," Ranis said.

"And I assume, if you are now sharing this with me, you know its worth?"

"An approximate value, yes," Ranis smirked. "He might look old for his kind, and broken now, but he is one of their senior commanders. He knows things about Hallowvale and its defenders that even my dear brother does not."

"Wonderful," Vitur said, making a show of lifting Lysander's head to better inspect him. Though she hid it well, Ranis could sense the tension in her. She hadn't come here expecting this, and she was now having to choose her words carefully. She had yet to work out if Ranis was plotting behind his brother's back – simply keeping the knowledge of this prisoner from Drakan was dangerous, and Vitur was now complicit in it. Ranis found watching her try to hide her sudden caution almost amusing.

"Just listen to what he can tell us," he instructed her, deliberately playing on her fears. He motioned her to one side and moved so that his face was just in front of Lysander's, snatching him by his thin, matted white hair to keep his head tilted back.

"Look into my eyes, Lysander," he whispered, dropping the tone of his voice while tapping into a keening noise that rose from deep within his throat, a sound not consciously audible to humans but effective in dulling their thoughts. "Hear my voice, and converse with me."

One of Lysander's eyes was glued shut by blood and bruised swelling, but the other snapped open and fixed on Ranis, who murmured a low, slow incantation, further easing aside the shattered remnants of the justiciar's mental defences, the words matching the heartbeat Ranis could hear thudding in his ears. He put one hand lightly on the human's cheek, their eyes now inches apart, his whispers mere susurrations, the ancient tongue of Vampyrium incomprehensible yet alluring to mortal ears.

He saw Lysander's eye lose focus.

"Now, tell Lady Vitur what you told me," Ranis said, taking a step back. "Tell her about the paths into Hallowvale, the ones that do not pass through any gateway."

"The tunnels," Lysander said slowly, his voice a dry rasp. "There are many tunnels beneath the city."

"Go on," Ranis said, casting a sideways glance at Vitur. He could feel her tension, but also her anticipation.

"Some were built below the palace, to allow the royal family to escape if need be," Lysander said. "Few know of them, so they have few guards. There are more all across the city. Under the citadel, under the bank, the arboretum. They link with sewers and crypts and other hidden spaces."

"Isn't all that just fascinating?" Ranis said to Vitur, who mustered up a smile.

"You really have outdone yourself this time, my vyrelord," she said, putting a hand on his arm. He fought the instinctive desire to bat her away.

"I think we may have found a means to bring this drudgery to a speedier conclusion," he said. "Shall we inform my brother?"

He was being outright cruel now, practically taunting her – did she follow his lead and risk accusations of treason in exchange for the glory of being the one who broke open Hallowvale, or did she play the safer hand, satisfied that Ranis would include her when he shared his discovery with Drakan and reaped the rewards?

"We should tell him," she said eventually. "The sooner Hallowvale falls, the sooner we can feast."

Typical Vitur, falling down on the side of caution. Ranis had predicted as much, in fact he had intended to tell Drakan from the beginning. Now though he had Vitur as collateral. If the information proved unreliable or any plan built around it failed, he would ensure she was the first to take the blame, even if the trade-off meant allowing her some of the glory.

"Come then," he said. "The broods have been instructed to gather, so that gives us the perfect opportunity."

He hissed an arcane phrase and Lysander's head slumped forward like a puppet whose strings had been cut, the hypnosis broken.

"Don't worry, old man," he whispered in the justiciar's ear. "A few more hours and I'll be sure you receive your just reward."

✦ ✦ ✦

The vyrelords and ladies attended their master as they had done most nights since arriving outside the city, flocking to the toll building that Drakan had made his lair. The structure lay on the road just west of the city, a place where merchants had paid the tithes required to trade within Hallowvale before passing the walls. The main room, where the emporoi once queued before the tithing table, was spacious enough to accommodate the most senior vyre.

There was a vault beneath the floor, used to store the tithes prior to their transportation into the city. That was where

Drakan emerged from, a hush falling as, despite his great size, he materialised before his underlings in absolute silence.

Drakan had only attended a few such gatherings since the siege lines had been completed, and when present he rarely spoke. He seemed bored with proceedings, happy to let the legion progress with the siege at their own pace. Where he went when he was absent, none knew.

Ranis was relieved to find his brother attending. Revealing what he knew would have been considerably less impactful had he been absent, and now that Vitur knew it would be a matter of hours before it became common knowledge. Everything was falling into place.

Instead of speaking right away, he allowed the mortals to go through their usual dull reports. Senior legionary officers were present, as they were at every such gathering, describing the latest progress in the siege works. Ranis was almost wholly unaware of what they were saying, his focus fixed on Drakan.

His attitude was the same as it had been since the start of the invasion. He seemed disinterested. He sat in the tithing chair behind the table at the end of the room and simply stared into the ether, as though watching or listening to something that no one else, even his fellow vampyres, could detect. When the mortals delivered their reports, they addressed Vanescula, who was stood at his right side and to all intents and purposes was acting with his authority. The captain of the vyreguard, Korgax, stood on Drakan's left.

Vanescula, always Vanescula, Ranis thought bitterly. His sister did so love to be second, after their older brother.

Well, the time had finally come to change the hierarchy of the House of Drakan.

"I have a report to make," he said when the legionary officer had finished speaking, cutting over Vanescula before she could call upon the next speaker. "One that I think we should all hear."

He took to the centre of the floor, gratified by the fact Drakan was now deigning to look at him as he spoke.

"I have lately come across information that, if used wisely, could bring an end to this siege within a matter of days, if not this very night."

There was some hissing and ticking. Ranis pushed on, giving his sister the sort of self-satisfied smirk he knew would infuriate her.

"There is a weakness within the city's defences, one which I now have complete knowledge of. There are tunnels beneath Hallowvale, including their citadel and under the royal palace of the upstart icyene queen."

Now the room was gripped by full on, chirring unrest. Vanescula's voice cut through it, cold as a frost witch's curse.

"How do you know this?"

"You are not the only one with a mind for strategy, my sister," he said, intending to wring every ounce of enjoyment he could out of the moment. He half expected Drakan to demand he stop being so obtuse, but His-Dark-Self simply watched his little brother, red eyes unblinking.

"A prisoner was taken by the brave soldiery of my cohort," he went on eventually, deigning to cast a glance at the legionary officers present. "A senior commander among the

Saradominist vermin. He has proven... amenable to my lines of questioning."

"Where was this prisoner taken?" Vanescula pressed. "And who are they?"

"Lysander, justiciar of the unicorn," Ranis admitted. "He was captured as the Saradominists fled from that hilltop they wasted so much sweet, fresh blood defending."

"The hill was taken almost two weeks ago," Vanescula pointed out. "And you are only telling us about this now?"

Poor Vanescula. For all her supposed skill when it came to positioning herself within the Drakan court, she was terribly predictable when she got angry.

"I wished to ensure the prisoner was of some worth before troubling my Lord Drakan with him," Ranis said. "But after interrogating him, and seeking the advice of the noble Lady Vitur, who has been of great assistance to me in this matter, I believe what he has told us is pertinent."

He swept his arm to indicate Vitur, who was standing off to one side. She smiled and inclined her head to the gathering, happy to play a part in the plan.

"The Saradominists have little presence in these tunnels," Ranis went on. "If they can be broken into, we will have a way into the city that bypasses the walls. No part of Hallowvale would be beyond us."

"Everybody out."

They were the first two words Drakan had spoken since the beginning of the meeting.

"Everyone, except Ranis," he added.

Nobody said anything. Ranis felt an intoxicating flush of triumph as he locked eyes with his sister and watched her accept that she had lost this particular battle. She dared linger longer than everyone else but, finally, turned and stormed out, refusing to meet Ranis's gaze.

Soon it was only the two males of the Drakan line left in the tithing room. Even Korgax of the vyreguard had withdrawn.

Ranis began to speak, intending to reassure Drakan that he had not kept Lysander's existence a secret out of scorn towards his older brother. He never got the chance to explain. Drakan moved, faster than even a fellow vyre could follow, out of his chair and over the tithing table. Ranis found himself pinned to the floor beneath the powerful weight of his brother, one hand holding him by the throat, another snatching his wrist.

He choked, trying to get the words of contrition out, knowing better than to struggle. Drakan ignored him, simply bringing his hand up against Ranis's face. He sniffed deeply, around the tips of Ranis's clawed fingers.

Then, as suddenly as he had struck, Drakan let go. He disappeared through the tithe house's door and out into the night, not having said a single word.

Ranis lay on his back, panting, staring up at nothing as he tried to work out what had just happened.

Drakan had been scenting him for blood. His sense of smell was more potent than any other vampyre's. He could pick up a trail from the slightest fleck.

Ranis snarled and scrambled to his feet. He dashed out after his brother, taking wing as soon as he was outside, realising what he was about to do.

+ ◆ +

Ranis was too late.

By the time he caught up with Drakan, Lysander was already dead.

Ranis's brother stood in his tent, relinquishing the justiciar's broken neck just as Ranis rushed inside. He stared from the body of the human to the hulking vyrelord, and uttered a single word, riven with anger and disbelief.

"Why?"

"To teach you a lesson you should already know," Drakan said. "To not keep secrets from your master."

Ranis did something he immediately regretted. In a fit of fury, he tried to strike his brother.

Drakan caught his arm by the wrist and simply held him. Ranis went very still.

"Were anyone else watching us, you would be dead right now," Drakan told him.

"Forgive me," Ranis said hoarsely.

"I will consider it," Drakan said, and let go. Ranis hurried back a few paces, as though doing so would protect him.

"He was valuable," he said bitterly, looking past Drakan at Lysander's limp corpse.

"Another reason to make an example of him," Drakan said. "Do not worry. I ensured he lived up to his full potential. You did well to capture him."

Ranis damned himself for feeling pride. Each of the three siblings – Ranis did not consider the fourth, the coward

Draynor, to be a true Drakan any longer – possessed their own, preferred style of manipulation, and mixing threat with praise was Drakan's. Ranis wished he wasn't beholden to him, and wished he did not feel delight whenever his brother seemed to notice him.

"Then we'll use the tunnels?" he asked hopefully.

"We shall," Drakan said. "We will dig our way into them, and strike from below, directly at the icyene queen and her family. With them slain or taken, the city will fall."

That was what Ranis had wanted to hear. Even if Drakan had slain his trophy, all the vyrelords had heard him reveal the tunnels' existence, and all would know that when they stormed Hallowvale from below, it was Ranis's plan that was being enacted. Everything was still going as he had hoped after all.

"Let me lead the attack," he said, hoping to secure the glory he craved.

"You shall," Drakan said. "But I will send Korgax with you."

"I have no need of a matron to hold my hand while I…" Ranis began, trailing off when he looked at Drakan.

"You are not to slaughter everyone you meet above the tunnels. It is unlikely the queen herself will be there, so taking her kin prisoner will be of greater service than raw killing. I trust Korgax will remind you of that."

Ranis knew better than to argue further, realising it was time to cut his losses.

"Just tell me when we reach the tunnels, my lord," he said.

✦ ✦ ✦

Vanescula sought out Drakan as the day began to dawn.

She was permitted by Korgax to descend into the vault beneath the tithing house. She briefly thought she had managed that rarest of things – finding her older brother while he was slumbering. All vyre, even the greatest, preferred to sleep in the caskets that their kind inhabited on Vampyrium, and failing that, in bare soil. The floor of the vault had been packed with the latter, but when Vanescula stepped down onto it, she could find no sign of Drakan in the loamy darkness.

"Why do you disturb me?" Drakan demanded from behind Vanescula. She turned in a flash. Drakan loomed over her, his expression cold and hard. If he had been slumbering, there was no sign of it.

"My apologies," Vanescula said, offering a bow. "I was… troubled. I came seeking clarity."

"Let me make assumptions," Drakan responded. "You are distraught that our brother has achieved something, and concerned that he will use his success to usurp your power among the other vyrelords?"

"You knew, didn't you?" Vanescula demanded, refusing to be drawn by her brother's incisiveness. "Ranis hasn't managed this by his own. And even if Vitur has played a part in concocting his scheme, I don't believe they could have been aware that there were tunnels beneath Hallowvale, while you were not."

"I did not consider it a particularly great feat of logic."

"That's why you've barely lifted a hand since the start of the invasion," Vanescula went on. She was angry, and knew she was dangerously close to speaking out of turn, but she detested feeling like a fool.

"The siege doesn't matter, does it?" she said. "Not really. It's a distraction. The Blood Altar lies in the tunnels under Hallowvale, and reaching it is your only concern."

"True," Drakan allowed. "Ranis has proved useful in one sense. His prisoner knew the location of the altar, though Ranis had not the wit to ask about it. He does not know the old stories. Now I need only access those tunnels, and it will be mine."

"You would let Ranis claim it alongside you?"

"Of course not. I will indulge his little plot and allow him to try and seize the icyene queen and her family. The Blood Altar may be the true prize here, but taking them will unlock the city. Hallowvale must still fall for my plans to reach fruition."

"You could have slain Efaritay," Vanescula pointed out. "But now capturing her is the objective?"

"Not just her, but her family," Drakan said. "The queen is a slave to the love she has for her little human husband. If her family are threatened, she will submit, and when she does the city's fall will be even more assured. But one way or another, I will have the altar."

Vanescula considered her brother's words, then spread her arms.

"And where do I fit into all of your carefully laid plans, my lord?"

"You will know if I have need of you," Drakan said. "This sting you have suffered is good for you. If you were too prideful, you would become like Ranis. Always consider the wider game being played, sister."

There was truth in that, Vanescula supposed. Ranis had made his play, yet the arrogant fool was still oblivious to the true reason the vyre had marched upon Hallowvale. There were still plenty of moves to be made, and a little time to make them.

Vanescula inclined her head once more and retreated, leaving Drakan to the darkness of his lair.

TWENTY-FOUR

◄◆►

L uken could not find Akeron in his chambers.

He had gone to assist the archpriest in getting dressed and preparing for the day's duties, as he did every morning, only to discover the room abandoned. Visions of Zamorakian infiltrators and the pale, terrible monsters from his nightmares filled his thoughts.

He hurried through the Hallowed Sepulchre's upper corridors, wondering if he should alert the hypaspists of the unicorn. Instead, he found the last thing he expected after leaving the dorm wing.

The place was abuzz with activity, not congregants or a service, but the priesthood, seemingly out in full force. They were working throughout the corridors and chambers of the temple, mostly at the many stone statues that populated the holy spaces. They seemed to have opened recesses in the plinths or were packing some sort of material into cavities concealed in the mouths or arms of the figures.

"Have you seen the archpriest?" Luken asked one of the priests he recognised, Istarkus. The Saradominist directed him to one of the second-level corridors where, sure enough, he found Akeron. The archpriest was fully dressed and busy directing the efforts of more church laymen by the torchlight burning in the lower levels, snapping at them to pick up the pace.

"There you are," he said brusquely as he caught sight of Luken. "You're late!"

"I couldn't find you," Luken protested.

"Well, now you have," Akeron said. "Stay close. I have something I must show you."

"What is this?" Luken asked as he joined the archpriest. "What are they doing to the statues?"

"Preparing them for what is to come," Akeron said.

"What does that mean?" Luken asked, refusing to be dissuaded by Akeron's usual gruff opaqueness.

"They are setting traps," Akeron said. "To slow down the vyre and keep this ground hallowed for as long as possible."

Luken began to say that surely the vyre wouldn't ever reach the Hallowed Church in the first place, but he stopped himself, realising he sounded like a child. Akeron's inference was clear. From the reports that trickled into the city from the walls, the Zamorakian assaults were relentless, near-constant. The longer the siege ground on, the more likely it was that the defences would crumble. Luken had tried not to think about that – it filled him with gut-churning fear – but he knew he would soon have to face reality.

The priesthood of Saradomin were preparing for their last stand.

"Follow me," Akeron said. He still held his star staff, and with a muttered word he ignited it, summoning Saradomin's glory. Grasping it, he led Luken towards the nearest stairwell. They began to descend.

"This sacred space was built by the icyene, as you well know," Akeron declared as they went. "But do you know the tenets that must be adhered to if it is ever threatened with destruction, or worse, defilement?"

"No," Luken admitted.

"That is as it should be," Akeron said. "After all, you are still a junior illuminator, and diligent though you are, such grave matters are still beyond you. But not for much longer. The humans occupy the upper crypts, and the icyene the lower, but which is lowest of all?"

"The tombs of the priesthood," Luken said. "And the grand hallowed coffin, the final resting place where each archpriest is interred after their passing."

"So you have been paying attention," Akeron said with the barest hint of humour. He was starting to wheeze as he continued to descend, struggling on the seemingly endless stairs, but when Luken tried to offer an arm he warded him away with a grunt.

"I will be making my final journey to that coffin soon enough, vyre or not," he declared. "Perhaps I'm making it right now!"

"Do not say such things, archpriest," Luken said sternly.

It was growing colder and darker the deeper they went,

Akeron's staff now the only source of light. They were about to pass by the fourth floor, the lowest point he had ever been within the Hallowed Sepulchre. The fifth and final level was forbidden to junior illuminators. Luken kept close to Akeron, not daring to voice that fact.

They stepped out into a long, low stone corridor. Alcoves lined it, some bearing more graven statues of icyene and human holy men and women, others stone sarcophagi. These were the final resting places of the most senior priesthood, Luken knew, filled with the sacred bones of those who had kept the light of Saradomin alive in Hallowvale, down the centuries.

As they had done below the palace, the torches set into the walls flared into life as they began to pass through the crypt. It was painfully quiet – Luken felt as though the mere scuffing of his feet were loud enough to awake the hallowed dead.

Would he too be interred down here one day, amidst the stony silence? Given current circumstances, he found it unlikely.

Akeron led him on, to the heart of the Sepulchre's depths. A ring of torches ignited around the centre of an open chamber, brightly illuminating the object lying between them. It was another sarcophagus, the grandest Luken had ever seen, a great slab of stone painted blue, its flanks inlaid with precious stones that formed the Stars of Saradomin, a holy constellation that glittered in the firelight.

"This is where my mortal remains are set to spend the rest of eternity," Akeron rasped. "It is a great honour."

"Of course, archpriest," Luken said, voice small as he gazed from the tall pillars reaching up into the flickering shadows of the chamber's vault, then back down at the hallowed grand coffin. He didn't dare ask Akeron why he had brought him down here, in defiance of the sacred rules.

"When I lie in that, it will be atop the bones of those who have gone before," the archpriest carried on. "An ossuary, secured by the stars of the Lord of Light. And if the vyre breach the defences, I will do so while still living."

Luken stared at him, wondering if he had misunderstood.

"What do you mean, archpriest?"

"The commandments are clear," Akeron replied, looking at the sarcophagus rather than Luken. "If the forces of darkness overrun the city, the priesthood of the Hallowed Sepulchre are required to arm its defences, then inter themselves in its depths. That way none will be able to disarm them, and the sanctity of the Sepulchre will remain. The vyre filth will not defile our flesh and blood."

"That is insane," Luken said. Akeron shot him a withering look.

"It is holy writ, boy. All the priests are preparing for this end. We who have tended to this place all our lives. We are ready to finish it at the appointed time, and in the correct way. None of us will fail in this sacred duty."

"Saradomin will not let this happen," Luken said, feeling a bitter upwelling of emotions. "He cannot! There is still time for him to come!"

"Saradomin sees a picture bigger than all of us," Akeron said. "Whatever happens is his will, and by it the light shall endure. Do not forget that. Do not question it."

Luken fought back tears, cleared his throat, and looked Akeron in the eye.

"Will that be my fate as well? Am I to be interred?"

"No."

"Why not? I know I am only a junior illuminator, but I am still part of the clergy. In time I would have become a full priest. Do you not think I am worthy? Have I not shown my faith in the Lord of Light? All my life, this is all I've ever known."

Akeron cracked the base of his staff off the floor, ending the mounting diatribe before it could go any further.

"I have a duty," he said. "So do you, and it is not to know only darkness in your last, suffocating moments. Do not forget the value of the knowledge you hold."

"The Blood Altar," he said.

"Yes," Akeron wheezed. "Justiciar Lysander did not return to Hallowvale. He led the rearguard, and was surely slain. That means you and I are the only people in this city who know of the Blood Altar's existence."

"What must I do?" Luken asked, a sudden, cold clarity gripping him, thawing the icy panic he had known just before.

"I have been doing further research, based on your suggestion," Akeron said. Luken frowned.

"What suggestion?"

"You talked of the power of the Everlight, and how it might be used against the altar. I have explained why I would not dare destroy the artefact itself, lest it unleash something terrible. Perhaps though, we might break the means of accessing it. The skulls that act as a ferry between the tunnels and the altar's chamber. That is the duty I am giving to you, should the city fall."

"How?" Luken asked. "You said yourself, we cannot move the Everlight below ground, and I am no sorcerer or rune-caster."

"The Everlight is not the only tool of Saradomin's grace we have in our possession," Akeron said, raising the star staff. Its light intensified, making Luken blink.

"You will bear this after I have been sealed away, down into the tunnels," the archpriest said. "You know the Prayers of the Seven Dawns? And the First and Final Wisdom of the Book of Light?"

"By rote."

"Then you have the power to summon the light of Saradomin's star, if your faith is pure."

"But is it?" Luken wondered. To his surprise, Akeron gave a wheezing chuckle.

"The fact that you doubt yourself probably means it is. Here—"

The archpriest proffered his sacred staff to Luken and, after a moment of reverent nervousness, the junior illuminator accepted it.

"Speak the hallowed words, boy," Akeron instructed as the light shining from the staff flickered and dimmed. Luken started to recite prayers he had learned as a child, gripping its haft and trying to focus on the glory of the Lord of Light. Sure enough, its illumination became stable again. Luken stared up at it in awe, amazed at the thought that he was carrying the staff of the archpriest himself.

"Is it truly faith, or sorcery?" he asked.

"Where one ends and another begins is not a matter for us to debate," Akeron declared before taking the staff back. "What matters is that you are as worthy of the Lord of Light as I am. When you reach the portal of the skulls, call upon our god and strike it with the staff. That is the only hope I have for damaging the way to the altar."

"What if it doesn't work?"

"Then we will have done all we can. You must save yourself."

Luken was silent, and Akeron gripped his shoulder.

"This is a last recourse," he said, clearly trying to lighten some of the burden he had heaped upon Luken. "Hope is not yet lost. The walls are strong, and our defenders are brave. The Everlight still shines. As long as it does the vyre will not walk the streets of this city, nor flock through its skies."

"But if the light goes out…" Luken said, no longer shying away from the awful reality he found himself in.

"If darkness falls, you must come and find me," Akeron said.

TWENTY-FIVE

———◆◆———

The dead had been digging for some time.

They had started on the south-western corner of Hallowvale, in an old graveyard beyond the city walls, close to the southern coastline. The first cohort had encamped there, and their palisades hid the shambling corpses as they delved ever deeper and further underground.

Such workers needed neither rest nor sustenance, only stopping their grubbing when brittle bones finally snapped and the foul magics maintaining them flickered and snuffed out. Labour that would have taken a mortal force weeks was being conducted in days.

Drakan permitted Vanescula to visit the dig site. Together they descended into the earthen tunnels created by the undead, ignored by the procession of limping, festering corpses as they scraped and burrowed, or hefted caskets full of soil back towards the entrances.

"You started as soon as the siege lines were complete?"

Vanescula wondered, noting just how advanced the work was as she peered along a crosscut, then stepping lightly aside as a headless corpse stumbled unsteadily past carrying a basket full of soil.

"Of course," Drakan replied.

"And the bombardment, the assaults, all just to keep attention elsewhere? Even the boats?"

She was referring to the rafts and small transports being visibly constructed by the legion on the nearby coastline.

"For the most part, yes," Drakan said. "All a distraction. We will need to cross the water at some point though, if the Everlight is to be snuffed out."

Vanescula considered how ingenious her brother was, but then that was why House Drakan had achieved the power it now enjoyed.

"Are we beneath the walls?" she asked.

"Nearly. We are digging deeper, to avoid the foundations. We don't want to cause damage to them. A collapse will raise the alarm."

"But if that happened, we could storm it."

"The outcome would be doubtful. Striking from below, less so. Besides—"

"The altar is the reason we are here," Vanescula said, daring to pre-empt her brother. "Will you join the attack then? Surely you cannot trust Ranis to secure the altar?"

"It was Ranis's prisoner who confirmed its location to me," Drakan said. "You should stop underestimating your brother. But no, he will not claim the altar. He does not yet know of it. He will lead the attack on the citadel, and Korgax will make sure he takes prisoners and does not stray. While he does, I will claim the true prize."

"And what would you have me do?" Vanescula asked, not daring to voice her desire to be with Drakan when he reached the Blood Altar, but hoping it was clear.

"You will do what you are good at, and wait. I do not know if I will be able to put the altar to work immediately. We may require patience. Hallowvale will not fall in one day, not before the will of its people is broken."

◆ ◆ ◆

Efaritay found an unexpected figure in the arboretum when she went to sing once more to the blisterwood.

At first she stood, frozen in fear, convinced she was being visited by a spectre from her recent nightmares, or that the Zamorakian necromancers had succeeded in raising the dead within the sanctified walls. There was a man before the blisterwood, framed by its thick white trunk. He was armoured and spattered with dark, dried blood, his posture hunched with exhaustion. It was only when he turned that Efaritay recognised her husband.

"Ascertes," she exclaimed, rushing forward and gripping him by the shoulders. "Are you injured?"

Ascertes stared up at her, his expression cold.

"No," he said eventually. "I thought I'd find you here."

Efaritay let go, feeling stung.

"Someone must grow the blisterwood," she said immediately.

"The blisterwood is no use against human legionaries," Ascertes said. "I have hardly seen you since the day you returned to the city. We need you at the walls, Efaritay. *I* need you."

Efaritay bowed her head, giving up on pretence.

"Forgive me," she said. "I… I fear I have failed."

"Why?" Ascertes demanded. "Why do you remain here? If I did not know you better, I would think you are afraid."

"Who is not afraid?" Efaritay said, looking her husband in the eye. "We are surrounded by terrors and abandoned by our god."

"Then all is lost?" Ascertes asked angrily. "Should we go before Drakan, kneel and plead for terms? Ask him to spare the city once he claims it?"

"Do not speak his name," Efaritay snapped. "You have not faced him in battle. I have!"

"And you lived," Ascertes said. "Let none say you are not a mighty warrior. Let none say we cannot resist him and his kind."

Efaritay shook her head vigorously.

"He… He was not trying. He was taunting me. All of us. He killed the royal guard like they were children. He could have killed me too, but he did not seem to care. It didn't matter. It felt like all of this is just a game to him."

"He is the worst of the vyre," Ascertes said. "A monster. You cannot expect him to think as we do."

Efaritay was silent, wondering how she could articulate her fears, the terrible malaise that had gripped her since that night.

"His hubris will be his undoing," Ascertes went on. "He underestimates the resolve of you, of both of us. Of all the defenders of Hallowvale. We will not let this city fall."

She looked down at her husband, bloodied and battered, still defiant, still burning with resolve. For all the light the icyene supposedly held within them, she had always felt it was humans who burned the brighter over their short existence.

She embraced him tightly.

"Rest," she told him. "Go to the children. I will see to the walls."

"I left Babel commanding the defences," Ascertes said. "It is hard to convince him to leave his planning sessions. He is withdrawn, like you. You marched beyond the walls to break the vyre, but it seems you are the ones who have returned broken."

"Then I am thankful I have you to fix me," Efaritay said, trying to press on with her renewed resolve, and not think about the beast beyond the walls. "Tell Larina and Safalaan I love them, and I will see them soon."

✦ ✦ ✦

Ranis flexed his hands, feeling his talons distend, then bared his fangs in a grin.

"Remember, His-Dark-Self desires prisoners," Korgax said. Ranis's vicious smile evaporated, and he glared at the captain of the vyreguard.

"Were you not one of my brother's favourite pets, I would rip your fangs out right here," he told him. Korgax said nothing back, looking perfectly unintimidated.

The vyrelord glanced at the pallid swarm of vyre filling the tunnel behind him. It was a mixed brood, his own and Verzik Vitur's. The vyrelady herself had insisted on accompanying them, seemingly intent on cementing her role as part of the plot, especially now that it had been approved by Drakan.

Ranis had been impressed with how quickly the animated corpses had worked. Drakan had told him earlier that evening that they had broken through to one of the passageways that Lysander had revealed beneath the city. Ulf's were-pack had been sent ahead, loping through the depths beneath the city, scouting out the warren of tunnels the besiegers had just gained access to.

It was everything Ranis had dared imagine when Lysander had first spoken of the passages. The ground below Hallowvale was a labyrinth, with the escape tunnels under the citadel and palace and old crypts intersecting with cellars and sewer systems. The vyre would be able to travel north, almost following the line of Hallowvale's walls, eventually reaching the passages and dungeons under the citadel itself.

Ranis could sense from the sub-vocal keening of the rest of the swarm that they were ready. He pulled on the metal cap he had taken into the confined space instead of his crested helmet, and looked to the werewolf crouched, in a semi-bestial form, at the point where the tunnel dug by the corpse-slaves broke into one of Hallowvale's subterranean passages.

"You know the way?" Ranis demanded of the beast. She had been the one who had located the lower levels of the citadel. Ranis hadn't bothered to ask for her name. He wasn't even sure if werewolves had names.

The beast nodded.

"Lead on," Ranis ordered.

◆ ◆ ◆

Night was falling, the hills beyond the Everlight's radius shrouded in darkness.

Rhea stood on the ramparts, looking out, beyond the Zamorakian lines. She was hunting for a hint of light there, a glimmering from beyond the nearest ridge. Any sign that they were not alone. That Saradomin was coming.

She had put that hope from her mind for so long, just as she had instructed Mardin. She didn't want to give in to the weakness she saw in the likes of Phosani. She didn't want to be a warrior whose foundations were built on blind hope. But hope was rapidly becoming all they had left.

The Zamorakians were preparing for another assault. Their numbers meant they could throw some cohorts against the walls while leaving others to rest, ensuring near-constant attacks. The garrison tagma did not have the luxury of doing the same – soldiers snatched what rest they could atop the walls, sleeping with their backs to the parapets, doing their best to ignore the rain of stones and bolts that battered at the defences during the brief interludes.

The Zamorakian artillery had fallen silent, which meant the next wave would be upon them in a matter of minutes. Rhea's existence had become a blur of constant bloodshed, driven by raw aggression and the will to survive. She knew she had no choice other than to keep fighting. She wouldn't let the Zamorakians break her, not here, on the walls of the Hallowed City.

"They're coming again?"

Rhea looked to the side, and was startled to find an icyene next to her. It was the queen herself, her spear glimmering in her grasp. Rhea was so numb she hadn't even noticed her approach.

"Yes, Your-Winged-Majesty," she said hastily, saluting the star upon her breastplate. She realised the icyene had been moving along the wall, speaking with the defenders she passed. It had been weeks since any of them had last seen the queen, but she had reappeared earlier that day, like the sun rising again. The last Zamorakian attack had barely made it to the walls, Efaritay and her royal guard descending on them as they scaled their ladders and slaughtering them.

"I see you have been blessed with a shard of the blisterwood," the queen said, noticing the length of sharp timber held in Rhea's belt.

"A gift from the king, Your-Winged-Majesty," Rhea said. "I was privileged to fight alongside him during the first assault."

"Then I'm sure you brought honour to the Wolves," Efaritay said. She seemed about to carry on down the line, then stopped, gazing down at her. Rhea remained dutifully silent.

"I must ask something of you," the queen said eventually. "A request, rather than an order. I fear the end is coming, and I must make… provisions for when it does."

"My queen, I'm sure…" Rhea began, but Efaritay quietened her before continuing.

"If the walls are breached, the city will fall into chaos. I know you are a veteran, that you will have seen such horrors before. If all else seems lost, I must ask you to leave your position and seek out my children, Larina and Safalaan. Do your best to see them to safety, outside the city. They mean everything to me, and more besides. They bear within them the future hope of our people, human and icyene united. I speak not only as a mother, but as the queen. The vyre must not be allowed to extinguish our future."

"Your-Winged-Majesty, surely I am not fit for such a task," Rhea said, dreading what Efaritay was ordering her to do. She was coming to terms with dying here, with her fellow Wolves, giving her life to defend her people and, in doing so, not having to endure the sight of their destruction. Efaritay's 'request' felt like a betrayal. "Would you not rather entrust their safety to the royal guard?"

"They will protect them to the end, of course," Efaritay said. "But that may not be enough. I do not want to entrust them to my fellow icyene alone. I have spoken with you before, have heard multiple times of your exemplary service. I know this is a burden, but it is still one I must ask of you. It is my duty, as much as it is yours."

Rhea could not find a response. She could not deny her queen.

"They are in the eastern wing of the citadel," Efaritay said. "Though they may yet be moved to the palace. Will you go there, when the end comes?"

"I will, Your-Winged-Majesty," Rhea found herself saying. What choice did she have? She was a warrior, and she had been given her orders. Efaritay rested a hand on her shoulder briefly.

"You will have my eternal thanks, and the thanks of all our people, Rhea," the queen said. Then, she was gone, moving off down the line.

Rhea had no time to ponder her queen's command. The next Zamorakian wave was coming.

TWENTY-SIX

———◆———

It was growing late.

Ascertes closed and locked the shutters in Larina and Safalaan's bedroom. At the start of the siege he had insisted on keeping them open, so that the Everlight's protection would always be shining on his children. They had been unable to sleep though, and he had eventually permitted the traditional closing during the so-called 'late hours', when the humans of the city slept. Like their mother, Ascertes' children needed less sleep than him, but more than an icyene. They were in every way a blend of the two peoples, and that, according to Efaritay, was their strength. Between her and Ascertes, they had forged the beginning of a Saradominist dynasty that could truly unite humans and icyene.

"Is mam coming to visit as well?" Larina asked hopefully. They had run at Ascertes screaming when he had walked in, throwing themselves into hugs. He had found himself laughing and picking them up, and trying to hide his tears.

There was nothing more precious to him than his family; amidst the blood and brutality of the Zamorakian storm assaults, he had almost lost sight of that, but it came rushing back with their embrace. He was suddenly thankful Efaritay had told him to come here, that he had taken the time to take off his armour, unbuckle his sword, and remind himself why he'd been fighting so hard. He just wished he could do so without the guilt at the thought of her returning to the walls. He hoped what he had said in the arboretum had helped restore some of what she seemed to have lost. She needed to lead.

"Mam is commanding her brave warriors again," he told Larina as he turned back from the shuttered window.

The chamber they were staying in was in the easternmost wing of the citadel, furthest from the assaults pounding its west side. He had spoken with Efaritay about moving them to the palace, but though it was out of the way of direct assaults against the walls, they had agreed it was too vulnerable to attacks from the bay. The Zamorakians seemed to be building boats and rafts on the coastline to the south. So in the citadel they would remain, locked away with their chaperone and a few members of the royal guard.

"It's nearly time for your bed," he told them both with pretend sternness. Safalaan began to loudly complain, and Ascertes was about to reassure him he'd read them a story, maybe even two, when he heard a sound from beyond the chamber door.

It was a voice, raised, urgent. Frowning, Ascertes strode over and opened the entrance to the corridor.

He was met by the icyene guard who had been stood outside, Lyrana, and another of her comrades, Klepas. The latter had seemingly just arrived. Ascertes noticed he was bleeding from a gash along one arm.

A horrible chill gripped him.

"My king, these corridors are not safe," Klepas said. "There are intruders in the citadel."

"Where?" Ascertes demanded.

"I was patrolling the lowermost corridors with Kellos. They seemed to come out of nowhere. Kellos tried to hold them off while I sounded the alarm. I fear he is dead. They are vyre, coming from below."

There was suddenly no time for the fear or the uncertainty, only for action. He turned and spoke to the chaperone, Esme, trying not to shout, not wanting to panic Larina and Safalaan.

"Take the children up the nearest flight of stairs, now. Keep going until you reach the throne room. Raise the alarm as you go, say that the lower corridors have been breached by vyre. If you are cut off, barricade yourselves in the nearest chamber. Go, now."

Safalaan began crying. Esme scooped them against her flanks with commendable haste, her expression grim, determined. Ascertes knew she would die before any vyre would touch either his son or daughter.

"Lyrana, go with them," he ordered the icyene guarding the door. "Klepas, I must ask you to remain with me. We must buy them time."

"Of course, my king," Klepas said dutifully.

"Go with your children, my king," Lyrana urged. "Klepas and I can hold them!"

"No," Ascertes said. "I want an icyene with them. Now go!"

Esme, the children and Lyrana began to hurry out into the corridor. Ascertes spoke to Klepas.

"Do you prefer to fight with your doru or your xiphos?"

Klepas blinked, then recognised Ascertes had no weapon.

"Xiphos," the guard said, and offered his spear to the king. Ascertes took it.

Esme and the children hadn't even made it to the far end of the corridor before the vampyres struck.

Ascertes heard them coming, and only just had time to swing the spear into a defensive guard. There was a scrabbling and a hissing sound from the set of spiral stairs they were facing at the end of the corridor, rising up out of the darkness. Then, before Ascertes could do anything more, a blur of movement.

Klepas saved his life. The first vyre came out of nowhere, a ghastly, pale face and bared fangs, with an ear-piercing shriek. The icyene slammed it back with his shield, matching its speed and checking its charge.

Suddenly the whole end of the corridor was full of hissing monstrosities. Ascertes had never encountered a vampyre before. They fitted every grim and terrible tale he had heard, their speed shocking, their faces born from the stuff of nightmares, but Klepas swung his sword in a wide arc and stamped forward with his shield, trying to hold them off. They hissed and cringed, as though blinded by the icyene, and when one tried to grapple with the guard it had its limb ripped off in a gout of dark blood.

Ascertes tried to lunge past Klepas to aid his defence, but his spear tip failed to find any of the monsters. Then one was on the icyene, seemingly overcoming its revulsion at the winged being. It snatched Klepas's wrist as he swung his xiphos and lashed its talons across his face, gouging through even the cheek pieces of his helmet.

Klepas screamed and reeled back, blinded by blood. Ascertes stabbed at the one that had wounded him, but it dodged effortlessly, ignoring the human to snatch one of Klepas's feathered wings and throw him against the wall.

The icyene's defiance was at an end. The vampyres swarmed him, shrieking, burying him in rending fangs and claws. Ascertes stumbled back, daring to look along the corridor, catching sight of his children just disappearing up the next set of stairs, Lyrana bringing up the rear.

The vyre were too fast. They'd be on them in seconds, once they ripped themselves away from Klepas.

But as he looked to his family, he caught sight of the single, shuttered window between himself and the stairwell.

Idiot. Why hadn't he thought of that?

Turning his back on the vampyres, he began to run.

It was less than a dozen paces to the slender window port, but he knew after the first step he wouldn't make it. The vyre raced after him, unrestrained now that they had brutally extinguished Klepas's light. He wasn't going to be able to reach the window before they tore him apart.

Ascertes roared, and threw the spear.

It struck the shutter, a clumsy, glancing blow, but with enough force to splinter the bottom part of the wooden covering.

Light – the glory of the Everlight – lanced through the gap. It wasn't enough to reach either Ascertes, or the other end of the corridor, but it created a barrier of brilliance, a wall of illumination between them and the stairwell his children had taken.

Ascertes fell, a hand around his ankle, another clawing at his thigh. He tried to scramble to the light, but was dragged away along the cold flagstones, his ears full of hissing and chittering.

With one final defiant shout, he was hauled back into the dark. He fixed his thoughts on his wife and children and prepared to die.

✦ ✦ ✦

Ranis wiped the bitter blood of the icyene from his lips and snarled.

"Mortix, go."

The vampyre thrall looked at him, letting out a keening noise that indicated her fear.

"Risk the light, or die by my hand," Ranis spat at her, fangs bared. "And I promise you, I will make it slow."

The thrall stared for a second at the light blazing in through the broken shutter, cutting the corridor in half. It had been a clever move by the human, Ranis allowed. He should have been quicker.

Mortix finally found her courage and attempted to dart

through the light. She was only exposed to it for a split second. It was enough. As she passed through, her flesh ignited, and she became a howling ball of flame that tumbled to the floor on the other side, reduced to mere ash in a few heartbeats.

The other vyre around Ranis hissed. The Everlight was even more potent than the sun, charged with the raw power of Saradomin. Just gazing on the beam spilling in through the gap made Ranis's eyes ache and his skin feel like it was burning.

They could not pass this way. Even worse, his keen hearing could detect shouts and the running of feet from the floors above. The alarm was being raised, and soon the lower levels of the citadel would be swarming with icyene.

Had he made a mistake? Maybe he should have insisted a full assault be mounted through the tunnels, rather than a mere raid, an attack they could have overrun the citadel from below and ended the siege at a stroke. He had feared that if he had suggested such a thing, Drakan would have decided to command it himself, or worse, given it to Vanescula. Ranis was the one who had discovered the tunnels, and he deserved the glory. A raid had seemed like the subtler suggestion.

He looked down at their prisoner. The man was being restrained by several members of the brood, and was pale and shaking, his eyes wide. He was probably wondering why he hadn't suffered the same fate as his icyene comrade.

"It's him," Vitur said with an excited hiss, pushing through the mass of her underlings. "It's the king!"

"Ascertes," Ranis hissed. The man looked up at him, and Ranis grinned.

He had hoped to take them all, but the king of Hallowvale would surely do, for now.

"Bring him," he ordered.

✦ ✦ ✦

Efaritay roared and kicked the Zamorakian legionary off the Sunspear, sending the body plunging back off the wall.

She looked for another, but there were none. The attack was faltering, broken. The ladders were being cast from the walls once again, the bodies of the Zamorakians thrown after them. She raised the Sunspear towards the retreating enemy, her blood coursing with the rush of battle.

The foe kept coming, and they kept killing them. Let them come, she thought. Let them dash themselves to bloody ruin on the walls of her city, while their vyre masters starved, cowering out there in the dark. Her certainty had returned, rekindled by the fire of battle.

"My queen," said a voice, drawing her from her defiant reverie. She stepped away from the parapet and found herself being addressed by a young icyene messenger. He was wide-eyed and pale in the Everlight's glow.

"Urgent word from Strategos Babel, Your-Winged-Majesty," he said. "The lower levels of the citadel have been breached. Zamorakians are attacking from the tunnels. Your presence is required immediately."

Efaritay tried to process the news. There had to be some sort of mistake.

"The Zamorakians are beneath us?" she asked.

"Yes," the messenger said, nodding emphatically. "The strategos had already directed reinforcements below, but he prays you attend him in the throne room!"

Terrible fear gripped Efaritay, and she immediately took off from the wall, taking wing down to the citadel's main courtyard, then in through the doors and towards the throne room.

The place was filled with icyene, most of them royal guards. A number of them closed ranks protectively around Efaritay as she arrived, but she waved them angrily away. Only then did she see what she had so desperately hoped to find.

Larina and Safalaan were just before the throne dais, huddled against their chaperone, Esme. Efaritay swept to them and pulled them to her, giving the Sunspear to the nearest guard. They were tearful and whimpering, and Safalaan resisted at first.

"You're alright," Efaritay said, trying and failing to hide the tremor in her voice. "You're safe. Nothing can hurt you here."

She knew those words weren't true, but she said them anyway. She needed to believe them as much as they did.

"My queen," said a familiar voice. It was Babel. The strategos appeared harried, afraid. Still holding her children against her, Efaritay looked at him, and was surprised to find him struggling to find the right words.

The terrible, plunging sense of horror returned. She stood up, turned around, searching among the faces for one that was out of place, one that wasn't icyene. Unable to find it, she spoke.

"Where is my husband?"

✦ ✦ ✦

Ranis threw Ascertes to his knees before the tithing table and spread his arms in triumph, Vitur standing cautiously in his shadow.

"Behold," he declared to Drakan. "The king of Hallowvale! I make him your prisoner, my brother, to do with as you will."

Ranis knew he was being painfully grandiose. He was trying to hide how afraid he was. Would Ascertes be enough? Would the queen fight on? He should have been swifter, then perhaps he could have captured their brats as well.

He dared admit none of that to Drakan, awkwardly lowering his arms and watching his brother warily as the hulking vyrelord rose from behind the table and paced round to where the human was crouched. Ascertes was shaking, and didn't raise his eyes.

"This is what you bring me?" Drakan demanded eventually, turning his gaze on Ranis. "The enemy's stronghold at your mercy, and all you return with is one cowering mortal?"

Ranis couldn't find an answer, and when he began to stammer something Drakan simply carried on over him.

"No matter. This little offering will have to be enough. Send word to the broods. Have them gather their full strength on the edge of the encampment before the westernmost gate. It is time we broke these fools."

TWENTY-SEVEN

———◆———

Efaritay reached the walls, the soldiers crowded there hastily parting.

She could see nothing at first beyond the Everlight's glow, her eyes still adjusting to the darkness beyond it. As they did so, she began to discern figures in the nebulous twilight space where the Everlight faded and the night began.

"My queen, please wait," she heard Babel calling as he hurried along the wall after her. She wasn't listening.

She stepped up onto the parapet and took flight.

It felt like a nightmare, surreal and unimaginable. Ascertes was down there, bound to a pole driven into the ground in front of the Zamorakian siege lines, just outside of bow range from the walls.

He wasn't alone. The monster was with him too, standing slightly off to one side, hunched over, motionless. Waiting for her, Efaritay knew. Behind were its minions, a great swarm of vyre, a pallid host lurking at the edge of night.

The Sunspear's light shone, carrying a fragment of the Everlight into that shadowy space between night and artificial day, making the vyre ahead hiss. It picked out Ascertes' face as he looked up and beheld his wife descending towards him.

"Go back," he shouted. "For the light's sake, Efaritay!"

She alighted in front of Drakan. The vyrelord rose up to his full, fearsome height, gazing upon her with eyes that gleamed wickedly in the Sunspear's glow.

They looked at one another, Efaritay wondering if he could hear her heart hammering in her chest, could taste her anger, could smell her fear.

Eventually, Drakan spoke.

"I will not harm you. Go to him."

Efaritay watched Drakan for a little while more, then did as he said. She went to Ascertes.

"Are the children safe?" were his first words.

"Yes," Efaritay said. "They're both unharmed. They're in the throne room now, surrounded by the guard."

"I'm sorry," Ascertes said. There were tears in his eyes. "I didn't think they'd do this. I didn't think they'd let me live."

Efaritay had a powerful urge to embrace him, but dared not before Drakan. She could feel his terrible eyes on them, watching, calculating. He was a predator, and she knew that everything he did was bent towards catching his prey.

"You have nothing to be sorry for," she told Ascertes. "You protected our children with your life. They are safe. I'm the one who should be sorry. I have been weak, so weak. My mother would be ashamed."

She looked at Drakan, forcing herself to meet the gaze of the thing that had infested her nightmares.

"Release him," she said.

"Perhaps," Drakan replied. "If you give me what I want. The city."

"The city is not mine to give."

"You are its queen."

"I reign in Saradomin's name. Hallowvale belongs not to those of royal blood, but to the light itself."

Frustration passed over Drakan's pale, bestial features, and Efaritay instinctively gripped the Sunspear tighter.

"If you cannot give me the city, you have nothing to negotiate with."

"You can have me. A prisoner exchange. Take me, and release my husband."

"King or queen makes little difference to me, icyene. It is like for like. I am not here to break even. I come seeking profit, and you are not in a position to negotiate a better deal for yourself."

"So you say," Efaritay declared, her voice defiant, despite her fear. "Night and day your mortal slaves have attacked the walls at my back, and every time they have been repulsed. These defences have never been breached. They will hold until our Lord of Light comes and burns you, and every blood-sucking night-spawn that cringes in your shadow."

Drakan laughed.

"Brave words," he said. "And well spoken, but meaningless all the same. Saradomin is not coming. Your god of wisdom has lost sight of everything else bar destroying Zamorak.

He grows desperate since Zamorak snatched the Stone of Jas from him. He will sacrifice this city and everyone in it, including you and your family, believing that when Zamorak is defeated he can simply return and reclaim it."

Efaritay knew in her heart that he was correct, but she could not accept it, not in front of him.

"I came here to negotiate, so let us negotiate," Efaritay demanded. "Release my husband, unharmed. In exchange you may not only claim me as prisoner. I will swear fealty to you. I will betray my oaths, abandon my faith. You will have turned the queen of the icyene. You may do with me as you will."

Drakan cocked his head to one side as he watched her, like an avian or a curious hound catching a scent.

"You will kneel here, in the sight of your own warriors atop your walls?"

"I will," Efaritay said. "But you must swear a binding oath that Ascertes will not be harmed, and that he will go free. And it must be a blood oath."

Drakan bared his fangs. Efaritay realised after a surge of panic that he was smiling.

"You know the ancient ways of Vampyrium then?" he asked. "A great vyre such as myself will not – cannot – make a blood oath lightly."

"And that is why I demand it," Efaritay said. "And furthermore, you will promise me that no harm will come to my children should the city fall."

"You overplay your hand," Drakan hissed dangerously. "You are the one seeking terms, not I. If I will it, I can summon the were-packs and have them rip your precious husband apart before your very eyes."

"I am not afraid to die," Ascertes exclaimed. "Do not do this, Efaritay! You are our city's last hope. Don't throw it away for me!"

"The city will endure under you," Efaritay told him. "You are as strong as I. Stronger, in fact. The past weeks have proven that. You will lead, and this darkness shall not overcome you, or our children."

She wished there was another way, but she could not find it. She wouldn't be able to endure knowing the vyre had Ascertes, knowing the terrible things they could do to him. She would rather suffer it all herself, than have to explain any of it to her children.

The only terror left to her, was the certainty that she would never see any of them again.

"I will give you my oath," Drakan said. "By the blood, I swear to you that your husband will live, and that he will go free. I give you no other promises, though if it eases your mind, I do not intend to slaughter the inhabitants of your city. I am here for a greater goal. Do you accept this oath?"

Efaritay nodded. Drakan raised his forearm, and sank his long fangs into his own flesh. Black blood welled up, running down his white skin and pattering onto the soil. He pulled his fangs free, and spat a hissed word in the dark tongue of Vampyrium.

"It is done," he declared. "And now you will fulfil your own part of the bargain. Kneel."

"Don't," Ascertes tried one last time. "It's not too late! Please! Fly back to the walls. Protect our children!"

"You have already protected them better than I have," Efaritay said. "And you will do so again."

She knelt. Disgust filled her, a sickening revulsion. She found herself considering planting the Sunspear's silver base in Hallowvale's dirt and driving herself onto it, mingling her blood with Drakan's and finally escaping this horror. But that wasn't an option. She set the spear down beside her, and lowered her head, fixing her gaze on the black blood the vyrelord had spilled in his promise to her.

The hissing of the vampyres behind Drakan rose, like the susurration of some huge serpent, the sound – Efaritay assumed – of their approval.

"Renounce your station," Drakan commanded her. "And give me your oath of fealty. Swear your loyalty to His-Dark-Self."

She could feel thousands of eyes on her, not only the Zamorakians and their vampyre masters, but the gaze of her soldiers and loyal guards, of those who had spilled their own blood and seen their comrades slain to end this scourge. She was betraying them, she knew, even if she told herself that they could endure without her, that she had only given up herself and not the city. All for love.

"I abdicate the throne of Hallowvale," she said, feeling like she was choking on the words. "I am no longer its queen. I renounce… Saradomin, and his light. I am your servant… the servant of Your-Dark-Self."

"For eternity," Drakan added with a low, ticking rattle, leaning forward so he was stooped over her, the sound of his vast brood rising to a fever pitch.

"For eternity," Efaritay breathed.

"Rise," Drakan commanded. The former queen obeyed, looking at her new master. His terrible face showed none of the triumph she had anticipated. He wiped some of his dark blood from the puncture wounds in his arm and pressed it against her forehead with his thumb, almost tenderly. She shivered.

"It is done," he said. The vyre let up a shriek, the chilling noise transfixing the cold night air and ringing back from the walls, walls Efaritay found she did not have the strength to turn and look upon.

"Release him," she told Drakan. Instead he stooped and, to Efaritay's shock, picked up the Sunspear.

Drakan grimaced, as though touching the blisterwood haft of the weapon brought him terrible pain – Efaritay had not thought he would be able to touch it at all. Again, she found herself in dreadful awe of the power of the monstrosity.

As she watched, the spear's light began to dim. Its silver blades no longer shone with lustre, and the blisterwood haft darkened, its white wood taking on a grey patina, as though it were finally withering with age. And as it died, the small radius of light it was casting about Efaritay shrunk. The vyre horde were advancing, beginning to surround her. Their presence made Efaritay's skin crawl, but she dared not try to snatch her weapon back.

Soon the spear had lost all of its brilliance, just dull steel and silver, its glory snuffed out by the master of Vampyrium.

Drakan let out a low hiss and flexed his fingers around the haft, then spun the weapon, as though testing its weight.

"An acceptable offering for your new master," he told her, then made a piercing, shrieking sound that sent ice down her spine and made her cringe in pain, her ears aching.

The vyre fell upon her from all sides, snatching her and dragging her into the darkness of the deep night.

"You swore," she screamed at Drakan as she was snatched away. "You swore on your own blood he would go free!"

"And he will," Drakan snarled back at her. "And soon. Soon, you will wish that he had died."

TWENTY-EIGHT

———◆———

Burning with raw frustration, Archon Babel struck his hand against the parapet.

He had known Efaritay was a fool when she had agreed to marry that human whelp. She could have chosen him instead and secured a strong icyene legacy that would last for millennia. Instead she had degraded herself – degraded all of them – by offering herself to that weak little man, and granting power to humans throughout the queendom.

It had led them here. This betrayal, the fruits of her foolishness, enacted for all to see. It marked the end, Babel was certain. Their end too, if he did not act.

"Sound the call for all icyene officers to attend me," he snapped at his salpinx blower. The young icyene was just staring down at the darkness beyond the Everlight, which the queen had disappeared into. He didn't snap out of his horrified trance until Babel fully turned to face him.

314

"The officer's call," the strategos barked, then strode past the horn blower as the notes pealed out across the walls, heading for the throne room.

✦ ✦ ✦

Rhea found Phosani on the wall just below the jagged spur of stone that was all that remained of the north-western tower.

"Orders, commander?" she asked the justiciar. Phosani said nothing. She was simply standing and staring into the dark.

It was the same all along the wall. They had all witnessed Queen Efaritay depart alone, down to where the Zamorakians had staked out the king. Rumours had swept through the ranks of how vyre had struck the citadel from below, through half-guarded tunnels that none had believed they could access. A stupid mistake to make. They had seized the king, had almost seized the royal children too. Rhea couldn't help but remember the promise she had made just hours ago to Efaritay, the oath she had taken to protect them.

Briefly, Rhea had thought Efaritay intended to battle the monstrosity she assumed was Drakan, but instead she had done the unthinkable. She had surrendered.

Now everyone on the wall seemed paralysed by fear and shock. Rhea had sought out Phosani, but the White Wolf didn't even seem to be aware of her presence.

Rhea felt a stab of anger. This was no way to react to such betrayal. There should be anger, and defiance, the kind of fury that would help ensure they all lived at least another day. Instead she could see only a crushing, deadly despair.

"Justiciar," she snapped at Phosani. The White Wolf finally looked at her, and Rhea was aghast to see tears in her eyes.

"We are lost," Phosani said, her voice as cold and hard as midwinter frost.

Rhea stared at her, trying to say the right words, words that would rally her old commander, remind her of her duty, give her hope.

But she couldn't find them. Instead, she simply turned, and walked away.

✦ ✦ ✦

Babel's icyene subordinates had filled the throne room.

The strategos could sense their fear, and was determined to quell it. Their pathway to salvation was obvious. All they needed was the courage to take it.

"Queen Efaritay has surrendered herself to the vyre," he told the assembly. "In doing so she has betrayed us, and the entire city."

The icyene stared, some speechless, others looking dour and resigned.

"It is clear Saradomin is not coming, and that the humans are beginning to tire," he carried on. "It will be another day, two at most, before the Zamorakians breach the walls. When they do, it will not matter that the Everlight is stopping the vampyres from taking wing or walking in the open. Drakan's human legionaries will sack the city. That is now inevitable, despite all our efforts, and the sacrifice of every brave icyene who has fallen thus far."

"Then you're saying we must prepare for one last stand?" one of the officers asked.

"No," Babel said firmly. "I'm saying that the time has come to save what we can. There is no reason for us, our warriors, or our families to remain here and perish with the humans. We can leave this place anytime we desire. We need but take wing."

Now the silence that filled the throne room really was one of shock. Babel pressed on, not wanting to be thought of as treasonous by his subordinates.

"A new day is about to dawn. If we take wing now, the vyre will not be able to stop us. We fly west, towards where Saradomin's great hosts are mustered. All of us. We carry our swords to serve Saradomin another day, and we ensure our people can endure for many generations yet."

"Traitor," shouted a voice, ringing from the chamber's high roof. Babel froze, glaring out over the assembly. They parted, and he saw just who had spoken. Not an icyene, of course.

"Traitor," Larina and Safalaan's ugly human wetnurse, Esme, repeated. She and the children had been brought into the throne room for their own safety, and with Efaritay's sudden, initially unexplained departure they had not moved. Larina and Safalaan were staring from behind Esme's skirts at the icyene, looking scared and confused. Just the sight of the half-human whelps caused Babel's anger to seethe.

Esme seemed intent on matching it as she continued to shout up at him.

"You dare call your queen a traitor? When you now conspire to abandon the people of this city? Those who have called it their home alongside you for centuries? Is your blood so much purer and more precious that you would not mingle it with ours at the end?"

"Efaritay betrayed us," Babel shouted, no longer trying to contain the hatred he had held onto for so long. "Because she was weakened, weakened by her misplaced love for her human pet! She was like an oak plagued by deep-rot, mighty on the outside, but hollowed out and wasted within. That is what acceptance of your kind does to us. It has undermined the strength and stability of Hallowvale since she first took Ascertes' hand in marriage! Why should we die alongside you, when we can all live?"

"And will you leave these children to perish?" Esme demanded, her hands on Larina's and Safalaan's shoulders. "Just because they weren't blessed with wings like you? Is their blood tainted, impure, because they are half human?"

"I would abandon no one," Babel declared, ruffling his own feathers angrily. "So by all means, tell me how their lives can be saved? Yours too? Show me an end that isn't a meaningless sacrifice?"

Esme held Babel's gaze, her face ruddy with fury, but she said nothing more.

"Remove them from the hall," Babel ordered the commander of the royal guard, Calix. The icyene didn't move.

"You would disobey your strategos?" Babel said.

"I take orders from the queen or the king," Calix responded, his tone guarded. "And if they are not present, from their heirs. I will certainly not remove them from their own throne room."

"There will be no need," Esme said. "I will not make them witness any more of your cowardice, Archon Babel."

She left, taking her precious charges out into the courtyard. Babel watched them go, trying to crush the shame and humiliation he felt, trying to latch onto the truths he had spoken and not wonder where they were going or what would become of them.

Fundamentally, what he had said was right. To let every icyene in the city die just so the humans felt as though they had not been abandoned would be a monumental waste, yet it seemed he was the only one brave enough to say it. That was fine, for he was a leader, a general, trusted by Saradomin for his strategic wisdom. He would wake his people from this nightmare, and ensure not another one perished by Zamorakian steel or a vyre's fangs.

"Return to your commands and spread the word," he instructed his officers. "Tell your warriors to go to their families and ready them. Everyone who can take wing must prepare to. Nothing must be taken but a little food. We need to travel light and fast. Any who cannot fly will have to be carried. Otherwise they cannot be saved."

"I will not go," Calix said. "But nor will I think less of any who wish to save their families. If I had children of my own, I suspect I would do the same."

"Do as you wish," Babel told him coldly.

"Is this an order, strategos?" another of the senior officers, Parathakos, asked.

"It is," Babel said. "I will report what has happened here to Saradomin himself, and if there are any repercussions, I will bear them in their entirety. I will embrace it all gladly if it means saving our people."

That seemed to be enough for the rest. There were nods, and expressions that had been despairing now took on an aspect of grim determination.

"Go and spread the word," Babel repeated, knowing it was too late to turn back now. He would save them, and face the shame for the rest of his existence if need be.

"We fly with the dawn."

TWENTY-NINE

———◆———

Drakan watched the icyene leave Hallowvale as the sun rose, and his kin fled to their dark burrows, cellars and shaded pits.

At first it looked as though the cursed Everlight was expanding, swallowing up the Zamorakian siegeworks immediately west of the towering walls. It became clear that the illumination belonged to the icyene themselves, rather than the works of their god. They came in a vast, continuous flock, thousands of them, flying in arrowhead formations, warriors on the outside and their families within, guarded against any vampyre who would dare brave the strengthening daylight.

They were fleeing.

He had expected nothing less from them. For all that other vampyres feared them and their untiring light, Drakan knew that most icyene were cowards at heart. He knew it because it was the same cowardice he had seen many times in his own people. A vampyre, regularly blood-nourished, could live almost as long as an icyene, and that blessing brought with it the fear of a sudden, unexpected end, from accident or from a killer's blade. Hoarding life as they did, they feared death more than the likes of humans, who to Drakan seemed to live their lives in a joyous, foolish, headlong rush. They had no shortage of courage, because they knew that no matter what they did, death would find them sooner rather than later. Sometimes Drakan envied that. Sometimes he tried to think like a human and grasp moments other vampyres would cower from.

"Your friends are abandoning you," he told Ascertes. The king of Hallowvale was standing in the doorway of the tithing house behind Drakan. He made no response to the mild taunt. His eyes were vacant, jaw slack. Drakan had hypnotised him after his wife's submission. It would be necessary for what he had planned.

Efaritay herself was being held by a section of his vyreguard in the vault below. Now that the icyene were abandoning the city, she had served her purpose. He had no doubt he would find future uses for her, but her part in his current plans was ended.

The icyene were still flocking overhead. Fearing at first that they were about to be attacked, the Zamorakians had stood to, but now that it was clear what was happening they started to shout and jeer, beating weapons on shields and taunting their hated, fleeing enemies. A few loosed crossbow bolts, but the icyene were flying too high.

Their escape did not trouble Drakan at all. They would soon become Zamorak's problem, which meant they would not be his. Success here was all that mattered.

He let out a shriek, its piercing noise pitched specifically to awake Vanescula from wherever she was hiding from the new day. She was strong enough to suffer the light for the little while it would be necessary to receive her instructions.

She arrived eventually, her flinching discomfort relieved by the sight of the fleeing icyene.

"They would really abandon the humans?" she wondered.

"Everyone has a breaking point, and the icyene's comes faster than most," Drakan said. "Now, all that remains is to break the humans."

✦ ✦ ✦

The next Zamorakian assault began not long after dawn.

Rhea had expected it as soon as she had realised what the icyene were doing. While everyone around her had stood in bleak, disbelieving silence as the founders of Hallowvale had flown over their heads and away beyond the Zamorakian siegeworks, Rhea had found herself raging, shouting up at the flocks. Hatred had gripped her, disgust more potent than any she had known. It was the worst of betrayals, almost unthinkable.

Eventually, she spent her wrath, and joined in the silence of the others as they stared impotently after the escaping flocks. The last had passed by, and their glittering lights had melded with the constellations still showing amidst the remnants of the night, out to the west.

Then the assaults had resumed. Drakan's legion were throwing their all into it, across every section of Hallowvale's walls.

The Wolves held their part of the line. It was hopeless. Almost half of the sphendonitai seemed to have simply disappeared, deserting their positions and fleeing down into the city.

To Rhea's grim satisfaction, none of the Wolves in her section abandoned their posts.

She drove back and killed one legionary who had made it over the parapet, pinning him back against the wall and carving down through his shoulder with her kopis. Next to her Mardin, Klaxar and Alcindies were heaving at a weighted siege ladder, trying to shove it back from the ramparts.

She stepped between them and added her strength, bellowing with effort as, finally, they were able to tip it past its upright axis and send it plunging back into the mass at the base of the walls, legionaries tumbling, screaming, from its rungs.

There was no time for even brief exultation. Another Wolf, Diana, was shouting for her attention. Her helmet was gone, and she was bleeding from a scalp gash as she gesticulated across the wall.

"The section south of the next tower has fallen," she panted. "The Zamorakians have overrun it. They're trying to push through the tower and reach this part of the walls!"

"Go back and hold the connecting door for as long as you can," Rhea ordered. "I'll bring reinforcements."

She set out across the wall, going north, avoiding the efforts of the Wolves to drive back the endless, rising tide.

As she went, she passed Damacleso, the Imcando, and the last of his fellow dwarf crew making their stand around their pyrokutor. The war engine had been wrecked by Zamorakian missiles, the parapet around it finally demolished, but they had refused to abandon their part of the walls.

"Have you seen the White Wolf?" Rhea asked the dwarf as he pulled his axe from the half-severed neck of the Zamorakian he had just brought down. He just shrugged.

"Keep going north, would be my best guess," he said.

Rhea carried on along the wall, shouting for Phosani as she went. She found her beneath the ruins of the northwest tower.

The White Wolf was sitting with her back to the parapet, her sword beside her and her head in her hands. Otrava and Insela were crouched on either side, seemingly trying to console her.

Rhea could not contain herself.

"What are you doing?" she shouted. "Get up and fight!"

"There's no point," Otrava shouted back, standing so she was between Rhea and Phosani. "It's over! We've been abandoned! First by Saradomin, now by the icyene!"

"This is pathetic," Rhea barked. "Shameful! Has everyone lost their courage? Will none of you deign to die standing, with your swords in your hands?"

None of them would answer her. Rhea glared at Otrava, addressing Phosani past her.

"I have orders from the queen herself, to defend her children. If you will not give me instructions, White Wolf, I will obey Efaritay's last command."

Otrava said nothing, and Phosani remained slumped against the wall. She might as well already have been dead. It would have been easier for Rhea if she were.

"May your name perish with you, coward," she spat, venting her anger with the bitter curse before turning her back on them and returning to her section.

There, she found Alcindies dead. He was slumped against the parapet, a crossbow bolt through one eye, his other wide with shock, one half of his pale young face a mask of blood.

Rhea stared at him for what felt like a lifetime. Then she looked up, discovering Klaxar and Mardin before her. Their expressions were grim, but Klaxar mustered one of her vicious smiles.

"I take it this is the end, then?" she demanded.

"Not yet," Rhea said, making her mind up. "Phosani and her lapdogs have abdicated command, so I'm following my last orders."

"Dare I ask what those are?" Mardin said.

"They came from the queen herself, before she... Before we lost her, she asked me to find the royal children, Larina and Safalaan, and get them out of the city."

Even Klaxar looked surprised.

"Do we even know where they are?" she asked.

"I was going to search the middle chambers of the citadel. They won't be in the lower parts because of the attack from the tunnels, and they won't be up around here. If I can't find them in the citadel, I'm going to the palace."

Mardin and Klaxar exchanged a glance, neither so much as flinching as a crossbow bolt cracked off the parapet and bounced up past them.

"Did the queen ask you, or order you?" Mardin asked.

"Should it matter?"

"Probably not. Dying here or in the streets makes no odds to me, personally."

"You're always so cheery, Mardin." Klaxar grinned as another bolt whistled overhead.

Rhea looked at those Wolves still fighting, still struggling – warriors she had served alongside for years, now abandoned to a meaningless death. Rhea had never stepped back from a fight, had never turned her back while the Wolves were facing their foes.

But she had her duty, and for once it didn't involve facing the foe head-on and killing them.

"With me," she shouted, rallying the nearest Wolves to her just as another ladder slammed home against the parapet, roaring legionaries beginning to scramble over the top of the stonework.

For the first time in weeks, they met no resistance.

✦ ✦ ✦

The legionaries rushed at Insela and Otrava, and the two Wolves moved to block them from reaching Phosani, but did not raise their weapons.

"We surrender," Insela shouted.

The Zamorakians came up short, the fire in their eyes momentarily dimmed by confusion. They did not witness surrender often, especially not from the Saradominist soldiers who wore the pelts of beasts.

They seemed uncertain about what to do, until one, marked as a centenarius by his helmet's crest, pushed his way forward, brandishing his spatha.

"Down on your knees, dogs," he demanded in crude Icyenic, his grizzled face riven with hatred. "Now!"

"If you're going to kill us, we'll meet our ends standing, not kneeling," Otrava said defiantly.

It looked as though the centenarius was going to grant Otrava her wish, until the White Wolf pushed her aside. Phosani had roused herself from the despair that had gripped her. She faced the Zamorakian officer unflinchingly, her helmet off and silver hair about her shoulders.

"Do you know who I am?" she demanded.

"I don't need to know you to kill you, dog," the centenarius spat, planting his spatha's tip against Phosani's breastplate. The justiciar didn't flinch, but continued to glare into the Zamorakian's eyes.

"I am Phosani, commander of the ordo of the wolf," she said. "These walls have been entrusted to my care. They belong to me."

"Not anymore," the centenarius snapped, though even he now sounded hesitant.

"If I yield them to you, you will surely be rewarded by your masters," Phosani carried on. "But I can offer you more than just this wall."

"Do not play games with me," the centenarius growled, stepping in closer, shifting his spatha so its blade was pressed to Phosani's throat.

The cold steel held no fear for her. She had already made

her choice. In truth it had been made for her, by the god who had deserted her, and the queen who had betrayed her.

"I can ensure you win a greater prize," she said. "The daughter and the son of Queen Efaritay and King Ascertes. The heirs of Hallowvale."

◆ ◆ ◆

Drakan walked Hallowvale's underworld, scenting his way through the warren.

This was the second time he had walked it. The first had been as Ranis had led his little invasion of the citadel, a useful distraction for him to forge alone and unnoticed into the city's depths. He had located what he needed that first time, but now, as Hallowvale fell, he would enact the next part of the plan.

The stench of blood infused with the arcane was intoxicating. He found it almost impossible not to be drawn to it. He had brought only Ascertes and Korgax, the former walking with the flat-footed, vacant gait of the hypnotised. He would permit no one else in these final moments, not even Vanescula. He was about to discover if all his work had been in vain, if the great future he imagined not only for himself, but all his kind, would be realised. He had long ago forgotten what true fear felt like, but he suspected what he was experiencing now was something akin to it – anticipation bordering on the painful.

He spoke words of power when he reached the right length of tunnel, summoning magics riven with the blood-darkness of Vampyrium. They transported him and his companions in an instant to a stone chamber, bearing at its centre a rock that had been fashioned by some ancient hand to look like a pair of skulls, fused together.

He tried to remain calm, to treat this as any other hunt. After all this time, it would be supreme foolishness to make a mistake because he was too hasty.

The skulls were a portal, and the portal was open.

"Guard this place," he instructed Korgax, who nodded. The vyrelord looked at Ascertes.

"Place your hand on the skull," he instructed the enthralled human. He mirrored Ascertes' movements, stirring up the blood magics running through his veins as he did so, calling to what he sensed lay beyond.

The transportation was so instantaneous he didn't even register the rock's touch. If the blood-fuelled potency around the portal had been strong, it was almost overwhelming in the chamber he was transported to. He panted and shivered, burning with the desire to feed, to gorge himself of the magic-infused blood surrounding him.

Control. Now, more than ever. The portal had carried Ascertes through with him, and he snatched the king of Hallowvale and hauled him towards the centre of the chamber.

There, the source of this glorious energy waited for him – the Blood Altar. The stone ran eternally with vital essence, its bitter, coppery stench a delight to Drakan's senses. It was power in one of its rawest, most primordial forms, and now Drakan would control it. And with it, he would make something new.

Gripping the back of Ascertes' head, he plunged the human's face into the blood welling up from the centre of the altar.

Even Drakan's hypnosis was not enough to keep Ascertes docile while he drowned. He began to struggle, but it was useless in the vyrelord's grasp, like a child trying to break free from his father. Drakan simply held him down, spitting words of darkness that melded with the magic energies that flowed through the chamber.

Ascertes' struggles began to lessen. Eventually he became still. Drakan continued to hold him under until his incantation was finished. Then, he waited.

It didn't take long. He felt Ascertes twitch. He let go of the back of his head. Suddenly, with a terrible, gargling shriek, the former king of Hallowvale surged upwards, gasping, eyes wide and white in the mask of crimson covering his face. He stared at Drakan, panting.

"You are reborn," the vyrelord told him. "Tell me what you feel."

"Hunger," Ascertes rasped, struggling to speak. "Ache."

"You are one of our kind now," Drakan told him, feeling a surge of satisfaction stronger than any he had known for millennia. "A child of Gielinor reborn as a son of Vampyrium. The first of a new breed, one that will remake this world."

Ascertes – or the thing that had once been Ascertes – looked down at his trembling hands, then up once more at Drakan.

"Master," he hissed.

"Kneel," Drakan instructed.

The creature did so.

"Tell me your name," Drakan said.

"I… I do not remember. I am… so hungry."

"You have returned to me a new being," Drakan said. "It will take time for your mind to reorder itself. Your memories will return, but do not be concerned. You are Ascertes Hallow no longer. In time you will take a name that befits what you are now. A name worthy of a warrior of Vampyrium. You will swear your oaths to me. Swear that you will serve me and no other for as long as you exist. Acknowledge me as your creator, your thrall-father, and your vyrelord."

"I acknowledge all of those," the creature declared. "You are my master, I am your servant. I will do whatever you desire."

"Of course you will. Now, go from this blessed place, and feed. That is my first command. After you have done that, things will be easier."

"Thank you, master," Drakan's creation said. He rose, unsteady at first, but slipping into a stooped, predatory gait as he moved away from the altar and towards the markings on the floor that indicated the portal that would take him back to the depths of Hallowvale. Then he was gone, and Drakan was alone in the chamber of the altar.

Finally, he allowed himself to give into his craving. He drank, gorging himself on the altar's sorcerous blood. He felt it running through his veins, revitalising him. He was mightier than he had ever been, riven with blood magics. He was Drakan, not merely lord of Vampyrium, but the father of a new race, creator of life.

He had done the unthinkable, had proven that the glories of Vampyrium need not be confined only to those born there. The work might not yet be complete – he sensed that his new creation still lacked something, some vital spark, and in that moment he experienced an uncomfortable sense of doubt. Was what he was now doing doomed from the beginning? Or would all of Gielinor drink as he now drank, and rejoice in the day he had overcome death itself?

Finally he pulled back, panting, snarling, shaking. He could not lose himself any longer. There was more to be done. So much more.

He had to stop the frenzy of bloodshed he knew would come with the city's fall. His vyre were starving after weeks of scanty nourishment, and with few icyene and soon no Everlight to check them, he knew that slaughter awaited the humans of Hallowvale.

But that was not what he willed for them. Ascertes was only the beginning. Drakan would remake all of this city in his image, and when it was done, he would have founded an empire that would rule Gielinor.

THIRTY

◆

The bells announced the beginning of the end.

The clamour started close to the western walls and spread through the city, translating from the market to the Saradominist quarter, where the shrines took it up. Eventually the mighty bell of the Hallowed Church above them began to sound, the deep, sonorous clanging that had once called the faithful to worship now heralding their doom.

Luken was eating alone in the refractory when he heard the sound. He felt a tightening in his gut, a flush of cold fear.

It could only mean one thing. The walls had been breached.

He abandoned the bread and cheese he had been eating and hitched his himation up before hurrying out of the refectory.

Akeron was in the upper hall. His face was grim, set. The priesthood was gathered around him, conversing in low tones. Luken made eye contact with him as he approached, but the archpriest shook his head, once, causing him to pause on the chamber's edge.

"Brothers and sisters," Akeron called out, bringing the nervous discourse around him to an end. "You know what the bells portend."

"Are we sure the walls have fallen?" one of the churchmen, Deacon Asklipus, called out. "What if it is only a rumour that has gotten out of hand?"

"Brother Tomath has come from the Shrine of Celestial Contemplation, by the western gate," Akeron said, gesturing at a flushed priest standing by him, his tonsured pate glistening with sweat. "He has seen the incursion with his own eyes."

"It's true," Tomath said, still short of breath. "I saw Zamorakian soldiers in the streets, fighting to reach the gate from the inside, no doubt to open it. The walls above me were being overrun, and soldiers of the city tagma were fleeing by. I came straight here."

"If the Zamorakians are within the streets, it is over," Akeron stated. "With the icyene gone, none will be able to resist them."

Luken had been asleep when the icyene had fled. Several pale-faced youths in the dorms had described how they had watched huge flocks of them rising into the sky with the dawn. At the time they had mistakenly believed they were going out to attack the Zamorakians, but word had quickly spread through the quarter that it was nothing less than a betrayal, that the founders of Hallowvale and its supposed guardians had not only given up all hope, but chosen to abandon their brethren to the dark.

He had felt a strange sort of resignation at the news, but now that was replaced by raw fear, the knowledge that what he had been dreading was arriving.

"We must begin final preparations," Akeron said to the priesthood. "The Zamorakians and their beastly masters must not be allowed to defile the sacred resting places and holy relics within the Sepulchre. We must complete our work here, for the glory of Saradomin."

Luken tried not to think about the irony of a priesthood sacrificing themselves for a god who had abandoned them. Such thoughts were surely unworthy. If Akeron did not presume to judge the decisions of their deity, then who was he to question them?

The archpriest led the assembly in a short prayer, then dismissed them. Luken knew they were going to set the final traps throughout the Hallowed Sepulchre, then consign themselves to death, yet none of them showed any hesitation.

He hurried through their midst to Akeron's side. The archpriest reached out and took hold of his arm, that familiar, bony grip.

"Are you ready, boy?" he asked. Luken found he could only nod, not trusting himself to speak.

"The junior illuminator must be interred too," Deacon Asklipus said. He had spotted Luken, and now paused as though to harangue him.

"If he lives and is taken, he may disclose the nature of

the traps," he went on. "All our deaths would then have been in vain."

"He will disclose nothing," Akeron said sternly. "The junior illuminator will be seeing that I am properly interred, with proper honours. Or would you deny me the end befitting an archpriest, deacon?"

Asklipus looked like he might argue, but then thought better of it. He hurried on his way.

"Come," Akeron said to Luken. They set off down through the Hallowed Sepulchre, the base of the star staff tapping the cold flagstones. They passed the priesthood as they descended, priming the cunning internal mechanisms that had been crafted by the icyene centuries ago into their statues and altars. Luken wondered if the traps would really be enough to keep the vyre at bay.

"Are you ready?" Akeron asked him as they went.

"Yes," Luken said.

"Don't lie to me. I've known you since you were knee-high to an Imcando."

In truth, Luken was battling not to break down in tears. It felt like a nightmare, like another of the horrors that plagued him almost every time he laid his head down in his dorm room. Yet there was nothing he could do to wake himself. He could just carry on, every step surreal, every moment spent battling with denial.

"I'm scared," he blurted out.

Akeron stopped. They had just reached the lowest level. To Luken's surprise, the archpriest turned and embraced him.

"I cannot make promises," he said as he did so. "You are not a child anymore, so I will not lie to you. I do not know what will become of you, or of this great city. But I do know you'll have a better chance in the tunnels than you will in here."

Luken sniffed and nodded, burying his face in the archpriest's shoulder.

"I am sorry it has come to this," Akeron went on. "None can see the future with any certainty, not even wise Saradomin. If I had known what doom would befall us, I would have sent you far from here. But this is the end the choices and actions of others have crafted for us. For you, there is still a chance of something more. Do not give up on that, even when you are alone in the dark. The lives of many may yet rest upon your courage."

He broke the hug, and Luken managed to nod, his head bowed.

"Come now," Akeron said. "We must hurry. Time is running out. The vyre are coming."

He led Luken on the route they had taken before, pausing in the deepest depths of the Sepulchre.

"I told you there was a route into the tunnels from here," he said as he paused at a graven icyene statue set into an alcove in the wall. "This is the one you must take."

He worked his way round to the small gap between the rear of the statue and the wall itself, tracing his fingers over the stonework. He pressed on one, smaller than those around it. There was a grating sound, and part of the wall levered away to one side, creating a small black opening just large enough to crawl through.

"Don't worry, it gets bigger," Akeron promised as Luken stared at it. "Here, you will need these too."

He produced the blood talisman and the map. Luken took them reluctantly, still not really believing that any of it was happening, still yearning for some reprieve.

"Come now, and let us finish this," Akeron said and, taking him by the arm, led him to the sarcophagus at the heart of the Hallowed Sepulchre's depths.

◆ ◆ ◆

The walls were overrun.

For all the frenzy involved in storming the city, the fourteenth legion kept its discipline. The cohorts that took the ramparts fought down to the gateways, intending to open them for the rest of the legion.

Dorien and the hypaspists of the owl fought to the end holding the western gate from both outside and in. When the last of the roaring Saradominist warriors finally fell, their bodies were hastily dragged to one side so the heavy doors could be swung inward, admitting a rush of fresh Zamorakian infantry. That was when the true carnage began.

The invaders ran amok through the streets, hunting fleeing Saradominist soldiers. One group of hoplitai made a last stand on the steps of the city's bank, while another, led by an icyene called Zephas, who had refused to abandon the city with his kin, put up a fierce resistance in the square outside the arboretum. The doors of the great dome itself remained stoutly barred, the Zamorakians unable to gain entry even after the last of the defenders outside were hacked down.

The most desperate resistance occurred around the Everlight. When the icyene had abandoned the defence of the tower, Justiciar Aliya and her Lions had rushed out to the archipelago in an effort to protect it. Though icyene, Aliya had refused to flee the city.

She arrived just ahead of a flotilla of boats bearing Zamorakian legionaries. Built in the southernmost siegeworks over the previous weeks, they disgorged their warrior cargos on the shores beneath the brilliance of the Everlight.

Aliya's magic surged as she summoned flames to meet them. Legionaries were immolated as they charged up the white rocks and marble steps towards the tower. Some boatloads were set alight before even reaching the shore, the armoured Zamorakians aboard given a choice of burning or drowning.

Aliya was the most potent sorcerer on either side in Hallowvale, but she alone was not enough to hold back the rising tide. Her small force of hypaspists fought stubbornly at her side, forming a cordon on the steps around the Everlight, preferring to die rather than permit the sacred tower fall into the hands of the Zamorakians.

Wreckage from the assault beached itself along the southern shores of Hallowvale, and some of the boats, diverted by the changing currents, landed within the city walls. Those on board stormed inland, rising up through the narrow lanes and winding streets beyond the docks and wharves, most of them pushing towards the palace.

It was one such group that Rhea and her little pack of Wolves encountered just two streets short of the palace doors.

The Wolves had the advantage of surprise – they had emerged from an alleyway right into the midst of the Zamorakians. They slaughtered their prey. Besides Mardin and Klaxar, there were five others left with Rhea. She had told them briefly of what she hoped to do. None seemed convinced it would succeed, but all accepted that it was her duty to try, and therefore their duty to aid her. She was silently thankful they were with her.

Klaxar finished the last legionary with a brutal swing of her labrys. Blood spattered up the store's front and ran dark and thick between the cobbles underfoot.

"We have to keep going," Rhea said. "The palace is close."

When they had first abandoned the walls, they had searched down through the citadel, hoping to find Larina and Safalaan there. Instead, they had come across an icyene Rhea recognised as the captain of the royal guard. He had chosen to stay behind and was headed to the walls when Rhea met him. He claimed the royal children had been taken by their chaperone from the citadel, though he didn't know where.

The palace seemed like the only option. Rhea had set off with her small following through the city as it descended into chaos. Deserters from the walls coupled with people fleeing blindly from their homes down towards the docks to the south and east meant most of the streets were impassable, so they had to take back alleys and travel north at first before they could turn down, beyond the arboretum and past the market square.

They turned a corner and found the palace ahead. There was no sign of the icyene guards, and the great front doors lay open.

Rhea had the terrible sense that they were too late. She led the others into the shadow of the pillars that supported the front of the structure, racing up the steps and through the doors, trying to ignore the tiredness in her limbs.

She had never seen the inside of the palace. It had an austere majesty to it, corridors of white marble and busts of past icyene rulers interspersed between tall windows.

Some were shuttered. Others admitted the dazzling brilliance of the Everlight, but Rhea knew it couldn't be relied on – who knew how long it would be before the Zamorakians overran it and snuffed out Saradomin's glory?

Despite the open doors, there were no signs of a struggle. Rhea paused in the entrance hall, its floor dominated by a sprawling mosaic of Saradomin bequeathing his star to a crowd of noble icyene, and listened.

Nothing. She dared call out, her voice echoing back from the cold stone.

"My name is Rhea, of the ordo of the wolf! I am a soldier of Saradomin, charged by the queen to bring her children to safety."

There was no reply.

"Search the rooms," Rhea ordered the other hypaspists.

THIRTY-ONE

◆—▶

"Help me with it," Akeron instructed Luken as they stood once more before the grand hallowed coffin. The junior illuminator hesitated, then put his shoulder to the slab covering the sarcophagus, heaving it far enough to one side to expose the interior.

The cold stink of the grave reached Akeron, old bones and mouldering cloth. He shivered. As majestic as the grand sarcophagus was, its contents were anything but glorious – the raw fodder of mortality, great men rendered down to the bare truth.

"Surely there's another way?" Luken asked. Akeron ignored the boy. He could not be weak now. Not here at the end, when it really mattered.

"Help me up," he rasped, his throat dry. Luken's reluctance was obvious, but still he obeyed. Limbs trembling, Akeron managed to pull himself up the star-littered side of the sarcophagus and clamber into it, so he was standing inside. The bones of his forebears crunched underfoot.

He stood, looking down at Luken, not knowing what to say. He loved him, he realised, loved him as the son he had never had.

It would do no good admitting that now. He doubted the boy would survive. He was still so young, so foolish and naïve. His good heart deserved a better fate that this. But young or not, he had a duty as well. Akeron had no choice but to burden him with it. His only hope was that it might yet prove Luken's salvation, his means of escaping this doomed city.

"Do not wait," he told him. "Move the slab into position, then go. The vyre will be upon us soon, but you can still make it out if you hurry. Do what you can to break the portal, but after you have tried, save yourself. That is my last instruction to you, Luken."

The youth was crying. Akeron was too spent for tears. He grasped the boy's shoulder one last time, then handed him the star staff. Luken took it in trembling hands.

With some difficulty, Akeron lay down in the sarcophagus. The remains of former archpriests dug into his back, as though they were prodding and taunting him.

"The slab," he rasped.

"Light be with you, archpriest," he heard Luken whimper. Then there were the sounds of his struggling, and the scrape of stone on stone.

Little by little, the illumination of the torches was replaced by solid darkness, until finally the last sliver of light was gone.

Akeron lay shivering, alone but for the dead. None had met their end like this, though all would have known that, if the Hallowed Sepulchre was ever threatened, it was their duty to do what Akeron was doing now. He was sure none of them would have hesitated. That was all the comfort he had left.

All he could hear was the beating of his heart and the rasping of his breath. He wondered if the air would run out first, or whether it would be the thirst that would kill him. He found himself praying for the former, knowing it would be quicker.

He shifted slightly, the bones still digging in. All else was silent. Was Luken still there? Surely he was already gone? If so, it was too late. Too late to cry out, to scream, to plead to be set free. Too late to ask why their god had abandoned them all.

Akeron almost groaned in despair. Almost. He forced himself to stay silent, to try and control his breathing. That was when he noticed something his eyes had been unable to pick out when the slab had first been heaved into place.

There were lights on the reverse side of the grand hallowed coffin. Little shards of lambent crystal that glowed with their own faint illumination. When the icyene had first carved and fashioned the stone tomb, they had done more than just decorate its exterior. They had inset stones into the inside of the lid, creating a constellation of stars that would look down forever upon the hallowed dead.

Saradomin hadn't abandoned him, the archpriest realised. He had been here all along, waiting for him.

Tears in his eyes, Akeron said his final prayer and lay still.

✦ ✦ ✦

Luken stood for far longer than he should have.

Akeron's instructions had been clear, but how could he go? How could he abandon the man who had raised him to this terrible fate?

He knew what Akeron would have said. This was no worse than what many in the city would suffer – better, perhaps. Hallowvale had fallen, and Luken's nightmares were coming to kill them all.

He gripped Akeron's staff tighter, finding it still warm to the touch where the archpriest had been holding it. He was still alive. Luken still had the strength to heave open the sarcophagus lid once more, drag him out.

But he couldn't. He had been given a duty of his own to fulfil, one just as great and terrible as the sacrifice the priesthood were now making. If he failed, if he hesitated any longer, he might have rendered it all in vain.

He screwed his eyes shut and tried to articulate a prayer, something Akeron would have been proud of. There was no answer. There never was, he realised. He was alone, but that could be no excuse.

Luken might fail Saradomin, but he could not fail Akeron.

He drew out the map the archpriest had given to him, and hurried to the statue that would admit him into the underworld.

✦ ✦ ✦

Hunger.

He had never known anything like it. It was a void at the core of his being, driving out every other sensation, every other thought. Hunger, and the desperate urge to quench it.

He couldn't remember his own name. He had been told it by his master, but it had no importance, not anymore. All that mattered was the void, and his need to fill it.

The darkness around him hid nothing. He could see, not as he might once have, but in hues of crimson, blotches of red discolouration that seemed to bloom and spread like blood across his vision.

Blood. He craved it. Nothing else could quench the hunger. He had wished so desperately to drink from the crimson altar, but his master's will had denied him. His master was powerful beyond all comprehension. Not even his hunger could make him deny it.

He could smell blood. Hear it too. The rush of it through veins, and the delicious thudding of the heartbeats that drove it, an endless feast just waiting to be gorged on.

They were somewhere above, but growing closer. He was lost, but the beats led him, the tattoo of vitality that would save his soul and help him remember. Once the hunger was gone, he was sure, he would be himself again.

THIRTY-TWO

———◆———

As Rhea's companions searched through the palace, she did her best to fight off her doubts. Where else would a chaperone take the royal children? The Hallowed Church perhaps? The remaining hypaspists of the unicorn would still be there, perhaps that was a better bet for safety? Or maybe they would seek shelter in some humble dwelling or abandoned shop, hoping to hide the identity of the children and escape during the chaos of the city's sack?

And if Rhea couldn't find them, then what should she do? Make a small, futile last stand in the palace when the Zamorakians arrived? Try to make their own escape?

A shout from Klaxar ended her uncertainties. She rushed along the corridor and burst into the room her companion had entered.

Before Rhea were the heirs of Hallowvale. Their chaperone had secured them in what looked like a dining chamber, dominated by a long table and chairs framed at the far end by another high, slender window depicting Saradomin presiding over a grand feast. They were huddled before it, backlit by the multi-hued brilliance streaming through the stained glass.

The chaperone had opened the door for Klaxar. Rhea's old companion was crouched and smiling at the children, trying to reassure them, her efforts incongruous considering the labrys she had laid down beside her, its head still glistening with Zamorakian blood.

"We're going to get you to safety," Rhea said as she entered, trying not to startle them. The children's eyes were wide with fear.

"Where is mam and da?" the boy – presumably Safalaan – demanded.

"The icyene have abandoned us," the chaperone said, her voice coloured by anger.

"I know," Rhea said. "And the walls are overrun, which is why we have to hurry."

"How can we get out? Isn't the city surrounded?"

"Only on land. Zamorakian boats have been landing at the docks all afternoon. If we can make it to one, we can use it to get out."

A voice from the doorway disturbed Rhea. It was Mardin.

"Zamorakians at the front doors," he said grimly. "We've barred the entrance, but there are bound to be other ways in. I recommend we get out, before this turns into a siege."

"We need a route," Rhea said to the chaperone. "Can you lead us?"

"We might have to go down," the woman said. "There are tunnels beneath the palace. One goes to the southern shore."

Rhea gestured for her to guide them. Esme headed towards a side door, shepherding the children with her. Before they could reach it, Rhea heard a shout and the familiar clash of steel from outside.

The Zamorakians had already found another way in.

"The door," she barked at Mardin who, with another hypaspist, Helas, stepped hastily inside and swung the entrance to the dining chamber shut.

"Follow the children," Rhea said to them and to Klaxar. "See they get out."

"Don't be stupid," Klaxar snapped, swiping her labrys from the floor and casually shouldering it. "This is your little quest, not ours. Get after them!"

Rhea knew it was madness to argue, though still she hesitated. Just then there was a solid impact against the far side of the door, shaking the dark timber. Helas and Mardin immediately threw themselves against it, battling to keep it shut as it continued to shudder under a rain of blows.

"We need to block it!" Klaxar shouted as she and Rhea added their strength to their efforts.

"Table's too big to shift," Mardin grunted, a particularly brutal blow momentarily staggering him before he drove himself back against the woodwork. "Chairs won't be enough."

Before Rhea could answer, the assault on the door suddenly ceased. The hypaspists remained braced against it, fearing a trick. Instead, a voice rang out from the other side, muffled but unmistakable.

"Rhea, is that you?"

It was Phosani.

Rhea looked at Mardin and Klaxar, who stared back at her.

"Open the doors, Rhea," came Phosani's voice again from the other side of the dining chamber entrance. "That's an order."

The voice unmistakably belonged to the White Wolf, yet there had been no sounds of a struggle, no indication that she had arrived and driven off or killed the Zamorakians who had been pounding at the doors just seconds earlier.

"There are Zamorakians in the palace," Rhea called out. "I cannot risk letting you in."

"You'll die if you don't," Phosani snapped. "Open the doors, and live."

"Have you really fallen so low?" Rhea demanded. "After all these years, have you thrown your lot in with the Zamorakian scum?"

Even after all Rhea had seen, after witnessing the collapse of Phosani's faith and courage over the past weeks, it seemed impossible that she would betray the cause they had fought for together for so long.

"This is your last chance, Rhea," shouted another voice she knew – Otrava.

It was less difficult to imagine the likes of her and Insela betraying their oaths. Rhea felt an unexpected pang of guilt. She should have shielded Phosani from their influence, should have told her that they did not seem worthy of joining the pack. They were not true Wolves, not worthy of the legacy of courage and duty borne across the years by the ordo.

"Open the doors!" the traitor shouted. Rhea looked at Mardin, Klaxar and Helas as they stayed pressed side-by-side against the timber frame, and shook her head.

The assault against the doorway resumed, even more furious than before. Rhea felt the timber shivering against her shoulder as she looked to the other entrance into the chamber, where the chaperone and her precious charges were hesitating, unsure if they should continue alone.

The dilemma was clear. Abandon the door and Phosani and her new allies would break through, but how could Rhea leave the children and their minder to wander unprotected with the palace overrun? They wouldn't make it out of the next chamber, let alone down to the tunnels they had spoken of.

"Leave the door, follow the children," she hissed at the others over the hammering. "One holds each doorway in turn, as we go. Understood?"

"Give me the honour of this one, justiciar," Helas said fiercely. Rhea nodded, noting how he had addressed her. She had never wanted such an honorific, had never desired command. All of her life, she had served, the good soldier. Now, it seemed, she was the only one left to give orders.

A part of the door splintered, the blunted tip of a spatha punching through dangerously close to Klaxar's head.

"Now," Rhea shouted, and threw herself back.

The doorway burst open almost immediately. Rhea, Mardin and Klaxar dashed across the chamber to the far door as Helas stood his ground, bellowing as he lunged with his doru.

"Go," Rhea shouted at the children. Klaxar got ahead of them as they dashed through the next door, Mardin and Rhea both stopping in it.

There was no time for an argument. A crossbow bolt cracked off the white wall beside them, not a Zamorakian one. Helas was already down, another bolt through his throat. It was the work of Insela, the treacherous lieutenant grimacing as she reloaded her weapon. Otrava was with her, and Phosani, the White Wolf's helm gone and her hair unbound, her face a cold, pale mask. Black-armoured Zamorakians flooded in through the doorway around them, charging at Rhea.

Fury the likes of which she had never known gripped her. She roared and met the first legionary, letting the thrust of his spatha jar off the star on her breastplate and slide past her as she lunged in and took the man's throat. Momentum caused them to collide in the doorway, his hot blood jetting across her cheek. She shoved him back into the next man, swung at him, forcing him to defend himself, driving him back.

"Face me," she bellowed at Phosani. "Face a true soldier of Saradomin, you treacherous coward!"

Perhaps there was still some spark of pride left in her old commander, for the White Wolf let out a roar of her own and drove past her new allies, striking wildly. Rhea parried, kopis and xiphos clashing.

How many times had they sparred together? How often had they fought in the line almost side-by-side, resisting the Zamorakian hordes? In a heartbeat, all fellowship was forgotten, all kinship cast aside, replaced by hate and rage.

Rhea went on the offensive, a flurry of strokes that Phosani met. Neither had their shields anymore. Rhea's mind went back to their last training session together, in the old icyene shrine that had become the Wolves' armoury.

Footwork. She saw Phosani's counter before she made it, giving ground so she was back in front of the doorway as the traitor turned defence into attack. Rhea parried a crosscut, scraping her blade down that of her opponent, trying to slash her kopis across Phosani's face.

It had once been her duty to keep her justiciar sharp. Now, it was her duty to break her.

Phosani twisted both her blade and Rhea's aside before the kopis could connect, then tried to drive back in while Rhea's guard was open.

Rhea had no time to parry. The xiphos bit deep, gouging across her breastplate and leaving the star of Saradomin cut in two. It had held though. Phosani's strike hadn't found flesh.

Rhea had been anticipating Phosani committing to striking through her guard. She had trusted to her armour, trusted to the emblem of her god to protect her while she, in turn, lashed at the traitor before she could recover.

Some instinct, born out of decades of combat, or perhaps dragged to the fore from some past session with Rhea, caused Phosani to throw herself back at the last instant. The wicked tip of Rhea's kopis caught her cheek. Had she not moved, the blow would have cleaved Phosani's skull in half from left to right.

She reeled away, clutching the red wound. Rhea saw the follow-up in her mind's eye, saw her kopis take the former justiciar in the throat, carving her open to her spine and turning the silver hair about her shoulders crimson.

Instead, she was forced to parry as Otrava came at her from her left side, yelling furiously. Rhea's rage redoubled and she drove the other traitor back with a flurry of blows, but there were too many of the Zamorakians now, the weight of them forcing her back. She parried, taking more hits against her armour, and suddenly there was a hand gripping her shoulder, dragging her back through the doorway she had been defending.

Mardin shoved her into the corridor beyond the dining chamber and slammed the door shut. She began to protest, shouting that it wouldn't hold them, but her voice was buried by the crash of shattering marble. Mardin had heaved the bust of some icyene noble standing next to the doorway over, and it now fell across the doorway, half blocking it. The timber of the door itself began to splinter as the Zamorakians beat at it furiously, but the broken stone visage of one of Hallowvale's ancient founders ensured it stayed shut.

"By the light," Rhea panted. Mardin had broken the dark fury that had gripped her, and she now turned, looking to see if the children were in the corridor as well.

"Klaxar has taken them on," Mardin said, indicating a set of stairs leading down to what Rhea presumed were the lower levels. "If we hurry, we can catch up."

They ran for the steps, the door beginning to split apart behind them. Vengeance against Phosani would mean certain death, and that would mean Rhea had abandoned her own duty. She prayed silently to a god she had rarely sought out, that she would have an opportunity to face the White Wolf again after she had gotten the children out.

They reached the bottom of the stairway. A tunnel-like passage lay ahead, less grand than the corridors above, built from sloping brickwork and devoid of windows.

"Get back!"

Rhea heard Klaxar's shout ring out along the tunnel, followed by a clattering noise, then a scream that sounded like one of the children.

Mardin began to run and Rhea followed. They rushed down the stairs and burst into a chamber at the tunnel's end. It was a subterranean confluence, three different entrances all leading in different directions, all going down.

Something had risen up out of one of them. It took Rhea a moment to realise that she recognised it.

Ascertes. The king of Hallowvale, taken by the vyre. Now he had returned, alone, but changed utterly. His once-noble clothes were stained with mud and blood, his face as white as a corpse. More blood glistened black in the torchlight across his mouth and chin, and his eyes gleamed like a predator's in the darkness.

He bared his teeth, and Rhea saw fangs, wet with vital essence. Klaxar's blood. The hypaspist was on her knees, labrys fallen beside her, both hands clutching her throat as she tried to stem the flow from her torn neck.

The chaperone was now the only thing between the bloodied king of Hallowvale and his children. She spread her arms protectively, warding away her former ruler, seeing what Rhea only now understood.

Ascertes was no more. Somehow, the vyre had infected him, tainted him with their predatory nature. His eyes alone spoke the truth – there was no comprehension in them, no awareness, only a terrible hunger.

He was fast, too fast for Rhea to follow. He had the chaperone by her throat, and by the time either of the two remaining Wolves had taken a step forward, had thrown the brave woman against the nearest wall with a brutal crunch.

Rhea and Mardin charged across the chamber, but they were too slow. The creature snatched Larina as she managed to shove her younger brother back. Rhea's sword was driving towards the corrupt human, but she was forced to check it so it didn't strike the girl instead.

The beast sunk its fangs into Larina's pale, slender throat. Rhea cried out in horror.

"Da!" Safalaan shouted. The voice of Ascertes' son, and the taste of his daughter's blood, seemed to do more to break through to the man he had once been than the threat of Rhea's sword. She saw his eyes widen and lose that terrible gleam, even with his fangs at Larina's throat. He broke the death-grip, looking about like a man awaking from a drunken stupor, his gaze travelling from Safalaan to Larina, in his arms, limp and unmoving.

"No!" Safalaan screamed.

The exclamation came out as more than just rage and despair. The child seemed to shine, a sudden and luminous brilliance that flooded the chamber.

Ascertes shrieked and flinched away, blinded by the light of his son. Still clutching Larina, he darted towards the darkness of one of the stairwells. Rhea made to pursue, but by the time she reached the upper steps the creature had already vanished, carrying Larina with him.

"Go after her," Safalaan shouted. "Get her back!"

"She's dead," Mardin said, his voice dull with despair as he looked at Rhea. "As will you be if you go down into the dark after that thing."

"That was the king," Rhea said, still horrified by what she had just witnessed. In her time fighting the Zamorakians she had encountered many undead nightmares and unquiet spirits, but never had she seen or heard of a human transformed into a vyre. Werewolves were said to be the biproducts of vampyric efforts to create a servant species, but Ascertes had clearly been something else entirely.

Mardin was right – Larina was gone, and there was no further time to ponder what terrible fate had befallen her and her father. Instead, Rhea hurried to Klaxar's side. Mardin had already helped her to sit up against the wall and was stemming the worst of the bleeding. Rhea looked at the amount already spilled and the glazed look in her old friend's eyes. It was too late.

"Sorry," was all Klaxar could grunt, spitting blood.

"Save your strength," Rhea instructed her. "We'll get you out."

"No," Klaxar managed, grimacing with the effort. "Give me my labrys. I'll hold them."

It was clear Klaxar wouldn't be able to stop the Zamorakians, but it was also clear she had minutes left, at best. Rhea bowed her head briefly, mastering the bitter surge of sorrow that swelled within her. Then, she picked up the powerful axe and placed it in Klaxar's hands. Her grip was still strong.

"You deserved a better end," she told her.

"Doesn't... make a difference," Klaxar said. "Get the boy out."

She looked at Safalaan, who had sat down nearby, sobbing into his arms. The sight of the boy helped drive out the exhausted sense of failure gripping her. She still had a duty to do, and she would rather die than admit to final, crushing defeat.

She moved over and took him by the shoulders.

"I'm sorry about your sister... and your father," she said to him. "But we need to keep going."

Those probably weren't the right words. She had never raised a child, had rarely even spoken with one. How could she bring comfort to one who had witnessed such horrors?

She looked to the chaperone, who lay where Ascertes had thrown her.

"She's dead," Mardin said, following her gaze. "I checked her."

"She was brave," Rhea noted, not knowing what else to say. This city was full of the brave, and the cowardly, and soon all would be equally dead. That was the truth of it.

There was the sound of voices, echoing down from the corridor they had left behind. It had to be the Zamorakians.

"Go," Klaxar hissed.

"Which tunnel?" Mardin asked Rhea. There were three sets of stairs leading further down. It seemed unwise to take the one Ascertes had vanished into. The other two amounted to the roll of a die.

"Left," Rhea decided. "Come on."

She pulled Safalaan to his feet. To her relief he didn't struggle, and stayed upright as she guided him towards the stairs. She paused while Mardin joined her, carrying a torch retrieved from one of the brackets in the wall. She looked back at Klaxar.

"It's been an honour," she told the hypaspist.

Klaxar didn't manage to say anything, but was able to summon up one last bloody grin.

Rhea saluted her, tapping two fingers to the scarred star of Saradomin on her chest, then led Mardin and Safalaan down, deeper into the cold, bitter depths.

THIRTY-THREE

◆◆◆

Vanescula paced.

She was with her cohort on the edge of the siegeworks, not yet committed to the assault. She had been there since Drakan had instructed her to oversee the attacks on the walls, before vanishing without further explanation. She could only assume he had gone to the Blood Altar. She yearned to join him in the quest, but she had been given clear instructions, and she did not disobey her brother. So, instead of hunting through Hallowvale's depths, she was receiving messengers from assault parties and snapping out orders for them to take back. She was fully armed and armoured, but felt impotent and cut adrift, unable to pass into the radius of the Everlight even as her underlings overran the walls.

That, at least, she hoped would soon change. The flotilla the legion had been busy constructing had set out for the small cluster of islands to the south-east of the city, intending to storm it and snuff out its accursed light. Once they did, and darkness finally fell, the vyre could descend and truly finish the siege.

Another panting runner brought news. The fourth cohort had finally breached the citadel itself. Vanescula, squinting into the light, could see that the western gates were now open. The defences were being overrun and still, there was nothing she could do besides commit more reserves and order the cohorts to secure more of the walls and then push on into the city.

In her anxious, frustrated state, she didn't notice Drakan until he landed right in front of her.

"My lord," she said hastily and bowed without thinking. The master of the vyre rose to his full, imposing height and furled his wings. He spent a few moments looking out over the city before addressing Vanescula.

"I have found what we seek," he declared. "And it is glorious."

Vanescula knew what he said was true. Fresh blood still glistened on his lower face, and she could sense how its power infused him. He was stronger than ever. She envied him deeply.

"The altar is below the city?" she asked, trying to keep the hunger from her voice.

"It is," Drakan confirmed. "I have left Korgax guarding its entrance. But you will not visit it yet. You have one more duty to fulfil first."

"Have I not done enough?" Vanescula snapped, despite herself. "Am I not worthy to sup the same blood as my own brother?"

Drakan looked at her levelly before answering.

"That is for me to decide. The altar offers more than just its arcane blood. It allows us to remake mortals in our image."

"You have managed this?" Vanescula asked, shock cutting through her anger.

"Yes. Ascertes is no more. What was once the king of Hallowvale we now count as kin. He stalks the deeps, looking to feed. And now that we know it can be done, the time has come to change not just one or two mortals, but this entire city. In time, all of Hallowvale will drink the blood and bear within them the immortal glory of Vampyrium."

Vanescula could hardly imagine such a thing. A whole city of vyre, a kingdom of their own, Vampyrium recreated on Gielinor. And why stop at Hallowvale?

"Now you truly understand," Drakan said. "And you see also why our lesser kindred must not be allowed to slaughter at will. They may feed, of course, but the majority of those within the walls must be spared. It will mean little if I rule over a kingdom of corpses."

"So be it," Vanescula said, accepting her brother's will once more. "I shall go to the broods and tell them to... restrain themselves."

"Make it clear that excesses of bloodshed will not be tolerated," Drakan said. "But do not yet tell them of the altar. Not until the city is ours."

"As you wish, brother."

✦ ✦ ✦

Hallowvale burned.

The legion was under orders to avoid damaging the city or massacring its inhabitants, but there was only so much restraint that could be shown. Fires caught and spread amidst the chaos, black, broiling plumes of smoke beginning to climb into the sky, hazing the Everlight's glory.

Above the citadel, the city's blue and gold standard was torn down by cheering Zamorakian soldiers and cast from the walls.

In the Saradominist quarter, legionaries stormed the shrines and temples, hauling down statues and shattering mosaics while shedding the blood of the Lord of Light's priesthood.

Around the Hallowed Church, the ordo of the unicorn made their last stand. Monokeros had been honoured with the rank of justiciar after the loss of Lysander, and he and his hypaspists gave their lives to keep the doors to the Church barred for as long as possible. When the last of them fell, the Zamorakians attempted to break open the entrances, but they had no tools to aid them, and couldn't gain access.

When they eventually did, the first ones over the thresholds were immolated by the traps awaiting them.

To the south-east, the Lions were making a stand of their own. Aliya, exhausted and with her runestones burned out or spent, withdrew with the last of her hypaspists inside the Everlight. The Zamorakians fashioned a crude ram from the wreckage of one of their boats and used it to batter down the doors. The pristine white marble of the tower's stairway ran red with blood as the Lions fought ferociously for each and every last step.

In the end, it was not a Zamorakian who snuffed out Saradomin's light. Aliya, alone now, reached the arcane controls at the pinnacle of the tower, just beneath where the blinding luminance was surging forth. She knew that the Zamorakians would try to break the Everlight, and she knew that none would be able to work its complex machinery, crafted by Saradomin himself. If she turned it off, they might not know which parts to destroy. Perhaps, one day, it could be brought back to life.

It was her last act as justiciar of the lion. She spoke the sorcerous words and shifted the machinery that would douse the Everlight. Then, as it started to flicker, she took one last look out over the city, then threw herself from the tower's pinnacle.

And suddenly, the light was gone. For the first time since it had been built, darkness fell over Hallowvale. Night swept in, and claimed that which had been denied to it for so many centuries.

With a shriek that chilled the blood of every mortal that heard it, the vyre rose.

THIRTY-FOUR

———◆◆———

At the bottom of the next flight of stairs Rhea found another tunnel, this one carved from bedrock rather than built from brick. For a short way Mardin's flame was their only illumination, but abruptly the torches fixed to the jagged walls began to ignite as they passed them, seemingly aware of their presence.

"Sorcery?" Rhea wondered aloud, keeping a tight hold on Safalaan.

"Looks like it," Mardin answered. "An icyene trick, hopefully." He kept his own light aloft.

They came to a crossroads. Rhea paused, trying to picture their progress in her mind relative to the directions of the different branches.

"Have you ever been down here?" she asked Safalaan. He shook his head, sniffing.

Rhea chose the left-hand branch. It soon became clear the tunnel was descending deeper still, its slope leading them far below Hallowvale. Rhea doubted they were directly under the palace any longer.

Mardin, leading the way, came up short, and gestured with his free hand to wait. Rhea looked past him and saw that there was firelight coming from around a bend in the tunnel, indicating that someone there had already ignited the torches further along. A second later she caught the sound of hurried footsteps, echoing along the passageway.

She caught Mardin's eye and brandished her kopis. The hypaspist nodded and pressed back against the wall, ready to sweep out and cut down whatever was approaching. It seemed unlikely it could be anything other than more Zamorakians.

Rhea held Safalaan close, and put her hand over his mouth, not wanting him to give them away with even a whisper. A shadow was thrown against the far wall, the footsteps right on them now.

With a snarl, Mardin lunged.

◆ ◆ ◆

Luken hurried through the darkness, trying not to panic.

It was one thing to be led by Akeron through the tunnels under the palace, but another to try to travel almost the entire length of the city's underbelly from north to south. The passages were not as uniform as the ones he had seen before, most just dirt and bare rock and no arcane torches, bending and winding like a rabbit's warren. At times they opened up into what seemed like abandoned cellars and forgotten crypts, long sealed off from above. At one point the passages crossed through one of the old sewer systems that serviced the icyene quarter just east of the citadel.

Luken became lost. At one point he doubled back, growing frantic, as terrified now at the thought of wandering forever in this dark, cold underworld as he was of what he might find lurking around the next bend.

After wandering aimlessly he sat down against the tunnel wall and wept. As he sat snivelling, he noticed the light of Akeron's staff, still clutched in one hand, starting to glimmer. Up until then it had been a constant glow, his only companion in the dark. Now though it was flickering.

His panic resurged as he thought the light was about to go out, but his eyes ran to where it was falling, against the far wall. The flickering picked out something in the rock face he had missed. Rubbing his eyes, he pulled himself up and peered closer.

A crude version of a Saradominist star had been carved into it, along with a small circle in each quadrant.

Luken stared, then fumbled for the map stuffed in the cord securing his robes. He held it up to the light of the staff, pinning it to the stone so he could trace a grubby finger along the parchment, then looking back up at the design on the wall next to it.

The star and four gold coins. According to the chart Akeron had given him, the symbols were carved into the tunnels directly below the city bank.

He knew where he was. He traced the lines, south, towards the palace, and the twin skulls.

The light of the staff had stopped pulsing. It was constant

again, steady. It had been guiding him, Luken decided. The power of Saradomin, or perhaps just one last assistance from Akeron. The thought of the old archpriest rekindled his courage. Against all odds, Akeron had not abandoned his faith. Neither would Luken. He gripped the staff more firmly and held it up, using it to ward away the darkness that seemed to creep and coil all around him.

He reached the next waypoint on the map, and then the next. Light kindled ahead of him, not the lambent illumination of the star staff, but the flicker of flames. It was a torch, set into the wall, lighting up at his approach. That at least meant he was closer to the palace, in amongst the oldest tunnels excavated by the icyene.

Almost there. He began to hurry, footsteps echoing ahead and behind, giving him the uncomfortable sensation that he was being followed.

He swept around a bend in the tunnel, and thought he had died.

Something surged at him from the flickering shadows, firelight gleaming ruddily from bared steel. He screamed involuntarily as he was driven back against the opposite wall, convinced that a Zamorakian was about to run him through.

"Wait!"

The voice was a woman's, and it stayed the hand of his would-be killer. Luken kept very still, gripping the staff, staring like a trapped rabbit at the wolves that had snared him.

The one with a sword pressing against his gut was a man, while a woman stood behind him, clutching a boy against her side. Both the adults were clearly warriors, garbed in steel and leather. Luken felt as though he recognised the woman, but more importantly, he noticed the battle-scarred star of Saradomin emblazoned on her breast, the same one sewn into the front of Luken's grubby blue robes.

"That's the archpriest of the unicorn's assistant," the woman said, surprised. "Let him go."

The man removed the threat of his sword, and Luken abruptly remembered where he knew the woman from. She was Rhea, the lieutenant to the White Wolf, one of the hypaspist commanders. He had seen her during the early days of the invasion, in the council sessions held in the citadel.

"What's your name?" she demanded.

"Luken," he responded, voice dry. "I... I'm junior illuminator to Archpriest Akeron."

"He is fleeing," Rhea's scarred companion said darkly. "You came all this way from the Hallowed Sepulchre? How did you find the tunnels?"

"I am not fleeing," Luken exclaimed, anger at the false accusation momentarily overcoming his fear. "I am on a holy quest!"

He stopped himself before going any further, remembering his duty. The pair frowned, clearly not believing him.

"Archpriest Akeron gave me his staff," Luken declared, brandishing the glowing relic defiantly. "I am to perform a vital task."

"In these tunnels?" Rhea asked.

"Yes."

"And what is this task?"

"I have sworn an oath upon the light of Saradomin not to say."

"Convenient," the man grumbled, looking back at Rhea. "We should just leave him."

"What is happening at the Sepulchre?" Rhea asked.

"Final preparations are being made to preserve it," Luken said. "The priesthood are sacrificing themselves, so that none will know how to breach their defences."

That caused the pair to exchange a look. Rhea nodded at Luken; he realised she had noticed the map crumpled in his fist.

"You know these tunnels?" she asked.

Luken wondered how much he should admit to. He cleared his throat, and nodded.

"I have been entrusted with a way through them, yes."

"And does that include a way out of them, once you complete whatever your quest is?"

"Yes."

"Then we'll need to make use of your knowledge," Rhea said. "Do you know who this is?"

She patted the shoulder of the boy at her side. His face was tear-streaked, and he had been gazing up at Luken with dark, solemn eyes. Luken shook his head.

"This is Prince Safalaan, heir and now quite possibly ruler of Hallowvale. Queen Efaritay herself charged us with getting him and his sister to safety. We have already failed her, but we will not fail him."

"You're using the tunnels to get out of the city?" Luken wondered.

"We're trying to reach the docks, but we don't know the way," Rhea admitted. "The Zamorakians have already overrun the palace, and there are vyre down here."

Luken looked sharply at her, trying to weigh the possibilities against the dangers.

"I can show you the way to the docks, if you protect me until my task is complete," he said.

"And what is your task?"

"Would you make me break an oath made to our god? It is vital. That will have to be enough."

"Very well," Rhea said finally. "Lead on."

The junior illuminator led the way, his staff combining with the torches to fill the underworld with light.

Rhea didn't know if following him was the right thing to do. After Phosani's cowardly betrayal, and Ascertes'… change, she didn't trust anybody but Mardin.

But she didn't know the way. The chances of wandering the tunnels until the Zamorakians or the vyre found them seemed far higher than finding the right way out. She contemplated taking the map Luken seemed to be using, but that would risk damaging it, and she wasn't sure she would be able to read it anyway.

For better or for worse, their fate was in the young Saradominist's hands.

They carried on for an age, until Luken came to such an abrupt halt Rhea almost ran into him.

"We're close," he whispered, his voice hoarse. "But do

you hear that?"

Rhea was about to say she hadn't, when she caught a low hissing sound, growing rapidly louder. It reminded her of the noises she had heard during the battle above Hephaston's mill.

"Vyre!"

She threw Luken and Safalaan to one side. Something slammed into her with bone-jarring force, sending her sprawling across the tunnel floor.

Pain shot through her arm, and she heard her kopis clatter away. She rolled, snarling, reaching for it with her other hand. The hissing had been the sound of vyre wings.

It was fast, faster than the tainted Ascertes. She heard a roar, a roar that became a shriek.

The light glowing from Luken's staff flickered, and the flames of Mardin's torch flared, then guttered. Rhea managed to get onto her knees and snatch her sword, twisting in time to see the last of her old friends dying.

The vampyre ripped Mardin's throat out in a jet of blood. The creature was heavily armoured, but it used its fangs and talons, its monstrous strength and speed overpowering the veteran Saradominist soldier in an instant.

Rhea screamed and threw herself at the creature, but it ducked a swing of her kopis and tossed Mardin against her, then snatched her wrist and slammed it into the tunnel wall. As Mardin's blood gouted over her she cried out, feeling bones in her hand crunch, her kopis falling again. The creature let go and she had no choice but to shove Mardin aside, terrified that the vyre was about to tear Safalaan apart.

It was Luken, and not Rhea, who stood between the heir to Hallowvale and the blood-drinking horror. The skinny youth raised his star staff in trembling hands, shouting a prayer.

The light emanating from the staff redoubled in intensity, and the vyre let out a shriek, shielding its face with one gauntlet. Rhea hoped that it would flee, the way Safalaan's light had caused his father to, or perhaps even immolate beneath the sacred illumination, but neither happened.

The vyre recovered. Luken's desperate pleas to his god were cut off as it snatched his throat and pinned him to the wall, shrieking, fangs glistening black with blood. Safalaan, screaming, ran at the terror and beat his fists against its armoured flank, but it didn't even seem to notice.

Mardin was on the floor, choking, dying. Rhea's right hand was in agony and her kopis had skittered away across the tunnel floor. She reached down with her left, and as she did so, remembered what was lodged in her belt.

The blisterwood shard. She snatched it from her waist and lunged with a roar at the vyre, just as it prised Luken's staff from his grip and cast it across the tunnel.

Darkness fell as the light of Saradomin went out, but Rhea had followed instinct honed by decades of battle. She had gone for one of the weak points in the vyre's armour, at the joint between shoulder and arm, and even in the dark she found her mark, just as the creature turned on her.

The blisterwood punched through the vampyre's pale, cold flesh, skewering under its arm, punching between its ribs.

The thing let out a howl so piercing it seemed to burst Rhea's eardrums. She clutched at her head with her uninjured hand and stumbled back, letting go of the blisterwood.

She could see nothing, she felt only incredible pain and could hear only a terrible ringing. Then, light flickered once more, not the illumination of Luken's staff, but the angry glow of firelight.

The vyre had ignited. Flames burst across it from where the blisterwood was impaling it, and its shriek became a roar of combustion as it burned from the inside out, cooking inside its armour.

It staggered, releasing Luken, and by the time it fell with a clatter of armour, its body had been reduced to ash and smouldering embers, the stink of its immolation making Rhea choke, then vomit.

She put her left hand against the cold, unyielding stone of the tunnel wall, steadying herself as the darkness returned. Luken scrambled past and retrieved his staff, hoarsely panting the prayers that summoned the light.

The vyre was no more, just ash heaped within an empty suit of blackened armour. Rhea noticed something glinting white among the remains, and stooped, finding the blisterwood shard whole and unburned. She slipped it back into her belt.

Mardin was dead. He lay in the middle of the tunnel, eyes staring unseeingly up at the ceiling, blood pulsing in a slow, dark trickle from his torn neck.

Rhea crouched over him, clutching her broken hand. She was silent, until she felt the tide of her emotions break over her. It brought with it a shout, rage and sorrow, a deep, primal exclamation of pent-up grief that echoed away through

Hallowvale's desolate depths, repeating over and over before it finally, slowly faded away into the darkest crevices of the underworld.

She wept, shedding tears not just for Mardin, or for Klaxar, but for every friend she had known down the years who had died like this, for a god that had abandoned them all.

She felt a hand on her shoulder. She looked up, at Luken. His expression was grave. Safalaan was standing beside him, holding his hand.

"I need to finish my quest," the junior illuminator told Rhea. "Before it's too late."

He crouched down in front of her and held up something he was wearing around his neck. It was a talisman with a glittering ruby in its centre, fashioned to look like a drop of blood.

"This will transport us to where I need to be," Luken said. "Touch it, close your eyes, and focus on your heartbeat."

"Where is it taking us?" Rhea demanded.

"A place of blood and darkness," Luken said. "One which I must seal off."

Safalaan put his hand on the talisman, next to Luken's. His eyes were red-raw, yet he wasn't crying anymore, his young face stony and defiant.

Slowly, Rhea reached up with her left hand, and placed it against the talisman.

THIRTY-FIVE

———◆———

Luken took a long, slow breath, and tried to find the right words.

The talisman had worked. He was standing in the chamber of the twin skulls, along with Rhea and the prince.

Something had happened when the vyre had attacked them. It was as if, overwhelmed, he had forgotten to be afraid. He had known he was about to die, and fear had suddenly felt like an insignificant and meaningless emotion.

He tried to maintain hold of that feeling of inevitability, and the sense of unassailable calm it had brought with it.

Rhea was holding the child close and they were staring around, taking in the chamber of rock they had been transported to. Luken took back the talisman and strode to the skulls, raising the star staff as he went.

What now? Akeron had claimed the staff and its light could break the portal to the Blood Altar. But how? He remembered the archpriest's insistence that, if he found he could not break the skulls, he should save himself. Perhaps that was all this was? Perhaps Akeron had simply wanted to offer Luken a way out?

But he had to try. He stood before the leering stone, gripped the archpriest's staff two-handed, and began to pray.

The words were ancient and holy, the most powerful invocations of the Book of Light, spoken in the tongue of the icyene. Luken had known them almost all his life, each catechism as familiar to him as the halls and corridors of the Hallowed Church.

He called on Saradomin, called on the divine power manifesting as his light. He prayed for deliverance, for strength, and above all for the glory of his god to show itself by turning away the dark, by breaking the strength of the forces of evil. His voice was firm and strong, and the light of the star staff blazed, filling the chamber.

Yet the skull stone remained unchanged.

Luken approached it, holding the staff over it, chanting, feeling the power his faith gave him. The light bathed the rock, but it remained otherwise untouched, the twin skulls seeming to mock Luken.

His words faltered. He turned to prayers of his own, taken not from the sacred texts but from the heart, calling on Saradomin and his righteous glory to break this gateway to so infernal a place.

The light coruscated about the star that tipped Akeron's staff. Still though, there was no sign of any effect on the portal.

The last words of Luken's prayer became a roar of frustration. He swung the staff, slammed it against the rock with all his strength, not caring if the holy relic shattered, venting the fear and sorrow and uncertainty of the past weeks in an instant of raw passion.

There was a crash like thunder and a burst of light so brilliant it blinded Luken. He was flung back, landing painfully on his back. As the noise reverberated around the chamber, he thought the roof was caving in, expecting to feel the weight of Gielinor itself come crashing down on him.

He remained uncrushed. He clutched at his eyes with one hand and groped about with the other, finding his feet as his sight slowly returned.

The star staff had shattered into a hundred shards, each splinter pulsing with a rapidly fading light. They illuminated the skull portal, broken. Luken's strike, and the arcane discharge he had unleashed, had riven the skulls almost in two, leaving a jagged, black crack between them that smoked in the aftermath of the ferocious blow.

"Is it done?" Rhea asked softly. She and her charge were unharmed, the child clutched in her arms, staring wide-eyed at the portal.

"I... I think so," Luken managed.

He knew the only way to be sure would be to touch one of the skulls and see if it transported him to the accursed chamber, but he did not dare do that. Whether it was broken now or not, what more could he do?

Ears still ringing, he mouthed a prayer of thanks to Saradomin and scooped to retrieve as many shards of the broken staff that he could fit into the pockets of his himation.

Then, after one last glance at the portal and its twin, terrible grins, he pulled out the blood talisman and held it out for Rhea and Safalaan to take.

◆ ◆ ◆

The throne room lay deserted before Ranis.

He grinned, pacing slowly through it, gazing at the towering statues and pillars and the mosaics, and the grand, circular window that framed its far end. He mounted the dais before it, looking between the two thrones, and chose the largest.

The city had fallen. The loss of the Everlight had made sure of that. Now the broods were descending on the cowering inhabitants, and victory was at hand.

Drakan himself was abroad too, disciplining the vyre. Ranis didn't care much for that. He had restrained his own need to feed, and had entered the citadel with all haste, intending to stake his claim. He would be remembered as the first vampyre to have penetrated the very heart of the enemy's stronghold.

He sat down on the throne.

He had barely come to rest when he detected movement in the chamber's doorway. He surged immediately back to his feet, thinking that Drakan had come to claim the throne.

But no, it was just his accursed sister. He hissed softly.

Vanescula laughed as she swept into the hall and noticed the startled expression her brother was trying to hide.

"Am I interrupting your coronation?" she taunted.

"Shouldn't you be scurrying around, begging our kin not to take what is rightfully theirs?" he countered. "Does my brother still demand we spare the cattle?"

"Oh, poor Ranis," she said, pouting at him as though he were a young broodling. "You still don't know?"

Ranis bristled, trying to fight off the detestable feeling that his sister currently held some kind of power over him.

"Know what?"

"We did not come here to conquer, or at least, it is an afterthought. There is more to this city than you know."

"What do you mean?"

"The Blood Altar," Vanescula declared grandly, flashing her fangs in a smile. "It lies beneath Hallowvale."

"That old myth?" Ranis scoffed, but Vanescula just laughed at him.

"Only a myth to short-sighted dolts like you, Ranis. Our brother has tracked it down. He has visited it, has partaken of its power."

"Impossible," Ranis breathed, feeling dumbstruck.

"And there's more," Vanescula said, clearly delighting in driving home her victory. "The altar offers us more than just its arcane blood. It can be used to change mortals. To transform them. To grant them the blessings of Vampyrium."

"It… turns them into vyre?" Ranis asked, no longer certain if his sister was playing some elaborate joke.

"Yes," Vanescula said, raising her arms triumphantly. "That little human you captured, Ascertes – Lowerniel has already taken him before the altar and turned him. In the coming days, all in this city will experience the same! Hallowvale will become more than just a subjugated stronghold. It will become our new home, remade at the dawn of a new age!"

As his sister's words rung through the desolate throne room, Ranis battled the urge to strike her. What she claimed sounded as magnificent as it was impossible, and yet, one matter rendered it all detestable to him. He had known nothing of it. Their brother had confided in Vanescula and not him. Now she held the advantage, once more carried the prestige. All his efforts since the start of the invasion to advance his position had been in vain.

He stood silent, glaring with tightly fettered hatred at his sister. She seemed to sense his thoughts and, still smiling, reached out and placed one hand gently against his cheek.

"Do not be upset, little brother. We can carry on our contest for a thousand years and more. But we shall do it here, as lords and mistresses of what will become the greatest and most terrible city in Gielinor."

✦ ✦ ✦

Drakan returned to the tunnels under the city.

He had left the altar to ensure his vyre didn't massacre the city's inhabitants, and in that regard he had done what he could. Starving and exultant, the broods had descended on the crowds of refugees clogging the eastern docks and streets, and quenched the worst of their murder-lust.

Hallowvale was Drakan's city now, and its people were as much his subjects as any of the vyre.

The death of the Everlight had ensured that. He had crouched atop the walls of the citadel and let loose a victorious shriek as darkness had blanketed the city, his cry so piercing it caused windows below to shatter.

As always, the moment's exaltation had been fleeting, driven by the constant desire to keep going, to keep hunting. Dawn was not far off now – the legion had orders to secure suitable nesting sites within the city for the vyre to retreat into. The proper work of subjugation would not begin until the next nightfall.

Drakan would not wait until then. He commanded the first of the prisoners taken during the storming of the walls to be brought by the vyreguard, and descended with them into the depths. Drakan could scent the alluring blood-stink of the altar as strongly as before, yet when he cried out through the tunnels, expecting Korgax to answer, there was no response.

His instincts, honed by thousands of years of predation, stirred.

He left the vyreguard behind, sweeping through the passageways. Not only could he not hear Korgax, but he could sense others. Heartbeats, three of them. He bared his fangs, slashing through the dark, surging like a storm of wings and talons into the section of tunnels saturated with blood magics, the ones that allowed access to the altar's portal.

He found Korgax, reduced to a heap of ash within his fallen armour.

He should have left more than just the captain of the vyreguard. In his hubris, he had thought no mortals would find their way to this place, but some had, and they bore the power of Saradomin, or the icyene – something inimical to his kind.

He scented the air, listened again. The heartbeats were growing fainter. They were fleeing.

He spat an invocation, furling his wings about him in a flurry that stirred up Korgax's ash. In an instant he was in the chamber bearing the portal, the only means of accessing the altar.

It was broken. The twin skulls had been split apart. To Drakan's vision, the space was still saturated with the light of Saradomin.

He hissed with frustration, half-blinded, and lunged forward to press both hands against the skulls.

The space around him flickered. One moment he was in the chamber of the Blood Altar, another he was back with the skulls. After a few seconds more of uncertainty, the flickering ceased. He was still standing before the portal.

Drakan snatched his hands back, not wanting to be trapped in some liminal space between the two.

The gateway to the altar was broken. He could fix it, he was certain. But not immediately. Not without great study, and care.

Hallowvale had fallen, but a new age of darkness would not be born tonight.

Drakan howled with rage. Then, calling upon the blood magics, he returned to the tunnels and threw himself after the ones who had done this – three little heartbeats, fleeing for their lives.

✦ ◆ ✦

"There," Rhea shouted, pointing with her uninjured hand.

They had stumbled from the tunnels to find themselves beneath the palace, with the first hint of dawn on the horizon. Rhea had smelled sea salt and felt shingle crunch under her feet, leaving behind the cloying sewer-reek that had befouled the final few passages.

She felt hope then, almost unwelcome after so much suffering, and it redoubled when she spotted the boat, beached against a rock on the shingle. The slender shore around the south-eastern tip of the city, beneath the palace, was littered with the detritus of the seaborne Zamorakian assault that had been launched against the islands bearing the Everlight.

Luken made an ungainly rush over the shingle, almost tripping in his robes. Rhea urged Safalaan after him and hurried to catch up. They put their shoulders against the damp timber and began to heave.

With a crunch, the boat shifted slowly down towards the waves. In the dark it was impossible to tell if it was damaged – they would just have to trust in durable Zamorakian craftsmanship.

As they reached the shallows, a horrific sound came echoing from the tunnel opening at their backs. The shriek of a vyre. Rhea and Luken exchanged a glance, the young Saradominist pale and wide-eyed in the faint light of dawn.

"Into the boat," Rhea snapped, lifting Safalaan up over the side with some difficultly, wincing at the pain in her hand. She was waist-deep in the water now, its icy chill embracing her. She pushed the boat further out before trying to drag herself up.

One-handed, she would have fallen back if Luken and Safalaan hadn't snatched at the straps of her breastplate and dragged her on board.

"Oars," she panted. To her relief, Safalaan located two in the bilge.

"Take the rudder," she told the child, relieved he was aiding their efforts. "Point it this way, like this."

She directed him before indicating that Luken should take the starboard side with his oar while she took the port, using the crook of her injured arm instead of her hand.

"We're going south," Luken pointed out. "Shouldn't we follow the coastline? This boat will never survive out in the open sea."

"The vyre fear water," Rhea said, hoping that part of the old tales was true. "We need to put as much of it as possible between us and whatever is coming. Then we'll turn west."

"Look," shouted Safalaan.

Rhea turned back towards the shore – something had emerged from the tunnel under the palace. It was huge and pale. She remembered the beast Queen Efaritay had submitted to before the walls. It could only be Drakan.

She thought the monstrosity was going to take flight, knowing that it would tear them apart in a heartbeat. But as it began to unfurl its huge wings, light surged from the east. It shone past the Everlight. Rhea thought the ancient tower had been restored, but it was something even more potent.

Dawn had broken. It struck the shoreline and the waves lapping at it, the brilliance of a new day breaking over a city of darkness. That was a light even the greatest efforts and foulest magics of Vampyrium could not snuff out. The light of Gielinor itself.

The thing did not retreat, as Rhea had hoped, yet it hesitated.

"Keep rowing," she snapped at Luken. They were far out now, the waves rocking the boat back and forth. Between them stretched a watery expanse, the oceans of Gielinor anathema even to the lord of all vyre.

Drakan furled his wings. He continued to watch, making no gesture, giving no sound.

To Rhea's surprise, Safalaan surged to his feet in the back of the boat, shouting towards the dire figure.

"I will come back! Remember me!"

Rhea snatched him and pulled him down, telling him to keep at the rudder.

On the shore, the vyrelord raised one fist. Salute or mockery, Rhea didn't know. All she was sure of was that Lowerniel Drakan had heard the child's promise.

EPILOGUE

◆━━◆◆━━◆

They beached the boat not far west of the rearmost Zamorakian siegeworks. Rhea was confident the attentions of Drakan's legion were on their newly conquered city, and that they wouldn't be patrolling the area to their rear.

They pressed inland a little way, into a forest that rose to a low hill. Rhea had them pause by a small stream, where they quenched their thirst.

Luken began to rip the skirts of his himation. When Rhea asked why, he gestured to her arm.

"To bind it," he said.

She accepted his help, strapping her limb against her chest. The injury ached, and her inability to flex her fingers left her in no doubt that the hand was broken.

She'd had worse.

"We need to keep going as long as there's daylight," she said. "We'll build a brush shelter when it starts to get dark.

No fires though, not until we've put at least another day between us and the city."

Luken nodded and took a breath, as though he was about to say something of great importance.

"Might… I stay with you?"

The question caught Rhea by surprise – she hadn't even considered sending the young priest away.

"For the time being," she said, secretly thankful that she had someone else to help look after Safalaan.

The boy had gone a little way further up the slope and climbed onto a boulder, and now seemed to be looking back over them.

"Don't wander," Rhea called up to him, walking around the boulder with Luken. "This place isn't safe."

He didn't respond, and Rhea looked in the direction he was gazing. She realised there was a break in the trees lower down the slope, and it meant Hallowvale was visible, stretched out beneath them.

She had never seen it without the Everlight's glory shining over it. The buildings had lost their lustre and the walls were scarred and cratered. Pillars of smoke rose across the city, and in the distance the Everlight stood, dull and dead.

It was the saddest sight Rhea had ever seen. She refused to linger on it.

"There is no time for sorrow," she told Safalaan. "That is something you will learn. We must keep going. Always."

"I meant what I said," the child said, not taking his eyes off his home. "I will go back, for mam and da and for my sister. For everyone."

"I believe you," Rhea said. "And I hope I'm with you when you do, my prince. Now come. We keep going."

Luken offered to carry Safalaan on his shoulders, and with a solemnity that would have been endearing but for the circumstances, the child accepted. They set off up the slope once more, Rhea pausing just briefly to look once more upon that fallen city and its extinguished light.

Then, she turned her back on Hallowvale, and kept walking.

ACKNOWLEDGEMENTS

From *Robbie MacNiven:*

My thanks go out to the team at Titan, especially my editors Michael and Daquan for their hard work seeing this novel through from start to finish. Also to the talented team at Jagex, particularly Tim and Mel, for being so open and approachable, and for helping me delve into the deep depths of RuneScape's lore.

From *Jagex Ltd:*

Many thanks to all those who assisted in the development of this book.

     At Jagex Ltd, in particular: Kate Blacklock, Tim Fletcher, Matt Parrish, Andrew Macdonald, Mark Montague and Ed Pilkington.

     Plus all those who read and inputted into various drafts of the manuscript including Aeternus Lux.

     With additional thanks to B-hive Associates Ltd.

ABOUT THE AUTHOR

Robbie MacNiven is a sci-fi and fantasy author and a historian from the Scottish Highlands. Besides novels for franchises such as Warhammer 40,000 and Marvel's X-Men, he writes audio dramas, comic scripts, has worked on multiple digital games, and sometimes finds the time to pen non-fiction military history.

For more fantastic fiction, author events,
exclusive excerpts, competitions, limited editions and more

VISIT OUR WEBSITE
titanbooks.com

LIKE US ON FACEBOOK
facebook.com/titanbooks

FOLLOW US ON TWITTER AND INSTAGRAM
@TitanBooks

EMAIL US
readerfeedback@titanemail.com